BEST FRIENDS *For Never*

OTHER TITLES BY TEAGAN HUNTER

SEATTLE SERPENTS SERIES

Contemporary Sports Romantic Comedies

Body Check

Face Off

Delayed Penalty

CAROLINA COMETS SERIES

Contemporary Sports Romantic Comedies

Puck Shy

Blind Pass

One-Timer

Sin Bin

Scoring Chance

Glove Save

"Game Changer"

Neutral Zone

TEXTING SERIES

Contemporary New Adult Romantic Comedies

Let's Get Textual

I Wanna Text You Up

Can't Text This

Text Me Baby One More Time

*Textin' Up My Heart (*novella*)*

SLICE SERIES

Contemporary Romantic Comedies

A Pizza My Heart

I Knead You Tonight

Doughn't Let Me Go

*A Slice of Love (*novella*)*

Cheesy on the Eyes

ROOMMATE ROMPS SERIES

Contemporary Romantic Comedies

Loathe Thy Neighbor

Love Thy Neighbor

Crave Thy Neighbor

Tempt Thy Neighbor

STARS SERIES

Contemporary Upper YA Emotional Romances

We Are the Stars

If You Say So

STAND-ALONES

Contemporary Romantic Comedies

The DM Diaries

BEST FRIENDS *For Never*

TEAGAN HUNTER

This is a work of fiction. Names, characters, organizations, places, events, and incidents are either products of the author's imagination or are used fictitiously. Otherwise, any resemblance to actual persons, living or dead, is purely coincidental.

Published by Montlake, Seattle

www.apub.com

ISBN-13: 9781662519482 (paperback)
ISBN-13: 9781662519499 (digital)

Cover design by Letitia Hasser
Cover photography © Wander Aguiar Photography

Printed in the United States of America

For all my favorite fictional small towns.
Thank you for giving me a place to disappear to.

CHAPTER ONE

Noel

"I love you. Don't you see that, Josette? I love you, but I can't wait forever. So tell me you love me, too, or this is over."

"I . . ." She rolls her tongue over her bottom lip, her baby-blue eyes boring into me. Her honey-blond hair doesn't move an inch as she shakes her head. "It's not that simple, Riley."

"It is." I slide my palm over her cheek, cupping her face as she nuzzles into my touch. "It *is* that simple, Josette. Love me back. *Please.*"

Her lips part, those words I want her to say sitting on the tip of her tongue.

But they never come.

No, it's something far more jarring.

"Cut!"

Like a rubber band being snapped against a wrist, the world is brought back into focus, and the set buzzes to life around me.

You'd think I'd be used to it after spending the last ten years on various movie and TV show sets, but getting lost in the world of make-believe is easier than some people think.

"Bridget, that was amazing!" The director shoves his headphones off, letting them fall around his neck, then rises from his chair and crosses over to me and my costar. His eyes are big, bright, and excited as he stares down at the woman next to me. "You were flawless. The emotion . . . It was breathtaking. Heartfelt. Gut-wrenchingly perfect. Everything I was looking for. I have no notes. Just give me that same thing for the next take."

He pauses, then sucks in a deep breath before turning to me. That sheen of excitement? It's gone, and I know I won't like what I hear next.

Just like I haven't liked it the last eleven times he's come over here. We've run this scene repeatedly, and he's still unhappy. But then again, so am I.

"Noel," he starts, disappointment lacing each letter of my short name. Seriously, how is it possible he sounds that displeased in just one syllable? "Listen, that was good. Really good. It's just . . ."

Another heavy inhale. Another dramatic pause as he steeples his fingers together, resting them under his chin, his lips falling into a flat line.

I grind my teeth. If my agent could see me right now, he'd smack me upside the head for messing with my moneymaking smile. Then again, he's not the one having to stand here and get criticized in front of an entire set when you've just given the performance your everything.

"I need *more*," he continues, pointing his steepled hands at me. "It's still coming off a bit stiff. I'm not feeling that . . . emotion, that *depth*. We need those to make the audience believe this is real. You need to be on the same level as Bridget here, or else the audience won't root for you two, and we need them to root for you. Got it?"

He's talking to me like I'm a child. Like he's the one in charge. And I guess, technically, he is in charge here. This is his movie. His shit show. I'm just starring in it.

My first instinct is to tell him he's a fool if he thinks anyone will believe this trash writing is real. That he must be higher than giraffe titties if he thinks this is going to make viewers do anything except laugh or hide behind their hands with secondhand embarrassment.

That wasn't a heartbreaking scene. It wasn't a tear-jerking moment. It was a demanding one—a love-me-or-else sort of scene. At this point, *I* don't even want to root for my character.

But I've been in the industry long enough to know that my first instinct when it comes to a director is usually not the direction I should be going if I want to keep the peace and remain employed.

Play it safe, Noel. Always play it safe, especially when millions of dollars are on the line.

So that's what I do.

I nod, then shoot him my best smile—the one I always save for the cameras—and tell him, "You got it, David."

He seems relieved, squeezing my shoulder. "Thanks, Noel. You're the best. We're going again in five." He marches back to his assistants and the crew, already barking orders.

Our makeup artists rush onto the scene, their brushes poised and ready, as I turn back to my costar and they begin caking on our powder to help cover up the sweat forming at our hairlines.

"You good?" Bridget asks, not even flinching at the brush near her right eye.

"I'm good," I lie to Bridget, ignoring it as they pat here and there so I'm not shiny from all the sweating I'm doing. Why the hell did we have to film in Georgia again? In the middle of June? It's humid and hot even with us shooting indoors on the soundstage, all thanks to the unbearable heat outside, and I'm getting increasingly agitated as the day progresses. I'm from the Pacific Northwest. I'm not used to the mugginess the South provides.

She arches a brow. "Are you, though? That was . . ." She slides her eyes over to the director, who is now yelling at Darius, a PA who probably hasn't done a damn thing wrong.

"Embarrassing as hell?" I scoff. "Yeah, I know. But he was right. I sucked."

"*You* didn't suck. This dialogue does. It's crap."

She gets it.

I thought maybe it was just me, but no. Which is not a good sign. Not a good sign at all. If the actors aren't even connecting with the scene, it's not going to hit with audiences either. Reshoots after this inevitably fails testing are not an option, thanks to my agent booking me out the ass for the next six months, all starting with a trip I really, really don't want to take.

I shove that thought aside. It's not something I need to be thinking of right now. I need to focus entirely on this next take so I can nail it and we can get out of here faster. We are just four scenes away from wrapping this film, and the whole crew has agreed to work over the weekend in hopes of finishing early. The last thing I need is to mess this up and let everyone down.

Bridget peeks over at the crew again before stepping in closer and lowering her voice. "Go off script," she says.

"Oh, so you *want* me to get fired."

She laughs, lifting her eyes skyward. "Please. As if David would ever fire you. He'd lose the movie like *that*." She snaps her fingers for emphasis. "You're the whole reason the budget got bumped up so we could film the first part of the movie on location in Paris. You're not going anywhere."

I don't even bother refuting her words. She's right. I *am* the reason the budget was expanded. The studio's last movie didn't do as well as they hoped, so they cut the financing for this one. Then I came onto the scene, and millions of dollars were suddenly available.

I guess that's the kind of pull you have when riding a hot streak and landing roles left and right after your big-budget movie sweeps the awards season.

But the trophies on my shelf aside, going off script is not an option with David Richards, the multi-award-winning director famous for his epic, sweeping romances, running the show. As much as he's known for his two-plus-hour-long sagas, he's even more notorious for hating it when his actors improvise. He says a script was written for a reason, and we're expected to follow it to a T. He's already kept us to 4:00 a.m. three times this week because he wasn't happy with a speech my character's brother was giving—he kept leaving out too many filler words.

One Night is expected to be this generation's *The Notebook*, taking the audience by storm and being quoted for years. I can't blow this just because I can't move past some crappy dialogue and deliver the scene like it needs to be delivered.

"Trust me, Noel, it's not you," Bridget tells me as if she can read my mind. And maybe she can at this point. We've been working side by side nearly nonstop for the last eight weeks. The only real breaks from one another have come in the form of three-hour naps between takes or when David rushes off to his trailer to correct the script. "It's this speech. It's too . . . choppy. It needs work. David is just afraid to admit it."

I glance at Kris, one of the makeup artists, and their eyes connect with mine. They point their brush at Bridget. "I'm with her on this. That speech didn't evoke a single reaction from me except annoyance. If a partner said those words to me, I'd be gone in a flash. But I don't play games." They shrug, then continue working on my face like they never said a word.

"Thanks, Kris," I mutter. Bridget smiles victoriously. "Oh, shut up. Stop looking so proud. I'll . . . I'll think about it."

"Thinking about it and doing it are two different things. Come on, Noel. You can do it. Pull from experience. I know you have some heartbreak in your past." Bridget rakes her eyes over me. "There's no way you look like you and don't."

This wouldn't be the first time Bridget flirted with me during this shoot. If we weren't costars, I'd consider it. But I have a rule against dating anyone I work with, and I'm not planning to bend that anytime soon.

"I bet you have girls crying and mooning over you left and right. Hell, the boys too," she continues, her eyes still drinking me in. "Probably you were the king of your high school, turning down prom dates hourly."

I laugh at that. I was most certainly *not* the king of my high school. I wasn't what you'd call popular, but I wasn't entirely on the outskirts either. I was the sought-after lead for every school play, and in the tiny town I hail from, that held *some* weight.

"I was a theater geek."

"So? I've met theater geeks. They're usually the freakiest of them all. Ask me how I know." She bounces her brows up and down.

I shake my head with a smile. "You're too much, Bridge."

She shrugs, not bothered by my words. And why would she be? She's been in this industry since she was nine years old, getting her start on the Family Channel, and she then went on to do what nearly every childhood star does—have a public nervous breakdown and go wild. She's been in the headlines more times than I could ever dream of, though it's been mostly bad over the years. This movie is supposed to be her big comeback, showing the world she's not just another former childhood star turned rowdy partyer.

Which means I have to do it. I have to go off script, not just to save myself from delivering those horrible lines but also to save this movie for Bridget.

My brain kicks into overdrive, and all the possible ways I could play this scene flow through me at once. I know where I can tweak it, where I can make it better.

I heard rumors that the last actor to pull a stunt like this with David was banned from ever starring in another of his movies. That led to him being barred from other sets and branded as "undirectable." Not saying he's been completely blacklisted, but I don't believe it's a coincidence he hasn't been a lead in a serious film since.

It's a risk. A huge one. If I'm going to do this, I'll have to be sure I can pull it off or risk facing David's wrath.

"Just think about it," Bridget says as the makeup crew finishes.

They scurry off the set, a fake front lawn that'll be transformed into a dramatic nighttime scene during edits. David demands a quiet room, then counts us in.

"Action!" he calls, and the set is frozen. The cast, the crew—everyone—is quiet and unmoving, all eyes on us as Bridget and I get back into the scene.

I take a deep breath and blow it out slowly, shaking my hands out to ease the tension rolling through me.

I sneak a peek over at David. He's watching me intently, commanding me with shrewd eyes not to screw this up.

Come on, Noel. You've got this. Do what Bridget said. Pull from experience. Make this better. You deserve it. She deserves it. The crew deserves it. Hell, audiences deserve it. You can do this.

The director clears his throat, indicating he wants me to get a move on.

Another inhale. Another exhale.

Then I step toward my costar, who has fully transformed into Josette—the woman I've been wrongfully lusting over for years—and I slip back into my character's shoes.

"You left me, Josette. I was ready. I was there. I was waiting. I *have* waited. For ten years now, yet you never showed. And even now that you're here, you're not really here with *me*. You're miles away."

"He's my husband, Riley," Bridget says, perfectly playing off my improv.

"You think I don't know that?" I toss my hands into the air. "You think I'm not painfully aware of that every day? I'm so damn aware of that it's sickening. He's your husband, and he's my brother. You don't think that eats at me constantly?"

"Then how can you ask me to choose? How can you stand here and ask me to be with you over the man I took a vow with?"

"Because I loved you first, Josette! *I* loved you *first*." I grab at my chest to emphasize my heartache, stepping into her so close she has to tip her head back to meet my eyes. "I loved you first," I repeat, quieter this time. "And it's not fair. It's not fair that he gets you when you were never his to have. From the first moment I saw you, I knew you were mine and I was yours." I run my knuckles over her cheek, and she presses into my touch as if we've rehearsed this before.

"Just because life threw us a few curveballs, it doesn't mean that can't still be true. We can still be together. You can still choose me."

"I . . ." She shakes her head. "It's not that simple, Riley."

"It *is* that simple. And you want to know why?"

"Why?" she whispers, her eyes glistening with unshed tears.

"Because you're mine. You've always been mine. You always will be mine. You know it as well as I do. Even if you walk away today, even if you go back to him, you'll still belong to me, and I'll still belong to you. So why not spare us more heartache, huh?" I smile softly, ensuring it doesn't reach my eyes to play up the sadness in the scene. "Why not give in and do what you want, not what *they* want you to do? Why *not* choose me, Josette?"

She swallows thickly, a single tear slipping down her cheek, something that isn't in the script either. "I . . . Riley . . ."

I rest my forehead against hers. "Please. *Please.*"

"I need time."

"Time?" I laugh wryly. "You've had ten years, Josette. It's now or never."

"Please . . ." She splays her hands against my chest, then fists my shirt like she's desperate to hold on to me. "Just one night, Riley. Just one. That's all I need. Besides, you waited ten years. What's another twelve hours?"

She laughs softly, and I shake my head.

"Twelve hours? That's going to feel like days." I press my lips to her forehead, then step away. "One night. If you don't come find me, I'll know, and I promise I'll disappear from your life for good."

She lets out a choked sob. "Don't say that."

"I have to say that, baby. I can't keep having half of you."

"Riley, please. I—"

I hold up my hand to stop her. "No. I've made my choice. Now you make yours."

She sniffles, nodding as she wipes at her cheeks. "Okay."

I take a few steps, then stop and turn back to her. "One night, Josette," I remind her.

She lets out another soft cry as she wraps her arms around her waist. "One night," she echoes, and I leave, walking past the camera and out of the shot.

I brace myself, ready for David to come unglued, but it doesn't happen. The set remains quiet, and I swear all eyes are on me as I stop in front of the director.

He stares at me, his dark eyes blank, not giving away his feelings.

Then, as soft as I've ever heard him say, he tells the crew, "Cut."

And the set bursts back to life.

I blow out a wobbly breath, shaking off the character and bracing myself for the hell that's about to rain down as the rest of the crew moves around. From their furtive glances, it's obvious that they are pretending to do their jobs but secretly eavesdropping, waiting for the same thing I am.

David rises from his chair, his headphones now around his neck as he steps toward me. He works his jaw back and forth, and I just know it's going to be bad. So, so bad. There's no mistaking this tension rolling between us. He's pissed.

Fuck. Why couldn't you play nicely, Noel?

"David, listen. This was me. I was the one who—"

He lifts his hand, shutting down Bridget's attempt to take the blame. "Save it, Bridge. Noel here can make his own decisions." He crosses his arms over his chest. "Can't you, Noel?"

One thing I refuse to do is be intimidated by him.

So I answer, "Yup, and I stand by them."

His nostrils flare.

Then just like that, all the tension dissipates, and David gives me the biggest smile I've ever seen.

"You should. Because *holy shit,* Noel, that was incredible. Magnificent!" He grabs me by the shoulders, giving me an excited shake. "I don't know where all that came from, but that was . . . *Wow.*" Another jostle, then he lets me go. "The angst . . . The emotion. It was perfect. Just what I was looking for. Audiences are going to be blown away by that. Hell, even *I* was sucked into their relationship. Truly some great work."

I'm stunned. Speechless.

David claps my shoulder. "Seriously, great work, Noel. We might need to bring you in to look over our next script if that's the kind of stuff you can pull out of nowhere." He laughs, then squeezes my shoulder. "Let's take a break for dinner, then we'll reconvene at seven."

He leaves me standing there staring after him, my mind still reeling.

It's not until Bridget throws her arms around my neck that I realize she's still beside me.

"Noel! That was amazing! I can't believe you pulled that off and didn't lose your job. I mean, I doubt he could have fired you now with just a few days left in the shoot, but still. That was incredible!"

She hugs me, and it's only when her hands wander a little too close to my ass that I pull myself from my stupor, removing myself from her embrace as politely and quickly as I can.

"Thanks, Bridge," I tell her, putting at least a foot between us. "I don't know where it came from."

"I do! You're a rock star! You totally pulled from real life, didn't you?" She pokes my stomach. "I knew you had it in you. I knew there was heartache in there somewhere that you could use."

I chuckle softly, subtly taking a step back. If only she knew. "Yeah, maybe."

"So, I'm going to head back to my trailer. You're more than—"

"Agent!" I interrupt, not wanting her to say those next words. I really don't need her inviting me back to her trailer. I've managed to keep us in public spaces over these two months and intend to continue doing so until we wrap. "I have a call with my agent. I'm sorry. Maybe next time?"

It's a lie. I don't have a call with my agent. In fact, I don't have any plans other than to go back to my trailer and sleep until our next scene. If I'm lucky, I'll grab a quick snack from craft services, but I'm not holding my breath on that one.

Bridget gives me a saccharine smile. "Sure. Next time."

She shoots me a wink, then flounces off, calling out to her on-screen husband, who I'm pretty sure I saw leaving her trailer last week when they thought no one was looking.

I blow out a relieved breath, scrubbing my hand through my hair, not caring if I messed it up. The team will have to fix it before the next scene anyway.

"Great job, Noel," Darius tells me as he passes, that clipboard I'm almost certain he sleeps with under his pillow in his hands.

"Thanks," I mutter, exhaustion setting in as I head toward my trailer.

Holy shit. What a day so far.

I've been up since 3:00 a.m., it's nearing 6:00 p.m., and we still have two more scenes to get through today, so we won't be done until at least eleven. And that's *if* we manage not to screw anything up and get through them quickly.

As I walk through the set and out toward the lot, a few people call out, telling me how amazing that was or that I made the scene better.

It's a relief. I thought for sure David was going to blow a fuse and come unhinged on me—hell, I still can't believe he didn't—so it feels good knowing it worked for everyone, our own built-in test audience included.

I climb the steps to my trailer, letting the door slam behind me, then flop down onto the couch, where I plan to spend my entire dinner break in a deep, deep sleep.

My body sags against the sofa, which is easily the most uncomfortable piece of furniture in the world, but right now, it feels like heaven, and my eyes grow heavier by the second.

Fuck, this feels nice. So nice. Too nice.

I'm nearly asleep when a shrill sound pierces the air.

I peel my eyes open, glaring at my phone on the counter. Most people are attached to them, even on set, but not me. I always leave it in my trailer, tucked away so that I can focus solely on shooting.

I sit forward, able to grab my phone off the counter with my movement because the trailer is so tiny compared with how tall I am, then settle back into my original spot.

Unsurprisingly, my screen is filled with notifications. Emails, texts, missed calls, and social media shit I really could not care less about.

I swipe everything away, ignoring it all, not just because I don't *want* to deal with it but because I'm too fucking *tired* to deal with it, then set an alarm so they don't have to pound on my door repeatedly to get me up.

I'm nearly asleep when the damn thing goes off again, and I snatch it back up, glaring down at whoever interrupted the short amount of time I get to myself.

My assistant.

I click on his name, and our text thread fills my screen.

Vince: As requested, the first-class flight to Seattle is booked for Thursday at 12:20 p.m. Car pickup is scheduled.

Vince: Okay, turning off my professionalism for a moment . . .

Vince: Fucking wild you have to fly, then drive three hours to that little town you call home. Small town life is weird.

I'm suddenly very awake.

Not because of Vince's lack of professionalism, which I admire about the guy, but because this is all becoming too real.

Bridget was wrong about pulling from experience.

I didn't break a single heart in my day.

Everything I just said? All that shit about wanting to be chosen? About waiting? About wanting?

It's what I wish I would have said to my former best friend before I did just what my character promised—disappeared from her life for good.

Until now.

CHAPTER TWO

Parker

"Are you sure you ordered the right one?"

"I'm positive I pointed to green, Parker."

"But *which* green?"

"There's more than one?"

I sigh, shaking my head at my business partner. "You're exhausting, Ax, you know that?"

He grins, his dark brows lifting high. "Only because you remind me daily." He scratches his thick red beard. "Though I did order green. I'm not sure why they sent . . . Well, I'll be honest. That looks like baby shit."

I wrinkle my nose, staring at the paint can's offensive color. The *wrong* color. "It really does." I jut out my bottom lip. "I wanted sage."

"Sage, shit. Pretty close, no?"

I cut him a glare. "Not even kind of close, Axel."

He chuckles, still messing with his beard, a nervous habit I've caught on to over the years. It doesn't mean he's lying, but it does mean he knows he messed up. Again. "Well, I tried. I guess we'll need to reorder if you can't work with this one. It will set us back a few days, but I suppose it'll be worth it."

He *supposes* it'll be worth it? There is no way I'm going to smear this hideous green on the walls of Rossi Café, which I've spent the last two months perfecting. I have everything planned around sage, not . . . well, whatever this ugly color is. We have no choice but to reorder, which means we'll have to tell our clients we're behind schedule . . . *again*.

I replace the paint-can lid, smacking it into place with my rubber mallet with more force than I'd typically use.

Axel doesn't miss it.

"You mad?" he asks from behind me.

I shrug. "No. Yes. No. I'm not really sure."

"I'm sorry I screwed up."

I slam the mallet against the lid a few more times—not because I need to, but because I want to—then exhale and turn around.

"It's just frustrating because you're right—this *will* cost us a few days. Which means I'm going to have to disappoint Gianna again. Greta again. Heck, I hate disappointing anyone, and I feel like that's all we've done lately. First, there was the wrong lumber on the Krueger house. Now it's the wrong paint for the café *after* having to pull out and replace the wrong countertops. That's a lot of major screwups in the last eight months. If we keep this up, we'll be out of business before the end of the year, and we'll never get to complete the theater project I've been dreaming about for the last decade."

And I really don't want to blow my big dream. I've been working toward it for far too long to let it get messed up now.

Axel's brows are now nearly touching his hairline. His brown eyes are wide, and his lips curve up just slightly. How has my outburst *amused* him? This is serious!

"How are you smiling right now?" I bark at him.

"Oh, this?" He points at his grin. "It's just a coping mechanism because I'm a little scared you're going to hit me."

I rear my head back. "Hit you? What? Why would I *hit* you?"

He darts his eyes downward . . . right to the rubber mallet I'm still holding. The same one I've been pointing and swinging in his direction this entire time.

"Oh." I tuck my hands into the pockets of my overalls, securing the mallet safely inside. Honestly, it never occurred to me to hit him, but now that he's mentioned it, maybe a good whack upside the head would do the guy some good. Perhaps teach him not to keep messing everything up.

I sigh, shaking away the thought. That's not entirely fair. This is *our* business. We've said that from the start. Yet I haven't bothered to look at the finer details of things, like orders and invoices, and instead focused solely on the design aspects of the business. And if I'm keeping my head buried in the sand, then at some point, this becomes my fault too. All it takes is a simple request to review things and ensure he's ordering the appropriate materials.

"I'm sorry," I tell him. "It's just—"

"I know," Axel interrupts. "I know how important this is to you, and I *promise* I will do better. Things have just been a little hard at home with Mary and the kids, you know? Lots of late nights and very little sleep. It's been tough trying to keep up with it all."

Warmth spreads through me, and it's the same thing that always happens whenever Axel talks about this adorable little family he's created. He's a good dad. A doting one. A much better father than I ever had, that's for sure.

And while I love how important his family is to him, this is still our business, and we need to learn to run a tight ship despite the outside noise.

"I know that. I do. But we all have things at home distracting us."

Those dang brows of his lift high again, and this time they say, *Are you serious?*

Heat creeps up my cheeks. Fine. So my *at home* problems are a little different from his. I have a destructive cat who loves to knock over the

Christmas decorations I refuse to take off my fireplace mantel. Axel has four-year-old triplets and another baby on the way. But we're still dealing with distractions. That counts, right?

He laughs, crossing the café and returning to the front window he's spent a good deal of the morning reframing after an incident with the glass. He begins packing his tools, a sign we're done for the day. "I'm not trying to use it as an excuse. Yes, it has been kind of rough lately, but I still have a job to do, and I need to learn to do it right. And not just for you and the business—which, by the way, is doing great, and we won't be broke by the end of the year—I need to do it right for our clients too. They deserve that."

I sink back against the counter with relief because *he gets it*.

I shouldn't be surprised. He's been a good partner since Day One, never making me feel like anything other than his equal.

If someone had told me when I was eight years old that one day, I would not only be friends with Axel Cooke but also running a successful renovation company with him, I'd have laughed right in their face.

The red-haired mammoth standing before me with three—going on four—children, who likes to spend his weekends coaching Little League baseball or peewee soccer or baking cookies for the local nursing home, is the same guy who used to make fun of me for being a theater geek almost daily. He's the same guy who would "accidentally" look at my tests in science class and then tell the teacher *I* cheated off *his* paper. The same one who once loudly regaled the whole cafeteria with a story about how the one time we played spin the bottle in sixth grade, I kissed him and cut him with my braces, ensuring I wasn't kissed again until I was in eleventh grade.

He was a thorn in my side throughout school, but when I needed someone after my best friend left town, surprisingly it was Axel who was there to help pick up the pieces.

It's pretty spectacular what getting out of a petty high school environment can do for someone's personality.

"Thank you," I tell him. "It's just that with the theater project coming up . . ."

"You think I don't know that's what has you stressed?" He dumps one of his many drills into his beat-up leather tool bag. "If I added up all the hours I've spent listening to you go on and on about that damn theater, then added the triplets' ages together, we'd be about even."

"Are you saying I talk about it too much?"

"It's your dream. There's no such thing as talking about it too much."

His words warm me. Who would have thought such a sweet guy was hiding behind all those insults over the years?

"You're a really good friend, you know that?"

My words have the opposite effect on him, and he groans, rising to his feet. "Stop saying shit like that to me."

"Why?" I ask, pushing off the counter and setting about cleaning up my workspace, a much smaller task than his since I've basically been here all day, installing the coffee station and putting up the herringbone tile on the backsplash behind it. "It's true. You're like the *best* friend ever."

"We're adults, Parker. We don't use the term *best friends*."

"That's bull poo, and you know it."

"Just say *shit*," he says for likely the thousandth time in our friendship. "You're an adult. Adults cuss."

"Just like adults don't have *best friends*?"

"Exactly," he calls over his shoulder as he kneels and grabs a stack of lumber we're done with and then tosses it onto his shoulder like it weighs nothing, pushing himself to his feet like he didn't just add at least a hundred pounds to his already massive frame. Who needs to hire a big crew when I have six-foot-six Axel around to do all the heavy lifting? I swear, the man looks like he benches buses for fun.

"You're just saying that because you're embarrassed that Potty Parker *is* your best friend."

You have *one* accident just *one* time and you're forever branded as the girl who peed her pants on the playground.

The nickname haunted me all through elementary, middle, *and* high school, and I had nobody to blame but myself.

Axel snorts out a laugh. "That's embarrassing for you, not me, *Potty Parker*."

Hearing the name roll off his tongue so effortlessly sends a wave of mortification through me, and I pick up the nearest thing to me—my rubber mallet—and chuck it right at his back.

Being the giant he is, it bounces right off as if I never threw it at all.

"Did that even hurt you?" I call after him as he pushes through the front door of the unfinished eatery.

"Tickled!"

"Darn it!"

He laughs, the door closing behind him. I watch as he carries the lumber to his truck, his shadow monstrous behind the plastic we have covering the windows so as not to spoil the remodel's big reveal.

My phone, which is tucked into my front-center pocket, buzzes against my chest, and I don't even have to look at it to know what it is. It's the same notification I've been getting every day for six months at this time—a countdown.

It's just as much a reminder of how behind I am as it is a ticking clock to the one thing I've been wanting for over a decade.

I look around the space that's filled with workbenches and boxes of tables and chairs that still need to be put together, covered with dust from all the drilling and sawing. It's Monday evening, and this project *must* be completed this week. We're running out of time, and we still have to finish the molding, complete the accent wall along the back of the café, mount the display cases, paint the walls, *and* decorate this place from head to toe by the wee hours of Friday morning at the very latest.

Because Friday? It's the Big Day. The day we kick off the theater renovation.

Our small town has been without a theater since I was eighteen, which, in my eyes, is a true travesty.

Erected by one of the town's founding families, the Goodman Theater was once an integral part of the community. When I was younger, I'd heard so many stories through the years of the elaborate plays that were put on there that I knew I had to be part of it.

Sadly, the theater was not the same magical place it once was and deteriorated more and more the older I got. Fewer and fewer people wanted to put on plays no one attended. It was finally closed for good when a huge storm blew through town and caved the roof in.

Finally, after countless meetings where I went toe to toe with some of the most influential names in this town, too-close-to-call votes, and a generous donor, a massive renovation of the theater that was such a staple in my childhood has finally been approved.

I've been fighting for this day for so many years, yet now that it's so close, I'm looking forward to it less and less. Not because I don't want to head this project—I really do. After all, I genuinely believe theater has the power to change lives, especially since it changed mine. Watching performances on that stage was once my favorite thing to do, and I want the town to experience that aliveness again.

No. I'm not looking forward to it for a whole different reason.

The donor—an anonymous one I still know nothing about—had one stipulation and one only: the theater is to be named after the now-famous actor who got his start on the very stage.

That ultra-famous actor? He's my former best friend.

The one who pulled the same stunt my father did—left town and left me behind. The guy I haven't seen in ten years. The guy who, in so many ways, is responsible for who I am today.

The guy I am absolutely terrified to see again.

I didn't want to invite him, but if I wanted this theater built—which I do more than anything—I had to. So I assigned the task to one of the other committee members and shoved it out of my mind to deal with later.

Well, later is almost here, and that old gnawing feeling of guilt has been steadily rising for weeks.

"Earth to Parker!"

A giant hand waves in front of my face, and it's so beefy it's enough to pull me from my stupor.

Axel's back. And from how deeply his brows are tucked together in concern, he's been back for a while and I've been ignoring him. He's even standing on the other side of the table, which means I completely missed his massive, thudding footsteps when he came back inside. That's how in-my-head I just was.

I wish I could say it's the first time that has happened, but it's not by a long shot.

"You okay?" Axel asks, twisting up his lips.

I nod, grabbing my sketches and trusty iPad, stuffing them into my work bag, and slinging it over my shoulder. "Yup. Tired. Long day."

His perceptive brown eyes narrow slightly, probably because I'm talking in short sentences, a tendency when I'm annoyed. I hold my breath, silently begging him to let it go and not hold me here for questioning, because I'm not so sure I want to get into it right now. It really has already been a long day, and I'm not in the mood to rehash my past and all the reasons I don't want to see my old best friend. Even if I weren't heading up the theater project that will bear his name, in a town this small, our paths would have no choice but to cross.

I guess with all the bad luck I've had lately, the universe decides to throw me a bone, because Axel *does* let it go.

My shoulders sag in relief.

"I feel that. Are you still coming for dinner tonight? Mary's making lasagna."

"And miss my favorite meal in the whole wide world that my mother doesn't need to know about because she'll be completely jealous I don't love *her* lasagna the most? Of course I'll be there. Seven?"

He nods. "Bring some wine?"

I huff. "It's like you don't even know me, best friend."

He groans, which only makes me smirk. I love pushing his buttons entirely too much. "Get out of here before I *accidentally* call the paint store and *accidentally* order the wrong color for the walls again."

I gasp. "You wouldn't dare."

"Try me."

He has those darn eyebrows lifted high, and I know him well enough to understand that means only one thing—he's serious.

"Fine, fine. I'll stop," I promise, retreating toward the door with my hands held up in concession. "But I'm bringing white wine tonight for dinner."

"White?!" he calls as I open the door. "You know I like red with my lasagna!" he adds as I step through it.

"Parker! Parker! Dammit, Potty Parker, come back here!" he hollers as I let it close behind me, cackling the entire time.

He should know me well enough by this point to understand one thing—I'm serious.

◆ ◆ ◆

I wish I could say I did the responsible thing when I got home—took a shower and changed for dinner at Axel and Mary's place so I wouldn't look like a complete mess. But I did neither.

Instead, I ignored the Christmas cards and tinsel that Pumpkin, my orange tabby, knocked off the mantel again and plopped down on my couch to snuggle with him.

That was my first mistake, because I *know* this couch is my kryptonite.

The number of movies I've started on this hunk of junk? Hundreds.

The number of movies I've finished? Two and a half.

I always, always, always fall asleep anytime I lie down. I don't know what it is, but this lumpy old thing becomes the most comfortable piece of furniture ever, and I drift off into sleep as if I've just finished a

32k—or whatever those marathons are that those weirdos who actually enjoy running compete in.

It's my couch's fault that I'm racing around my small one-bedroom house like I am now, running late for something very important.

"Ugh, I'll be so annoyed if Axel even *thinks* about eating my slice of lasagna, Pumpkin," I say to my cat, who, admittedly, I talk to entirely too often.

I suppose that's what happens when you live alone for so long. You start talking to your pets like they're real people while telling everyone who will listen how lonely you *aren't.*

I'm not lonely—not really. I have great friends and a booming renovation business, *and* I'm about to work on the project of my dreams. Who cares if I spend my nights alone or hang out with my cat? That's not lonely. It's just . . .

Oh, heck. Who am I kidding? I am a little lonely, especially now that Axel has gone all family man. Sure, he still includes me in everything, and we're just as close as ever, but I know he needs his own space.

I push the thoughts away, saving them for another time when I'm not running late.

I hop on one foot as I slide my lace-free shoe on the other, then grab my favorite flannel jacket, which I got for a measly three dollars at the thrift shop, toss my cross-body purse over my head, and make a beeline out the door.

I'm in such a hurry that I don't even take the time to fully admire the beautiful summer we're having. It's mid-June, and the flowers are in full bloom. Borgen Avenue, the main street that goes through the small town of Emerald Grove, is lined with happy couples out on a stroll, and nearly every business has its door propped open to welcome evening guests for shopping or dinner.

It's one of my favorite things about this town—how welcoming every little nook and cranny feels. Walking into one of the cozy, usually family-owned businesses is like being wrapped in a warm hug.

Sometimes, that warm hug is all you need to lift your spirits. Or at least, it's all *I* need.

I pass by my mom's pottery shop and pause. She's at the counter helping a customer, showing the old woman handspun vases that were just finished last week.

My mother glances over at the window as if on cue, sending me a soft smile. *That* feels like a warm hug too.

I'll never know how she's always had that superpower. I just know I'll never tire of it, because my mother is the greatest mom in the world. Life's thrown a lot at her—from losing her own mother early to going on tour with her band at nineteen, then falling in love with a guitar player who, as it turned out, wasn't cut out for small-town living and left her a single mother to an eight-year-old.

She's been through the wringer, but she's strong and fierce, and she's all mine.

Dinner? she mouths.

Axel's, I respond.

She nods, then holds her thumb and pinkie finger up to her ear, like she's talking into an old landline phone, indicating she wants me to call her later.

I nod, then connect my hands in a heart and continue on my way.

My mother is originally from Emerald Grove, and her love for this place is exactly why she wanted to move back when I was eight—so she could raise her daughter in the same small town that always meant so much to her. As much as I love it here, she loves it even more, putting her entire heart and soul into every volunteer opportunity she's come across to keep it thriving. Despite her heartbreak, she's done it all with a smile. Her commitment and endurance are easily my favorite things about her. She's the most amazing woman in my life.

Well, *one* of the most amazing. Noel's grandmother takes a close second spot.

"Hey, Parker!" Fran from Francine May's Pies calls from her open shop door. I've been to more birthday parties in this town that serve Fran's pie than I have parties that serve cake. And really, it's no surprise. Wafts of cinnamon, apples, fresh cherries, and sugar delight my nose as I pause. The place smells heavenly, and I'm beyond tempted to ruin my dinner for a slice of pie, but I resist . . . barely.

"Hey, Fran." I wave at her. "Gotta jet, but I'll be in tomorrow."

"I'll save you a slice of marionberry!" She shoots me a wink as I keep moving forward.

I'm only stopped twice more—once by Dr. Z, who reminds me I need to get in for a checkup, even though I haven't been a patient of his since I was fourteen, and then by Terry, who wants me to read his script, as he believes it's the perfect piece for our opening night at the theater. That makes me feel good because I *knew* this town could benefit from the rebuilt theater and that people would be excited about it.

I waltz into the grocery store with a grin; wave to Peggy behind the front counter, who gives me a curt nod; and then head straight for the wine aisle.

If I hadn't taken that sweet, sweet nap, I would have had more time to peruse the bottles and find us something fun and new to try, but now I'm going to play it safe and settle for an old favorite.

Looks like Axel is getting his precious red wine after all.

I grab the brand I know he loves, then a bottle of white *I* love just to mess with him and turn toward the front.

Only there's nowhere to go, and I smack straight into something hard.

When did Peggy put a wall here?

Did I get turned around?

"Shit."

It's one word.

One single, tiny word.

And it's enough to rock my entire world.

I tip my head back, looking up, up, up and right into the eyes of someone I once thought would be in my life forever.

Into the eyes of someone I was wrong about. Someone I haven't seen for ten years.

Right into the ocean eyes of Noel Carter, my former best friend.

And the boy who broke my heart.

CHAPTER THREE

Noel

Fade In

Interior—Grocery Store—Evening

We find a man and a woman standing in the liquor aisle of a dimly lit local grocery, Jill's Bait & Tackle. The store doesn't sell bait or tackle and isn't owned by anyone named Jill.

Noel Carter, a man fresh off a plane and a three-hour drive, who is in desperate need of something alcoholic to drink, stands poised and ready to grab a bottle of booze.

Parker Pruitt, a messy-haired woman wearing paint-stained overalls and carrying a reusable grocery bag that's certainly seen better days, is Noel Carter's former best friend. She clutches two bottles of wine to her chest and stares up at Noel with wide eyes.

If I were reading a script, that's precisely what it would say about my current predicament.

After my stellar improvised performance, David trusted me to do more of that for the rest of the shoot, which led to us wrapping two days early.

Usually, I'd take that time to rest and recuperate, maybe catch up with friends, have a fancy dinner, or hit up my favorite theater in LA that only shows old movies. I certainly would have had time to prepare for returning to my hometown. But one call from my grandmother with the promise of banana nut bread, and I knew I was going back to Emerald Grove early.

I know it's a small town—entirely too fucking small, if you ask me—and our seeing each other was inevitable, but the last thing I expected on my very first night back was this.

Parker stumbles backward, her mouth agape, and reflexively, I reach out to steady her. My fingers curl around her bare arms, and we're standing so close that the scent of freshly brewed coffee the owner always keeps going is long gone. All that's hitting my senses now is her perfume—a mix of honey and wildflowers.

Her hazel eyes, which I haven't seen in so long yet still feel so familiar, seem darker and brighter all at once, and that smattering of freckles across her nose is more pronounced than it was all those years ago. There are a few traces of aging, a new line here and there, and an air of wisdom has replaced that innocence she always carried. Her cheeks are less full, and she no longer wears those damn Mickey Mouse earrings she never took off. Her auburn hair is as haphazard as ever, in a chaotic bun atop her head, and she's in the same overalls that I swear were a staple when we were teens.

Despite all that and the years that have passed, she still looks like the same Parker she's always been.

It's like I've been sucked back in time and we're standing in the halls of our high school by our lockers, and she's telling me about the latest mean thing Axel Cooke has said or how she swears she's going to fail her math test, even though she always had the highest grade in the class.

"Dick."

The word tumbles from her lips so smoothly, like she's said it a thousand times before, and it takes me a moment to catch up.

Did Parker, the woman I have never, ever heard cuss before, call me a *dick*?

More than that, how am *I* the dick in this situation? Last I remembered, she was the one who turned me down, not the other way around.

I open my mouth to remind her, to let all the words I've been holding over the years finally tumble free, when a shadow falls over us.

"Good evening, Parker. How are you?"

I'd know that rumbling voice anywhere.

I turn and look right into the eyes of my old high school principal.

Parker wasn't calling me a dick. She was talking to him. Relief floods through me at the realization.

"Mr. Dick. I mean, Dick. I mean, Principal McMichaels." I stumble over my words.

Christ. It really is like I'm back in high school.

Parker snickers beside me, and I ignore her, straightening my back and tipping my chin up.

The old principal laughs, waving his hand. "Please, Noel. Dick is fine. You're not my student anymore. But wow. This sure gives me flashbacks, seeing the two of you together like this again. It's been a long time since that's happened." He drops his eyes to the space between us. "I'd always hoped you'd find your way back together."

I follow his gaze, and only then do I realize I'm still holding on to Parker.

I didn't even notice I was still touching her, and I don't want to think about *why* I didn't notice.

Instead, I drop her arm, putting as much space between us as possible, even knocking into the next shelf in my haste to get away.

If Dick notices, he doesn't say anything.

"How is Mrs. McMichaels doing?" Parker asks, her voice as sugary as the maple syrup she loves to drown her waffles in.

"Oh, you know my wife. Can't keep her down for long, not even for a knee replacement. I meant to tell you how much we appreciated the cupcakes you sent. They were incredible. Very kind of you."

"Bah. It's nothing. And really, it was all my partner's doing, not mine. I just sat by and snuck about six cupcakes as he made them."

Dick laughs. I don't.

I don't because all I can focus on are two words.

Partner. He.

She has a *partner*. She has a *he*. She has someone to bake her cupcakes.

Parker continues talking to Dick, but I don't hear a word of it. All I can do is stare at her, watching her full lips move, the way they stretch when she smiles with nothing but sincerity, the way her hands wave wildly as she chats, the way she tosses her head back on a laugh, and how her eyes shine brightly, despite the gloomy lighting hanging overhead.

Once again, I'm struck by how familiar it feels, while being so different.

I guess that's what happens when you haven't seen someone since they were a teenager and now they're nearing thirty. Things stay the same and change all at once.

"Well, I'd better stop yammering and get this milk back to the house before my wife hobbles down here to find me."

The older man turns toward me with a smile, but it's not warm. It's reserved, never reaching his eyes, and his lips hardly moving. Odd, because I was never on his shit list as a student. I was a model kid, except for that one fight with Axel.

He extends his hand to me. "It was great seeing you, Noel. It seems like you've made a successful life outside of Emerald Grove."

It sounds like a compliment, but it feels awfully like an accusation.

He's upset I left, and a part of me gets it.

The people who leave Emerald Grove come back. Always. I can count on one hand the number of people who have left and not returned, including me. Once I had my diploma, my plan to head to LA was in full motion, and my career is all I've focused on since. Sure, I've seen my grandmother over the last ten years, but I always flew her out to me and never came back here. All other ties to this place were cut. People who were once such major parts of my life just stopped existing in it. I'm sure to the townspeople it feels like I abandoned them, even when I didn't mean to. I was just a kid with one thing on his mind—making his dreams come true.

I slide my palm against my old principal's, and instantly, he grips my hand with a strength you'd never expect from a man his age. "Thank you. It was great seeing you again, Dick."

"Try not to stay away so long next time, huh?" He gives my hand another hard squeeze and shoots Parker one last *genuine* smile before leaving.

If a director or producer had done that to me, I'd have squeezed back just as hard and stared them down, letting them know I wasn't going to take their shit. But getting into a pissing match with an eighty-year-old man isn't exactly my style.

Parker's shoes squeak against the floor as she shifts, and I'm all too aware that we're alone again.

We haven't been alone since . . .

I clench my jaw, not letting myself think about it. I've done a good job of pretending it never happened, and I don't want to ruin that streak now.

"Well, this is incredibly awkward."

A smile tugs at my lips before I can stop it. Parker always did like getting straight to the point.

And she's right. This *is* awkward.

It's not that I didn't plan to see her while I was here. I had no doubt she'd be at the ceremony on Friday as they break ground on the new theater. But I didn't anticipate running into her this soon on the trip. Or for this long. Or standing so close to her.

I turn toward her. We may as well get this over with now.

I clear my throat, running a hand through my hair just because I can. There are no hair-and-makeup teams here to yell at me not to. "How are you, Parker?"

She blinks up at me. Once. Twice. Three rapid ones.

"How . . . am I?"

I shrug. "Yeah. Like, how are things with you?"

Another blink.

She rolls her tongue over her bottom lip, the one I know tastes like peppermint all year long. "I . . ."

She shakes her head, stopping herself, and laughs lightly, then again, and again until suddenly, it's not light anymore. It's loud, obnoxious, and scathing. Can a laugh even be scathing?

She tosses her head back, grabbing at her belly as she continues to cackle.

I look around the small store, thankful there's nobody around to witness this except Peggy behind the front counter. But her nose is glued to the tiny TV she keeps back there with her, and she is paying us absolutely no attention.

Which means it's up to me to get Parker to stop . . . well, whatever this is.

"Uh, Parker?"

She either doesn't hear me or doesn't care that I've said anything. She simply continues to laugh.

I shuffle closer. "Parker?"

Still laughing.

"Park?"

Still. Fucking. Laughing.

It's gone past scathing and has landed safely in the infuriating category. Is this some trick to chase me away? To get me to leave? Because that's exactly what I'm about to do.

Hell, it's what I *should* do after the way she ended things between us all those years ago, casting me aside like I never meant anything to her, especially after I told her how I truly felt about her. Her rejection was painful enough, but what came next—her throwing away our friendship—was even worse.

I step away, ready to turn, but I can't leave. Why can't I leave?

Is it because I want to know why she thinks this is so funny? Or is it because it's Parker, and I haven't been this close to her in ten years?

I don't know the answer, but I know I'm tired of this.

"Dammit, Peter, would you stop?"

I don't know why I say that or where it comes from. I haven't said that nickname since I left this town.

But that doesn't matter because it works.

Parker goes silent, and I instantly miss her hysterical, slightly terrifying laughter.

Because this version of her? It's much scarier than the laughing.

Her back is ramrod straight, and her gold-speckled eyes narrow, losing that lively sparkle they've always had. She takes a step toward me. Then another. Again.

My back hits the shelf behind me, the liquor bottles rattling. *Why the hell does this tiny town have two full aisles of booze?* Oh, right. Probably because there's nothing else to do here than drink to help cope with the fact you live in the middle of nowhere.

"Don't."

It's one word, but it says so much.

"You don't have that right anymore."

Then she turns on her heel, leaving me in the middle of Jill's Bait & Tackle, my mind reeling and my heart hammering.

What the hell just happened?

"Noel? Is that you, bub?"

"I sure as shit hope so, or else we're going to have a serious talk about who you're leaving your door unlocked for, Lou Lou."

"Boy, I swear . . . ," I hear her mutter. She hates it when I call her Lou Lou, so I do it as often as possible.

I smile for the first time since Parker walked out of the grocery store.

There are so many reasons I never want to return to Emerald Grove, but my grandmother, Louise Hutton, or just Gran as everyone calls her, has never been one of them.

I take off my shoes, listening as she slowly rounds the corner from the kitchen, where, I have no doubt, she's been cooking all day. My stomach growls at the thought of her warm, buttery banana nut bread. Or maybe it's because I haven't eaten since this morning, which feels like forever ago at this point.

When she finally comes into view, I get a glimpse of her for the first time in six months, and my smile slips before I can catch it.

Has she always looked this frail? So tiny? So . . . breakable?

I can't remember a single time in the years I spent living with her that she's ever looked as fragile as she does now, and that includes the time she broke her foot hiking and spent weeks in a cast. Not even that slowed her down.

But seeing her now . . . She looks brittle. So . . . well, *old.* I know that's what happens to us all, but it's hard to reconcile that the woman before me is *my* grandmother, with her back hunched over just slightly and her winter-white hair that, up until now, she's always kept colored.

If someone said the word *grandmother*, this is what I would imagine. It's funny, because yes, even though she's always been my grandma, she's never *looked* like a grandma until now.

She winces ever so slightly as she hobbles closer, but I don't dare bring it up. She's sensitive about these things, and I don't want to piss her off when I only just got here.

"Well? What the hell are you staring for? Get over here and hug me already."

And just like that, my smile is back.

Oh, yeah, this is definitely her.

I cross the tiny entryway and sweep my seventy-eight-year-old grandmother into my arms, hugging her small frame tight, never wanting to let go. Much like she has for my entire life, she smells like fresh-baked sweets with just a hint of that damned aloe vera rub she swears can cure any ache or pain. Even though I think she's a little ridiculous for rubbing it on so often, I don't think it's a scent I'll ever tire of.

I hold on to her longer, not just because I've missed the hell out of her, but because I'm not so sure I want this to end just yet. I'm more than aware that my time with my grandmother is dwindling, and I don't know how many of these hugs I have left.

"Dang, bub, I know you missed me, but you want to let me go before your Kitchen Sink Cookies burn?"

"Shit. Why didn't you say so before?" I release her, nodding toward the kitchen. "Quick. Get back in there."

She swats at me with a roll of her eyes before following my instructions. I stay hot on her heels, tagging along, eager to get my hands on my favorite cookie.

I step into the kitchen that's been the same since I moved in when I was seven, and my jaw drops. "What the fuck?"

"Noel Benjamin Carter!" my grandmother admonishes. "I haven't added chocolate chips to this zucchini bread yet, and I swear I'll make 'em right out of that dish soap over there."

She gives me a stern glare that has me holding my hands up in surrender.

"Sorry, sorry. It's just . . . What the hell—*heck*—happened in here?"

"What?" She waves her hand around the room. "You don't like it?"

"No, it's not that. It's just . . . It's different."

She lifts a shoulder, and I try not to notice how much of her bone I can see stretching against her shirt with the gesture. "Sometimes change is nice."

For my entire life, this kitchen has had bright-yellow walls, the cabinets have always been chestnut, and her fridge was a white retro style. Only it wasn't just a style, it was authentically retro, and she had to have someone out to fix it at least once a year.

But now those once too-vivid walls have been painted a subdued light gray, the cabinets repainted white, and the old fridge has been swapped for a sparkling new modern one. Hell, even the rooster-print hand towels that used to hang off the stove are gone.

I understand change happens, maybe more than most, but it almost feels like a part of my childhood has died with the makeover.

"It looks great, Lou Lou."

With lightning-quick reflexes, like I didn't just watch her shuffle down the hall with a grimace, she whips her hand towel at me, and I catch it as effortlessly as she's thrown it.

She holds out her hand. "Now give it back."

I laugh, handing it back to her, then make my way over to the kitchen table, which is thankfully still the same, and settle into the chair. It creaks the same way it always has, bringing me even more comfort.

"There was no way I was getting rid of that table—too many memories," she says, almost reading my mind as she continues folding in the ingredients for her zucchini bread.

It's always like this when I see her. The last time she came to my apartment in LA, she baked for six hours straight, and when she left, I had a counter full of sweets. And when I flew her out to that set in Vancouver, she wandered off and worked in the craft services department for half a day before I found her. Got her name in the credits for that one. "And we kept the stove too," she continues. "My recipes are fine-tuned to that old lug. I'm old enough to know not to mess with a good thing."

Oh, but you did. The kitchen was perfect before.

"It was a good kitchen that served me well for many years, but I figured I'd give it a chance at a new life. We all need chances sometimes."

I don't miss the true meaning of her words. Her comments are directed at my leaving Emerald Grove for LA. In her own way, she is telling me to get over the change like she got over me leaving.

"Well, it looks great. Really. I like the color on the walls."

"Thanks. We had a lot of fun picking that out."

I let my eyes roll over the kitchen, looking at every detail and trying to discern what's different and what's stayed the same. The eclectic signs she once had littering the far wall are gone save for a handful of them, and they're now artfully arranged instead of squeezed wherever they'd fit. The bird clock that used to chirp insufferably every hour is now gone—one change I am definitely not mad about—and has been replaced by a simpler, less noisy design.

"Do you want Cornflake Cookies too?" she asks out of nowhere, though I shouldn't be surprised. She'd always had a one-track mind when I lived here, and that's what she can bake next for me. I know she's going all out now because she's missed me. It's how she shows her love, and I'll gladly accept, especially since I never get home-baked goods like this back in LA.

I chuckle. "You've already made banana bread, Kitchen Sink Cookies, and zucchini bread."

She peeks at me over her shoulder. "So . . . ?"

"So of course I want Cornflake Cookies too."

She winks. "That's my boy."

"Do you want any help?" I ask, rising from my chair. I'm already pulling my sleeves up, ready to dive in.

"Not a chance, bub. You came all the way out here and even flew in early for little old me. Let me spoil my only grandbaby."

I resume my spot with a grin, not even bothering to fight her about calling me a baby when I'm pushing thirty. How can I when she's clearly so happy to have me here, even whistling that old, comforting tune she always has? I have no idea what it is, but she's done it for as long as I can remember.

I watch her work, and she asks me about the movie I just wrapped filming, so I fill her in on the plot.

"Do you like it?" she asks after I've finished, her hands busy pouring the zucchini-bread batter into the loaf pan.

"If you'd have asked me that a few days ago, I'd have been on the fence about a good portion of it."

"I sense a *but* in there . . ."

"But after the director let me take a few liberties with the dialogue, I loved every minute." Honestly, Bridget's advice to pull from past heartache might have been a little *too* good. Because after that, it was like this whole new side of me was tapped into, and the words that spewed from me came a bit too easily. That, in turn, opened some old wounds I'd much rather leave closed.

Of course, running into said old wound earlier this evening didn't help either.

"Proud of you, kid. You're doing good work."

"Thanks. I wish everyone in town felt that way. It should make Friday pretty interesting."

She slides the zucchini bread into the oven, then crosses her skin-and-bones arms and rests against the counter. I wish she'd take a proper break and sit with me, but I know her too well. She's not going for it.

"What do you mean?"

I drag my hand through my hair. "It's nothing."

She laughs. "Oh, sweet boy. I've known you from the moment you tumbled out of your mother's vagina—"

"For her sake, I really hope that's not true."

"—and for as long as I can remember, when you're uncomfortable or nervous or don't want to upset someone, you run your hand through your hair like you just did. So spill it. Not like I'm going to tell anyone your business."

I laugh, barely stopping myself from doing it again, then fold my arms over my chest, mirroring her post. "Fine. I ran into Mr. McMichaels at Jill's."

"Dick?"

Oddly, hearing my grandmother say *dick* is less jarring than when Parker said it. Probably because even though she likes to get on me about cussing and often threatens me with washing my mouth out with soap, my grandmother is just as bad about it, especially in the right setting.

Parker, though . . . Well, I've never heard her cuss. Ever. It was always as cute as it was frustrating.

"Yes, Dick. Feels weird calling my former principal *Dick*, doesn't it?"

"If any of my old teachers were still kickin' it, I'd likely call them Missus. Humans are weird."

"Mm-hmm," I agree.

"So what'd Dick say that upset you?" she continues.

"I wouldn't say *upset*. It was just a vibe. Like he wasn't so happy with me leaving Emerald Grove and not coming back."

"Well, you have been away an awfully long time, and you know how the town feels about that sort of thing."

My shoulders deflate, that bit of guilt I always feel about leaving my grandmother behind nagging at me. "I know."

"Now, you know I don't mind, so don't go doing that whole sad-sack thing. I'm glad you went off and found something you love. That's all I've ever wanted for you. All your *parents* ever wanted for you." She lifts her drawn-on brows pointedly. "And they'd be damn proud of you for doing it."

I know she's right. My parents *would* be proud of me. I can feel it to the depths of my soul, and I wish like hell they were still around to see me now, but they died way before acting was even an idea I had for my future.

Emotion climbs up my throat just thinking about them. Sure, they've been on my mind over the last ten years—and they always will be—but being back here reminds me even more of what I lost.

It was a simple trip to Seattle, one they'd made several times before. It was supposed to be a night of fun. Instead, it ended in tragedy, leaving their car wrapped around a tree on the winding road leading into town and me without the two most important people in my life.

Everything changed after that. Not only did I lose my parents and have to move across town and in with my grandmother, but I also lost a bit of my childhood too. I started to look at life—and Emerald Grove—a lot differently after that.

"So who gives a hoot what old Dick says," Gran continues, pulling me back to the present. "They might be a little standoffish, but the people in this town still love you."

"Not all of them."

In a silent question, she tips her head to the side, and I sigh.

"Parker," I explain.

And really, it's all the explanation she needs. She's more than aware of my history with the auburn-haired girl from down the street. We were practically attached at the hip from the moment Parker moved to town, and we kept that up until the night I left for LA.

Then ten years passed, and here we are—nothing but awkward encounters at the grocery store.

"Oh." She says it so simply and definitively, and I'm thankful because the last thing I want to do tonight is rehash the horrible reunion from an hour ago.

Instead of pressuring me to talk, she lets it go, spinning on her heel and pulling items from various cabinets. I've watched her make them enough times to know she's getting ready to make the Cornflake Cookies.

This time, no matter what she says, I am helping. It's been too long since I've stood beside her in this kitchen, baking. We used to do it all the time, and I miss it far more than I realized until just now.

I rise from my seat, stepping next to her, towering over her tiny five-foot-two frame.

"All right, Gran. Put me to work."

And that's what we do for the next few hours—make cookies and have dinner before turning in for the night.

Maybe this trip back to Emerald Grove won't be so bad after all.

CHAPTER FOUR

Parker

"Oh, this is bad. This is *so* bad."

I step back from the wall I've been working on for the last six hours, and there is one thing I am absolutely certain of . . .

I hate it.

I was trying to create something different and eye-catching by alternating vertical slats of dark and light wood of different lengths, but it's not turning out how I wanted it to. It definitely draws the eye, but not in the way I intended. It's . . . flat. I need something that wows. Not this.

"It's hideous," I say out loud to nobody but myself. "Why did I think this was a good idea?"

"Because it is."

I jump, my wet paintbrush flying out of my hand, and gray paint splashes against the floor, splattering out for at least two feet. Thankfully, I was of sound enough mind in the wee hours of the morning to cover the newly laid hardwood, or else that would be a whole other project we'd have to take on today.

"Axel! What the heck?" I glower at the man standing in the doorway of Rossi Café. I carefully step out of the way of the mess I've made so I don't track the paint anywhere else. "I didn't even hear you come in."

"Clearly not, which is saying something because that bell is loud as shit."

I ignore his statement. "What are you doing here?"

"Um, working?" he answers, sauntering inside like he owns the place, which he most certainly does not. "I think the better question is, What are *you* doing here? You're never in this early."

"No, the *true* better question is, What's in that container you got there? It looks an awful lot like leftovers. Did you bring me leftovers?" I clap my hands, bouncing on my heels. I'm unsure if my reaction is purely based on excitement for the world's best lasagna or because I'm so tired I'm a little delirious at this point.

Oh, who am I kidding? *Of course* it's because of the lasagna.

"Why, yes, Parker, this *is* lasagna."

I race toward him, but when he holds up a beefy hand, I screech to a halt—literally, my shoes skid across the shiny new floors, emitting a piercing noise.

"Ew. That was terrible," I mutter.

"Want to know what else is terrible? You didn't bring my wine. You're lucky I found a bottle stashed deep in the fridge, but I still want answers." His brows pull tightly together. "Where were you last night? You are never a no-show. What gives?"

There's no mistaking the worry in his gaze, which makes me feel ten times worse than I already do for bailing. But after that horrible encounter with Noel, there was no way I was going to be able to go over to Axel's and pretend everything was fine in front of him, his wife, and his kids. I wouldn't have been able to play Auntie Parker and dream up stories about princesses who find their happily ever after when mine was ripped away from me. And it would have taken just one look from my best friend, and he would have been asking—

"Whose ass do I have to kick?"

That. He'd have been asking that.

Just like I didn't want to deal with it last night, I don't want to deal with it now. Truthfully, I feel ridiculous even being upset about the whole thing. From bumping into Noel to laughing like I'd lost my mind to getting upset over a silly nickname. It all seems absurd in the light of day.

"It's nothing."

"Right. Tell that to the tears welling up in your eyes. Either you tell me who I owe a beatdown to or I promise I'll not only eat this lasagna in front of you but also tell Mary you hate her cooking, and she'll never invite you over for dinner again."

I gasp, my hand going to my chest. "You wouldn't dare!"

"Oh, I would *so* dare." He tries to cross his big arms, but he's still holding the leftovers, so he fumbles a few times before finally giving up.

It's just comical enough to cause a laugh to bubble out of me, the noise so sudden and foreign feeling it surprises me, which makes me sad, and then suddenly the tears that were stinging my eyes begin to drip down my face, and I feel ridiculous all over again.

I *hate* feeling ridiculous.

But I love that my big lug of a best friend doesn't hesitate to cross the café and circle his arms around me.

"Dammit, Park," he mutters, his chin bumping against the top of my head as he pats my back. "What's going on? I haven't seen you like this in a long, long time."

I know what he's referring to, and I find it funny that the reason I'm crying now is the same reason I was crying then—Noel.

"It's—"

"Don't you dare. Don't say it's nothing. I saw the *Gazette* this morning."

I groan into him. "I don't understand why they think putting a fancy name like *Gazette* on it makes it anything less than a gossip rag." I sigh. "I guess everyone knows now."

"Oh, if it's in the *Emerald Grove Gazette*, then everyone definitely knows that Noel Carter is back in town several days earlier than planned. I assume that's why you didn't come over last night?"

I nod, stepping out of his embrace. "Yeah. I, uh, ran into him at Jill's in the liquor aisle."

He winces. "But there's only one way in and out of that aisle."

"Yup. Trapped."

He shakes his head. "What happened? Did he say something to upset you? Because if he did, I swear, I'll—"

"Beat him up? Jeez, you're violent today, you know that?"

"It's the lack of sleep. Makes me aggressive." Then almost as if on cue, he lets out a long yawn. "But also, yeah, I'd kick the ass of anyone who messed with you, Park."

"Even if it's Noel?"

He curls his lip up in disgust. "*Especially* if it's Noel."

"He's a famous actor. He could sue you for ruining his face."

Gone is the sneer, replaced quickly by a grin. "So you're saying I'd win the fight, huh?"

I roll my eyes, shoving at him. "Shut up."

"Shoving me? Wow, and you called *me* violent today."

"Keep it up, and I'll lob something at your head again," I promise.

"And I'll withhold this." He holds up the lasagna I almost forgot about. I lunge at it, but it's pointless. For someone so gigantic, he sure does move fast with little effort.

He holds the Tupperware container just out of my reach—even on my tiptoes—and shakes it lightly.

"Ah, ah, ah," he says. "Tell me what made you so upset that you couldn't bring me my wine, and *then* you can have your pasta."

"You already know."

"You did not get so upset you couldn't come for dinner just because you ran into Noel. Something else had to have happened. Remember, I know you, Parker, so spill."

"I don't want to. It's . . . embarrassing."

"Embarrassing? What'd you do, flash him?"

"Axel!" My cheeks heat just thinking about doing something so outlandish. "Why would I do that?"

He shrugs. "I don't know. It was the first embarrassing thing I thought of."

"Oh, so you think I should be embarrassed by my boobs?"

Now Axel's cheeks are turning red. No, his *whole face* is.

"Please, can we not discuss your boobs?"

"You started it," I point out.

"And now I'm ending it, so let's move on to where you tell me what awful, embarrassing thing happened."

I huff. "Fine. It was . . ." I blow out a breath, drawing this out far more than I should because saying it out loud will make me feel like a fool for getting so upset that I spent a few hours wandering the streets before I finally came here and worked through the night. "He . . . *HecalledmePeter.*"

"What?" he asks, and I can't blame him. I rushed those four words out like they were one.

"He called me Peter," I say more clearly this time. "I know it seems ridiculous, but—"

"Peter was his nickname for you."

I tip my head to the side. "How did you know that?"

"Um, on a good day, there are about two thousand one hundred people who live in this town, Parker. *Everyone* knows he used to call you that. Why do you think we all started calling Mr. Donaldson's dog Boy?"

"What does Mr. Donaldson's dog have to do with this?"

He gives a look that says, *Come on, now. Think about it.*

I think back to when Mr. Donaldson brought home a new puppy and how excited he was and how the town went a little wild with buying dog toys and how he named it—*oh my gosh!*

Peter. He named the dog Peter.

"The whole town changed a dog's name for me? Because Noel used to call me Peter Parker?"

My obsession with Spider-Man started when I was young, back when I was convinced I looked just like Mary Jane, thanks to my hair.

This carried over well into moving to Emerald Grove. Naturally, Noel picked up on it, and soon after I moved here, he started calling me Peter because of my love for the web-slinging hero and my name. It stuck from the time I was eight until . . . well, until he left.

I haven't been called it since.

Axel shrugs like it's no big deal when it really is. "We kind of like you around here."

Like me? *Like me?*

That sounds an awful lot like love to me.

It's touching and completely unexpected. And it makes me love Emerald Grove even more.

"We're totally Team Parker around these parts."

That part I don't like. Team Parker? As if they have to pick one of us? It shouldn't be that way. They shouldn't "pick me" because I stayed and Noel left. Is that why Dick was so rude to him last night? Because he left? Because of me?

"So, he called you Peter, and it freaked you out, so you went home and panicked there?" Axel guesses, pulling me from my thoughts.

"Sort of. First, he asked me how I was doing."

"He . . ." Axel blinks slowly. "He asked you how you were doing? Like you're an old acquaintance and you weren't obsessed with each other at one point? Like ten years hasn't gone by since you last saw him?" he asks through clenched teeth. "As if he didn't just walk out on you like your . . ."

He doesn't finish that sentence, but we both know what he was going to say.

Like your father.

It's no secret to anyone in this town what happened to my mother and me. One day, my dad was here, then the next, he wasn't. Everyone knows he walked out on us before breakfast, never to return. We just all like to pretend it didn't happen, bury it down deep, and never talk about it.

Or at least that's what I like to do.

"I wouldn't say we were *obsessed* with each other, but yes," I say, pretending Axel didn't just almost bring up the catalyst of my abandonment issues.

"That's . . ." He inhales sharply. "Well, it's fucking bullshit, is what it is. I'm kicking his ass."

Before I realize what's happening, Axel spins on his heel and is halfway out the door before I move.

"Wait, wait, wait!" I reach for him, snatching the tail end of his work shirt and tugging at him to stop. "Don't. Please."

"Why not?" he asks, whirling around, his face red, and not with embarrassment this time. Now he's mad. Big-time. "Why shouldn't I? He leaves you high and dry after telling you he loves you, then breezes back into town like nothing happened, making you cry, and I'm just supposed to be okay with that?"

I want so desperately to squeeze my eyes shut against the truth of what he just said, as if doing that could magically make it *not* true, but I don't. Axel means it when he says he'll beat Noel up, and that's the last thing I need right now.

"No. You're not. I'm not either. But this is a little much, don't you think?"

He sighs, then lets me pull him back into the café, effectively giving up on his mission. While I'm touched this is his reaction, I don't want something stirred up just because I couldn't handle seeing Noel again, the one person who I never thought would break me like my father did.

Boy, was I wrong about that.

When I'm satisfied Axel won't try to take off after my former best friend again, I return to my paint-splattered corner, pick up my brush, and set it inside the tray. There's paint dotted along the wall, but it doesn't matter. It will have to be repainted anyway because this is not turning out how I wanted.

"Did I know he'd be coming back to town? Obviously. I lead the restoration committee, and this is my project. We *had* to invite him. But did I expect to have a few more days to prepare for it? Definitely.

Do I wish our long-awaited reunion had gone differently, maybe involving some apologizing, a bouquet of roses, or a pony? I know it's a tall request and perhaps a little ludicrous, but yes. But last night was my fault, not Noel's. I shouldn't have let him get to me or let his simple question mess with my head. I should have handled it better, like a mature adult would, just as he was trying to do."

"I'm sorry, but that's still bullshit, Parker. Not just the pony part—because what the fuck?—but also, you deserve an apology for what happened. You don't deserve to have him blow you off like you're some random person from his past. You're more than that to him, and you deserve more than that. Like an explanation for never coming back, for fucking starters."

I exhale heavily. He's right in some ways, but I also understand why Noel reacted the way he did. It's not like I handled last night perfectly either. Heck, I haven't handled *any* nights perfectly, especially not when he left all those years ago.

"We were both in shock, that's all."

"Stop making excuses for him. That's the same thing you did when he left."

"I'm not making excuses. I'm just saying—"

The bell over the top of the café door—the one Gianna and Greta insisted on keeping because it belonged to a great-great-Rossi-someone-or-other many years ago—dings, and we turn toward the entry.

Of course, Axel and his ginormous self are right in front of the door, blocking my view of whoever just walked in.

"We're closed!" I call out to the person I can't see. "We're remodeling and will be open—"

"You."

It's one word uttered by Axel, but it's all I need to know who just walked through that door.

"Uh, Axel, hey," Noel says. "Been a long time."

"Not fucking long enough, Hollywood," my business partner growls, stepping toward Noel, who I'm suddenly very worried for.

"Axel!" I hiss at him, lunging toward him to stop whatever madness is about to ensue. It takes him a second, but he stops.

Probably because he knows that even though I'm only five foot six, and much, much smaller than his frame, I'll still kick his butt if he messes up my jobsite by fighting.

His big shoulders hitch up and down, his free hand making a fist at his side.

I step up beside him, coming face-to-face with Noel for the second time in less than twenty-four hours. How can you go a decade without seeing someone, and then suddenly, they're everywhere?

I place a hand on my partner's shoulder. "You can go now."

"What? Not a chance. There's no fucking way I'm—"

I glare up at him, daring him to keep going.

To my surprise, he doesn't.

Instead, his chocolate gaze darts around my face like he's looking for any sign I'm in trouble or not serious, but I am serious. So, so serious. I don't want this to turn into something it doesn't need to, like them fighting or Axel coming to my defense.

"Okay," he relents. "Okay. But if you need me for *anything* . . ."

"I know." I nod. "I know."

"Okay," he repeats. Then he looks—no, he *sneers*—over at the guy who used to be my whole world. "I'd say it was good to see you, but that'd be a damn lie."

A laugh bubbles out of me before I can stop it, which earns me a smile from Axel and a scowl from Noel, but I don't mind.

"I'll see you later, right?" the giant asks, and I know he's really saying, *I'll be back for the details and to make sure I don't need to make good on my promise of fighting him.*

"Yes," I tell him. "But Axel?"

"Hmm?"

I nod toward the Tupperware in his hand. "My dinner from last night, please?"

His eyes narrow, but he's not about to deny me right now.

He hands me the lasagna and wraps me in a quick hug.

"You have thirty minutes," he whispers before releasing me.

I smile, loving how protective he is, and then with one last glare at our surprise guest, he leaves. And I'm alone with Noel Carter once again.

We stand there awkwardly for far too long for two people who know entirely too much about each other.

I know he wore superhero underwear until he was seventeen, that he slept with a night-light even longer, and that he always had to hug his grandmother before bed, or else he'd be up in the middle of the night because he couldn't sleep. Heck, I've seen him projectile vomit SpaghettiOs before. We're far from strangers.

But right now? Right now, it feels like we've never met before.

"So, is—"

"I was—"

We start and stop at the same time.

But instead of that self-conscious chuckle that usually follows situations like that, we go back to silence.

And I absolutely hate it.

Why is this so hard? Why can't we just talk? Why did he have to be gone for ten years?

Oh, right. Because *Hollywood.*

And right now, he looks every bit like he's from Hollywood, with the light scruff lining his face, his styled midnight hair, perfectly fitted dark-wash jeans, black button-down shirt, snazzy deep-brown leather jacket, and matching boots. It's like he just stepped off a movie set or out to lunch with whatever starlet he's linked to this week.

He looks so similar to—yet different from—the boy I grew up with.

"Is this your place?" he asks, looking around the messy restaurant.

Out of everything I thought he'd say, that was not what I was expecting.

"This is Rossi Café. Surely you haven't been gone long enough to forget that."

It's a dig. He knows it, and I do too.

Regret eats at me for stooping so low, but it only lasts a moment, mainly because it feels good to finally acknowledge out loud to him that he's been gone for far too long.

"I remember. It's why I came here. Was craving one of those—"

"Italian Rossi breakfast sandwiches, double the ham and extra cheese," I finish for him. I've heard him order the exact meal a hundred times before, and I've likely ordered it for him a hundred times more.

This place is an old haunt of ours, which might be part of why I want so badly to make this café perfect for Gianna and Greta now that they've taken it over from Gianna's parents. That and because it's a staple in this town, passed down from one Rossi to the next. It's vital to our community, just like I believe the theater is.

"You're early."

"Pardon?" he asks. His eyes, the perfect mix of blue and green, catch the morning sun just right, making them brighter and clearer than they already are.

"For the ceremony. You're early."

"You . . . know about that?"

I huff out a laugh. "This is Emerald Grove. Everyone knows about it."

"This town likes to talk too much."

"You can say that again."

"This town likes to talk too much," he repeats.

I glare at him, and he smiles back, and I hate that I like it so much. It's different from the smiles I've seen him give in interviews. While I might have been upset with Noel, I never wanted to see him fail, and I've supported everything he's done in his career so far, even suffering through that terrible werewolf show he did.

His eyes wander around the café before settling on me, and I wonder what he sees. Does he still see the same awkward girl from high school? The one who worshipped him and followed him everywhere? Or does he see the independent woman I've become? The one who has been hardened by life? Who has most definitely fully recovered from the heartbreak she's suffered at his hands?

"So if it's not your place, then what are you doing here?"

I wave my hand around. "Working."

He doesn't look as surprised as I expected him to. Instead, he grins. "You're renovating it?" I nod. "Why does that fit you so perfectly?"

It's probably because I spent much of my youth designing and building the sets for every play at the Goodman Theater. It was the place I escaped to whenever life got too overwhelming or I remembered that the person who was supposed to love me unconditionally bailed. I loved losing myself in the set design so much that when it came time to buy a house, I got a fixer-upper and tackled the project myself, using it as a form of therapy to cope with the hole Noel left in my life.

Well, it wasn't all me. Axel helped too. It's what led us to realize we made a great team and gave us the confidence to form our business together.

"It looks really great in here," he says. "Can't believe it's the same place where we once ate six meatball subs in one sitting."

"We? *You* ate five and a half of those six."

"I was a growing boy! Besides, that's still teamwork."

Teamwork.

It implies that we used to be a team, and we were.

It's a hard reality to swallow now that we feel like strangers.

I turn away from him, uncomfortable with that realization, and march back to my all-night project—the accent wall for the back of the café that's not coming out how I wanted. I can't decide if it's me who sucks at designing or if I don't like it because I got zero sleep last night and desperately need some.

"Did you make this?" he asks, stepping up beside me as I stare at the wall full of mismatched wood, only one corner of which is painted gray.

"Yes."

"I like it."

I frown. "It's not turning out how I wanted."

"Well," he says, folding his arms over his chest, "let's tackle it one thing at a time. What's jumping out at you first?"

A few simple words, and just like that, I'm taken back in time to when we used to stand on the stage of the old theater and stare up at my set pieces. He'd say the same thing he just did, and we'd work through whatever was bothering me. This typically ended with me realizing I was being silly and that the scenery I'd just spent so long on looked great.

This feels like a mirror image of that.

"It's the slats," I say, allowing myself to dip back in time. "I think I should have gone with a different angle or a more uniform look, which is why I started painting it."

"You're getting ahead of yourself, Peter. One thing at a time."

There's that nickname again—*Peter.*

I've gone years without hearing it, and now I'm being called it twice in less than twenty-four hours. Hearing it now is less jarring than last night, but it still doesn't feel as good as it once did, that heavy feeling settling into my stomach just like it did in Jill's.

I ignore it. "The angle, then."

"It's very . . ."

"Plain?" I finish for him.

"A little. What's going over here against the wall?"

"A couch. Gianna and her wife wanted a space where people here for a quick treat could relax."

"Hmm," he purrs, widening his stance.

I try my best not to notice how it makes his jeans fit tighter against his legs or how it reminds me of simpler days when he used to stand and think with me for hours at the Goodman Theater, trying to get a set design right.

I don't notice any of those things.

"Then what about not going all the way to the bottom?" he suggests. "Sort of gives it a waterfall effect, which is appropriate for Emerald

Grove." He gives me a crooked smile, probably because I know what he's referring to far too well.

Tucked away on a trail leading out of town is a waterfall that all the locals and very few tourists know about. While the town has been picking up a lot of steam lately and gaining popularity thanks to new vacation rentals, we're usually just a pit stop on people's way to the Olympic National Forest. Most don't stick around long enough to see this place's true beauty, like Rockaway Falls—a double waterfall that's worth the hour hike one way.

I can't count the number of times Noel and I hiked out there for the day. If we weren't at the theater, we were at the Falls. It was our little slice of fun away from the busybodies in town who were always ready to spy on us and report back to Gran or my mother.

The urge to make the trek to our old stomping grounds washes over me something fierce, a pull I haven't felt in many, many years.

"*And* it would mean you get to save a lot of the work you've already done," he continues. "Keep the natural wood look to really make that waterfall effect pop. And I'm sure you could find somewhere to repurpose the boards we pull up so you don't waste materials. I know how much you hate doing that."

He's right on both counts. I hate wasting materials, and with just a few minor adjustments—take a few boards out here, readjust a few there—I can salvage it to make a stunning accent wall that I know everyone will love, me especially.

The Falls and this café have always held a special spot in my heart. This wall will only make me love them both even more.

"All right. You've convinced me."

"Knew I could."

He sheds his leather jacket, tossing it onto the dirty counter nearby, like it probably didn't cost as much as two months' worth of mortgage payments, and then rolls his long-sleeved shirt up to his elbows.

I hate that I'm not focusing on *why* he's doing this and instead just watching how his veins jump with every move he makes.

I don't pull my eyes away until he claps his hands, jerking my attention back to him and not his very, very toned forearms.

"Let's get to work."

Then before I can say anything, he drops to his haunches and begins removing boards.

When did he even pick up a crowbar? Better yet, why am I letting him stay?

I must be more tired than I thought, because instead of asking him to leave, I join in, grabbing my own crowbar and setting to work.

We work wordlessly for the next I-don't-even-know-how-long. Noel peels off pieces of wood, his fancy jeans pressed against the wet paint splatters on the floor like he doesn't have a care in the world, even though we both know those pants cost entirely too much for labor like this.

We're nearly done prying off the first section of slats when Noel breaks the silence.

"So, you and Axel, huh?"

"Me and Axel," I respond. "Who would have thought?"

"Definitely not me," he mutters, using a little too much force, sending the plank he was working on flying across the room.

I stare at the board as it finally settles near the front door.

Is he mad I'm friends with Axel? It's not like he was *that* terrible in high school. Sure, he could be a jerk, but that was so long ago.

"Because of high school and your rivalry?" I ask, turning back to Noel. "Because he's changed a lot since then, you know. We all have."

He sighs, ripping off another piece of wood, again with a bit too much force. "Oh, trust me, I'm aware."

He pushes to his feet, carefully putting his crowbar under the painted wood strips so I can replace them with the natural ones.

I follow him up, and though I'm used to working next to a man who towers over me, I'm *not* used to working next to Noel. It instantly feels different standing here with him than it does with Axel. He moves differently, not just because he has less finesse than someone who does this for a living. It's more than that. Or maybe I'm just paying more attention.

Instead of staring at how his arms flex with every careful pull of the wood, I work my bar behind a slat and pull. It doesn't budge.

"I guess I just didn't expect you and Axel, of all people," he continues, wrenching off another piece and breaking the one next to it. "Here, I got it."

He reaches over, our hands barely brushing as he takes over pulling.

"Me and Axel? What do you mean?"

"You know . . ." He trails off with a shrug. "It's just that you two never got along, so I'm shocked you're a couple now. But you're right, people change, so what do I know? Maybe he's a great guy."

"Oh, he *is* great, but we aren't together."

He gives me an incredulous look, and I laugh.

"He's *married*."

He stops what he's doing, staring down at me in shock. "Married?"

I nod. "Yup. With triplets and another baby on the way."

"He reproduced?"

I smack at his arm. "Hey! Be nice. That's my business partner you're talking about."

"I'm sorry, but you two own a business together?"

"Yep. Cooke & Pruitt Renovations. Axel handles the construction and I do the designing. The tourist influx has increased a lot over the years, thanks to all those people who live in camper vans and travel out this way, so more and more people were looking to invest in rental properties for extra income. We saw the need so we jumped at it, and our company was born. Now we do commercial stuff too."

I don't know why I'm rambling to him about my business with Axel—maybe because I'm immensely proud of everything we've built—but I don't miss the way Noel's eyes shine with that same look he used to give me.

Pride.

"That's . . . Wow. That's incredible. Truly." He rips off the last of the painted wood and then sets his tools on the worktable. He dusts his hands off on his pants before placing them on his hips. "I can't believe the Axel you're talking about is the same one who used to snort chocolate milk in the cafeteria, or the same one who would pretend I was invisible and walk through me with an *Oh, sorry, I didn't see you there, Nerdy Noel.*"

I cringe a little thinking about the stunts he used to pull, like terrorizing the town farmers' markets by letting loose any wild animal he could get his hands on or smashing up people's gardens, but that hasn't been the guy I know in a long, long time. Now he tends to half the community rows in our town garden, especially for the older folks who can't get out there as often. And he's the first one there setting up the market every third Saturday of the month.

A lot of credit for his transformation goes to his wife and how, the moment he met her, he knew Mary was the one and wanted to be someone she deserved. But I like to think it was me who was a good influence on him first.

Either way, it's safe to say he's nothing like the guy Noel remembers.

"I promise he's changed. He's matured. He's not that same guy from ten years ago."

"I'll believe you," Noel says, not looking like he does in the least.

"Good. And just so we're clear, there is absolutely *nothing* going on between us. We're friends. *Best* friends. He's like a brother to me."

"Don't," he bites out, and the ire behind his words shocks me.

Where the hell did that come from? "Don't what?"

His jaw tightens, and his eyes grow darker by the second. "Just don't."

I cross my arms over my chest, frustrated now because it all clicks into place what he means—don't say Axel is my best friend.

And honestly, how dare he? After all this time, he thinks he can just come back to town and pretend like nothing happened, that he can waltz in here and work beside me like we haven't not spoken for years?

Guilt gnaws at me because I'm responsible for that last bit, too, but still. Too much time has passed for him to act like he has a say in how I live my life or who I'm friends with.

"What ticks you off the most? That I have a new best friend? Or that it's Axel?" I scoff. "You were gone for ten years, Noel. *Ten years.* I'm allowed to have a new best friend."

"I know!" he shouts. His chest rises and falls with hard breaths, his sea-colored eyes now black, like stormy waters. "I know how long I was gone. I'm very fucking aware of it. I . . ."

He pinches the bridge of his nose as if he's already tired of this conversation, even though we've only just cracked the ice wall built between us all this time.

The ice wall that *I'm* to blame for. He might have been the one to put physical distance between us, but I'm responsible for the emotional detachment.

I did what I thought was best at the time, and even though it hurt, I'm not sure I'd have made a different choice.

He sighs, dropping his hand. "Don't equate best friends to sibling-like bonds. That's all I was meaning."

What? Why would that bother him? So I said Axel is like a brother to me. Big deal. There's no reason for Noel to be upset by that.

"Why not?"

He steps into me, so close that the scent of wood, paint, and construction is long gone. It's firmly replaced by spicy sandalwood. I hate it, yet I love it, because after all these years, after all the money he makes, he's still wearing the same cologne I bought him as a teen.

"Because I was your best friend once, Peter," he says quietly. "And I assure you, the feelings I have for you are not even in the same realm as sibling-like."

Have.

Not had.

He said *have.*

That throws me nearly as much as having him so close.

Without another word, he turns, waltzing from the shop and leaving his jacket and far too many questions burning the tip of my tongue.

And now there's no doubt I'll be seeing Noel Carter before the ceremony again.

CHAPTER FIVE

Noel

I left my jacket.

I realize it the second I step out of Rossi Café.

"Because I was your best friend once, Peter. And I assure you, the feelings I have for you are not even in the same realm as sibling-like."

What the fuck was I thinking, saying that? Where did it even come from? Why did I use the present tense?

And why do I want to march back in there and fight with her some more, even after all that?

We've always bickered, even when we were younger. She's stubborn when she wants to be and always has something to say. As much as those things have always exasperated me to no end, I might have missed them the most.

Hell, I think I might have missed *her* more than I've let myself believe.

I can't believe she's in business with Axel Cooke.

He was *my* friend first. We did everything together until we were eight. Then one day, Parker came to town, and the next, Axel and I were nothing. He turned into a bully, slinging insults almost constantly. I could handle his snide remarks about how I was a nerd for liking theater or how I'd rather spend my time watching movies than playing football. It was when he turned his ire toward Parker that I started to hate him.

So why, out of all the people, would she partner with him? And after all the shit he put her through? All the times he picked on her? Did that much really change in the last ten years?

I walk down Borgen Avenue, keeping my head low to avoid unwanted conversations, which means *all* conversations. I've never walked through a minefield before, but I imagine it's similar to navigating the main strip of Emerald Grove with everyone wanting to stop and chat or take selfies. And trust me, they'll talk about anything. I don't know the number of times I've been stopped so someone can ask after my gran, then suddenly the conversation takes a left turn and I'm being educated on the importance of ensuring my bowel movements are frequent but not too frequent and to add fiber to my diet to stay regular.

It's more than twice, which is two times far too many.

If they aren't stopping me for life advice or pictures and autographs, they're stopping to ask why I've been gone for so long, which is a whole other conversation I don't want to have. It's awkward, and people who were once friendly toward me are now cold and distant.

"Noel!"

I lift my head, unsurprised to find Leonard Figgins waving his arm eagerly as he darts across the street, struggling to juggle whatever's in his hands and that same messenger bag he used to carry around in high school smacking against his legs.

"Noel!" he calls again like he's worried I'm going to run away, though I don't know why. I've come to a complete stop and am staring right at him.

He screeches to a halt in front of me, running his hands over his hair and then shoving his glasses—also the same style he's been wearing since we were kids—up his nose.

"Noel!" he repeats, and I'm beginning to wonder if he thinks I don't know my name or something. "It's so great to see you. How's Gran doing?"

I'm unsure why he's asking me how my grandmother is doing. He lives here and sees her more than I do.

"Hey, Figs," I say, using the nickname he's had since he was seven.

His lips pinch together with displeasure. "Leonard, please."

"Right. Sorry. How are you, Leonard?"

"Oh, you know. I'm doing well. I'm the lead reporter at the *Gazette* now." He grins proudly. "It's so great to have you back in town. You're here for the Noel Carter Theater ceremony, right?"

I barely repress my groan at the mention of why I returned. Why does this damn theater have to be named after me? I want to find whoever this anonymous donor is and give them a piece of my mind.

"Yes, I'm just in town through the weekend."

"Only the weekend? Hmm. That's too bad. Doesn't feel the same around here without you."

Oh, I highly doubt *Leonard* here feels that way at all. He's hated me since ninth grade, when I beat him out for the lead in *The Importance of Being Earnest* at the Goodman Theater. Everyone in town knew acting was his passion—well, anything that gave him the spotlight was, really—so when he didn't get cast as the lead, he was livid and had his father, a prominent figure in this town who has his hand in multiple businesses, write the board to get him a spot on the school newspaper. He then went on to trash my performance and the play entirely. And the following year when I beat him again. He didn't even try out the third year—he just stuck to dissing me in his review, which is something he's kept up over the years. Gran's ranted several times about the articles he's done on my movies since I left.

It's safe to say the guy really has it in for me, so I'm surprised he's here talking to me, acting as if we're old buds.

"Anyway, how are you feeling about the new theater?" he asks, shoving his glasses up once more. "Excited? Eager? Maybe wanting something else to go in that beautiful and expansive space? Maybe something a little more economically positive for the community?"

He's smiling up at me, but there's a motive behind it, and I'd bet the Rolex on my wrist that he's searching for information, trying to get the latest headline out of me.

I should have known. The *Emerald Grove Gazette* has been a thorn in this town's side for as long as I can remember, always cooking up gossip, twisting whatever the townspeople say to stir up drama. It's fitting for him he'd end up working there. And if his thinly veiled questions are any indication, I'm sure an "accidental" meeting between us is nothing more than him following me around to get me to confess to hating the theater so he can derail the ceremony. It would make the most sense.

The only thing worse than a small town is a *bored* small town, and Emerald Grove is undoubtedly almost always bored.

But Leonard isn't about to get an attention-grabbing headline from me. As much as I hate this building being named after me, I fully support whoever wants to resurrect the old theater. I have far too many memories tied up in that place to see it go to waste. Besides, that stage is where I got my start. I wouldn't have my career if it weren't for it.

"*Excited* and *eager* are understatements," I tell him. "I'm positively *thrilled* for this town to have a new theater. We've been without one for far too long."

"But you've not been back to town since . . . How long has it been now? Nine, ten years? I think we've gotten by just fine without one, don't you?"

I muster up all my acting training so as not to react to his jab about my extended absence. "I might be the wrong person to ask about this, Leonard. I'm an actor, remember? I'll always advocate for the arts."

He's still holding his smile, but it's losing its warmth by the second. "Right. Sure. But we can all agree that bringing more revenue into this town would be a good thing, right? Like maybe a McDonald's or a gas station? A new grocery store? Or a strip mall, for example? We've got to get more options here. Put our money and resources toward something more immediately lucrative. Maybe someplace to compete with Jill's? Encourage Peggy to spruce the place up some?"

I might not live here anymore, but I know one thing—this town doesn't need sprucing up. Sure, it has its quirks, but that's what makes it such a unique stop for so many tourists. They don't want strip malls, fancy gas stations, or fast-food joints. They want the small-town cozy feel they're already getting. It doesn't need to be "fixed."

I guess I'm not surprised by his desire to bring in more commercial ventures to the town. I'm sure adding more businesses would cook up more drama, which would mean more buzz for Emerald Grove, and that's what he and the *Gazette* live for—the attention.

"I'm firmly pro theater."

His smile vanishes in a flash, and he turns his nose up at me. "I figured you'd feel that way, given who is involved in the rebuild and everything."

I have no idea what he's talking about, and I already hate myself for wanting to give in and ask him what he means, but I can't help it. I guess a little Emerald Grove gossip lover is living inside all of us.

"Given who is involved? What do you mean?"

"Oh, you didn't know?" he asks with faux innocence. "Why, the town's restoration committee is headed by our very own Parker Pruitt."

No. I would have known. *Someone* would have mentioned it to me at some point. When the mayor called me about the ceremony, he didn't say a word about Parker being part of this project. Granted, he didn't mention much other than telling me six times that he got my number from Gran and that he wasn't a stalker. He was strictly business, telling me where to be and when. That was it.

After seeing what she's done to Rossi Café, I should have known Parker was behind the restoration. She loved that theater as much as I did when we were younger, maybe even more. It was as much her escape from the real world as it was mine. We spent many hours working there before and after school and in the summers. It makes sense she'd want to restore it.

"Right. No, I knew that," I lie, praying he can't tell. "It's just early. I haven't had my coffee yet. I was going to stop at the café, but—"

"It's closed for renovations. Parker's heading that, too, you know. She's got her hands all over everything in town. If it's been recently remodeled, Parker probably did it. Axel, too, of course. Those two can't seem to go anywhere without the other." His eyes narrow.

There's definitely a story there, and I'd be lying if I said I didn't want to ask him about it, but I don't have the energy to get into it now. I barely slept last night as it is, and I really could use a coffee.

"Well, I won't keep you, Noel. I'm sure you've got lots to do to prep for the ceremony."

Considering I'm just there for the celebrity element and to say thank you, no, not really, but if it gets me away from Leonard and his questions . . .

"Yes, I still have so much to prepare, so I'd better get going. Great to see you again, Fi— Sorry. Leonard. Maybe we'll catch up again before I leave."

"Yes, yes. That's wonderful." Though his voice indicates he'd rather stick a fork in his eye than hang out with me.

I sidestep him, hustling down the sidewalk and far, far away from Leonard Figgins and his hatred for me.

By now, every shop on the main strip is open for business. I can feel every stare as I walk by Fran's pie shop, their curious eyes burning into my head. I think about stopping in because she's got the third-best cup of joe around, but it's too busy, and I don't feel like answering a million questions about being back.

My eyes catch the *Gazette* as I walk past the newsstand, and I groan at the headline on the front page.

> Actor Noel Carter Returns to His Roots—Will the Hollywood Heartthrob Stay This Time?

I'm not sure how they managed to write a ten-paragraph article about my coming back. Even Gran was surprised they got an article out so fast since she never told anyone I was coming in early.

Looking back, there is a slight chance *I'm* the one to blame for the article about my early arrival getting published so fast. Maybe I should have opted for something a little more low key than the Porsche 911 that Vince picked out for me, but man, was it fun on those curves on my three-hour trek here.

I keep walking, passing by Jill's Bait & Tackle and the bookstore, avoiding the few people who try to stop me. I cut down between Ruff 'n' Tough Dog Groomers and the local bar, Bigfoot's Hideaway, and pop out the other side in front of the one place I never could seem to stay away from—the theater.

I look out at the abandoned space, surprised at how tight my throat gets seeing it in this state, and I can almost understand why Leonard thinks it's best to tear it down and start fresh.

By the time I left, the doors were shuttered and Do Not Enter signs hung. The place was in rough shape due to the tree that fell through it, but nothing near what it is like now. Time has not been kind to it. The windows have been knocked out, the roof is caved in on one side, and there's obvious deterioration everywhere you look. It was already old when I was a kid, but now it seems ancient.

The only sign of life the building shows is the sparkling new sign that reads Future Home of the Noel Carter Theater.

Obviously, I knew it was being named that, but seeing it in person? It's a whole different level of mortification.

Really, a whole theater named after me? Sure, I found success outside of this town, but I'm still me. I'm still that same kid who used to run these streets until the porch lights came on, who used to hang toilet paper on the fountain just to have the chance to laugh as I watched someone try to fish it out, who used to help place the wreaths on light poles every November.

Having a building named after me feels ridiculous when I'm just me and these people have known me since I was born.

But if it means this town's arts community will be revived, I'll do it, even if Parker didn't tell me she was heading the committee.

Why didn't she say something? She had the chance earlier when we were working side by side in the café, which looks incredible now. Or why didn't she mention it last night? Or anytime over the last ten years? Hell, why didn't Gran ever bring it up? I know this project has to be years in the making, and yet I haven't heard a peep about it. I'll have to ask her about it later, but maybe after I've had my daily dose of caffeine.

Tucking my hands into my pockets, I head toward the south end of the strip, sticking to the residential side of things rather than the business side. Maybe that'll keep people out of my hair.

I pass a few houses with square signs stuck near their mailboxes. They have bold letters printed on them that read **SAY NO TO THE THEATER RESTORATION—SELL THE LAND!**

Huh. I guess Leonard isn't the only one who doesn't want to see the theater happen. I'm not surprised. It wasn't that big of a hit when I was younger, but I have no doubt that with Parker behind it, she has a plan to turn it into something everyone will soon love.

Goose bumps break out over my arms, thinking about her. Or maybe it's just because I left my damn jacket behind and the morning chill of the Pacific Northwest isn't something I'm used to anymore.

"I'll be darned," a smooth voice calls as I speed-walk past the signs.

It's familiar. It's warm. And it's a voice I haven't heard in far too long.

I skid to a halt, turning my face up to the house I've stopped in front of. My smile is automatic as I get a glimpse of the gal sitting on the front porch wearing jeans, a floor-length cardigan over a tank top, about twelve rings on ten fingers, and no shoes, as usual.

"Astrid."

"How are you, son?"

Son.

Never *Noel*, never *Kid*, never *Little Shit Who Kept My Daughter Out Past Curfew*. Always *son.*

"Doing all right. You?"

"I'd be a heck of a lot better if you stop lingering at the end of my driveway and come give me a hug."

I practically run up the short drive, taking the porch steps two at a time, and wrap the woman who was like a mother to me in my arms.

She smells like she always has—incense, coffee, and home.

That's what this place was to me. For the first six months Parker lived here, I never came over. Then one day, she told me her dad had taken off, and she wouldn't stop crying at school, so I walked her home to make sure she was okay. Astrid was sitting on the porch cradling a cup of coffee like she is right now and invited me inside, and just like that, this place became my second home.

"Come on, now. Let me get a good look at you," she says as she pulls away. She grabs my face between her hands, squeezing my cheeks as she looks me over. "Uh-huh. I see. You look good. Healthy. Your feet are clearly still working, your hands seem fine, and it sounds like your voice box is in working order. Right?"

"Yes, ma'am."

"Then how come you ain't bothered to call or come by in a decade?"

Of all the people disappointed in me for staying away for so long, Astrid being upset by it hurts the worst.

"I'm sorry," I tell her. "It's been . . . well, it's been an eventful ten years."

"I'd say," she says with a pointedly raised brow. She gives my cheeks another light squeeze before releasing me. "Have a seat. I'll grab you some coffee, and you can tell me everything I don't read about in the magazines."

"Yes, ma'am."

She disappears into the house I know like the back of my hand, and I settle into one of the mismatched chairs.

The smell of incense wafts out the door, and it takes me back to a time when things were a lot less complicated than they are now. A time when I used to slip off into imaginary worlds, play video games or charades, or sit at a dinner table full of laughter and love.

A time I miss more than I'd like to admit.

The screen door squeaks open, and Astrid comes out with two cups of fresh coffee.

I don't miss that she hands me the same mug I always used to call dibs on—the one shaped like a duck she found at a garage sale.

I accept it, taking a sip and not caring that it's hot as hell. It's worth the burn.

I sigh contentedly. "Damn. That's some great coffee."

"Best in town," Astrid agrees, taking a sip from her own piping-hot cup.

We sit quietly for several moments, just enjoying our caffeine jolt and taking in the morning. Even though so much time has passed, it's not awkward or uncomfortable. In fact, it almost feels like this is right where I've always been meant to be.

"So," she begins, "tell me how life is in Hollywood. Is it all it's cracked up to be?"

"It's great. I love it."

"Did you ever go to that club I told you kids about?"

"I did."

"And?"

"It's a gay club now."

"It was a gay club then too."

I chuckle. "Thanks for the heads-up."

"Didn't think you needed one." She shrugs, taking another drink. "So how are you really doing, son?"

There it is—her superpower.

I don't think Astrid Pruitt has ever been able to look at someone and not know when they're bullshitting her. She did it all the time when Parker and I were kids, and we never hesitated to be anything but honest with her. She made it easy to talk to her about everything from school to serious things, like when Gran had her breast cancer scare.

Astrid's always been there for me like I was part of her family, and I feel like a shitty human for not being there for her these last ten years.

I scratch at the scruff on my face that I've been letting grow over the last few days. "Honestly? Some days, I hate it. It's loud, things move really quickly, and the people are awful, but then I remember I get to make movies for a living, and all those bad things fade away. So my answer is a little complicated."

"Life's complicated."

I laugh. "That it is. How's Emerald Grove treating you?"

"It's been all right. Little quiet around here lately."

I know Astrid well enough to know she means it's been quiet here without me around, and I love her for it.

"Did you find everything you wanted, being away?" she asks.

When I devised my plan to leave Emerald Grove, Astrid was among the first people I told because I knew she would never ask me to stay. Much like she's always encouraged Parker to find her place in this world, she encouraged me to do so too. So when I told her the reason I was going, she nodded and told me I was making the best decision I could at the time.

When I left, I held on to that with everything I had, even if it meant hurting people I loved.

While I love Emerald Grove and have so many good memories here, I also have a lot of bad ones, like losing my parents when I was only eight. They loved this town but always wanted to travel more. Leaving felt like a nod to their missed adventures, so after high school graduation rolled around, I did just that, wanting to fill the void that losing them left behind.

Even though, after all these years of being away and doing what my parents always wanted—exploring the world—I still feel like part of me is empty and something is missing. Yet I don't regret leaving.

I sit forward, resting my elbows on my knees, blowing on my coffee. "Yes and no. I'm not sure I'll ever find what I want. It feels so . . . far away."

"You're too young to say that. I guarantee what you want isn't as out of reach as you think."

"Maybe," I say with a shrug, settling back into the chair. "Or maybe I should just give up and be happy with what I have."

She grins. "Or that too." She sips at her coffee. "I saw your last movie, you know."

I groan, squeezing my eyes shut. "Please tell me you fast-forwarded through—"

"You showing your naked behind to the whole world? Don't worry, Parker made sure to skip those parts."

Parker watches my movies?

"Come on. Don't look so shocked that she supports you," Astrid says, reading my mind. "Sure, things may be a little strained between you two now, but you'll always have her support."

"Strained?" I laugh. "That's a mild way of putting it."

She raises her brows in that disappointing way only a mom can. "The phone works both ways, you know."

"And you told her that?"

"You know darn well I did, son. You two . . ." She shakes her head. "You'll be the death of me one day. I just know it."

"Nah. You're never dying, Astrid."

"Do any of us ever really die? We just move on to another plane, but we're still here, just waiting for you to hear us screaming from the void."

I smile at her, not the least bit surprised by her feelings about the afterlife. I've sat at the Pruitt dinner table too often to be shocked by Astrid's free-spirited beliefs anymore.

"Never change," I beg her as she gets up for a coffee refill.

"It's too late to anyway. I'm old and set in my ways." She grins as she opens the door, her rings clinking against the handle.

After refilling our cups, she returns with the coffee carafe, sets it on the table between us, and settles back into her chair.

We sit there, letting the early-morning sounds fill the lull in conversation. I miss sitting on the porch like this, listening to the birds chirping and people greeting one another like old friends, which I guess they all are. Though I have a balcony at my penthouse in LA, I could never do this. The city is too full of shouting, horns blaring, and loud music rattling car speakers, not to mention the lack of privacy I'd experience there. The quiet is nice.

After a while, I tell her, "I guess I'd better get back to Gran's."

I try to hand her the mug back, but she waves it away.

"Keep it. It's yours anyway. Here." She tops off my drink with what's left in the carafe. "For the road," she says with a wink.

"Thanks, Astrid."

"Anytime. You know that. Right, son?" Her eyes search mine, because what she's really saying is, *I'm here for you no matter what.*

I swallow thickly, nodding once. "I know."

"Good. Keep it that way."

"Yes, ma'am," I tell her, kissing the top of her head. "I'll see you later."

"You'd better." Her tone is far from lighthearted. She really means it, and so do I.

I'm halfway down the drive when she calls out to me, and I turn and look up at the porch.

"It's Tuesday, you know," Parker's mom yells.

I grin, already knowing where this is going. "It is Tuesday."

"Well?" she prompts, her stare piercing over the top of her raised coffee mug. "Don't leave an old bird hanging."

"Still the same?"

"Every Tuesday for as long as I can remember."

For as long as I can remember too. Tuesdays used to be my favorite day because it meant dinner at the Pruitts' for Tater Tot Tuesdays. We'd make the most ridiculous things, and I'd love every minute. Even Gran tagged along for a few dinners, always bringing dessert with her. Then we'd sit in the backyard, swap stories, and sip hot chocolate until we were sixteen, when Astrid started letting us have the occasional "adult beverage."

Those summer nights were some of my favorites, one of the good memories about this place.

"Well?" she asks again. "Are you coming or what?"

I chuckle. "I'll be here, Astrid."

She shimmies in her chair. "Make sure you bring the wine coolers."

CHAPTER SIX

Parker

"I'm here, I'm here!" I call out to my mother as I barrel through her front door without knocking. Not that she minds.

For the second time in as many days, I'm running late.

I'm usually that person who's borderline obnoxiously early, but not this week, apparently. This is the week—one of the most important of my life—that I decided to throw all those years of being on time by the wayside and become a perpetually late arriver.

Honestly, if it wasn't for that damn couch, I just might have been on time.

Axel returned shortly after Noel left and grilled me for thirty minutes about what had happened. I think after the twentieth time I told him that all that had happened was that Noel had helped with the wall, he finally believed me.

It's a good thing, too, because the absolute last thing I wanted to get into was how Noel's parting words left me reeling.

I tried to ignore them all day, pushing them to the back of my mind, but all my efforts were fruitless. When I'd repainted the same spot for the third time, Axel officially sent me home for the day with a promise to finish painting the walls himself, since this time he ordered the right color. He swore he'd have everything cleaned up tomorrow so

I could spend Thursday mounting the display stands, moving furniture back in, and rearranging the place to my heart's content for the grand reopening after the theater ceremony on Friday, if I agreed to take a nap.

I was so tired I said yes. All it took was three minutes on my couch, and I was out for five hours, which is why I'm running in the door fifteen minutes late for Tater Tot Tuesday.

"We're in the kitchen!" my mother calls back over the sound of Carole King from the record player in the den.

We? Who else is here? It's probably Gran. She's been coming over sporadically for years, just like she used to when I was a kid. Tater Tot Tuesday is famous in these parts.

I don't know where my love of tots came from—maybe from school lunches—but I used to request them so often that my mother finally had to put her foot down and say we could only have them one day a week. And thus, Tater Tot Tuesday was born. We've hosted many people over the years, and sometimes it's just her and me. When I was younger, there were always at least three of us here. But it hasn't been that way in a long, long time.

I juggle the bag of toppings I brought as I take off my shoes. My mother didn't have too many rules growing up, but "no shoes in the house" was one that always stuck. Once I'm free of my flats, I pad down the hall, past the photos of me and drawings I've made over the years that line the walls, and head straight for the kitchen, where I immediately come to a halt.

Now I know why my mother said *we*.

It's not Gran, but he sure is related to her.

"Noel."

He and my mother are standing side by side, each working on their own dinner. A carton of wine coolers sits on the counter, one missing and one sitting right in front of Noel, already half-gone. Cheese, beans, meat, and various vegetables are spread around the countertop. It's safe to say that whatever this is, it was planned, and I was left out of the loop.

Noel's lips kick up into a grin on one side. "Peter."

"Peter?" My mother's eyes widen as she looks up at my old friend. "Wow. I haven't heard that name in . . ."

She trails off because we all know exactly how long it's been since she's heard it—the last time Noel was here.

"I hope you don't mind I invited Noel. But he stopped by this morning, and I realized it was Tuesday, and, well, I couldn't resist. Besides, it's nice to have both my kids under the same roof for a change." She nudges him with her elbow, her hands busy spreading Tater Tots in the bottom of a glass dish. "We just started, so scrub in, and we can get these all in the oven simultaneously."

She smiles at me brightly, and her smile would look entirely innocent to just about anyone else. But I know my mother, and right now, her smile says, *Play nice and yell at me later, darling.*

I smile right back, one that says, *Oh, I'm definitely yelling later because what the frick, Mom? I thought you were on my side!*

I set my bag of toppings on the island, then roll up my sleeves to wash my hands.

Mom's already set out a dish for me, so when I'm finished washing up, I dump my tots into the bottom and begin spreading them out how I like them.

I'm spreading the seasoned crumbled beef my mother made ahead of time when the music comes to a sharp end.

"Ah, crud. Gotta flip the record. You two keep going. Mine are ready, anyway," my mom announces, wiping her hands on a dish towel as she shuffles from the room. It's an apparent attempt at getting Noel and me alone together.

I love my mother more than life itself, but right now, I want to put her in a nursing home and never visit her.

No, wait. That's too mean.

I'll replace all her treasured photos with pictures of Clifford, the gardener from next door. They've been feuding for nearly fifteen years because he ran over her violets. He swore he didn't and that she's the one who killed them, and they haven't been able to let it go since.

Yes, that will be my revenge. She'll hate it.

"Well, that was obvious," I say once she's out of earshot.

"To be fair, subtlety has never been Astrid's thing," Noel remarks, and he wouldn't be wrong. She's never been one to shy away from telling it as it is or letting people know her exact feelings about things, like her strife with Clifford.

We work in silence for several minutes, me probably putting a bit too much force into throwing meat on top of my tots and Noel watching me like a hawk.

Why is he here? He hasn't bothered to show up over the years, and now, on his second day back in town, I can't escape him. What gives?

And why did he say those things to me this morning? Why did he get jealous of the idea of Axel and me together? Why did he imply that he still has feelings for me? Why does he have to keep calling me Peter? Why—

"Did they offend you?" he asks quietly.

I whip my head toward him. "What."

It's not really a question, more of a demand.

He dips his head toward the pan. "Your tots. Have they done something to offend you? Because mine haven't said a word all night, and I'm going to be pissed if you got the magic talking Tater Tots and I didn't."

It's a ridiculous thing to say, and it almost makes me smile. Then I remember that this night is mine, and he's intruding.

"Why are you here?"

"She asked." He shrugs, tossing a few tomatoes onto his already overly topped tots. Did he learn nothing over his years of attending Tater Tot Tuesdays? If there's one thing to avoid, it's too many toppings. They'll never crisp up the way I know he likes. They'll get mushy and gross within minutes. "I'm sorry. I wouldn't have come if I knew—"

"That'd I'd be here?"

"Well, yeah."

"It's my house. She's my mother."

"I know. I just . . ."

"I just find it funny that you've been gone for ten years, and suddenly you're everywhere I turn."

His hands stop, and for the sake of his tots, I'm glad. He sets the bowl of tomatoes down with a gentleness he wasn't showing the boards he was ripping off my wall this morning.

He turns to me, crossing one leg over the other, his hip resting against the island we've spent so many nights at, up late talking, doing homework, or making dinner as we are now.

"Why didn't you tell me you're heading the theater project?"

Of all the things I thought Noel would say, it wasn't that.

It's my turn to shrug. "I didn't think it would matter."

"You didn't think . . ." He shakes his head. "Of course it matters, Parker. You're the reason I'm back."

"No," I argue as I reach for the shredded cheese and spread a spoonful over the top of my tots. "The *donor* is the reason you're back. Trust me, naming this theater after you wasn't my decision."

"Why? Because it's such an awful thing to do?"

"Because it's tacky, and I know you agree, so don't argue."

He gives me no indication I'm right, but I know him well enough to know that I am. He hates the theater's new name as much as I do.

"Why not tell me?" he asks, this time more commanding and less gentle. "That theater . . . You know what it means to me."

"I know what it *meant* to you."

"For the love of . . ." He growls—actually *growls*—and, my gosh, is it the hottest thing I've ever heard. "Am I ever going to live this down? Am I ever not going to get punished for leaving and living my life?"

"I never said that."

"Well, it sure feels like it, and that's not fair. We *both* know it's not fair." He leans into me, that cologne of his hitting my nose, making me lose focus. "Because as I recall, I asked you to come with me, Peter, and you're the one who told me no."

My hands pause, and I swallow the sudden lump in my throat.

Just like he knows it's not fair that I'm upset with him for leaving, I know it's not fair for me to act like this rift between us is all his fault.

Because it's not. I'm to blame for a lot of it, and if he thinks the guilt of that hasn't eaten away at me over the years, he's wrong.

But I'm tired of feeling guilty. If we're going to get through this ceremony, we need to move on.

"You're right," I tell him, setting the cheese on the counter and turning toward him. "You're right, Noel. We should put this behind us. But if we do, that means we also put all things *Axel* behind us too. You're not allowed to be mean to my business partner."

"You need to tell that to *him*. I'm pretty sure that Goliath would have tried to fight me this morning."

I snort out a laugh, turning back to my tots with a grin. "Oh, he so would have. And it would have been glorious."

"Seeing me pummeled would have gotten you off, huh?"

Suddenly, I'm not laughing anymore. Or smiling.

No.

All I'm thinking about are the very real words Noel just uttered and how suddenly it's very hot in this kitchen.

It's the oven, I tell myself. That's what it has to be. No way is it because I'm now thinking of all the ways Noel could *get me off.*

"So sorry about that." My mother breezes back into the kitchen like she wasn't just waiting out in the hallway for a break in the conversation. She thinks she's so sneaky, but I'm onto her. "I had to change the record, then Larissa called, and you know how she loves to gab. She wanted to inform me that Noel was back in town, like I didn't know." She rolls her eyes with a grin. "Anyway, what'd I miss? Are our tots ready?"

I look at Noel's heaping pile of toppings, which will take forever to cook evenly, then at my pitiful mound, and nod. "Sure, let's get them in the oven. I need a drink."

"Oh! Noel brought wine coolers," she says, pointing to the carton of drinks on the counter.

Of course he did.

"Here, let me." Noel grabs a bottle of Watermelon Lime.

It's my favorite drink, and I haven't had it since the summer he left. Not since I got drunk on them and cried to my mother about everything that happened with us, how in love with him I was, and how I wanted to kiss him again so badly that I ached.

Sometimes I still feel that way.

Noel easily snaps off the lid and hands it to me. He remembers that I hate opening them because they rough up my hands. Funny for someone who works in construction, but we all have our quirks.

I almost have my fingers curled around the wine cooler when he jerks it back. "Ah, that's right. I almost forgot the taxes."

He puts the bottle to his mouth, closing his lips around it as he tips his head back for a drink. His Adam's apple bobs as he swallows, and I hate how much I enjoy watching it, almost as much as I hate myself for being so excited he remembered our ritual where he always takes the first drink or bite of my stuff as "tax."

"The only time taxes are a good thing," he says, wiping off his mouth with the back of his hand before handing me my wine cooler.

I clutch the bottle tightly, hesitating. I was glad he remembered, but now I don't know what to do. Should I wipe it off? Would it be weird if I did? I never used to before. Heck, back then, we used to share everything. Sandwiches, ice creams, drinks . . . It didn't matter because it was Noel, and nothing was ever weird with him.

Now . . . now it's different.

And if the way he's watching me closely is any indication, he feels the same way.

But I won't give him the satisfaction of making this awkward. Instead, I bring the bottle to my lips and take a drink like it means nothing. Like he means nothing.

But it does matter. *He* matters.

And that's the hardest part of it all.

◆ ◆ ◆

"Is it strange to say I've missed Tater Tots?" Noel pats his full stomach. Considering I once watched him eat five and a half meatball subs, I really shouldn't be surprised he finished off his overly topped tots *plus* half of mine, but I am. I have a feeling now that we're finished, he won't be moving from his Adirondack chair anytime soon.

We sit outside with a small fire while my mother cleans the kitchen. We tried to help her many times, but it wasn't until she threatened to change the locks on the house and never invite us over again that we gave in and hurried outside before she made good on her promise.

"Do they not have Tater Tots in California?" I ask.

"Of course they do. But I can't ever eat them. I'm always training for my next role, or we never go somewhere that has them. It's too lowbrow."

We.

I didn't miss that. I want to ask what it means, if he has someone back home waiting for him, but I'm not sure I have that right anymore.

Sure, he asked about Axel this morning, but maybe I have more manners than Noel.

"Vince, my assistant, is the bigger foodie of us, so I just let him handle reservations."

He makes reservations. That has to be for dates, right?

I push aside the thought.

It doesn't matter, Parker. Not your business.

The crackle of the fire fills the quiet that settles between us, and for just a moment, I let myself escape back into the past when we used to do this regularly. We'd open the windows and let the record player spin us something good, watch the fire, and just be. Sometimes, we'd talk, swap stories of all different kinds, tell jokes, or sometimes, we'd just sit like we are now. But no matter what we were doing, we were at ease with one another, just like we are in this moment.

"You can ask," he says quietly, breaking our little bubble of silence.

"Hmm?"

"You can ask if I'm seeing someone."

I shake my head. "It's none of my—"

"I asked about Axel this morning," he interrupts. "It's only fair you get to be nosy in the same way."

He has a point . . . "Fine. Are you seeing anyone?"

"No." The answer is so quick and automatic that it makes my heart soar with a happiness I haven't felt in a long time. "But I have."

And just like that, the happiness is gone.

It's silly, really, to think he'd never date or move on from fleeting feelings as a teenager. I knew he would, and heck, even I've dated a bit. But I still don't like it.

"Nothing serious," he continues, the firelight dancing in his eyes as he watches it burn. "Nothing that lasted. Nothing that ever meant . . ."

He doesn't finish his sentence, but he doesn't have to.

He means us. Nothing that ever meant something like what we had.

I'm not sure if that makes me happy or sad, and I don't have time to figure it out before the back door slams against the frame, and my mother comes bounding across the lawn.

"I just heard from the Community Hall, and they say we can host the first fundraiser there," my mother says as she takes the empty chair beside me.

"Fundraiser?" Noel asks. "What are we raising funds for?"

"The theater." Mom takes a sip of what I know is coffee spiked with bourbon. It's her go-to drink when she wants to unwind. She always says, "A nice nightcap for a nice day." "Even with the town's approved budget for it *and* the donation, we're still looking at a steep uphill battle to cover the rest of the renovation. We're going to fundraise for it."

"You're renovating on only half a budget?"

Half? Not even.

I shrug at Noel's question. "It's not a big deal. I know the town will come through."

Or at least I hope they do. Most of the town is on board for the restoration, but there are a few who have strong feelings opposing it. I'm hoping once they see how excited everyone else is about it, they'll change their minds.

"And if they don't?"

"If they don't, Parker plans to use her own money to cover some and take out a loan for the other part."

Noel sits forward, frowning over at me. "You're kidding."

"She's not," my mother answers before I can.

I hitch my thumb her way. "What she said."

"Parker, you can't do that. That's . . ."

"Farcical? Heedless? Perhaps even unhinged?"

"Are you finished, Ms. Always Wins at Scrabble?" I shoot my mom a glare before turning back to Noel. "It's my money, and I'll do with it as I wish."

"But that's *a lot* of money."

"I know that."

"I can—"

"Don't," I snap. "Don't."

He knows what I mean, just like I know what he was about to do—offer to pay for what the donation isn't covering.

But I don't want his money, and more than that, I don't *need* his money.

"Fine. But don't you want to use your savings for something else? A house? A car? A family?"

A family? Is he serious? There's nobody here I want to have a family with. Nobody except . . . I shake away the thought.

"I already own a house, and what do I need a car for? I don't go anywhere, and everything in Emerald Grove is walkable. A car seems like just another hindrance to the environment, is all."

"You tell him, sister." My mother holds her palm up, and I slap it. "I raised you well."

"But—"

"No. No buts," I cut in. "I've already made my decision. I've weighed this carefully and done all the math. I know this is what I want."

Noel stares at me, the flames glinting off the blue in his eyes. Finally, after what feels like several minutes, he nods. "Okay."

It's all he says about it, and I don't know why, but it feels like a weight has been lifted. I don't *need* Noel's permission or approval to do this, but I like that he trusts me enough to do this.

I know it's a big undertaking, but just as I'm confident in handling it, I'm also confident in this town. Sure, it took some time to get the council to approve it and give me a decent budget, but thanks to our donor, it seems we have interest, and that's what we really needed.

I don't expect the townspeople to front the entire bill and am more than prepared to take out a loan to cover the rest. I'm just hoping for as much as I can get before it comes to that.

I settle back in my chair, not even realizing I had sat forward in the first place. "Okay," I echo.

"Well, now that that's settled," my mother says, "how many people have we signed up for the bachelor auction part of the evening?"

"A what, now?"

"A date-night raffle!" my mother tells Noel with glee. "We've gathered all the single men in town and will raffle off a date night with them, along with several other services and items donated by local businesses. We thought of it after watching some Hallmark movie where the lawyer lady returned to her small town and fell back in love with her old high school flame, who stayed behind and became a lumberjack or whatever it is he was."

"A horse trainer," I provide. "No, wait. That was the other movie with a lawyer. Was he a baker? No." I tap my chin. "I know! He was a fishmonger!"

"Can you imagine that smell?" My mother wrinkles her nose. "No, thanks. I'd rather live in the city."

"I don't know. The city smells pretty bad," Noel offers.

"Good point," Mom says. "The last time I was in Seattle, it smelled like pee, fish, and weed. Now, the weed I didn't mind, but that pee and fish was not for me."

"It wasn't that bad, Mom."

"*You* went to Seattle?" Noel asks, his surprise evident.

It's warranted, though. I can count on one hand the number of times I've been outside Emerald Grove. That may sound ridiculous to some, but I'm perfectly content staying in my little corner of the world.

Noel knows that better than anyone.

"What? It was for a work thing with Axel."

Is it bad I like the way his eyes dim when I say Axel's name? That I like how a little wrinkle forms between his brows each time I mention that Axel is my best friend?

Probably, but I don't care.

"So, what? You fix up the town together and roam the state doing remodeling or something?"

"Or something," I say, not elaborating just to irritate him.

It works, and his grip on his bottle of Watermelon Lime tightens just a little.

"Well, if it's anything like the work you've done at the café, your success is well deserved."

My mother gasps. "You've seen the café? That's . . . That's . . . Well, that's a big load of crap!" She huffs. "Even *I* haven't seen it, and I got her the dang job."

"You did not! Axel and I"—I dart my eyes to Noel, and yup, the wrinkle is there—"got that job all on our own, thank you very much. We were having Rossi breakfast sandwiches"—*Did that wrinkle just deepen?*—"and came up with the idea right there in front of Gianna and Greta. They approved and asked us when we could start."

"Then you went and closed down the town's favorite breakfast and lunch spot for *eight weeks*." Mom pouts.

"It would have been six if Axel had ordered the right materials."

"Uh-oh. Trouble in paradise?" Noel questions.

"No. Our business is doing just fine. In fact, after the theater reno, we're thinking of updating the high school. Axel and I make *great* partners."

"I need a drink," Noel announces suddenly, shoving from his chair and stomping toward the house.

I watch him leave, his gait quick, like he's on a mission to escape as fast as possible.

My mother clucks her tongue once he's tucked safely inside the house.

I turn to her, brow raised. "Yes, Mother?"

"You're being mean."

"Am not."

"Are, too, and you know it. Teasing him with Axel's name like that. You know they have history."

"*I* have history with Axel, too, you know."

"Yes, but you've also had ten years of getting over it and discovering that he's matured and turned into a fine young man. Noel hasn't. It's still fresh for him."

I slink down in my chair. I hated being reprimanded as a kid, but somehow, it feels so much worse when you're pushing thirty. "Yeah, well, whose fault is that?"

"Parker . . . ," my mother says sternly.

I sigh. "I'm being petty."

"You are. And while you have a right to be upset about him not returning, you can't be upset about him leaving. You supported him then. You can't take it back just because he decided to stay gone."

"Like Frank decided to stay gone, right?"

She cuts me a sharp look. "Noel is *not* your father, Parker Bernice Pruitt. You know it as well as I do. Don't put what that man did onto him. That's not fair."

I swallow because I know she's right about that too.

It's not fair. My dad leaving and Noel leaving are two different things. But somehow . . . somehow, they feel an awful lot like the same.

My dad left suddenly in the middle of the night, leaving nothing but a note and a number to reach him. We never called it, and he never called us.

Noel's departure wasn't so sudden. He'd been talking about going for a long time. I guess somewhere along the way, I'd developed this thing in my head where I told myself he was just dreaming and that he'd never actually leave.

Then our senior year ended, and he told me with finality that he was moving away. I told him to go. Why wouldn't I? He was my best friend. Yes, it was going to suck for him to leave, but I wanted him to be happy. I wanted him to find that thing he always seemed to be missing.

The nights I've lain awake wondering if my father found what he was looking for rival the nights I've spent wondering if Noel found what he'd been after.

While I'll never have that opportunity with my father, I do have the chance with Noel. Maybe I should seize it.

"So tell me more about this raffle," Noel calls from the porch as the screen door closes behind him.

"Just give him a chance," my mother whispers. "Who knows? Maybe he's changed, just like Axel did."

"Yeah, maybe."

Or maybe it doesn't matter. We both know he's not sticking around. He's leaving after the ceremony, gone out of my life again so he can live his, I can live mine, and things can go back to how they were.

I thought it was what I wanted, so why does it scare me so much?

CHAPTER SEVEN

Noel

"Rise and shine, bub! Your ceremony starts in an hour!"

I groan, rolling over toward the door. "Five more minutes!"

Gran laughs, probably feeling the same as I am—like I'm back in my teen years, and she's waking me up for school or something I really don't want to do during summer break. "Not a chance. Get up, or I'll come in there and drag you out of bed myself. I'm making pancakes."

That has me feeling more awake instantly. I sit up, letting my *Spider-Man* printed sheets fall away. I thought Gran would have changed them to something else by now, but she hasn't. My entire room looks the same as it did when I left. It's completely ridiculous, though I can't help but appreciate it a little. My room was always my sanctuary, and she never came in without my permission, always preaching boundaries. To know she kept that up all these years . . . Well, it's just fuckin' sweet.

I pull myself out of bed with less reluctance than I'd have if no pancakes were on the way and shuffle to my adjoining bathroom, something I was very grateful for during my teen years here.

I take a quick shower, then dress in simple gray dress slacks and a button-down shirt, folding my suit jacket over my arm for later.

My stomach growls the second I pull my door open.

"Bacon!" I call out. "You made me bacon too? I knew you loved me!"

"And if you don't get in here, I'll eat every last piece."

I grin, scratching at the hair still dotting my face as I round the corner into the kitchen. "You wouldn't dare, Gran. I know you well enough to guess you made a pound, and your scrawny ass couldn't eat that if you tried."

She narrows her eyes in my direction from her spot at the table. "Can too."

I hang my jacket over my chair with a chuckle and head for the coffeepot. Caffeine is a must if I'm going to make it through this ceremony.

But the second I take a sip, I regret it. My grandmother can make almost anything I request, but coffee is not her forte. How she manages to mess it up every time is beyond me.

"Stop making that face, you little shit. I worked hard on that coffee."

"You shouldn't have to work hard on coffee," I counter. "It just happens or doesn't."

"Well, we can't all be coffee wizards like Astrid."

"She's not a wizard. She just understands there shouldn't be grounds in your coffee."

Gran shrugs. "We all have our strengths and weaknesses. My weakness is coffee. My strength is cooking. So sit your ass down and eat these pancakes I made specially for you." She points at the chair across from her.

I laugh, abandoning my coffee in the sink and parking my ass in the chair as instructed.

I load my perfectly fluffy pancakes with butter, douse them in syrup, and then shove a bigger-than-appropriate bite into my mouth.

A moan leaves me involuntarily, causing my grandmother to snicker, a proud smile curving at her lips as she sips her grainy coffee like it's not the most horrid thing in the world.

I'm too impressed by these pancakes to razz her about it. I cram another bite into my mouth.

Man, if my personal trainer could see me now, shoveling this sugar pile into my body, he'd kill me. Maybe not literally, but I'd definitely be doing burpees for hours.

I finish my stack of five flapjacks and a good portion of the bacon before I finally tap out.

"I'm done," I say, tossing my napkin to the table. "I can't. No more."

"Aw, you sure, bub? I made another loaf of banana bread . . ." Her smile may seem innocent, but she looks like the devil in a poorly made disguise right now.

I glare at her. "You're evil, you know that?"

She lifts her dainty shoulder. "You love me, and you know it."

"More than you know, Gran. More than you know." I pat my stomach. "Fine. Just *one* slice of bread, but then that's it. I have to get going for the ceremony."

"Ah, right. Don't want to be late for your big day. Here," she says, rising from the table. She cuts a quick slice from the freshly baked bread she must have made while I was sleeping and slides it onto a plate. She sets it down in front of me. "You eat this, and I'll finish getting ready."

"You're going?"

"You kidding me? Of course I'm going. Your grandson only gets a theater named after him once."

"Unless you're a Rafferty. I'm pretty sure Jude and Jasper have, like, four between them."

"Well, yeah. Have you *seen* that family? Hollywood royalty, I tell ya." She huffs like *I'm* the one out of line here. "Eat, relax, and work on your speech. I'll be ready in ten minutes, and we can mosey our way to the theater."

I halt, my fork halfway to my mouth. "Speech? What speech?"

She doesn't answer.

"Gran!" I call to her back. "Nobody mentioned a speech! What speech?!"

I swear I see her shoulders shake with laughter.

I love my grandmother, but sometimes . . . sometimes, I want to shake the old bird.

I pluck my phone from my pocket and scroll to a name I haven't touched in years. She has to have the same number, right? There's no reason for her to change it.

Me: Am I supposed to give a speech?

Dots dance along the screen almost instantly.

Parker: Who is this?

Fuck. Either she's deleted my number, or she did change hers, and I'm bothering a total stranger.

I don't know which option I hate more, but on the off chance it is her, I type back.

Me: Noel.

Parker: Noel who?

Me: Carter.

Parker: Hm. That doesn't ring a bell.

Parker: No. Wait.

Parker: Are you that guy who was in that movie where he showed his naked butt to the whole world? Not that I've ever seen it—I just heard about it.

Parker: Because if so, I'm shocked. I never expected THE Noel Carter to text little old me, a boring small-town gal from the middle of nowhere Washington, even though she did keep his secret that he did have a highly inappropriate crush on Tinker Bell and used to look her up on adult websites.

Oh, it's definitely Parker.

Is it strange to say I've missed her?

It's been two days since I last saw her. I left shortly after my fourth wine cooler for the night. Not because I was drunk—far from it, with those Kool-Aid knockoffs—but because if I had to hear about how amazing Axel was one more time, I would lose it.

I believe Parker is being 100 percent honest when she says she and Axel are just friends. I've heard enough about him and his wife around town to believe it.

No. It's the whole "best friend" label that grates on me. I am fully aware of how ridiculous, unfair, and even childish it is for me to be upset by it, but dammit, I still fucking hate it.

She may be friends with Axel, and he may have taken up the space in her life I left behind, but the one thing that will never change is that she belonged to me first.

I want to remind her of that, but I can't. That's too heavy a topic for one measly sip of bad coffee. Instead, I shove those thoughts and feelings back into the box I've kept them in over the last decade and let my fingers fly over my phone screen.

Me: First, I have it on good authority that you've watched my movies. Your mother claims you fast-forwarded through those parts, but just like you know things about me, I know things about you, and you're a butt girl. You might have acted innocent when she was around, but you watched those parts. I know it. You know it. We both know it.

Parker: How dare you!

Me: Second, there is no reason Tinker Bell should have had those proportions for a kid's movie! What did they expect to happen?

Parker: Pig.

Me: Butt lover.

Parker: What do you want, Noel?

Me: Was I supposed to write a speech for this thing?

Parker: No? Who said that?

Me: Gran.

Me: I knew she was just being mean.

Parker: But you panicked and bothered me while I'm trying to get this ceremony ready anyway?

I cringe. I didn't even think about that.

Me: Oops?

Parker: Just be here at 9 and have a few words prepared.

Me: So it IS a speech?!

Parker: No, you big baby. It's just a few words. You'll be fine.

Me: You know I hate public speaking.

Parker: You're an actor. Fake it.

Me: That's different.

Parker: Noel . . .

Me: Peter . . .

Me: Fine. I'll see you at 9.

Parker: Don't be late.

I grin. I like it when she's all stern and bossy. It's not a side of her that she used to show often, and getting her riled up so it would come out used to be one of my favorite things. I guess that hasn't changed much.

Me: Or what?

Parker: Guess you'll just have to see.

"Are you sure I'm not overdressed?" I ask Gran for the third time.

After her speech comment and Parker practically confirming I *did* have to give a speech, I started spiraling.

Just exactly how big is this event? How many people are attending? The whole town? Will there be cameras outside from the *Emerald Grove Gazette*? Am I overdressed? Underdressed? How long does my nonspeech speech need to be? How long is the thing going to run? Do I need to shake hands and kiss babies afterward? What, exactly, am I doing there?

"You're fine." Gran pats my arm with the hand she has looped over it. "You look great, bub."

I smile down at her. "You always say that."

"Always mean it too." She turns her nose up, daring me to contradict her.

She sure does pack a lot of attitude for someone so tiny, and I love every minute of it. She's always been this way—a little firecracker, ready to pop off when needed. I'm glad she hasn't slowed down a bit, even in her old age. Well, at least not spiritually. Physically, it is a different story. She's moving slower than she used to and has complained about her hips a few times. It's making me wonder if she's getting along out here by herself or struggling more than she lets on.

We wander down Borgen Avenue, passing by the shops that are usually full of customers at this time of day, but every window has some variation of a CLOSED sign.

Damn. I guess that answers my question about whether the whole town's coming to this thing.

"Are you nervous?" Gran asks, probably feeling the unease that's settled into my shoulders.

"About standing in front of the town I left ten years ago when I'm sure everyone here hates me? Nah. Not at all."

"I already told you—"

"They don't hate me, I know." I sigh. "Maybe you're right. Maybe they don't *hate* me, but they're mad at me for leaving."

"Well, you did stay away an awfully long time."

She doesn't say it to be mean. She's simply stating the truth.

At first, I stayed gone because of my career, which took off just a few months after I left. I'll be the first to admit I got lucky when I moved to LA. My roommate's uncle was the producer on *Deadman's Drop*, a whodunit teen drama that was supposed to be the next big thing. He got me a small role that, after only half a season, turned into something bigger thanks to social media and everyone falling in love with my character, a villain turned hero. I blew up practically overnight, and studios took notice. Offers started pouring in, and I booked movie after movie. Suddenly, I had money and could afford to fly Gran to me, so there was no point in coming back to Washington, especially not with how busy my schedule was. It was an excuse, my reason to stay away.

But over the years, my reason shifted to something else—I'd been away *too* long, and coming home would be far too weird.

Would the town accept me after being gone so long? Would Parker? Would they treat me differently now that I had fame and money?

There were so many what-ifs that I did the easiest thing possible: I stayed gone.

Running from my past and the heartache here was easier than facing it.

Now, though, after being back for just a few short days, I wish I'd had time to come back more often. Not just for my gran, but to stay connected to the people who used to mean so much to me. Like the Rossis, whose café I used to go to daily. I had no clue they retired and sold the café to their daughter.

Or Astrid, who was like a parent to me growing up.

Like Parker, who was . . . well, she was Parker.

I should have stayed in touch. I should have tried harder. I know that now.

The old theater comes into focus at the end of the street, and I gulp back my nerves at the size of the crowd gathered around.

"Holy shit."

"Dammit, kid, how many times do I have to tell you to watch your language?"

I smile down at my companion. "Sorry, Gran."

She winks. "It's all right. It's just a few people. Nothing to be worried about."

"Says the person who doesn't have to give a speech."

"You have to give a speech?"

I knew she was teasing about that earlier.

"Parker says it isn't a speech, but I am expected to say a few words."

Her ghostly white eyebrows lift. "You talked to Parker this morning?"

I narrow my eyes at her. "Why do you seem pleased by that?"

She says nothing, just grins in a way I don't like one bit. I want to ask her more, but the crowd's noise begins to swell, and soon we're being swarmed by townspeople.

I shake hands, smile, take selfies, and say *thank you* about a hundred times as I approach the stage they've erected outside the theater.

They got a stage for this? Damn.

I stop before walking up the steps, and there, standing on the other side of the stage, is Parker. Her auburn hair is twisted up in a bun that somehow looks classy and simple all at once. She's wearing a flowy skirt, a white top, and her trusty canvas shoes, which, if you look close enough, have paint splatters dotting their sides.

She's talking, her posture commanding the attention of the three people standing before her. She's not only heading this renovation on the construction side but also truly in charge of this whole project. People answer to her. They listen to her.

And I'm so fucking proud of her for it. She was quiet and shy in school unless you really got to know her, then she blossomed. Even at the theater, her safe place, she stuck to things that demanded the least attention, like set design or lights.

But now . . . she's changed. She's bright and cheery and respected, and now the world finally gets to see *my* Parker.

She turns and looks at me as if she can feel my gaze eating her up. Her eyes sweep down my body, and I know instantly something is wrong—I'm overdressed for this event.

"You lied," I say to my grandmother as Parker gestures to the people she's talking to that she'll just be a moment and begins making her way over to us.

"I did no such thing."

"You said I wasn't overdressed for this, and *that* was a lie."

"Oh." She rolls her lips together, then exhales a puff of air. "Well, fine. You just looked too cute and confident in your suit. I didn't want to ruin anything."

I groan. "Gran . . ."

"What? I care about you. Sue me."

"I'd take you for everything you're worth."

She shakes a wrinkled fist at me. "Bring it on, buster."

I laugh, shaking my head as I lead her to her reserved chair in front. "I'm leaving you here. Behave."

She rolls her eyes. "As if."

I want to tell her nobody says that anymore, but I know it's pointless. Gran is going to do what Gran is going to do.

With a heavy exhale, I straighten my jacket, take the two stairs leading to the stage with one step, and come face-to-face with Parker.

"Noel!" she says like she's surprised to see me or something.

"Peter."

Her hazel eyes narrow for a split second before she smiles, almost like she remembers we have an audience. And by audience, I mean the whole town is in attendance. Seriously, I don't think a single person stayed at home for this. Every single white folding chair is full, and it's standing room only toward the back. I see the owners of the bed-and-breakfast, Dick and his wife, Sue, who runs the car repair shop, and hell, even Peggy closed Jill's to be here.

Being with Parker is awkward enough. But having the whole town's eyes on us? It's almost unbearable.

She takes a tentative step toward me, folding her hands together in front of her.

"You look . . ."

"Completely overdressed? I know. Here." I shed my jacket, handing it over to her. "Hold this a moment, will you?"

I undo the button on my right sleeve and begin rolling it up. I lift my eyes to find Parker watching my every move. Her lips are slightly parted, her hazel eyes wide and locked in on what I'm doing. I move to the next, and she still doesn't look away.

It's not until I clear my throat that she finally looks up. Her cheeks turn pink almost instantly, but she doesn't offer an excuse or explanation.

No. She just meets my amused stare and barrels on.

"The ceremony will be quick," she says coolly, as if she wasn't just checking out my forearms. "A short speech from our mayor, Todd—"

"I know who Todd is, Parker. He used to babysit us, and we duct-taped him to a rocking chair once."

Her lips twitch with a hint of a smile. "Right. We did do that." She clears her throat. "Anyway, after that, I'll say a few words, then you'll go."

"You promise nobody is expecting anything epic?"

"I promise. They'll all be chomping at the bit for the closing Q&A session."

"You're doing a Q&A? With the *Gazette* here?"

She sighs. "Unfortunately. They were very pushy, and Todd wanted it, too, so what can I do?" She shrugs. "You ready?"

"We're going on now?"

"The ground isn't going to break itself. Which comes after your speech, by the way."

"Why are we breaking the ground again? Isn't it just a renovation?"

Parker shrugs again. "With some extensive work that needs to be done, yes. But Todd wouldn't let up on the idea. He said it would be 'more engaging,' whatever the heck that means. So we're doing it because I want my theater."

"Fine. Do I at least get to wear a hard hat?"

She looks up at my head, squinting as if she's weighing her options when we both know she's not. "You'll be fine."

"Wow. Just going to risk my safety like that, huh?"

"You're sticking a shovel into the ground. If you really want a hard hat, I'll have Axel grab you one."

I gnash my teeth together at the mention of the big oaf. "I'll live."

She gives me a deceptively sweet smile. "Good. Now, come on. Let's make this theater happen."

I follow her to the chairs behind the podium and wait for her to sit before taking the spot next to her. They're pushed tightly together, or at least that's my excuse for letting my leg rest against hers. Her touch is warm and familiar and so distracting that I completely miss the mayor walking to the podium and startle when he begins his speech.

"Thank you for coming today," Todd says. "We're excited to begin constructing the new Noel Carter Theater."

The crowd gives a polite round of applause, and Todd himself looks back to give me that enthusiastic thumbs-up only politicians can give.

I nod toward the crowd, but what I really want is to slink down in my chair and hide.

"You look like you're about to run away," Parker whispers as the mayor continues droning on. She leaned in, so close I can smell the peppermint coming from her ChapStick. "Don't run away."

"I'm not going to run away," I say as quietly.

"Good. Because you promised you'd do this."

"I know that. Unlike some people, I keep my promises."

It's a low blow—the lowest of lows. And I want to take the words back instantly, especially when Parker jerks back, her eyes full of hurt.

She turns her attention back to the mayor just in time for her to be announced.

"Everyone, please give a warm welcome to the restoration committee lead, the Noel Carter Theater project manager, *and* one half of Cooke & Pruitt Renovations, our very own Parker Pruitt!"

The crowd erupts into applause, much louder and longer than the one for my name, as she takes center stage and steps up to the microphone.

Unless someone is looking closely, they'll miss the shake of her hands, but I don't. I see it. She's upset, and it's all my fault.

She clears her throat. "Thank you, thank you. As I'm sure you *all* know by now since I've talked about it nonstop since I was eighteen"—the crowd laughs lightly—"I love this theater. It was my home away from home as a kid and throughout my teen years. It welcomed me when I felt lost, when I was sad, when I was happy, and when I didn't want to go home and listen to my mother sing Stevie Nicks off key."

Everyone laughs again.

"Ten years ago, I was devastated when they shuttered the doors. This building meant more to me than anyone else I knew." She glances back at me, catching my eyes and offering a small smile, one I don't deserve. "Well, just about anyone." She turns back to the crowd. "I've been lost without it, and I strongly believe this town has been lost without it, too, which is why I've annoyed you all for so long about resurrecting this old building. And now, thanks to an incredible donor who wishes to remain anonymous, we're finally breaking ground and are on our way to making theater a staple in this town once more. To commemorate such an incredible day, I'm pleased to welcome the namesake of our new theater, Noel Carter."

The applause this time is a little more enthusiastic, but still nothing compared with how they greeted Parker, and I'm not entirely surprised.

Parker turns toward me, and I try to catch her eyes as I make my way to the microphone, but they're completely blank as she claps with no real excitement behind it.

She's upset because I fucked up. Big-time.

Why? Why would I say that to her, today of all days? I'm such an asshole.

But I don't have the time to make up for it now.

I step up to the podium as the applause dies down.

"Thanks, everyone." I clear my throat, adjusting the microphone to my height. "Much like Parker, I spent my youth in this theater, and I can easily say that I wouldn't be where I am today without it. It changed everything for me, and I want nothing more than for another kid in Emerald Grove to have the same opportunity I did. That *we* did. I want them to have the chance to cry on that stage, to hear the roar of a crowd, and to find their passion, even if it isn't acting." I turn to Parker. "Maybe it's painting or set design, which leads to bigger and better things, giving them the skills to create stunning, totally showstopping projects." The barest hint of a smile tugs at her lips. "Or maybe it's directing," I say to the crowd now. "Whatever it is, I want them to find that same happiness I found here. I'm touched and completely honored to have the theater named after me. Thank you for giving me a place to find myself and a home to return to whenever I need to remind myself of who I am."

The gathered audience erupts into applause, my grandmother leading the pack as she shoots out of her chair and whistles loudly, just like she used to when I was a kid. It's equally embarrassing and endearing, even now.

I look to my left at Parker, who I assume has been standing by just in case I screw up, but even she seems impressed.

Not bad, she mouths.

I shrug, sending her a wink as the crowd's enthusiasm dies.

"All right," she says stepping back up to the microphone. "Let's get this theater started!"

Since he's heading the construction part, Axel and the mayor lead us off the side of the stage to a roped-off spot.

We stand in front of more cameras than I ever anticipated for an event like this, and right in the middle is Leonard. There is no camera in his hand, just a tape recorder, and he has a pinched expression on his face.

Someone hands me a shovel, and we gather for a few photos before Parker motions for me to proceed.

She wants me to do this? Fuck that. This is *her* moment. She's the one who has worked so hard for this. I'm just here for this ceremony, then I'm leaving town.

I shake my head, stepping up to Parker. "No. You."

Her eyes widen. "Me?"

"Yes. This is your project. It should be you doing this, not me."

"Don't be ridiculous, Noel. This—"

"Don't make me say it again." I lean closer. "This is your moment, not mine. Go shine, Peter."

She looks like she wants to argue, and I just know I'm about two seconds from hearing some excuse as to why she shouldn't be the one doing this.

"Par—"

"You know what? I will go shine," she says, surprising the hell out of me by taking the shovel and brushing past me like I'm nothing.

I swear, I've never been prouder.

She steps up to the center, and then with the broadest grin I've ever seen from her, slams the shovel into the ground. The crowd explodes into cheers. But I'm not watching them. I'm watching her.

Parker's shoulders relax for what seems like the first time in forever, and she blows out a long breath as she stands there, staring down at what she's accomplished. Sure, there's a lot of work ahead of her. But at this moment? At this moment, she just gets to *be*.

Be excited.

Be happy.

Be proud.

I don't think I've ever met someone more deserving than her.

Just for a moment, I want to stick around longer to see how it all plays out, watch her dream become a reality.

"She's fucking incredible," a deep voice says from beside me.

I look up to find Axel doing the same thing I'm doing—watching Parker with nothing but pride on his face.

"She is," I agree.

"Given how long you disappeared for, I don't find you qualified enough to say that, but this is her day, so I'm going to let it slide."

"I may have been gone for a while, but I still know Parker, Axel."

He laughs darkly as Parker begins taking questions from the media.

"No, you don't. You *knew* her, but I *know* her. I know the person she is, the woman she's become, a pillar of her community." He turns to me, and it's not often I have to look up to people, but I have to tip my head back to look into his dark, disapproving eyes. "I know her in ways you could never imagine because *I've* been the one who waded through the shitstorm with her. And I want you to remember that after your little weekend jaunt here, *I'm* going to be the one who is picking up the pieces after you leave. *I'm* going to be the one spending late nights with her while she tries to figure out what she's done to drive you away. *I'm* going to be the shoulder she leans on. So before you try to pull anything, remember that, *Hollywood*."

Axel isn't talking himself up. He's not letting me know that he's Parker's best friend, and I'm not.

No. This is a warning. A threat.

He's saying if I hurt Parker, I'm going to get hurt too.

And fuck me if I'm not full of equal parts anger and respect right now.

Angry, because if he knows Parker so well, he should know our whole story, know this isn't all on my shoulders. And respect because . . . well, how could I not? Not when he's so willing to step up for the woman I care so much about.

"You feel me?" he prompts when I say nothing.

"Yeah, Axel, I feel you. Loud and clear."

"Good. Because I'd really hate to break my promise to her about not pummeling you."

"Yes, I can see it's tearing you up inside just thinking about it."

"Never been more heartbroken in my life."

A hint of a smile cracks his lips like he's enjoying the thought far too much as we turn our attention back to the media frenzy still gathered around Parker.

Who knew this was going to be such a hot story? I expected some cameras and questions, but not for this to last so long.

"Parker, a moment?" the last person who should have been allowed here asks her.

"Leonard!" She smiles brightly at the journalist, but anyone with a keen eye can see it isn't genuine. "How are you?"

"Parker," he says, bypassing all pleasantries and moving into professional mode. "I assume you've considered how this theater won't bring enough revenue into the community and will strain our already limited resources instead? How this won't engage tourists and only the residents who already live here, who will inevitably grow tired of these homegrown theater productions, thus causing us to have to shut the theater down *again* in another few years?"

"Well, I—I . . . Of course, I . . . ," she fumbles, her response dying on the tip of her tongue.

I step toward them, ready to come to Parker's rescue, but Axel puts his arm out to stop me.

"Hang on," he says, still watching this unfold. "Let her answer."

Parker takes a steadying breath, then pushes her shoulders back ever so slightly.

"Thank you for your questions, Leonard. I love that you're so concerned about the theater and its longevity. Studies have shown that the presence of a theater in a town or city, no matter how big or small, enriches the lives of the people living there and creates a safe space for those who need it. I know that Emerald Grove is a tight-knit community, and surely, they want to create a haven for all who need one, right? I have full faith this town can come together and make this happen and keep the doors of this building open for all, for many, many years to come."

Leonard's jaw tightens at her answer. "So you want the townspeople to donate and resurrect this place on hopes and dreams because you had a happy youth here? What happens if you can't raise enough funds? Will the theater sit empty like it is now?"

"I don't believe we'll have any issues raising funds."

"Why?" Leonard counters quickly and sharply. This inquiry is becoming heated.

I try to step in again, but Axel still holds me back. I could easily shove him off me, but I know it'd create a scene, and I don't want to ruin Parker's special day.

And I fucking hate it. I hate sitting back and watching her get torn into like this. I want to help. I want to fix it. I want to be there for her.

"We have some creative ideas," Parker tells him. "We're hosting our first fundraising event, the Restoration Raffle, next weekend. I'm sure you've seen flyers all over town for it."

"We've also all seen the signs suggesting people *don't* want this theater to happen."

"Yes, true. I—"

"So while this all sounds great in theory, what happens if nobody donates?"

"I have faith the town will rally together and—"

"This sounds like you have a lot of *hopes* for this project but not a lot of cold, hard facts, or cash, for that matter." Leonard keeps pushing. "Do we really want to waste this generous donation—one that could benefit the town in much better ways—on your faith?"

"That's it," I mutter, and this time, when I push forward, Axel lets me go.

I stomp toward the ambush I'm watching unfold, not stopping until I'm next to Parker, who is struggling to answer Leonard's bullshit questions.

I place my hand on the small of Parker's back, and she jumps at the contact, peering up at me. Just like that, she's no longer tense. No. She relaxes into my touch.

"Ah, Noel. Just who I was hoping to speak with next. How do *you* feel about this restoration that could fail bearing your name?"

"Proud, *Figs*." I use the nickname he hates intentionally. He's riling Parker up, so why can't I rile him up? "Because I know without a doubt that it won't fail."

He shoots daggers my way. "And why are you so certain it won't fail?"

"Because I plan to help."

I do? Fuck me. What the hell am I saying?

Parker whips her head up at me. "You will?"

Her hazel eyes are so wide and full of such surprise and . . . Is that gratitude I see?

I can't let her down now. Not like I did before by never coming back.

I nod. "My schedule is clear for the next six weeks." It's not, and my agent is going to kill me for this, but the words keep coming anyway. "I'm staying in Emerald Grove to help raise the funds needed to complete the renovation, starting with the raffle next weekend."

"So you're auctioning off a date with yourself next weekend?"

Wait, what?

Leonard lifts the little recorder he's holding, eager for my answer, but that's not what I meant. Sure, I'll help, but auction myself off for a date? No way in hell.

"I didn't mean—"

"Yes!" Parker interrupts. "Yes. Next weekend, you can win a date with Noel Carter himself. Right, Noel?"

She bats her lashes up at me, and I know at that moment just how screwed I really am because I find that even after all these years, I still can't tell her no.

I sigh. "Yes."

I turn to Leonard and the whole media crew still gathered with their microphones and cameras poised, ready to catch this moment on film, so I can't back out.

"I'm auctioning off myself. A night with Noel Carter."

Leonard grins, and I hate it instantly.

"Splendid," he says.

Yeah. Splendid, indeed.

CHAPTER EIGHT

Parker

There aren't many people I don't like. I believe everyone deserves a chance, maybe even more than one in some cases.

But if I were forced to make a list of people I'm not so fond of, Leonard Figgins would top that list.

Who does he think he is? I don't remember him ever being so pushy. So cruel. He's asked questions about the theater project before, and sure, he's grilled me on it, but never to that degree.

Okay, so some of his questions were valid, and I totally understood them, but I have a plan. I've been saving up for this for years. Every penny I haven't spent on the absolute necessities has gone to this project, which isn't an insignificant amount. The business with Axel does quite well, and it's not that expensive to care for just me. I've built a nice savings. It's not enough to cover the costs the donation won't, but it's still enough to keep it going.

I'm prepared for this. I'm ready for this. And I won't have someone like Leonard try to knock me down before I've even started. I understand he was just doing his job and reporting on the happenings around town, but it still felt like an attack. I really shouldn't be surprised, given his dislike of me for being friends with Noel, who he always thought stole the spotlight from him.

After Figgins's heated questioning, no one else wanted to step up and grill me on the renovation, so the crowd dispersed quite quickly.

Now it's just me, Noel, and a few stragglers hanging behind, including Axel.

"I ever mention how much I hate that twerp?" He glares after Leonard, who is hurrying away, likely because he knows he's stirred up a storm.

"Me too," Noel agrees.

"Wow. Look at that. You two agree on something."

They exchange a quick look—one that I know holds much more meaning than I can decipher—and then look away just as fast.

I tip my head at Axel in a silent question, but he shakes his head.

"I'd better get going," he says instead. "Mary took the kids to the park, so I'm sure she could use my help."

"Oh." I frown. "I thought we were going to Rossi's afterward to celebrate."

"Rain check?"

I nod. "Yeah. Rain check."

Axel wraps me in his arms, hugging me tightly. "Proud of you," he whispers so nobody else can hear. "Knew you could do it."

"Thank you, but the hard work hasn't even started yet," I say as we pull apart.

"You kidding? *That* was the hard work. The rest of this? It's easy. We do it every day."

He's right. We do. The rest of this renovation? Easy peasy.

"See you in a bit."

He completely ignores Noel, who is still lingering, then takes off toward the park in the town center.

That leaves me and Noel.

"Where's Gran?" I ask him.

"She's walking back with friends. She was getting tired and insisted I stay out so she could nap in peace. Guess she's flashing back to our teen years when we'd play video games entirely too loudly and annoy her to no end."

"*You* were the loud one."

"Yeah, because *you* always cheated."

"Did not," I insist.

"Did too. Why else did I always call you Cheater Peter?"

I glare at him, but he smirks.

Silence settles between us, and it's awkward, something that's never happened with us before. I hate it.

"So . . . ," I say because I don't know what else *to* say.

"Yes, Peter?" His smirk is still in place.

I blow out a breath. "You didn't have to do that, you know? Step in and help. And you really didn't have to say you'd stay and help. I'm sure you've got plenty of . . . well, whatever you do back in LA. Movies and stuff."

He shrugs like it's no big deal when we both know it is. "I know. I wanted to."

"You wanted to raffle yourself off for a date night?"

"Well, no. *That* was your doing, remember?"

I wring my hands together and grimace. "I'm sorry. I sort of panicked."

"No shit." He laughs. "I guess I kind of deserved it after what I said."

I stiffen at the mention of the words he uttered to me before I took the microphone.

Unlike some people, I keep my promises.

In all fairness, he was right. I didn't keep my promise, and I've had to live with the repercussions for the last decade.

"I'm sorry. It was uncalled for."

"It's okay," I tell him.

"It's not. We said we were going to put all that behind us, and I shouldn't have brought it up."

"No, maybe not, but it was still true." I clear my throat. "Anyway, you don't have to do the auction. We'll figure something else out."

He shoves his hands into his pockets. "I'll do it."

"You will?"

"Yeah. I mean, I'm going to complain about it, but I'll do it."

I smile. He has that effect on me. One minute, I'm upset with him for calling me out, and the next, I'm smiling and laughing at his jokes. It's always been that way with us.

"I expect nothing less."

He turns his eyes up at the sun, squinting. "So, what now?"

"What do you mean?"

"I mean, what are you doing the rest of the day? I thought we might want to get together to come up with some other fundraising ideas."

He wants to *get together* with *me*.

It's a ridiculous suggestion. Completely absurd. Totally and utterly ludicrous.

And yet, I still find myself saying, "Sure. Let's go check out the new Rossi Café."

He folds at the waist, holding his hand out dramatically. "After you, my lady."

I roll my eyes, charging by him, leading us to the sidewalk. I don't take us to Borgen Avenue. I'm not sure I'm ready to stroll with Noel through the middle of town. Instead, I stick to the outer road, taking us the long way to the café.

We walk side by side, our arms brushing together every few steps. It's the same thing we've done so many times before, but it feels different now. Every step feels loaded, and every brush feels like it means something.

I wish we could turn back time and go back to when it was simple. I miss simple.

Suddenly, Noel pulls to a stop, and I instantly realize my mistake in taking us this way.

He steps up to the cemetery gate, the one I've been coming to every month for the last ten years, and stares longingly at the headstones.

We stand like that for several moments before he finally looks at me.

"You mind?" he asks.

I shake my head. "Not one bit."

He pushes the gate open, and we make our way down the small dirt path toward the back. It's the path I've walked so many times, so I stop when he passes by the turn he should be making.

He notices, turning back to me.

"Shit. It *is* that way, isn't it?" His shoulders fall forward in disappointment as he returns to my side. "Can't believe I forgot."

"Well, it has been a while."

He swallows hard, putting his head down, and we keep trudging along.

Halfway down, we take another turn, then walk past five plots before I stop. I let him go ahead, knowing he'll need this moment to himself.

Noel sucks in a deep breath, then turns to the old graves.

"Hey, Mom. Hey, Dad." He smiles softly. "Been a minute, huh?"

He crouches down, reaching forward to run his fingers over each letter in their names. I know because I've seen him do it so many times in our youth.

"Sorry I don't have any flowers. But I guess that's okay because it looks like someone already took care of that for me, didn't they?"

He glances over at me with suspicion.

I shrug in response, but he knows I kept up the tradition while he was gone.

At first, I did it because he asked me to. But after we stopped talking, I kept coming here. Maybe because it was a way to stay connected to Noel, or maybe because even though I never met his parents, they still felt like such important pieces of my life. Either way, I've kept it up for ten years and don't plan to stop anytime soon.

He offers a smile before turning back to his parents. I move away to give them privacy. Whatever he's saying, that's for them, not me.

Since it happened before I moved here, sometimes I forget that Noel lost his parents just like I lost my dad. Sure, his parents were taken from him instead of choosing to leave, but we were both left behind one way or another.

It's part of what helped us bond in the way we did all those years ago. I just never expected it to be the same reason we fell apart.

I busy myself with reading the other headstones in the cemetery, though I've done it a hundred times before, and wait patiently while Noel has his moment.

I'm unsure how much time passes before he finally joins me, his pinkie brushing against mine.

"Hey," he says quietly.

"Hey," I respond like a dolt. I move my hand away as subtly as possible, not because I don't *want* to touch Noel, but because I want to touch him far too much.

If he cares or notices, he doesn't mention it.

"Thank you, Peter. For taking care of them, I mean. That means . . ." He looks out over the top of my head, his eyes, which are rimmed red with unshed tears, narrowing for a moment before he peers back down at me. "It means a lot. I know those aren't fancy words, but they're all I have. So yeah, thank you."

He's right. They aren't fancy words, but they're exactly what I need to hear.

"Anytime."

He nods, then clears his throat. "So, lunch?"

I smile. "Lunch sounds good."

"Holy macaroni and cheese. I didn't expect this place to be this packed," I say as we squeeze—and I really do mean *squeeze* because this place is standing room only—through the front door of Rossi Café. "I don't know what I expected, but it wasn't this."

"You kidding me? The second I saw that wall, I knew this place was going to be fucking buzzing."

"That wall was your idea."

"Well, I guess I'm just that good."

I smack his stomach, and I really, really shouldn't have.

It's hard and bumpy, and *my gosh*, how many abs does he have under there? Sure, I've seen him shirtless in his movies—it's practically a requirement for every film of his—but I didn't think they'd be *this* nice in real life.

"Peter?"

"Hmm?"

"Are you feeling me up right now?"

I jerk my hand away, realizing that, yes, I *was* feeling him up.

Heat steals up my cheeks, and I duck my head in mortification.

He laughs, and I want to smack him once more, but I'm too afraid I'll accidentally start groping him again.

"Parker!"

Oh, thank heavens.

"Gianna!" I call out to the woman waving at me from behind the counter. "Come on," I tell Noel as I start toward her.

We make our way to the side of the front counter, and Gianna bounces over, her smile worth a million bucks. She shoves through the door we've built into the side and throws her arms around my neck.

"This is incredible, Parker!" She squeezes me tightly. "I cannot believe it. Everyone is gushing and cannot stop talking about the waterfall on the accent wall. And the wall color? Ugh. The sage is *so* perfect!"

"I'm so glad you like it, but, Gianna?"

"Yes?"

"I can't breathe."

"Oh!" She releases me with a laugh, and I suck in a breath of much-needed air. "Sorry. I just got so excited."

"It's okay. I'm really so happy you like it."

"I do. So much. Even more so today, now that there are customers here. Oh, and— Greta! Greta!"

Gianna waves her wife over to us, and Greta passes their employees to join us.

"Parker." Greta's smile rivals Gianna's as she wraps her arms around her wife's waist and tugs her close. "This is incredible. We love it. Thank you. Truly."

I wave off her words of praise. "It's nothing, really."

"Nothing? Are you kidding me? This is life changing. You've turned this dusty old café into something people will flock to see. It's . . ." She shakes her head. "I don't have the words for what you do for this community, always fixing up the businesses and now the theater too. It's . . ." She sighs. "It's truly awe inspiring."

My face begins to heat for the second time since I've walked in here. Thankfully, it's for something much less embarrassing this time.

"The waterfall was Noel's idea," I say, hoping to draw their attention to him.

It works, Gianna's eyes lighting up like she's just realized he's here.

"Holy shit!" She smacks her hand over her mouth. "I mean, shit. No. Fuck. *No.* Crap! Holy crap! *The* Noel Carter is in *my* restaurant."

He chuckles. "I've known you since we were babies, Gi."

"Yeah, but that was different. You were the dorky theater kid then. Now you're . . . well, you're *Noel Carter.*"

Greta rolls her eyes. "You'll have to excuse my wife. She's a fan." She sticks her hand out to Noel. "We haven't officially met yet, but I'm Greta. I've heard a lot about you."

"Nice to meet you," Noel says, shaking her hand. "Anybody willing to shack up with Gianna and handle her awful singing voice is good in my book."

"Hey!" Gianna complains. "I wasn't *that* bad."

"Babe, I love you, but you can't sing to save your life." Greta presses a kiss to Gianna's head. "Anyway, it was great to meet you, Noel, but I'd better get back to the front counter. In case you haven't noticed, we're a bit swamped."

"Of course. No problem." I wave her away.

"Can I get you guys anything? Our treat, of course," Gianna offers.

"Yeah, we'd love to treat you to lunch. Both of you," her wife agrees.

"I mean, I wouldn't say no to a sub."

"Yeah, of course. Anything special on it?"

"Double—"

"Everything and extra EVOO," Gianna and I finish for Noel.

He laughs. "Yeah, that."

He's a creature of habit. I've heard him order the same thing his entire youth, and Gianna's helped make the sandwich nearly just as long.

"One double meat, double cheese, extra EVOO Rossi Italian coming up," Greta says. She looks at me. "Your usual?"

"Please."

"You got it."

She hurries away, and Gianna turns to us.

"I'd better go help," she says. "Find a seat. We'll bring everything out once it's ready."

She gives me another hug before breezing back behind the counter. Noel and I shuffle through the packed shop toward the back. I don't miss how many people have their phones out and pointed our way. It's so strange. Is this what Noel deals with all the time? People watching his every move like this? I couldn't imagine how hard that would be to deal with.

"People are taking photos," I murmur to him as we approach a table tucked as far away from the prying eyes as we can be without sitting outside.

"Yeah, they do that. Just ignore them. I'll have my agent take care of it if they cause too much of a stir."

He pulls my chair out for me, and it reminds me of all the times he's done it before. He's always been a gentleman like that. I'm glad to see that hasn't changed.

"Thank you," I mutter as he takes the spot opposite me.

And that's the way we sit for several minutes—just there.

We don't talk. We just sit.

It's strange. We've been in this café together so many times before, but it's different now, and not just because of the new paint on the walls and the new layout. Everything with Noel feels like that now—the same yet different. I'm not sure how I feel about any of it yet, just like I'm not sure how I feel about him staying.

I haven't allowed myself to think about it much because what's the point? He's leaving again in six weeks. He's here to help raise funds, and that's it. That's all it means.

"Man, I didn't even think about it, but do you know how many Rossi breakfast sandwiches and subs I'm going to get now that I'm staying in town? Think it would be worth it just for that."

"Does Gran know this? That the only reason you're sticking around is for sandwiches? Not spending time with her?"

His eyes widen. "No, no. That's not what I meant. I—I—I—" he sputters, and I laugh at his attempt to fix his mistake.

I know he's not just staying for sandwiches. Or at least, I *hope* that's the case.

He sighs, giving up with a grunt. "There are other reasons too."

"Like my mother's coffee?"

"For starters." He grins, resting his arms on the small gray table we're sitting at. "So, tell me more about this theater. I suppose since I'm sticking around and helping raise funds for it, I should hear some of your ideas."

"Oh."

I don't know why his interest surprises me. Maybe because I thought he would use his name for clout and not do any of the hard work or care about what's happening. Why should he? He's taking off again at the end of his stay, never to think about this place again, I'm sure.

"Well," I start. "It's going to be a dual theater."

"People are going to be dueling?" He sits forward. "Are we talking about jousting or swords? Oooh. Or are you going with the Western theme—a good old-fashioned shoot-out? I'm partial to the swords. There's real art behind master swordsmanship."

I glower at him from across the table. "*Dual.* D-U-A-L."

"Oh." He settles back in his chair. "Less exciting—but continue."

"Anyway . . . ," I say pointedly. "We'll have two sections: one for plays and one for actual movies. We'll have to soundproof the heck out of it, and we'll only be able to show one movie at a time, but it's far better than the alternative, which right now means a three-hour round trip to see a movie."

Noel nods a few times. "I like it. It sounds doable and makes the space more functional than what Ms. Goodman used it for."

"Man, I miss that crabby woman," I say about our old theater director.

Part of the reason it took so many years to get the renovation underway was because of her unwillingness to part with the building. Even though it was sitting empty after the tree fell through it, she still didn't want to let it go. So it remained untouched until last year when she passed away and the property reverted to the town in her will. It then took another six months to convince the town council it should be used for a new theater. Of course, that led to me having to assure the others on the restoration committee it was a worthwhile project and that they should hire Cooke & Pruitt Renovations to head the project.

If it weren't for my anonymous donor and Axel and me working so hard to prove ourselves capable of handling such a project by renovating rental properties and businesses around town, I'm not sure I would have gotten the green light to get the project off the ground.

I only hope the rest of the town has as much belief as my donor and turns out for the raffle next weekend so I can prove Leonard and all the other cynics wrong once and for all.

"She hated me."

I gasp. "She did not! She loved you! She hated *me*."

"Then why do you miss her?"

I shrug. "Nostalgia."

Noel laughs. "I get what you mean. There's been a lot of that for me lately."

We both know what he's referring to—him being back. *Us.*

But we don't address it.

Instead, I tell him about my other plans—the concession stands, something Ms. Goodman was always against, how the movie club that meets in the park is already on board to rent the theater out monthly, and even my ideas for plays.

"You've spoken to the school board? Are they okay doing productions there, even if it means providing a chaperone? I know we always struggled with getting someone in there."

"Are you kidding me? Of course they are. Did you know their theater department hasn't been able to put on a real play in *five years*? They've just been sitting around on stools reading lines in the middle of the gym *after* basketball games. I already have three teachers signed up to volunteer. Besides, I think nobody wanted to do it before because of Ms. Goodman. She was so . . ."

"Mean?" he says with a laugh.

"*So* mean. Gosh, remember that time she threw the script at you? Like, straight up chucked it right at your head, then made you pick it up and give it back to her?"

"I can't believe she got away with it." Noel shakes his head. "Nowadays, there's no way that would fly."

"And with good reason. Our parents should have never allowed us back after that."

"Please. As if they could keep us away. We practically lived at that theater."

I smile. We *did* practically live there. In fact, one time, we even stayed the night there. Not on purpose—we totally fell asleep in the dressing room on a pile of clothes after a late-night painting session and got grounded for it—but still. It really was like our second home, even if it meant putting up with Ms. Goodman.

"I'm glad you're bringing it back," Noel says quietly, his attention on the tabletop. "I'm not sure I've told you that yet, but it's true. Those words you spoke during the ceremony . . . I feel them too." He lifts his eyes to me, and I don't think I'll ever get over how clear yet so stormy they are. "I know . . ." He exhales slowly. "I know I haven't been around, but no matter where I've been, I've always had a piece of that place with me."

My throat tightens with emotions I wasn't expecting, especially not sitting in the middle of the café.

It doesn't feel like he's just talking about the theater. It feels like he's talking about me.

Luckily, I don't have to respond, because Gianna chooses this moment to bring our food out to us.

"Okay," she says cheerily. "We have one Rossi sub, double meat, double cheese, and extra EVOO with a side of Rossi chips that I know you'll love." She sets the overcrowded plate in front of Noel. "And one meatball sub, extra provolone with two pickles on the side for you." She settles my plate in front of me. My sandwich looks wimpy compared to Noel's, thanks to all the extras he had added on there. "And finally, I brought your lavender lemonade, Parker." She turns to Noel. "I wasn't sure what you wanted, so I grabbed you a water, but if you want something else, just let me know and I can grab it."

"Water is fine. Thank you."

"Of course. If you two need anything else, flag me down."

"Thanks, Gi. This looks incredible. You really didn't have to—"

She waves off my praise. "Please. This is nothing. Now eat. Enjoy."

She tosses a wink, then hurries back to the front counter, which is still at least ten people deep. It's amazing to watch people leave, just for someone else to waltz in and fill their spot seconds later. I'm thrilled people love the makeover. Hopefully, it means continued good business for many years to come.

My lavender lemonade is swiped from the table the moment we're alone again.

"Hey! That's mine!"

I reach for it, but it's pointless. Noel's arms are too long, holding it perfectly out of reach.

"Sorry. Taxes."

I swear the world slows down as he closes his mouth around the straw, just like I swear I see his tongue poke out.

Don't react. Don't react. Do not react, Parker!

He takes a healthy sip, then lets out a loud and exaggerated *"Ahhh."* He licks at his lips. "Refreshing."

He sets my drink back down, and I glare.

"I hate taxes," I mutter, scooting the lemonade closer to me so he can't steal it again.

"Don't we all." He picks up his sandwich and takes a bite. "Holy fuck." He moans, his eyes rolling back into his head. "This is fantastic," he says around a mouthful of food.

It has no business being so hot, especially not when he has olive oil running down his chin, but it is. It *so* is.

I reach for my drink, praying he's too preoccupied with the sandwich to notice the shake of my hands, and gulp down half the cup in one go.

"So Greta said businesses, as in plural. This isn't the first place you've fixed up, is it?" he asks after his second bite. I haven't even picked up my sandwich. I can't. I'm too busy watching him.

"No. I redid the bookstore, Fran's, the frozen yogurt shop, and now this. It's not much, but it's helping them keep up with the latest trends."

"And those rental properties, too, right?"

"Yes."

"Anything else?"

I fidget in my chair, not liking where this questioning is going. Who'd have thought I'd be grilled so much today? "Some other projects here and there. Nothing . . . big."

"Hmm." He picks up his napkin, wiping at his mouth. "Anyone I know?"

I sigh. "Just ask, Noel."

"Fine." He sets his napkin aside and sits back in his chair. "Did you redo my grandmother's kitchen?"

I knew this question would come eventually. I'm not surprised Gran didn't mention the renovation to him. I visit her at least once a week, and we have a very firm *No Noel* policy. We don't talk about him at all—not a peep. We keep it strictly about us and the bond we've formed over the years. Sure, that bond exists because of Noel, but when we're baking in her kitchen together, we pretend he never lived there at all.

"I did."

"How much?"

I jerk my head back. "What?"

"How much did she spend on it?" he asks, pulling his phone from his pocket. "I want you to refund her."

There is no way he just said what I think he did. "Excuse me?" I ask.

"She doesn't need to spend her money on things like that. So, how much was it? I want to pay for it. I can transfer it now if you know your info, or write you a check this afternoon, whichever you prefer."

"You think . . ." I inhale sharply, trying to calm myself. I can't believe we're even having this conversation right now. "You think I'd charge your grandmother for a remodel? I practically grew up in that kitchen. She's the sole reason I even know how to make scrambled eggs. I didn't charge Gran a dime for that."

"Fine. Then what did you spend on it? I'll pay you back."

"I don't want your money, Noel."

I don't even bother trying to hide the venom in my words. How dare he think he can come in here and throw his money at me.

He tosses his phone to the table with a heavy sigh. "Then what do you want, Parker? Huh? You keep going around, doing all these great things, like resurrecting the theater, taking care of Gran's house, and putting fresh flowers on my parents' graves. What is it you want?"

"You! I want you!"

I freeze, almost like I've been hit by some fancy, techy, time-freezing ray gun straight out of *Spider-Man* or something.

Apparently Noel's been hit with it, too, because he sits unmoving. He doesn't say anything, just stares at me with wide eyes.

I hold my breath. Maybe if I'm not breathing, he'll forget I'm here, and maybe if he forgets I'm here, he can forget I just said that.

Maybe *I* can forget I just said that.

Ugh, why did *I say that? What the heck was I thinking? What the heck is* he *thinking?*

Then slowly, he blinks, and I suck in a desperate breath.

"Parker, I—"

"I have to go," I announce, shoving out of my chair. It's loud and undoubtedly draws attention, but I don't dare look back to find out. Or stick around, for that matter.

I push through the crowd and bolt out the front door, leaving behind my untouched lunch and Noel calling after me.

But I have to. I can't face him, not after what I just said.

And not after meaning it so much.

CHAPTER NINE

Noel

You! I want you!

Those four words have been playing on a loop for the last week. It doesn't matter what I'm doing, like having a conversation with Gran. They're stuck.

"—then Jackie Peeps said the Carolina Comets were taking the Cup this year, but I told her she'd been smoking too much of that whacky tobaccy and that the Seattle Serpents had it in the bag—"

You! I want you!

"Noel?"

You! I want you!

"Bub?"

You! I want you!

"Noel Benjamin Carter!"

I whip my head toward Gran. "What now, Lou Lou?"

She scowls at me, and I'm unsure if it's because I called her *Lou Lou* or because I wasn't paying a lick of attention to what she was just talking about. "Boy, I swear . . ." She shakes her mixing spoon at me, then turns back to the task at hand—baking enough to feed an army.

She's been in the kitchen baking away for tonight's raffle, which means the house has smelled amazing for days, and I've not been allowed to eat any of the delicious treats.

An absolute travesty, if you ask me.

It is almost as big a travesty as having Parker so close and not seeing her for a week. We've slipped right back into our old habit of ignoring one another, which is unfortunate, because I got a good ass chewing from my agent about extending my stay. But Aaron being Aaron, he made it work. He's already started fielding the questions that have popped up thanks to the photos of me some of the local high schoolers are posting on Instagram and canceled the red-carpet appearances and two interviews I had. All I have to do in exchange is read a script he's been trying to get into my hands for weeks.

It's the last thing I want to do, but it'll all be worth it if I can get Parker to talk to me.

When I saw her getting pie at Fran's on Saturday morning, she ran out the back door. When I saw her Tuesday morning at the town rummage sale, she hid under the booth where she was working. By Wednesday, I was wiped from helping out with various things around town—Gran had a whole list for me—so I stopped by Bigfoot's Hideaway for a drink, and I could have sworn it was Parker who disappeared through the kitchen doors and was never seen again.

On Thursday, I stopped looking for her, because one thing was clear—she would run no matter what.

"—I'm saying is that Jackie Peeps is wrong. How can you not root for your hometown to win the big hockey game?"

"Wait. You watch hockey, Gran?"

She stops mixing and peeks over her shoulder at me. "Yes! Where the hell have you been for the last ten minutes?"

"Sorry," I mutter. "I'm just . . . It's . . . I . . ."

She sighs, then sets her spoon down. She turns and heads for the table, wiping her hands on her apron.

"All right," she says as she sits across from me, where I've been bagging cookies for the last couple of hours. "What's going on? You've been a mopey little shit for the last week. Reminds me of that time Jessica or Julie or whatever her name was dumped you in eighth grade, and you boo-hooed for a week."

"Her name was Kelsey, and I did not cry for a week. It was one day, and it was my first heartbreak."

"Well, whoever she was, I hate her."

"You *just* bought flowers from her at the farmers' market."

"I did no such thing!"

I laugh. She did. We even joked about Kelsey's claim to fame, which is that she was my first girlfriend. Gran just has no clue who she is because she was never able to get her name right the whole three months that we "dated."

"Anyway," Gran says, cutting me a look that could kill if she wasn't so damn tiny and unintimidating. "What's on your mind, bub?"

I set aside the cookies I'm bagging and lock my fingers together, resting my forearms on the table. "Parker."

Gran's lips pull into a frown. "What'd you do, Noel Carter?"

"Hey! I didn't do anything!"

She arches a brow at me. "Why don't I believe you?"

"Because you've been in cahoots with Parker for years and never told me about it. Now you like her better than me."

She rolls her eyes with a huff. "Please. I love that girl like she was my own, but she's not my own. You are. I love you more, but that doesn't mean I want to see her hurt. So I ask again—what'd you do?"

"I really didn't do anything, Gran. We were having lunch after the ceremony last week, and we started talking about all the renovations Parker's done around town. She admitted to redoing your kitchen—something *you* could have told me, you know. Then I offered to pay her back for the project because I don't believe you should be spending your money like that, especially when I'm more than capable of taking care of you."

"First, I don't have to tell you shit."

I roll my lips together so I don't laugh at my grandmother saying *shit*.

"Second, I didn't tell you because I didn't think it was important who redid my kitchen."

"It's Parker. Of course I'd want to know."

She shrugs. "Third, even if I had paid for Parker's labor, it would have been my money to spend as I please. You might make the big bucks, but you don't need to take care of me. I haven't had a partner since your grandfather passed away—before you were even born—and I have been getting along just fine. I don't need anyone's assistance but my own."

If I weren't so worried she'd smack me for it, I'd reach over and high-five her for her empowering speech.

"And fourthly, you *did* do something wrong."

"How?!" I toss my hands into the air, completely at a loss.

"Because Parker is an incredibly independent person, and she doesn't need your money either. That business of hers she built is successful as hell, and this town wouldn't be doing half as well as it is if she didn't have the genius idea of renovating houses and using them as rentals for the tourists. Your offer was like a slap in the face to her, especially after you've been gone so long." I shrink farther down in my chair with each biting word. "You think you can just roll into town, act like you haven't spent the last ten years away, and throw money around to fix everything? That doesn't erase all the years, Noel."

As much as Gran always supported me in leaving, I knew deep down that a part of her was hurt by it. But this is the first time I've heard her so angry over it.

"I'm sorry," she says after several tense moments. "You know I'm glad you've found success. I really am. It's just . . ."

"I know, Gran. I miss you too."

"You've been gone so long, Noel. So, so long. Why?"

I gulp down the lump stuck in my throat. "You know why."

"Because of Parker? Because she wouldn't join you in LA?"

"It's more than that, and you know it."

"Fine. Then because you two kissed?"

I squeeze my eyes as the memories assault me. The kiss with Parker wasn't just a kiss. It was so much more than that.

It was a promise. Parker knew it, and I knew it too.

But then she went and broke that promise, and now here we are, ten years later.

"I know it's hard to let go of the past," Gran says. "But sometimes you have to if you want to build a future. You kids need to work out whatever's going on between you, because you've spent too many years of your life loving each other not to."

Deep down, I know she's right. Parker and I have too much history to just throw in the towel because we went and fell for each other.

But where do we start? How do we get back to what we had? Or even just our friendship? I miss that the most. I miss laughing with her with no discomfort. I miss sitting with her with no expectations. I miss being around her, and truthfully, I have since the day I left for LA.

How could I not? She's funny and smart and gets me on a level nobody else does. And even after all these years and the distance, she's still my best friend.

"Talk to her," Gran encourages. "Do it soon before these next six weeks fly by, you go back to LA, and another ten years pass without talking."

"I will," I promise her. "I'll talk to her."

And I intend to keep my promise tonight.

Parker might have been able to run and hide earlier this week, but tonight she can't. We're going to be trapped together in the Community Hall. Besides, she *has* to stick around. It is her event, after all.

I'm overdressed again.

Does nobody in Emerald Grove dress up for functions? At least a few people here are wearing dresses and suit jackets, but no other soul is dressed in a full tux like me.

"Gran, you let me overdress again." I scowl down at the woman on my arm.

She grins proudly, not even bothering to feign innocence. "I know. You just looked so damn handsome and had a little pep in your step for the first time in days. I couldn't ruin your good mood."

"Thanks," I mumble, though I don't mean it.

"Oh, don't be like that. You look great. I'm sure the bidders will agree." She winks up at me, and I'm not sure if I hate how excited she is for this torment I've subjected myself to or love how supportive she is no matter what.

"Wow, Noel! You look incredible," Fran says as she hands me the program for tonight. "Like a Hollywood movie star." She pauses, realizing what she's just said, then laughs. "Oh, right." She shakes her head. "Sometimes I forget. You're still just Noel to me."

I give her one of my red-carpet smiles. "Thanks, Fran."

"O-of c-course," she stutters, clearly affected by the grin.

I laugh as we make our way into the Community Hall, which has been overhauled to look like a fancy-schmancy event room instead of just where everyone gathers for bingo on Sunday nights. Tomorrow, this place will be teeming with folks who are ready to scrap over the winning pot. But tonight, it almost looks magical with its draping curtains, high-top tables covered in expensive-looking linen, and eye-catching centerpieces.

I have no doubt who put all the effort into this.

Like the universe is playing some cruel joke on me, the crowd parts, and directly across from me stands Parker.

"Holy shit."

She's next to Axel, who is holding a kid who looks to be about four, two identical ones standing next to him. Another woman, who I assume is Axel's wife, has her head tossed back and is laughing at whatever Parker's saying.

"Yeah, I'd say," Gran says, and I hadn't realized I'd said anything out loud. "She's beautiful, isn't she?"

I can't speak. Can't even nod along in agreement.

All I can do is stare.

Her eyes wander around the room, then land on me, and I see her stiffen, but not even that can distract me.

Parker's usually tied-back auburn hair is hanging loose around her shoulders in subtle waves, one side tucked daintily behind her ear. A knee-length, pine-colored dress clings to the curves she almost always hides underneath paint-stained overalls or T-shirts that are two sizes too big. She's wearing black high heels—a first since she didn't even wear them to prom—that make her legs look a mile long, and sparkly earrings dangle from her ears.

She's not just beautiful, she's stunning.

And now she's running away.

"Go." Gran unhooks her arm from mine and shoves me forward as Parker tries to disappear into the crowd. "I'll be fine. Talk to her."

I push through the crowd, ignoring people when they call out to me. I only have one thing on my mind, and right now, it's Parker.

I barely catch a glimpse of a green dress as the door leading to the basement closes.

"Noel, just the guy I was—"

"Rain check, Garth," I say to the owner of Bigfoot's Hideaway as I reach the door.

I throw it open without a care about the scene I'm surely making and step into the stairwell, letting the door close behind me.

"Parker! Park—"

There's a surprised squeak at my back, and I spin around to find her with her back pressed up against the wall.

She was hiding—*literally* hiding—behind the door.

"Crud," she whispers, and I grin.

"Yeah, *crud* is right. Are you really trying to run from me?"

She straightens, then lifts her shoulder. "I'm just getting some fresh air."

"In the stairwell that I know leads to nothing but a storage room for all the bingo tables?"

She notches her chin up. "Yes."

I roll my eyes. "Come on, Parker. You can't run forever."

"Why not? You did."

My jaw tics. *"I"*—I jab a finger into my chest—"didn't run. I told you where I was going. I told you where I'd be. *I* begged you to come, and *you* never showed. *You* stopped calling. *You* stopped answering the phone. *You* stopped being there for *me*."

"Because I was scared!" she explodes. "I was scared. You asked me to leave behind everything I knew and loved and follow you to LA like some lost little puppy. Why? So you could grow bored of the girl from your small-town life and take off again, leaving me alone to fend for myself?"

"I would *never* do that."

"Don't be so sure. People make promises all the time they can't keep. My father did it to my mother. He promised to love and cherish her, but when he wasn't satisfied with what this town could offer, he took off and left us and never returned. Like you. I knew you were never coming back the second you left, just like him."

Jesus. Is that what she thinks? Is that how she's seen this all these years? That I'm like her father, and I abandoned her? It was never supposed to be like that. I wanted her there more than anything. *She's* the one who didn't want to come.

I suck in a deep breath, running my hand through my hair. "Peter, I . . ."

She shakes her head. "It's fine. It's . . . fine."

"It's not," I tell her, stepping closer. "It's not fine. I didn't mean to stay gone. It's just . . . We stopped talking, and I thought . . ."

"You thought what? That I just forgot about you, like you forgot about me?"

My heart sinks. How could she even think that? There's no way I could forget her. She's Parker. She's . . . well, she's everything good about my life here. She's all my happy memories in one place. She's the greatest thing to ever happen to me. And yes, even despite the years, she's still the person who knows me the absolute best.

"You . . . think I forgot about you? I didn't. I could never forget you, Parker. Never."

"What else was I supposed to think?" She huffs disdainfully. "I've seen the tabloids. You were off in Hollywood, going to parties and falling into bed with actresses and stepping out of clubs at two in the morning and—"

I kiss her.

I step right into her, and I press my lips against hers.

It takes her about three seconds to realize what's happening, then suddenly, she's kissing me back.

She grabs the lapels on my jacket, holding me to her like she's afraid to let go, and I get it because I'm fucking scared too. I press her against the wall, cradling the back of her neck with one hand and her waist with the other as I explore her mouth with my tongue.

This kiss is different from our last one, not just because we both know what we're doing now.

It's different because this kiss is the culmination of years of pent-up anger and frustration and longing and missing someone so much your heart literally aches.

It's *that* kind of kiss.

I bunch the material of her dress up because I need to touch her more than I'm already touching her. I need to *feel* her. When my fingers brush bare skin, she tugs me closer, and I take it as a sign to keep going. I push the material up until it sits around her hips, then run the inside of my pinkie where her thighs meet.

She gasps into my mouth at the soft touch, and I pull away.

She looks gorgeous like this—her hair is disheveled from being pinned against the wall, her lips swollen from my kisses, and her eyes glassy with lust.

"Tell me to stop, Parker."

She shakes her head. "I can't."

"Then I won't."

It's all the warning I give her before I slide my hand into her silky underwear and take what I've wanted for so long—*her*.

She gasps as I glide my fingers through her folds and over her clit, then whines when I push just the tip of one inside her.

Fuck, she's tight. So damn tight. So warm. And so fucking perfect.

"Noel," she moans into my neck when I push in more and begin working her over with a single digit. She hooks her leg around my waist, pushing me deeper. I love the bite of her heel digging into my ass. "Please."

"Please what, Parker? Tell me what you want."

"You. I want you."

It's the same thing she said to me last week. The exact four words that have been stuck in my head since. But now . . . now they're so much more.

Our tongues collide in a fervent kiss as I fuck her with my finger, and *god*, she tastes so good. Like peppermint and home and all mine.

She bucks her hips against me, riding my hand like she can't get enough, and when I press my thumb against her clit, she gasps, wrenching her mouth from mine.

"Ohgodohgodohgod."

Sure, they're technically separate words, but they all sound like one.

"I'm so . . . so . . ."

"I know, Parker. I know."

And I do know because I feel it too. I'm as close as she is, only I don't have the luxury of coming right now—but fuck if I don't want to. My cock is straining against the zipper of my pants. It's the hardest I've ever been, and I know it's purely because of Parker and the little sounds she's making right now as she takes what she wants from me.

Her body tenses, and it's the only warning I have before she clutches my jacket tighter and comes undone around me.

I fuck her through her orgasm, letting her ride my hand the whole way through until the last shudder subsides and she's nothing but a shaking mess as she tries to catch her breath.

I kiss her lips, chin, jawline, and neck. I kiss her everywhere I can because I'm not ready to be done touching her yet. It's not enough, and I fear it will never be with her.

"Noel . . . ," she whispers as I nip lightly at her neck. "I—"

"Parker!"

The door bursts open, and I barely catch it before it smacks against me.

I let it close as Fran comes barreling into the stairwell, and I remove my hand from between Parker's legs, shifting in front of her to shield her from our intruder.

"Parker!" she calls. "Park— Oh." She stops, looking right at me. "Noel. Have you seen . . ." Her mouth drops open when she realizes that Parker is tucked against me. "Parker."

The woman in question pokes her head around me. "Hi, Fran."

The pie shop owner's cheeks grow redder by the second. "Hi, Parker. I, uh, I was just coming to let you know that we're getting started on the bidding. You know, in case you wanted to give the opening remarks."

"Right. I'll . . . I'll be out in a moment."

"Of course. I'll just, um . . ." Fran points out to the party. "I'll be there. I'll stall."

"Thank you," Parker says.

Fran gives me one last long glance as she pulls open the door just enough to squeeze through, then disappears.

The door clicking shut sounds like a shotgun in a small room—deafening and meaningful.

Parker pushes lightly against me, and I reluctantly release my hold on her, stepping back so she has just enough room to shimmy her dress back into place. She brushes against me with every movement, and I relish it.

When she's finally done, she looks at me for the first time.

"That was . . ."

"Yes?" I ask.

"Unexpected."

I don't think you can call ten years of waiting unexpected, but I don't tell her that. I brush her long auburn hair back from her face, tucking the strands back behind her ear as they were before I mussed them up.

"Do I look okay?" she asks softly. "Is my lipstick . . ."

"Completely gone and likely all over me? Yes."

She chews on her bottom lip. "I don't have my purse in here."

"It's okay. I'll sneak off to the bathroom."

She nods, blowing out a long exhale before pointing to the door. "I should probably . . ."

"You should," I tell her.

Except I don't move. I can't. Not yet, and not just because my cock is still straining against my slacks. It's more like I can't because I know as soon as I let her go, this moment is gone, and I'm not so sure I want to lose it yet.

I step toward her, my body snug against hers once again, and suddenly, everything feels right in the world.

"Noel . . . ," she says breathlessly. "What are you . . ."

I swallow her words, careful to keep my hands tucked by my sides so I can't slide them through her hair and we have to start this whole process over again.

I just need one more kiss. One more taste. One more minute of her being all mine.

I let my lips linger against hers until I can't any longer, and only then do I finally step away for real this time.

One step.

Two steps.

Three steps.

Four.

I need distance or we'll never get out of here.

She's sagged against the wall again, eyes squeezed shut as she tries to regain her breath once more.

She sucks in one last deep breath before brushing past me on shaky legs.

I grab her wrist as her hand lands on the doorknob.

She turns back to me, lifting her brow in a silent question.

"We should talk."

She swallows harshly. "Okay."

It's one word, a simple answer, and then she vanishes through the door and into the night.

I stand there for several minutes, staring at the spot she just abandoned, trying to talk myself down. Trying to figure out where the hell we go from here.

When I know I can't stay gone any longer without risking someone coming to look for me, I step back into the party smelling of peppermint and Parker.

◆ ◆ ◆

The Restoration Raffle is an official success, and we've only just started on the bachelor biddings.

The last I looked, we were up over $20,000. It's not the huge pot I've seen at other charity events and raffles I've attended, but for Emerald Grove, this is as big as it gets.

I'm not surprised that Parker is leading the pack. It's easy to get swept up in her and fall for her charm. It's no wonder people are clamoring to empty their pockets tonight.

"All right," she says into the microphone with a wide grin. To most, she probably looks completely put together and completely focused on the task at hand.

But to me? I can see where my hands played in her hair, spot the wrinkles on her dress where my fists held it up, and there is no mistaking the little red spot on her neck where my lips were attached.

Not to mention that every time her eyes scan the crowd, they linger on me for just a moment too long.

"Next up, we have Clifford Daws. Most of you might know Clifford as our resident go-to man for any and all things greenery, but tonight, he's offering up a special evening with him. You get to pick the day, and Clifford will take you to Lake Cushman on his boat for a romantic day on the water. We'll start the bidding at fifty dollars."

"Fifty?" Clifford says loud enough for the microphone to pick up. "I'm worth at least a hundred, dammit."

The crowd laughs, and Parker does her best to stay composed as she smiles at everyone.

"Well, then, folks, I guess we're starting at a hundred."

"Damn right we are," Clifford grumbles.

She bangs her gavel against the podium, and a few bids go up around the room. Soon Clifford's worth at least $175 and looking pretty damn proud of it.

I tune them out as I spy Parker's mother waltzing over to me with a cup of coffee in her hand. She can't even give it up for one night.

"Astrid, you look lovely tonight."

Parker's mother grins, then waves her hand over her floor-length dress, which looks like something somebody would wear to Coachella. "This? Bah. It's nothing. I thrifted it years back. Now, about you and my daughter."

"Pardon?"

She laughs. "Please. You can't fool me. But just so you know, if you two are going to sneak off together and pretend like nothing happened, you might not want to make googly eyes at one another."

I shake my head, ready to deny everything, but it's pointless, especially with Astrid's knowing look.

"It was nothing."

Her usually cheerful eyes narrow to slits in an instant. "It had better not be nothing, Noel. That's my baby girl."

In all my years of knowing her, I've never heard such seriousness from Astrid Pruitt. Sure, she's been like a mother to me, but like a fun mother who lets you do and get away with anything.

But right now . . . Well, she looks downright scary, staring up at me with sharp eyes.

She steps into me, lowering her voice. "If this is nothing . . ." She shakes her head. "Well, then, I don't think it's a good idea if you stay around, even if you did promise to. That's not fair to her—or you, for that matter."

"It's not . . . I just meant . . ."

"I know what you meant. I'm just telling you that you'd better know what you're doing when it comes to her. Parker is strong and resilient, but even the toughest people have limits."

I understand where she's coming from. I truly do.

But in all fairness, I didn't mean to hurt Parker the first time around. I was just looking for something more out of life. Something different that would allow me to really follow my passion for acting.

I think the hardest pill to swallow is that all this time, that thing I was looking for . . . it might have been right here.

I know I have to go back to LA after my time here is up, and I want to do that, but the rush to do so doesn't feel as pressing anymore, and I'm not quite sure what to make of that.

But that's not a problem I want to deal with right now. I have bigger things to worry about, like figuring out when I can get Parker alone again.

"Understood, son?" she prompts, wanting a response from me.

I nod. "Understood, Astrid."

"Good. That's good." She takes a sip of her coffee. "Well, I'm off to bid. But one last thing?"

"Yes?"

"My daughter's lipstick is on your collar." Then she throws her hand up and yells, "Five hundred for Clifford!"

I stare in shock as Astrid pushes her way to the front of the crowd, steps onto the small stage they've erected, grabs Clifford by the shirt, and drags him off into the crowd like he isn't her mortal enemy.

What in the hell just happened?

Apparently, Parker has the same thought, her mouth ajar and eyes twice their size as her mother moves through the bodies standing around. Half the people are laughing, and half are just as shocked as we are.

"Well, then." Parker laughs lightly. "I'm definitely going to need that story later."

The crowd chuckles along with her as she shuffles her cards.

She reads over the name and pauses, her eyes flicking toward me.

Fuck. I'm next.

She steps up to the microphone again, that same fake smile from before plastered across her lips.

"Next up, we have the man I'm sure most of you have been waiting for. Some of you may know him as Hollywood's heartthrob, but to many of us, he's still that same kid who had training wheels on his bike until he was twelve."

"And a half! He was twelve and a half!" Axel hollers from across the room.

I glower at him, and he just shoots me a grin. His wife swats at him, shaking her head, and I don't even know her, but I like her already.

"Sorry. Twelve and a *half*." Parker tucks her lips together to hide her grin. "Please help me in welcoming to the stage . . . Noel Carter!"

The room erupts in cheers, and I push off the high-top table I was leaning on and make my way to the stage. Several women in the crowd talk behind their hands, probably making their plans to bid. If I didn't want this theater to succeed for Parker's sake, I would immediately run in the opposite direction and book a plane ticket back to LA.

But I can't run. Not just because of the theater, but because there is no way I'm walking away after what just happened in that stairwell. I have to know if it was just a onetime thing or if it could be more.

The spotlight is blinding as I step onto the stage and wave to the crowd. I swear they cheer louder because of it.

I ignore it. I have my attention set on something else—Parker.

I step up to her, pressing a kiss to her cheek, not missing the way her breath hitches.

"You're going to pay for that later."

I don't know if it's a promise or a threat, but it elicits the tiniest of squeaks from her, and I'm satisfied either way.

Parker clears her throat. "All right. Let's get this started. We'll start the bids off at—"

"One hundred!" a woman yells from the crowd. I hold my hand to my eyes to see who it is, but I can't make her out.

"One fifty!" another woman adds.

"One seventy-five!"

It keeps going until it hits $750, Parker's eyes getting wider and wider with every bid.

It's our biggest bid all night, but I think they can do better.

I slide up next to Parker, sticking my head in front of the microphone. "Come on, now. We can do better than that, right? Think of how much joy this theater is going to bring your kids."

"Think of how much joy he can bring me for one night," someone in front says.

"Abigail!"

I recognize that voice. It's my tenth-grade teacher, which means that her daughter, who was a year younger than us in school, just said that.

She ducks her head down, but not before I throw her a wink.

What? It's for a good cause.

"One thousand dollars!" A new voice booms through the small space, and every hair on my neck stands up. Leonard Figgins elbows his way through the crowd. "I bid one thousand dollars."

I don't know why he repeats this, but it sends a hushed murmur through the crowd, and Leonard simply smirks.

Then it's crickets.

Nobody moves. Nobody says anything. And I'm pretty sure it means I'm going on a date with Leonard Figgins, where he will no doubt grill me on any- and everything, and I'll walk out a headline.

"Five thousand."

My head whips toward Parker, who is staring down at Leonard with sharp eyes and a face that says *Try me.*

"You can't do that," he tells her, fuming.

"What? I can't donate to a good cause?" she challenges.

"Yeah, can't she donate too?" someone says.

"Let her bid!"

The volume kicks up, and everyone agrees that Parker should be allowed to play along with everyone else.

"But you . . . you . . ." Leonard stomps his foot. "Ugh! I'm out."

Parker smiles victoriously. "Well, there you have it. Noel Carter, sold to the highest bidder—me."

She bangs the gavel, making it official.

I was wrong. I'm not going on a date with Leonard. I'm going with Parker.

And damn if I haven't been more excited for anything in my life.

CHAPTER TEN

Parker

This night is not at all turning out how I thought it would. I thought I would come in here, mingle with the guests while I avoided Noel, auction off the bachelors, then head home to comfort myself with a bottle of wine and fall asleep on my couch for the sixth time this week.

But no.

There was no avoiding Noel. He waltzed into the party looking ridiculously handsome—and completely overdressed—in a tux that clung to every inch of his body he clearly spends a lot of time working on. I knew right then that tonight would be my undoing.

A small part of me was relieved when he followed me into the stairwell. If we were going to talk about my little outburst last week, at least we'd be doing it behind closed doors.

I just didn't expect to be doing *it* behind closed doors too.

But he kissed me. He kissed me, and I was a goner—straight putty in his hands. I was wrong if I thought he was a good kisser at eighteen. It's nothing compared to the way he kisses me now—like he owns me.

Then his touch drifted lower, and there was no way I could tell him to stop. I couldn't have mustered the words if I tried. The way he touched me with such care and such need . . . It was unlike anything I'd experienced before. I've made myself come plenty of times on my own, but nobody else ever has. I guess I shouldn't be surprised that Noel was my first. He always knew me best.

"Really, Parker? Five grand?"

I snap back to the present to find Noel grinning down at me as the audience goes wild.

I just bid on Noel.

And I won.

"Little steep, no?"

"It was for a good cause." I shrug, trying to play it off like I bid only for the theater project and not because I couldn't stand the thought of him going out with someone else, especially not Leonard Figgins.

Sure, I know it wouldn't have been an actual date, and I have no doubt Leonard would have spent the entire evening badgering him with questions or trying to get a story out of him, but still, that wasn't the real reason I bid.

I wanted Noel.

No.

I *want* Noel.

And all to myself.

He leans down to me, so close his lips are brushing my ear. "You know, Parker, if you wanted me to touch your pussy again, all you had to do was ask. Not pay five grand for the privilege."

Heat steals up my cheeks, and his words go right between my legs to the very spot he's talking about.

Do I want that? Yes, please. More than anything.

Am I going to be able to stop thinking about it until it happens again? Not a chance.

Am I completely screwed when it comes to Noel Carter? Absolutely.

I gulp, turning back to the crowd like his words haven't ignited a fire inside me, and give them the best smile I can muster.

"That concludes our bachelor auction. Fran will be up next to start the raffle, so make sure you have your tickets ready. Thank you all for a wonderful evening."

The place breaks out in more cheers, whistles, and gushing. The second I walk off the stage, I'm bombarded by folks.

I usually love this. I love being part of such a small, tight-knit town. I love the camaraderie when everyone comes together, and I love their support.

But right now, the only thing I want is the six-foot-four man standing on the stage, smirking down at me with heat in his eyes.

Oh yeah. I am so, so screwed.

I stay late, until the last stragglers are moseying their way to the door.

But it's still not late enough.

Noel prowls around the room, making small talk with everyone and dumping trash into the bag in his hand.

When he said he would stay to help with fundraising, I certainly didn't think he meant picking up trash after the event.

I know it's just his way of staying close to me, though. How could it not be, with him sending looks over here every ten seconds?

"Parker, my dear," my mother says sweetly as she wraps me into her arms. "I'm so proud of you. You did incredible tonight. You put a good dent in the fund for the restoration."

"Yeah, but it's still not enough."

"No, but you've just funded at least two more weeks. Look at the positive side."

I know she's right, and I should be happy. But I can't help thinking that maybe Leonard was right. Perhaps asking the town to help pay for the theater is too much.

Sure, we're getting discounted labor from my and Axel's crew, but we still have to pay them, and the supplies we're using aren't free. Not to mention the cost of the screen, the equipment for the concession stand, and the chairs, and just overall not making it look like it's a thrown-together mess—we'll need at least another $500,000 to finish it out. It's a lot to ask of anyone, let alone the town that raised you.

"Breathe, Parker," my mother says softly. "Just breathe."

I suck in a deep breath, then exhale.

"We'll talk more tomorrow." She lets me go, her eyes glassy from the scotch she's undoubtedly dumped in her coffee over the last few hours.

"Oh, we are *definitely* talking tomorrow." I slide my eyes from her to Clifford, who is waiting nearby. "He your ride?"

"He sure is." My mother giggles like a teenager, and I wave her goodbye.

After saying goodbye to Fran and the rest of my volunteers, there's just one person left.

Noel.

We work silently for the next thirty minutes, picking up trash, taking down decorations, and moving tables back to where they belong while soft music plays in the background. I don't know where it's coming from, but I've never been more grateful for it. It's keeping me distracted from all the naughty thoughts running through my mind, like what would Noel do if I just walked right over and kissed him? Or shoved him into one of the chairs and crawled onto his lap? If I dropped the straps on my dress and shimmied out of it? Would he kiss me back? Would he ravage me the way I want him to?

The soft music that's been playing in the background comes to a natural stop, and it's our cue to wrap up the cleaning and get going for the night.

Noel saunters over to me, somehow making carrying a trash bag look like he's on a red carpet.

"So, Peter."

I don't even bother trying to hide my grin. "So, Noel."

"Do you have any plans tomorrow?"

"I was going to give my cat a bath, but that's about it."

"Your . . ." He shakes his head. "I'm sorry. Did you say you were going to give your *cat* a bath?"

I lift a shoulder. "Pumpkin's weird. He loves baths and hates normal cat things. Well, except for destroying any- and everything I leave on my countertops or mantel. He loves doing that far too often. He's weird."

"Sounds like it," he says. "So, cat bath but nothing else?"

"If you're asking to take me out, I suppose I could postpone Pumpkin's bath. He won't be happy about it, but you can explain that to him."

Noel presses his lips together, smothering a laugh. "I'll see if I can muster enough courage to break the news to him."

"Does that mean you're asking me out?"

"Yes, Parker, I'm asking you out."

"Where?"

"Pardon?"

"Where do you want to take me?" I ask him.

He laughs lightly, running his hand through his hair in that same nervous habit he's always had. "I, uh, hadn't really thought that far ahead."

"Not the city, please. I don't think I can handle that."

"No city, I promise. What about Rockaway Falls? I haven't been there in . . . Fuck, I don't even know how long it's been."

I do. We went for my eighteenth birthday and swam at the waterfall's base. It was cold because it was March, but we didn't care. We had fun and spent the whole day out there shivering our butts off, then ended up being late for curfew. My mother gave me concerned looks the rest of the week, and I know now it's because she was worried we were out there fooling around.

We were, but not in the way she thinks.

We weren't having sex. We were busy being young and free and having far too much fun for two people with no idea what heartbreak was ahead.

Oh, to be that naive again.

"Rockaway Falls sounds nice. The tourists haven't started coming in for the season yet, so it shouldn't be too crowded. I can pack a . . ." My words teeter as Noel begins shaking his head.

"Nope. You pack nothing. I'm taking *you* out on a date. I'll take of everything. I just need you ready to be picked up by eleven."

"Oh, thank gosh. Because I really wasn't planning on getting up any earlier than nine. I need sleep after tonight."

"Why? Someone wear you out?"

One side of his mouth hitches up in a proud grin, and images of us in the stairwell flash through my mind.

Did someone turn off the AC before they left? Why is it suddenly so hot in here?

I rock back on my feet, the heels I wore long gone and now sitting in the corner. "So tomorrow?"

He chuckles at my change of subject. "Yes, tomorrow. Speaking of, we about done here?"

"Oh yes. We didn't even have to stay to clean up. They have a crew that comes and does it. I just always feel so bad leaving it trashed, so I . . . What?"

His head is tipped to the side, and he stares at me with soft eyes.

"Do I have something on my face?"

He shakes his head. "No. You're just . . ." Another head shake. "You're something, is all." He looks around the mostly empty room. "You ready to head out of here, then?"

"Yes, please. My feet need a break."

Then suddenly, I'm being swept into the air, and I let out a loud yelp at the unexpectedness of it all as I throw my arms around his neck. Noel readjusts me, hugging me close like you see firefighters heroically carry women in the movies.

"What are you doing?"

"Giving your feet a break," he says like it's the most logical thing in the world.

He carries me over to the lone chair we haven't yet put away, then drops me onto it.

"Stay," he instructs, and I don't dare ignore his request as he crosses the room and fishes my shoes out of the corner.

He brings them back over, then drops to his knees and wraps his hand around my right calf.

His touch shouldn't matter. I shouldn't feel a thing, especially not right between my legs. But I *do* feel it, and it takes everything I have to remember to breathe as he slides my high heel onto my foot.

He does the same with the other, his thumb caressing my leg just a little too long before he drops it back to the floor.

He stands, then reaches for me again, and I hold my hand up.

"I can walk."

He arches a brow. "Are you sure?"

I laugh. "Yes, I'm sure."

Still, he offers to help me up, and I accept because I selfishly want to touch him again.

He pulls me to my feet and guides me toward the door, grabbing his tux jacket along the way. He slings it over his shoulder, and I admire him from the corner of my eye. His bow tie—since when did those get so attractive?!—is undone, his sleeves are rolled up to his elbows, and his jacket hangs off him so casually. Heck, even my lipstick on his collar is hot.

So, so hot.

"What?" he asks.

"*What* what?"

"You were smiling. Do *I* have something on *my* face?" He parrots my question.

No, but you have something on your collar.

"Okay, I swear your smile just grew. What are you thinking about?" He mock-gasps. "Are you thinking *naughty* thoughts, Parker Pruitt?"

I roll my eyes. "Please. You wish."

I push open the door to the Community Hall, leading us both through. I reach back in and shut off the light, then bend and grab the key cover that looks like a rock and lock the place up for the night before returning the key to its spot. It's likely a little absurd to anyone else that the key to this place is just sitting outside, but it's Emerald Grove. Nothing bad ever happens here.

"Can I walk you home?" Noel asks.

"No."

He chuckles darkly. "Oh, I'm sorry if you thought I was asking, because I wasn't."

Sweet crackers. Why is that so hot too?!

I'm still just worked up from earlier. It has to be that.

I point to the other side of the road, hoping that Noel can't see my finger shaking. "See that plump cat in the window?"

He follows my finger. "I see it."

"That's Pumpkin."

He swings his gaze back to me. "You live across the street?"

"I live across the street."

"Oh."

"Oh, indeed." I echo him for the second time. "So, good night?"

"Yeah. Good night, then."

He turns on his heel and begins walking away, and I . . . well, I can't believe it.

Is he seriously just walking away? After our kiss? After he had his fingers inside me? After *everything*? That's his response? I can't believe it. Can't fathom he'd do such a thing. I hate it and wish I had something to throw at the back of his head as he continues sauntering away.

But I don't. So instead, I settle for a foot stomp.

He hears it.

He stops, turning back to me, one hand tucked into his pocket.

"Something the matter, Peter?"

"No. Well, no. I . . . Yes."

"Well, which is it?"

I push my shoulders back. "Yes, something's the matter."

He marches back over to me, concern woven into his blue-green eyes. "What's wrong?"

"I just . . ." I swipe my tongue across my bottom lip. "Well . . ."

"Yes?" he prompts.

I huff. "Aren't you going to kiss me good night?"

He doesn't say anything, just stares down at me, his eyes losing all fear and turning darker by the second.

"No." It's one word, yet it's so pained.

"Why not?" I shoot back.

"Because, Parker," he says quietly, stepping into me until I'm forced to tip my head back to stare up at him. His cologne engulfs me, and I want to pull him closer and press myself against him so I can smell like him the rest of the night. "If I kiss you right now, I won't stop. And not stopping means I'm going to press you up against this building and fuck you. I really don't think our first time should be in public or against the Community Hall for the whole town to see, nor do I think you're ready to invite me into your home, especially not with all the things I want to do to you."

I gulp, too shocked to respond.

There was no doubt in my mind that Noel would want that, not after tonight. But to just come out and say it so brazenly? I was *not* expecting that.

He takes another step closer, his eyes boring into me. "Is that understood?"

I nod. "Understood."

"Good." He puts distance between us, and I miss his warmth instantly. "Go home. I'll wait here to make sure you make it safely."

"All the way across the street?"

"Humor me. Please."

"Fine." I walk backward away from him. "I'm humoring. Are you happy?"

"Ecstatic."

I turn around with a smile, making the *oh-so-long* trek back to my house, adding extra sway to my hips.

I can feel his eyes on me the whole way. How can a stare I can't even see be so intoxicating? So thrilling?

"Hey, Peter?" Noel calls when I'm about halfway across Borgen Avenue.

I pause, looking over my shoulder. "Yes?"

"Bring your swimsuit."

He laughs when my eyes widen, and I scurry along to my house, tucking myself inside and away from Noel Carter before I do something foolish, like invite him in.

I press my back against the door, holding a hand over my rapidly beating heart, trying to calm it down.

It's not going wild from the walk.

No. It's going wild for Noel, the thing it's always done where he's concerned.

Tomorrow, we're going on a date.

And I know exactly which swimsuit I'm going to wear.

"I really am sorry about your face."

I wince, looking up at the three lines cutting across Noel's otherwise perfectly sculpted cheek. He shaved for the auction last night, and I admit I was a little sad about it. But now, not so much. Not with the stubble that's already grown in.

He looks good like this. Older. More distinguished. Rugged.

He looks more like the Noel I remember and not the Hollywood version of him I've seen for the last ten years.

He ducks under a tree branch covering the trail as we head out to Rockaway Falls, then reaches up and runs his finger over the fresh cut from my cat. "It's okay. You know, when you said Pumpkin wasn't like other cats, I thought you might be kidding. But nope. He's really not like other cats. He's evil."

"Well, actually, in that regard, he *is* like other cats. All cats have a little bit of evil in them. It's sort of their thing. Like sometimes, I'll wake up in the middle of the night because I can feel eyes on me, and it's just Pumpkin sitting in my doorway watching me. It's eerie."

"This is why I'm getting a dog if I ever get a pet."

"You always did want one."

"Still do."

"Then why don't you have one?"

He shrugs. "I travel too much. Don't think it'd be fair to the dog."

"You could always be one of those people who takes their dog with them everywhere."

"Hmm. True. We could travel the world together. See the Pyramids or tour the Mayan ruins. I could get a baby backpack and carry him around whenever his little legs tire. Maybe his own pair of sunglasses so the *paw*parazzi don't bother him."

"That is entirely too much detail for me to think you're *not* kidding about this, especially that bit where you think there's paparazzi for dogs."

"What?" he asks distractedly, as if he were truly lost in his own little fantasy world. "Oh no. I'm totally kidding."

He's not, and we both know it.

Just like he wasn't kidding about breaking the news to Pumpkin that he wouldn't be getting his bath today, hence the scratches lining his cheek. He showed up at eleven sharp with a quick knock on my door. I let him in, giving him a short tour of my house, before introducing him to Pumpkin, who promptly swatted at him and slunk off to his bed.

"Stop staring at them," he says as he expertly navigates us down the beaten path the locals have carved out over the years. He's walking the trail like he does this regularly and it hasn't been a decade since he's been back here.

"I can't. I feel horrible."

"It's not your fault."

"But maybe it is. Maybe Pumpkin heard me talking about you over the years and picked up on some things, and now he hates you."

Noel stops abruptly in a narrow spot along the path, and I nearly run right into him.

"What? What's going on?" I ask, trying to see around him.

He turns, looking down at me. "You've talked about me over the years?"

"Oh, that." I wish I could hide my face right now so he can't see the pink tinge in my cheeks.

"Yeah. That. So?"

I sigh. "Of course I've talked about you. You were a huge part of my life for a long time. Then you weren't. I've complained a lot. I'm sure that's why he doesn't like you. Because of how *I* feel about it."

"And how do you feel, Parker?" he asks. "Do you like me? Do you forgive me for leaving?"

This isn't the conversation I planned to have today, but I suppose it needed to happen sometime. I guess now is as good a time as any.

"I . . ." I exhale heavily. "I told you last night I was scared when you asked me to come with you, and that's true. It terrified me more than I care to admit. Because what if you did get tired of me? What if things didn't work out with us? What if we ruined a beautiful friendship?"

"I don't—"

I hold up my hand to stop him. "Let me get this out, because if I don't, I'm not sure I ever will. I've only said it once before to . . ."

I trail off, not daring to speak Axel's name because I really don't think bringing him up on our date would be the best idea, but it doesn't stop Noel's jaw from twitching because he knows exactly who I'm referring to.

I push my shoulders back. "All those things scared me. *You* scared me. You were my person. The most important piece of my life aside from my mother. The last thing I wanted was to lose you in any capacity. But I knew. I knew that if you stayed here in Emerald Grove, you'd hate it and eventually hate me because *I* was why you stayed. So when you said you wanted to go, I encouraged it. I wanted that for you. But then you asked me to come with you, and I froze. Completely panicked. We'd just kissed for the first time, you told me you loved me, and you were leaving. My head was swimming with so much happening so fast. I couldn't commit, so I let you go with the promise I'd come to you eventually.

"But when you got to LA and got settled, you asked again, but I knew it was already too late. I could tell you were changing in the few short months you were gone. You were finally in your element, taking classes and working and doing all these auditions. You were happy. And I knew that I couldn't be the one to hold you back. I couldn't be the one to keep you from becoming the person you were meant to be. So I stopped calling. I stopped answering the phone. I stopped trying to hold you back because I wanted you to flourish. I wanted you to find everything you were looking for. I wanted you to be happy. And you were. I saw that in the magazines, the award shows, and everything else you've accomplished over the years. You got what you wanted, and I'm so, so glad. I just . . . I never intended for ten years to go by without a word. But the longer you stayed away, the harder it became to connect the version of you now with the version I know.

"So, yeah, maybe Pumpkin's heard me complain about you being gone because that part I *do* hate, but don't think for a second that I blame you for all this. I don't. I blame myself. This rift between us is all my fault because I couldn't grow up. Because I didn't want to leave behind the safety of Emerald Grove. Because I was too scared to tell you I was in love with you."

The last words tumble out of me, and for a second, I want to take them back.

Why wouldn't I? I just admitted to Noel that I loved him.

But then, the weight that's been on my shoulders since I was eighteen begins to lift, and I don't want to take it back anymore.

I feel free for the first time in years.

So why do I want to run and hide? Is it because Noel hasn't moved or blinked and is just staring at me like I've sprouted a second nose or something? Or maybe because *saying* I loved him brought back all those old feelings that maybe aren't so old after all?

"Look, just forget that I—"

"Stop," Noel snaps, and I clamp my mouth shut. "Just stop talking."

"I'm sorry. I didn't mean to upset you. I—"

Noel's lips are on mine for the second time in less than twenty-four hours.

His kiss is commanding, like he's not just kissing me. He's claiming me. *Owning* me.

Noel tips my head back, his fingers weaving through my hair and under the bun I have my auburn locks pulled up into as he tugs me closer, his tongue pushing into my mouth and tangling with my own.

He tastes like toothpaste and coffee and regret and hope all rolled into one.

The kiss is hard and fast and over entirely too soon, then he's wrenching his mouth from mine, his breaths coming hard and fast.

"What was that for?" I manage to get out once I regain my composure.

"Because. We were kids, Parker. Idiots. We led with what we *thought* the other wanted, and to what avail? Ten years of silence? Ruining a friendship that once meant the world to us? All we did was hurt one another. It's what we were trying to avoid, but it's exactly what we did anyway. And I'm sorry for that. So fucking sorry that I can't even begin to tell you. I've spent the last ten years beating myself up over our friendship falling apart and trying to find ways to repair it. I'm not sure we can, but I *am* sure that I don't want to hurt you anymore. That I want to be your friend again. I want . . ."

"What, Noel? What do you want?"

"You. I want you."

It's the same thing I told him last night, yet it still takes my breath away.

"M-me?"

He nods, his lips kicking up into a grin. "Yeah. Is that really so hard to believe?"

"Yes. You're . . . well, you're Noel Carter. You can't want me."

"Oh, but I do, Parker Pruitt. I really, really do."

His lips drop to mine once again, and this time, his kiss is softer, slower, and sweeter, but still so, so good.

I get lost in it. In the way he touches me, how hard his body presses against me, and how heavenly he smells.

He pulls away when he's had his fill, rubbing his nose against mine. "Come on. We still have a long hike ahead of us."

I nod, unable to say anything, too dazed by his kisses.

He's right. We do still have a long hike ahead of us. We're stuck together the rest of the day.

And that thought excites me as much as it scares me.

CHAPTER ELEVEN

Noel

Coming to the Falls was a bad idea.

It's not because it's busy—in fact, nobody else is here, and we didn't see anyone else on the trail coming in—and it's not because it isn't completely gorgeous out here.

It's because of the black bikini Parker is wearing.

Who could have thought something so simple could be so fucking sexy? I've seen women stripped down to nothing countless times. But this? This is a million times better in every way.

When we arrived at our favorite rock, she ripped off her plain baby-blue T-shirt, plopped down on the blanket I spread out, and immediately started munching on the grapes we brought along.

Since we've been here, I've barely looked up at the Falls. I haven't paid much attention to the vast swimming hole, which is the perfect shade of blue green. And I have hardly even taken in the way the sun's rays bounce off the surrounding trees.

I've been too busy staring at her, unable to say anything because I'm terrified that my next words will be entirely inappropriate.

"—tell you about how Jules from the frozen yogurt shop and Hank down at the library were caught out here necking?"

"What?"

She whips her head over to me. "Were you not listening?"

"Sorry. Distracted by the"—*Don't look at her tits. Don't look at her tits.*—"the views."

"It is pretty out here, huh?" She sets the now half-eaten bag of grapes to the side, wiping her hands on her shorts. "Anyway, I asked if Gran told you about Jules and Hank getting caught out here with their pants down. Well, they didn't actually have their pants down. Or maybe they did. I don't know. The rumors have been running wild, par for the course for Emerald Grove."

I laugh. "No, Gran didn't mention that, but I'm not surprised. Jules is a looker."

Parker rolls her eyes. "You always did have a thing for her."

"It wasn't a *thing*."

"Please. The number of times you went in there with no money in your pockets just to get a peek at her was sad."

"It wasn't that bad." I chance a look at her. "Was it?"

"It was definitely obvious."

I groan. "Do you think Jules knew?"

"Are you kidding? She *loved* the attention. I bet if you walked in there now, she'd faint."

"I did hear her bid at the auction last night." I scratch at my face before remembering my battle wounds from Pumpkin. "Maybe you should have let her win." Parker's hazel stare turns icy. "What? It's clear she would have known her way out here better than you did."

"Hey! I told you to turn right, but no, you wanted to go left."

"Because left was the correct way to go."

"Obviously it wasn't, or we'd have been out here an hour earlier. Have you really spent so much time in California that you've forgotten the way here?"

"I guess so." I shrug, though I don't love knowing that I *have* forgotten the path to one of my favorite places. It's just another reminder I've been gone for far too long.

"Do you like it out there? In LA, I mean."

I nod. "I do. There's always something to do, I've made some good friends, and the weather is perfect."

"Why do I feel like there's more you're not saying?"

I chuckle. "Because there is. The lack of privacy definitely sucks. I know it comes with the gig and all that, but sometimes it's just too much, you know? I can't even go to the grocery store without it being a whole thing. Constantly having my personal life splashed across the internet isn't exactly ideal either. But I love making movies, so I guess I just have to deal with it."

She shakes her head. "I don't know how you do it. I couldn't imagine. I don't *want* to imagine. That's not the kind of life I'd want to live, no matter how much I'm getting paid."

I understand why she'd feel that way. The media scrutiny is certainly not for the faint of heart. But to hear her flat-out say she'd never want to be part of my world . . . It makes me sad in a way I hadn't anticipated, because what does that mean for us? Does it mean Parker would still never come to LA? Does it mean she's already written off being friends after I leave?

The thought turns my stomach sour. I know Astrid said even the strongest people have their limits, but I can't stand the thought of Parker not talking to me again, especially after I just got her back. In just the short time we've been reunited, she's already engraved herself on my soul again, and I can't go back to how I felt before, like I was missing something vital.

I can't go back to a Parker-less life. It's that simple.

I shove the thoughts down, tucking them away for later, for a time when I'm not on a date with her.

She's here right now. We're together. That's all that should matter.

She settles back on her hands, the sun bathing her in light. "This feels incredible. I missed this."

Being out in LA for so long, I kind of forgot what it was like to miss sunshine like Washingtonians do. The dark, cloudy months can feel like they go on forever sometimes, and even those who are used to it and love it start to crave the vitamin D they're missing.

"It's nice," I say, but I'm not basking in the light like she is. I'm too distracted by her.

Her hair, which she took down when we arrived, is nearly dragging against the blanket. Her head is tossed back, and her face is turned toward the sky. Her eyes are closed, and her chest is pushed out like her heart is reaching for warmth as well.

She looks like a supermodel posing for a swimsuit ad, but it's not posed or fake. This is real. Raw. All Parker.

I still can't wrap my head around how she could think I forgot about her. Or how I could ever grow tired of her.

My entire life centered around her at one point. Hell, even when I didn't want to admit it, these last ten years have centered around her, too, in one way or another. Every choice I made, every role I took, everything I did, I thought about Parker.

I could never forget about her, and I damn sure could never get tired of her. I know she's got some issues with that because of her father leaving her, and I know that I have to do the same when I go back to my life in LA at some point, but I'm nothing like him. I intend to make sure she knows it.

"I can feel you staring at me," she says as my eyes drag down to the freckle that sits just below her tits, the one I've wanted to kiss for so, so long.

"Well, that top *is* doing wonders for your . . . figure."

She rolls her head my way, looking at me with a grin. "Perv."

I shrug, not the least bit apologetic about it, and don't bother pulling my eyes from her.

It's a far cry from when we'd come out here as teens. Back then, I'd sneak glances at Parker every chance I got. But that's just it. I would *sneak* them. I'd never look at her as brazenly as I am now, like a man starved for her touch and attention.

Parker's breaths grow shallower the longer I stare at her, her chest rising and falling rapidly.

I like that my stare affects her so much. That it is literally taking her breath away.

She shoots to her feet, taking off her shoes.

"It's hot," she announces. "I'm going for a swim."

She gives me her back, drops her shorts to her ankles, and steps out of them before jumping off the rock and into the water.

She disappears for only a moment before she breaks the surface, her long, wild auburn hair tamed by the water.

Rivulets snake down her face as she stares up at me. "Well? Are you coming?" She bats her lashes, her lips pulled into a grin on one side as she treads water. "Or are you chicken?"

It's the same thing she used to say to me when I didn't want to swim.

No. It's not that I didn't *want* to swim. I was scared she'd see exactly what effect she had on me.

But now? I don't care, especially not when I know the game Parker's playing. She's not the same shy and awkward girl from before.

She's bolder. Braver. And she's playing with fire.

I want to play too.

I shove to my feet, kicking off my shoes as I drag my shirt over my head.

There's no mistaking the hunger in Parker's stare as she gapes up at me. She drags her eyes down my chest, over the abs I spend a lot of time working on with my trainer, and straight down to the unmistakable bulge pressing against my board shorts.

Being in the public eye, I'm no stranger to being stared at.

But having Parker look at me like she is now . . . Well, nothing can compare to how good it feels.

It makes me want to kiss her again.

I jump into the water next to her, wrapping my hands around her waist as I break the surface. Her legs go around me in an instant, as if it was the most natural thing in the world.

She gasps as I settle her against me—right on my straining cock.

"Hi," I say.

She grins. "Hi. Happy to see me?"

"Always."

She giggles, and then suddenly, she's kissing me. It takes me a moment to realize what's happening. I've been the one to make the first move every other time we've kissed, so it's unexpected but not unwanted.

I kiss her back, my fingers tangling in her long locks, holding her to me as I coax her lips open with my tongue.

I float us over to the rock, pressing her back up against it, and we make out like I'm sure her mother thought we were doing all those years ago, Parker grinding against my hard cock with each bob in the water.

It's good. Too good.

"Peter," I growl against her lips when she does it again.

"Noel." She smiles deviously.

"You're playing a dangerous game."

"I don't know." She rubs against me again, and I hiss at the contact. "It doesn't feel dangerous to me. It feels good." Another swing of her hips. "So, so good."

"Keep it up," I mutter.

"Is that a threat?" Her nails scrape lightly against my scalp. "Because it sounds a lot like a promise." She ghosts her lips over mine. "And I thought you said you keep your promises."

Her words are my undoing.

Unable to hold back any longer, I kiss her hard and fast like I can't get enough of her, because I *can't* get enough of her.

She rocks against me, taking from me what she needs at this moment as I undo the top of her suit.

She doesn't complain or act surprised when I let it fall away. Or when I drag my lips down her chin and her neck and to the tops of her tits.

No. Instead, she leans back, giving me access to the parts of her I want as I hike her up higher and suck her beaded nipple into my mouth.

"Holy smokes," she calls out, and I grin around her. She can't even cuss right now in the heat of the moment when I have my lips latched on to her nipple.

I nip and suck at her, giving each breast the attention it deserves until they're wet and red from my beard scratching against them. Then I kiss my way back to her lips, brushing my tongue against hers as I tug on the tie of the suit bottoms.

"I want to touch you, Parker. Can I touch you?"

"Yes, please. I need . . ."

She doesn't finish the sentence. There's no point. We both know what she needs, because I need it too.

I pull at the string holding her suit together, and she pulls away just enough for it to float off into the water.

Parker's naked.

In my arms.

I have a naked Parker in my arms.

I could die in this moment and go straight to Heaven, and it still wouldn't compare to this.

I snake my hand between her legs, running my fingers through her slick folds.

"Fucking hell," I mutter, the water so clear that when I look down, I can see everything as I slide two fingers inside her. "You're so goddamn wet for me."

She nods, her head lolling back, and she moans when I brush my thumb against her clit. "F-for you."

She pushes down on my fingers, eager for more, and I oblige her request.

I play with her pussy, relishing the soft noises she makes as she fucks herself on my hand. Each sweet whimper, each cry for more, is like music to my ears. She made soft noises last night, trying to stay quiet to keep the party guests from getting suspicious. But now there's no need. She can be as loud as she wants. And fuck if the sounds she's making aren't the most beautiful melodies I've ever heard.

"Noel . . . Please . . . ," she begs. "I need . . ."

"Tell me, Parker." I stroke her clit again. Another gasp. "Tell me what you need."

"I need to feel you inside me. All of you."

It's not a request. It's a demand.

And I've never been so fucking torn before.

She presses her forehead against mine, her nails digging into my head. "Please, Noel. I want to come on your cock."

It's the most forward and provocative thing I've ever heard her say, and it would just be cruel not to give her what she wants.

But . . .

"We don't have anything out here."

She shakes her head. "It's okay. I'm on the pill."

"Yeah, but—"

"I've never been without a condom. Ever."

"Are you sure?"

"Yes. Are you?"

"I'm good. I've never been without either. I'm careful. Do you trust me?"

"More than anyone else."

Fucking hell.

"My shorts," I choke out. "Undo my shorts."

She drops her hand in the water between us, untying my shorts and shoving them down just enough, and then Parker's hand is on my cock.

Parker's hand is on my cock.

Holy shit. It's . . . it's everything I could have hoped for. Everything I've wanted. Everything I've imagined, over and over again. And I have imagined it. A lot. More times than I should probably admit. But that's because I've been head over heels for this woman since I was seventeen. That's a lot of time to make my own fantasies.

I'm not proud of the garbled sounds that leave me as she strokes me, her grip the perfect pressure I love. The perfect pressure I need.

It's too much. If she keeps this up, it'll all be over before it even really starts.

"Parker . . ." I gasp out her name before swallowing the lump that's formed in my throat. "You have to stop."

"Why?" she asks, stroking me again, her thumb brushing over the head of my cock.

I hiss. "Because I . . . *Fuck.*" She giggles as I groan when she does it again. "I'm going to come."

"Isn't that the point?"

I grab her wrist, stilling her movements. "Yes, but when I come, I want it to be inside you."

She gulps, then looks me square in the eye. "Then what are you waiting for?"

I take her mouth in a heated kiss, pressing her tighter against the rock we've spent so many summers on as kids, then tease her pussy with the head of my cock.

She tries to drag me closer with her heels, and I laugh. I know I'm being mean, but if she wasn't so lost in this excitement, she might notice my hands are shaking.

It's ridiculous that I'm nervous. It's not like it's my first time, but in many ways, it *feels* like it's my first time.

Parker is everything I've been waiting for, and I want this moment to be just right. I don't want to rush it. I want to savor it. I want to savor *her*.

"Please," she asks again, and my defenses are weakening.

I want to feel her so badly. Want to see how her body trembles under me. Want to hear my name tumble from her lips when I come inside her.

"I need you."

That's all it takes, and I slide inside her.

"Oh god," she moans, her eyes falling shut as I push into her inch by torturous inch. "I can't . . . It's too much."

"You can," I tell her, feeding her another inch as I kiss her jawline. "You will."

She nods, her breaths growing sharper by the second until I'm fully seated.

I pause, giving her a moment to adjust to my size. She fits around me perfectly, as if she were made for me, and I love the little noises she makes as the waves urge us closer together and force me to rock against her gently.

Her heels dig into my ass, her silent way of asking me to move, and I'm happy to heed her request.

I pull out, then push back into her softly. Unhurried. Painstakingly slow.

"Noel . . ."

She's not just saying my name. She's making a request, and I know what she's asking for, because I need it too—*more.*

This time, when I pull out, I thrust back in harder and faster, picking up my pace until I'm not sure where she ends and I begin.

I glance down, loving how we look together, and it spurs me on even more.

"Look down," I tell her. "Look at us." She rests her forehead against mine, looking down to see where we're joined. "Look at how good we look together. Look at how beautiful your pussy is, wrapped around my cock."

She groans, her whole body shuddering with delight as I drive into her again. "You can't say things like that, Noel."

"Why not?" I ask.

"Because it's . . . it's dirty."

"Would you rather I describe it to you, then?" I thrust into her harder. "Would you rather I tell you how warm and wet your cunt is as it's gripping my cock?" Another thrust. "How eager it is for me?" Another. "Or how good your tits look bouncing in the water as I fuck you? As I make you sweat for me? As I make you tremble?"

"Please . . . ," she whimpers. "I . . ."

I slide my hand between us once more and press my thumb against her clit.

"Or is it because it's me, Parker, your best friend? Is it so dirty because I'm voicing all the same thoughts you've had for years?"

"Noel!" she moans, squeezing her eyes shut as she gets just what she asked for—to come around my cock.

I fuck her through her orgasm, mine racing up my spine with just a few more thrusts, then I explode, a burst of bright-white light behind my eyes as I spill myself inside her.

It's magnificent. Heavenly. Dare I say, spiritual.

Every-fucking-thing I could have asked for.

I want more. I *need* more.

But not yet. Not now. Not when she's going limp in my arms, her eyes barely able to stay open.

I slow my movements, rocking against her lightly as our orgasms wane, then kiss her everywhere I can reach before starting again.

When she begins to shiver against me, I drag us both out of the water and lay her down on the blanket-covered rock.

I curl up next to her, wrapping her in my arms, and she comes to me willingly.

After a few quiet moments, she mutters, "So much for our first time not being in public."

I laugh. "Yeah, so much for that."

Then she's snoring. Softly and quietly.

I could stay here forever.

The thought flits through my mind so quickly I barely have a chance to register it.

All I know is that forever here doesn't sound as bad as it once did.

And I'm not sure how to feel about that.

CHAPTER TWELVE

Parker

Of all the times I've dreamed about making love to Noel Carter, not once did that fantasy include Rockaway Falls.

But that's exactly what happened.

I had sex with Noel Carter.

I had sex with my best friend.

I feel different and the same all at once.

Different because *Holy crap, I just had sex with Noel*, and the same because it felt so . . . natural. Right. *Perfect.*

"You know," he says, his fingers dancing along my naked back. We have no idea where my suit top went. After waking up from a brief nap, we searched for my suit for thirty minutes, but we could only recover my bottoms. I guess I'll be hiking back in just my T-shirt. "The first time I came out here was with my parents. They brought me here for the day."

"What'd you do?" I ask, though I already know the story. He's told it to me many times over the years, but I still love to hear it. The joy in his voice is worth hearing over and over.

"We had a picnic. Gran sent us here with tuna-salad sandwiches and a homemade blueberry cobbler. We ate and laughed, then took turns jumping off the top of the cliff before doing it all over again. We stayed out so late we had to walk back in the dark, my mother telling my father, 'I told you so, Jeffrey,' the whole way back. He'd respond with, 'Yeah, but we sure had fun, didn't we, Tiff?' She'd roll her eyes, but she'd still be grinning. That's what they always did—laughed at each other. Even when they were mad, they still laughed." He swallows roughly. "It was my favorite day out here for a long, long time."

"What knocked it out of first place?"

"You."

I smile against him. "My first time was with you."

"I remember. You fell about halfway down the trail and skinned your knee so bad that blood was running down into your shoe, but you refused to give up until you saw the Falls."

"I was awfully determined, huh?"

"You were. But that's what I've always liked about you. Even though you were quiet, you weren't going to stay that way. You were going to leave your mark no matter what."

"It's part of why I like design so much. Sure, I'm designing for other people, but I'm designing for me, too, and I always leave a little piece of me behind."

"I can see that. Like the waterfall in Rossi Café. That's not *them*. That's *you* and what this place means to you."

"It's you too. You helped me make it."

He drags his fingers over my back again, his touch so featherlight that goose bumps spring up over my skin. "I just helped you see it from a different perspective, is all."

"You've always been able to do that, you know. Bring out a different side of me. Make me courageous."

"Nah. That side has always been there. She just needs a little reassurance sometimes."

I like the way he talks about me. It's the same way he always has. Noel has never made me feel less than. He's never made me feel inadequate or slow or like I wasn't worth his attention. He's always lifted me up whenever I was down and done everything he could so I would see my worth as he does.

"You know what else she needs?" he asks.

"What's that?"

"Kisses."

Without warning, he swings me over on top of him, his hand going to the back of my head as he pulls me down for a kiss.

It's hard and searing, and it doesn't take long until I'm writhing on top of the obvious erection he's sporting.

"Fuck," he mutters against my lips. "What have you done to me, Parker?"

I don't think he's really looking for an answer, so I don't give him one. Instead, I roll my hips against him, and he hisses at the contact.

"I swear, you make me feel like a teen again. I'm entirely too fucking close to coming in my swim shorts."

I giggle. "Sorry," I say, but I don't mean it at all.

"You're not." He squeezes my hips. "And it's mean."

I arch a brow. "Is that so?"

"Hmm. It's so." He kisses me. "And I've been thinking, and I believe I know how I want you to make it up to me. How you could apologize."

"Oh, you've been thinking, huh? In the last, what? Three seconds?"

"What can I say? I'm quick on my feet."

I laugh, rolling my hips against him once more. He groans, his grip on me tightening. "What's my penance?"

"Up."

I stop moving against him, pulling away to look at him. "What?"

"Crawl up."

I tip my head, still not understanding.

"Straddle my face, Parker. I want your knees on either side of my head so I can taste your pussy that felt so good around my cock."

"Oh." It comes out breathless because I *am* breathless.

And I'm hot. So, so hot. Sitting on Noel's face shouldn't be so appealing, but it is. I want it.

"Well?" he asks.

I answer him by following his request, scrambling up and over him until my knees are caging him in.

"That's my girl." He reaches a single finger up, hooking it into my suit bottoms and tugging them to the side. "Now sit."

"What?"

He squeezes my cheek with his free hand. "Sit."

"I . . . I can't."

"You can." He clutches me tighter. "Sit."

"But I . . ."

"I swear, if you say something silly right now about how you're going to crush me, I won't lick your pussy, and we both know it's exactly what you want right now. Sit, Parker, and don't make me say it again."

There's something in his voice . . . a growl that I can't help but listen to, and I sink down, his mouth connecting with my core. I cry out in relief as his tongue snakes out against me.

I've had a guy go down on me once before, and it was so terrible I never let it happen again.

But this? This is different in every possible way.

He teases me, sucking my clit into his mouth just enough to torment me before releasing me again. He does it over and over, taking me to the edge, then backing off, until I'm grinding down on him with a wildness I didn't realize I had in me.

I've never felt like this before—this wild and brazen. He just came inside me not even an hour ago, and now he's licking at me like he'll never get enough.

I can't get enough either.

I throw my head back, my breasts exposed for anyone to see if they were to come out to the Falls, but I don't care. I *can't* care. Not when he's touching me like he is. Not when it feels so, so good.

He slides a single finger inside me as he draws my clit into his mouth once more, but this time he doesn't stop, and my orgasm hits me out of nowhere, sneaking up and slamming into me with a force I've never felt before.

I'm not sure how long Noel keeps playing with me, but eventually, my legs grow tired, and I can't keep myself held up anymore, and he relents.

He helps me back down, then rolls me to my back. He pushes his swim shorts down, then slides into me once more.

He makes love to me again, slowly and gently and at his own pace until I'm bucking against him, and he's sighing into my neck as he comes inside me.

I didn't know it could be like this. Didn't know it could be so good.

But I should have. Should have known that with Noel it would be different. It always is.

And that's the scariest part of it all.

When we hike back from the Falls, the town is dead, and I'm not surprised. It usually is around sunset, especially on Sundays. All the shops close around three or four, and the day becomes less about business and more about spending time with loved ones. I've always appreciated the work-life balance the community has pushed.

Noel carries our backpack stuffed with our wet towels and blanket. He's got our now-empty cooler in one hand and mine in the other.

Walking down Borgen and holding hands with Noel should be strange, but it's not. Another thing that feels as natural as breathing.

"So, good date?" Noel asks, grinning down at me.

My cheeks instantly heat as I remember everything we did this afternoon. "Good date."

"Do you want it to be over?"

"What do you mean?"

He shrugs. "I don't know. Was thinking we could make dinner at your place?"

My brows shoot up as we pass by Fran's pie shop, which is closed for the evening too. "You cook? Because I distinctly remember you setting off the smoke detectors over a grilled cheese sandwich—*twice*."

"First of all, I wouldn't have burned a thing if you hadn't distracted me."

"I was just doing my homework."

"Exactly, and it was incredibly distracting." He grins. "Second, I've come a long way since then. I can cook several things now, thank you very much."

"Like?"

"Well, breakfast, for starters."

"Everyone can make breakfast. It's called cereal."

"I mean *real* breakfast. Eggs, bacon, hash browns, waffles. That kind of stuff."

"Fine. I'll give you that. What else you got up your sleeve, Chef?" I tug on his plain mustard-yellow shirt as we walk by the local butcher shop that makes the *best* grab-and-go burgers. It shouldn't be a color that looks good on him, but somehow, it does.

"I can make pasta. And before you say that's just boiling noodles and opening a jar, I mean, I can make it *from scratch*."

"You make your own noodles?"

"Well, no. But I make my own sauce," he says proudly as we hook a left and cross the street to the side my house is on.

I nod. "You're impressing me more and more. What else?"

"Let's see. There's steak."

"Yummy."

"A mean French onion soup."

I wrinkle my nose as we pass my neighbor's yellow house, their front yard full of flowers that Clifford planted last year. "Pass."

"Reubens," he adds.

"And you're reeling me back in."

"Salmon, chicken, shepherd's pie," he continues, listing off foods as we turn into my short driveway that's more of a parking spot. "Oh, and of course, your favorite dish, la—"

"Mom!"

I quickly drop Noel's hand and take a step away from him like I just got caught doing something I shouldn't be doing.

I don't know why I do it. It's not like my mother would be upset if something happened between me and Noel. She loves Noel. She'd be thrilled.

But still . . . I want to keep this to myself for just a bit longer. At least until I know there's actually something to tell.

If she notices we were holding hands, she doesn't show it.

"Well, well, well," she says, rising from the chair on my front porch and walking down the front stairs to meet us. "If it isn't my daughter who I was just about to send the Coast Guard out to look for."

I roll my eyes. "You'd send Park Services, not the Coast Guard, Mom."

"Well, whoever. But I was just about to call them up." Her eyes drift down my body. "Nice to see you made it back in one piece."

I cross my arms over my chest, subtly trying to hide the fact that I'm not wearing a bra—well, bikini top. "We lost track of time."

A sly grin tugs at her lips. "I'm sure you kids did. Did you have fun?"

"We did." Noel coughs out a laugh, then bumps his shoulder against mine. "Peter, tell your mom how much fun we had."

I scowl at him for putting me on the spot, then turn a tentative smile to my mother, who can always read me so easily. "So much fun."

My mom chuckles. "Well, I just came over to talk to you about last night. I'll get out of your hair so you two can—"

"No!" I blurt out, holding my hands up to stop her. "No," I repeat, calmer this time. "Stay. I want to hear."

Her eyes flit between Noel and me, but eventually, she nods. "All right. If you insist."

"I do. I really do." I look up at Noel. "Do you mind?"

"Of course not. I should probably get home to check on Gran, anyway. I'm sure she's just bored to death without me around."

I didn't mean for him to leave, but now that he's suggested it, I realize I don't hate the idea.

Not because I don't want him around—I do. But I need some time to process what has transpired today. We took a big step, and I haven't entirely wrapped my head around its consequences yet.

"Thank you," I tell him.

He bends, pressing a kiss to my cheek. It's not completely out of the norm, but it's unusual enough for my mother's eyes to widen in surprise at the gesture.

"I'll text you later," he tells me, then wraps his arms around my mom before taking off.

I watch him go the whole way, unable to wipe the smile off my face, even when he turns the corner and disappears.

"So . . . ," my uninvited guest says, and I turn to her. "How was your day *really*, dear?"

I roll my eyes, walking past her and into my house. I should probably lock it, but nobody ever locks their doors around here. "Stop it. Get inside."

"What? I'm just curious. Can't a mother be curious about her daughter? Can't she wonder why she's walking home without a bra on?"

"Mom!" I hiss, pushing open the door and pointing inside. "Go."

She cackles as she waltzes by me.

I let the door slam closed behind me and march straight to my bedroom while my mother stops to give Pumpkin chin scratches. I strip off my shirt, grab a bra from my top drawer, and put it on before pulling a fresh shirt off a hanger and meeting my mother in the kitchen.

She's already at the coffee station working on making us a pot. She dumps the grounds into the filter, then closes the lid before reaching up and pulling two mugs from the cabinet above while I go to the fridge for my creamer.

I pour a bit into my mug, then plop down in a chair at the small, two-person walnut table I refurbished, while she stands with her back against the counter, watching me with a knowing grin.

"What?" I finally grit out after several minutes of her staring at me.

"Nothing." She lifts a shoulder, but I know her. It's not nothing. It's *never* nothing with her.

She always knows when something is up, and while I love it most of the time, sometimes—like right now—it's the last thing I want.

The coffeepot gurgles out the last of the fresh brew and Mom pours us each a cup before taking the spot opposite me.

"So, want to hear about last night?"

Oh, thank gosh. A subject change.

"Yes, please. Give me all the details. Every last one."

She sighs wistfully. "Well, as you can imagine, Cliff was—"

"Hang on, hang on. *Cliff?* He doesn't allow *anyone* to call him Cliff except for old Ms. Chan, but she doesn't let anyone boss her around."

"Yes, he lets me call him Cliff," she mutters with a grin. "*Anyway*, Cliff was surprised I bid on him. See, the thing is, we've kind of been . . . friendly toward one another lately."

"Friendly? Is that what the kids are calling it nowadays?"

She narrows her eyes at me. "What did you and Noel do today at the Falls, Parker Bernice?"

I sink lower in my chair at the use of my middle name and the reminder of *exactly* what went on today. "Tell me more about how *friendly* you are with Cliff."

"We're not sleeping together if that's what you're after."

"Yes, because I am *dying* to know about my mother's sex life," I deadpan.

"We're just . . . friends," she continues. "Now that I've been on my own for a few years, I've realized how much I've grown to dislike the quiet. Cliff's been living alone his entire life, and he seemed like he could use some company. One night, I noticed he was up late, so I went over with a carafe of coffee. We got to talking, and one thing led to another, and well . . ." She lifts a shoulder. "I guess we're going steady."

Going steady.

It's such a dated term, but it paints a clear picture of what's been going on. He's her boyfriend.

It's sweet. And completely unexpected.

Since my father left, I can't recall a time when my mom ever expressed an interest in dating. She's always seemed happy being single. In fact, I *do* remember several times she sang anthems about how freeing it was to be single.

Maybe it was all a front. Maybe she wasn't as happy as she's always let on. Maybe she's just as lonely as I've felt.

"Stop that, dear. Don't get that look on your face."

I peek up at her. "What look?"

"The one where you look all sad. I was happy with my years of freedom. I truly was. So don't think for a second that I regret them. I had fun and was okay with being focused on raising my talented, smart, and beautiful daughter. But you're all grown up now, and I'm all grown up, and I think maybe . . ." Another shrug. "Maybe it's time for me to cut loose a little, you know? Have fun. Maybe let my guard down and see what someone has to offer me."

She has my father to thank for being so guarded about trusting men again. I'd be a liar if I said I wasn't the same way myself—not just because of my father's abandonment but also because of Noel's.

Sure, I've let my guard down a little more over the years, but I still have reservations about letting people in—especially those who have hurt me.

I push those thoughts aside, wanting to focus on something happy, like my mother having a boyfriend.

"How long?"

"Hmm?" she asks over the rim of her mug.

"How long have you been dating Cliff."

Red fills her cheeks. "Oh, not long," she says dismissively.

I don't buy it.

"Mother . . ."

She huffs. "Fine. About six months now."

"Six months?!" I explode. "You've been dating Clifford Daws for *six months* and didn't tell me?!"

"Well, yes. It's not anyone's business who I date."

"I'm your daughter."

"You are, which means I'm still your mother and entitled to my privacy. But now you know all my juicy details, so let's talk about Noel."

I lift my head. "It's not anyone's business who I date," I throw back at her.

She lifts her brow in response, unaffected by my childish ways.

I groan, dropping my head against the table. "Let's not."

"Parker . . ."

"It was nothing," I say against the table.

"Then why did you just say you were dating him."

I lift my head. "Well, to be fair, it was *one* date, and it was for the auction."

"Right. And I'm sure it had nothing to do with the fact that you've been in love with this boy since you were, what, fourteen?"

I gasp. "I have not! I didn't even like boys then."

That's a lie, and we both know it. I definitely liked boys then, but mostly, I liked actors or musicians. I didn't like Noel.

At least, I don't *think* I liked Noel.

Sure, I noticed him, but I didn't *notice* him. Not really . . . Did I?

I shake the thought away because that's absurd. "I didn't have feelings for him until our senior year. You know that."

"You mean the kiss."

I swallow, remembering the pain that followed. It still stings, despite Noel's apology. His words were sincere, and I know he meant every single one. And I want to move forward, but kind words and an afternoon of bliss don't erase years of pain like some magic Band-Aid. "Yeah, that."

"Did you two talk about that at all? Or were you too busy doing other things?"

I ignore her second question, bringing my coffee cup to my lips for the first time. I take a sip, then blow on the brew because it's still too hot to drink.

"We talked," I tell her.

"And? Have you two worked things out?"

"We're not a hundred percent yet, but we made . . . progress."

It's not a solid answer, but she grins anyway, and it's the biggest smile I've seen from her since . . . well, last night when she dragged Clifford off the stage.

I can't help but smile back. Even though we certainly still have stuff to work through, I'm happy with where things are with Noel. And it's been a long, long time since I could say that.

"Do you think you can have what you had before?"

I don't know how to answer her because I'm not sure. I don't know if we can, but I don't necessarily know if that's a bad thing either. We were young then. We didn't know what we wanted out of life, and now we do. Maybe we can build something better than what we had before, even if Noel is leaving again.

Sure, there'd be a lot we need to discuss, but there's no sense in rushing into that now, especially when we don't even know what this thing between us is. Are we friends with benefits? Are we picking back up where we left off ten years ago? Or are we something else entirely?

I don't know, and I don't *need* to know right now. I'm enjoying myself too much to want to think it to death, especially since I'm not even sure if this *is* something more, if I'd be willing to give up everything to follow Noel to LA.

I push all the thoughts away for later when I'm not rocking an exhilarating post-orgasm high.

"We'll see," I settle on, then wave my hand. "Enough about Noel and me, though. Tell me more about you and *Cliff*."

A dreamy look crosses her features, and she sets her chin on her hand, that smile still present. "Well, I guess what really started it was . . ."

CHAPTER THIRTEEN

Noel

As I suspected, Gran had already turned in for the night when I got home from the Falls, and she was already off in town this morning, which I know thanks to the note she left attached to the fridge informing me she "needed a break from all the cooking" and to "fend for yourself."

I smiled, wrote back a quick note asking if she wouldn't be making any more banana bread, just to tease her, and then left for Rossi's Café with one thing in mind—Parker.

Yesterday was not what I expected, yet everything I wanted wrapped into one.

I want more of it. Not just the sex either. I want more of Parker. I want to laugh with her again. Play with her again. Have fun again.

As much as I enjoy my life in LA, it's never felt like home to me, not in the way Parker does.

I've missed that feeling far more than I realized.

I head down Harris Street, noting that almost all the anti-theater signs are now gone. Could it be the naysayers are finally getting on board?

I turn onto Borgen Avenue to find that the town is already buzzing with people, and to my surprise, they wave instead of putting their heads down or turning their noses up at me like they did when I first arrived.

It feels . . . good. Better than I expected it would. I knew there was a chance people would be angry with me for leaving, but I never thought my neighbors I've known my whole life would ignore me. Now, though, they're warming back up to me, and it reminds me of how I used to feel walking down these streets—safe.

"Noel!" Fran calls as I walk by the pie shop. "You hungry?"

I pat my stomach, already walking through the front door because the delicious smell wafting to the sidewalk is too irresistible. "Always. What do you have on the menu?"

She waves me over to the front counter, pointing at the display cases that show off the perfectly round pies she likely baked fresh this morning. From the smell of it, she's still using her mother's famous cherry pie recipe, which calls for just a bit of bourbon and only the best Rainier cherries.

"We have our staples: apple, cherry, and, of course, marionberry, which we all know is a Pacific Northwest classic. Then we have our specials: peach cobbler, blueberry cobbler, coconut, and white chocolate with graham cracker crust. And finally, our mixes: blue raspberry, white chocolate coconut, and apple coconut, which I know sounds a bit wild, but it's *so* delicious."

I stare down at the many options, unsure of which one to get because they all sound so damn good, and my stomach is already growling. I didn't eat dinner last night, and after yesterday's workout at the Falls, I need sustenance soon.

I look up at Fran. "Do you happen to know which one is Parker's favorite?"

Her eyes widen for a moment before a grin breaks across her lips. "I sure do. It's—"

"Apple coconut," a voice booms from behind me.

I turn, tipping my head back to look at the giant. "Axel. Nice to see you."

He grunts. "Hmm." He shoves by me and points right at the apple-coconut pie. "Get that one. It was her creation."

"Parker came up with it?"

He nods. "She and Fran here were tipsy on whiskey sours down at Bigfoot's and were talking pies. They got hungry, snuck off to the kitchen here, and created this monstrosity."

"Hey! I'll have you know it's our second-best seller so far this summer." Fran pushes her chest out, her nose tipping up in the air. "Everyone but *you* loves it."

"*Everyone* is wrong. Coconut is the devil's dandruff."

"Actually, I believe that's cocaine," I interject.

He sneers at me. "You'd know, wouldn't you, Hollywood?"

I draw in a deep breath, trying to keep my cool for Parker's sake. I know she loves Axel, but man, do I want to punch him right now. And why wouldn't I want to? He keeps taking shots at me. It's only fair I fight back, isn't it?

"I'm getting real—"

"There you are!" Parker comes blazing in through the door. "I've been looking all over for you, Axel. I— Oh. Noel."

Gone is the contempt I feel for Axel. It's swiftly replaced by elation.

Parker's here.

Her eyes dart between Axel and me, and she carefully steps up beside me and places a calming hand on my arm, as if she can feel the tension radiating off me. "I didn't realize you'd both be here. Is everything okay?"

"Fine," I answer before Axel can. "I was just grabbing us some pie."

"For breakfast?"

"Yep."

"I knew I liked you." She pushes to her tiptoes and presses a kiss to my cheek.

She does it so effortlessly that I don't think she realizes it's happened until Fran lets out a little squeak.

The baker smacks her hand over her mouth, eyes wide. "Sorry," she says behind her hand.

Parker shrugs, either pretending not to be affected by Fran's reaction or honestly not caring.

That would make one of us.

I care, and Axel cares too—if his flared nostrils are any indication.

"So what are you getting me? Because I hope it's—"

"Apple coconut?"

"Yes! How'd you know it was my favorite?"

"Axel."

She launches herself at the giant, hugging an arm that's nearly as big as a toddler. "Oh, Axel. You really do love me, don't you, best friend?"

He shakes her off, his lips turned down into his bushy red beard. "Stop it. It's too early for this."

"You're going to admit it one day." She grins up at him while he continues to frown. It's his eyes that give him away, though. He adores her. It's clear for anyone to see.

While I might never understand their friendship, especially given their history, I can see that it's as genuine as it comes and that Axel truly cares for and wants the best for Parker.

I guess that makes him okay in my book.

"So, a slice of apple coconut and what else, Noel?" Fran asks from behind the counter.

"Cherry. It's been far too long since I've had it." I toss my thumb toward Axel. "And whatever the big guy wants. I'm buying."

"A whole white chocolate and peach cobbler, then a slice of marionberry, please, Fran," he requests with a smirk in my direction. "That's okay, right?"

Dick.

I give him a tight smile. "Yep. Perfectly fine. Anything for my *good friend* Axel here," I say, laying the sarcasm on thick. We're far from being friends, and Parker is the only reason I'm letting him get away with this. I turn back to Fran. "Ring me up."

"You got it," she says, jovially punching the buttons on the screen with a bit of hum.

I'm sure she's feeling extra cheery right now, what with selling this much pie before 9:00 a.m.

Fran gives me my total, and I hand over my black card, then turn to Parker. "What are your plans for today?"

"I'm heading to the theater. Want to join?"

Axel stares daggers at me over the top of her head, but it doesn't stop me from telling her, "Of course. Can't think of a better way to spend my day. Except for maybe at the Falls."

Parker blushes, no doubt remembering yesterday, while Axel says, "Then take a hike."

I ignore him, collect my slices from Fran, and then follow the duo out the door.

I wasn't sure what I wanted out of the day, but now I can't imagine spending it any other way—seeing Parker and annoying the hell out of Axel.

It's the perfect combination.

"Wait, wait, wait. You're telling me the next fundraiser is a drinking competition?"

"I guess if you really, really want to break it down to basics, then yes. But it's more about the bowling than anything else."

"How so?"

Parker swings her legs back and forth as she shovels another bite of pie into her mouth. We're sitting on the stage, enjoying our breakfast and coffee we grabbed from Rossi Café while Axel bosses around a crew as they work on replacing the walls.

Looking out at the now-empty theater . . . Well, fuck. It's got me feeling all sentimental. The last time I was inside was the night before I left, and I was too wrapped up in Parker to really appreciate it. Seeing it like this now takes me back to all the hours I spent on this stage and how much this place contributed to the person I am today. It's strange seeing it so bare, but I know Parker is going to build it back up to something even better than before.

"I don't know," she says. "It just is."

"But you *want* people to buy the beer, right? Because the proceeds from every purchase go to the theater fund."

"Well, yes, but—"

"So it's a drinking competition."

"No!" She huffs, then laughs. "Yeah, fine. I guess it is a little bit. But we're still hosting trivia, bowling, and having fun, so that's something, right? Plus, it's not just the proceeds from beer sales. It's the food too. I still can't believe Garth is doing all that."

I snort. "I can. That guy has had a crush on you since sixth grade."

"He has not!" she argues, but there's no real indignation behind her words. She knows I'm right. "He's just nice to *everyone*. Plus, he was a theater kid too. He's sympathetic to the cause, that's all."

I roll my eyes, sipping my coffee, which is *almost* as good as Astrid's. "Whatever you say, Peter." I wipe my mouth with the back of my hand. "Can't believe they let him keep that slogan. I saw it the other day, and my jaw about hit the ground."

She tips her head to the side. "What? Not a fan of 'Bigfoot's Hideaway: Come See His Balls'?"

"Oh, *I* love it. It's hilarious. I just can't believe Leonard Figgins Senior let it get pushed through."

"I think he was absent when we took that vote. It's why it's important to go to every town meeting. You never know what's going to be on the ballot."

"Clearly."

She scrapes the last piece of pie off her plate and pops it into her mouth with a noise that shouldn't be legal to make in public. It's borderline pornographic, and I should know—it's the same little noise she was making yesterday when she came on my face.

She drags her tongue across each prong of her fork, making sure to get every bit, and I watch her, barely holding back a groan . . . and a boner.

I clear my throat, shifting my attention to anywhere else.

Axel's crew is working fast, and I feel bad just sitting here with Parker while they do all the heavy lifting, but then she belches, and I know I'm right where I'm supposed to be.

"My goodness. Excuse me. I don't know where that came from." She pats her lips with her napkin. "Guess that pie was just that good."

She's always been like this with me—comfortable enough to be herself. I can't count the dates I've been on over the years where it's obvious the woman I'm out with is pretending to be someone she's not. I don't want that. I want real.

I want Parker.

"So does that mean you're coming to the event?"

"I said I'm here to help fundraise, and I meant it."

"I know, but . . ."

"But?" I ask, bumping my shoulder against hers. "What's on your mind?"

"Well, you're leaving." She shrugs, looking down at where her legs are bouncing off the stage. "I know you're only here for six weeks, and I don't want to monopolize your time."

She can't be serious.

"Hey," I say softly, reaching over and tipping her chin up toward me so she's forced to look into my eyes. "I'm here for you, Parker. You know that, right? I'm staying for you."

"I thought you were staying for the theater. Because you believe in it."

"I believe in *you*."

Her eyes widen, and I feel her swallow sharply. "Oh."

"Is that really such a surprise?" I ask, dragging my thumb across her soft bottom lip, unable to stop myself from touching her.

"Well, no. I mean, maybe. You've always believed in me. I just . . ." She shrugs again. "I don't know. It just feels different now."

"Because of yesterday?" She nods. "I don't know about you, Parker, but yesterday didn't change anything for me. Not when it comes to you. I still have all the same feelings about you I've always had. What we did . . . It didn't change any of that. Wait. No. That's not true."

Her brows crush together. "It's not?"

"No. It made me want you more. And I already really, really wanted you," I say, leaning in closer and pressing my lips to her cheek.

Her breath hitches, and I grin against her, kissing her again, all the way to her ear so only she can hear what I'm about to say next.

"You have no idea how badly I want to fuck you on this stage, Parker," I whisper. "I wanted to do it ten years ago, and I want it even more badly now that I know what you taste like."

She lets out a small gasp.

"If we were alone right now, I'd do just that. I'd roll you over and slide between your legs. I'd eat your pussy until you begged me to let you come, then I'd fuck you until my name echoed around these walls. Then I'd do it all over again just because I could."

She gulps, and the sound is so audible that a few crew members look over to see what's happening.

Parker waves at them, and I laugh, then pull away. Her chest is heaving, her pupils are dilated, and a tiny bead of sweat sits just at her hairline.

"Something wrong, Peter?" I ask her innocently.

She squeezes her eyes shut, shaking her head. "I hate you."

I laugh. "You do not."

"I don't. I really don't. Though sometimes, I think it would make things easier."

I'm not sure what that means, but I don't want to get into it now—not with Axel barreling into the room.

He stops just a few feet from the stage, his eyes locked only on Parker, pretending I'm not even here.

"We've got a problem," he tells her.

Gone is the playfulness. Parker's hackles are now raised. "What's wrong?"

"Come look."

Then Axel turns on his heel—still not sparing me a glance—and marches back out of the room.

Parker hops off the stage, and I scramble after her and Axel.

We skid to a stop when we find him standing in the middle of the entryway, his head tilted toward the ceiling.

"See that?" He points to the hole ripped through the ceiling. Fluffs of pink insulation that look like they've been covered in dirt hang out. "That's—"

"Asbestos." Parker groans, her hands going to her hips. "Crap. Crap, crap, crap."

"How bad is it?" I ask, not entirely following along. I know how to use a hammer just enough to get me in trouble, but beyond that, I'm out of my element, and I have no idea what any of this means other than there's a hole that shouldn't be there.

"See those nasty gray and brown spots up there? Where it's not all bright pink? It means we're going to have to pause and get a team in here and make sure there isn't more anywhere else," Axel explains. "Will probably set us back a few days."

"And cost us several grand." She sighs, and I want to step up and comfort her, but I know she doesn't need my rescuing right now. Or my distractions.

"Hey," I say, tugging on her elbow.

She turns to me, her eyes full of worry, and I hate it so damn much. I wish she'd just let me help. Let me give her the money to finish this place exactly how she wants with no sacrifices, but I can't do that either.

"I'm going to head out. Let you and your business partner get this settled, okay?"

She smiles softly. "Okay. I'm sorry. It's just . . ." She waves her hand toward the mess she's just discovered.

"See you tonight?" I ask, and she nods. I move to press a kiss to her forehead, but when I catch Axel watching us from the corner of my eye, I change my mind.

Instead, I step back and give her an awkward wave, then head back to the theater to grab our trash.

I'm just about back to the entryway when I hear unmistakable muffled voices through the door.

I pause, listening in even though I know I shouldn't.

"It's not what it looks like."

"Really? Because it looks like you two are dating."

"And what if we are?" Parker challenges Axel.

I grin, able to imagine her clearly. I bet her shoulders are pressed back, and her chin is pushed up, just begging him to keep questioning her.

"Then that's your business, I guess. But I'm just saying, I remember what happened before when he left, which he *will* do again."

"I know how it was, Axel. I was there too. I lived it."

Fucking hell. The pain in her voice . . . It's not what I expected. My heart was fucking crushed when I left and I realized Parker was never coming out to LA. But I had people to distract me and pull me out of it. I had a shiny new town to explore. Parker had what she's always had, and I can imagine living here with reminders of us all around had to be tough.

I hate that I hurt her, but I can't go back and change the past, no matter how badly I want to.

"I know," he says. "I know. I just . . . Fuck, Park, I just want the best for you, all right? You've had enough heartbreak between your dad leaving and Noel leaving. I don't want to see you go through that again."

"And *I* don't want to go through that again, but this is my decision."

Axel doesn't respond immediately. Then he sighs. "I'll respect that. Just . . . don't forget, okay?"

"I won't."

"Good."

I kick open the door, announcing my presence, and Parker jumps, but not Axel.

No. He stares me down hard, his beefy arms crossed over his chest.

"Later, Peter," I tell her, this time not giving a fuck and stopping to press a kiss to her head.

"Later," she mutters, blushing.

"Axel." I nod to him.

"Hollywood," he responds.

He knows I heard every word. He *wanted* me to hear every word.

It's another reminder that he's been there in ways I haven't.

It sucks, but it just reinforces what I need to do over these next few weeks—make sure that when I leave, Parker knows exactly how I feel about her this time.

Parker: How mad are you going to be if I say I have to cancel tonight?

I stop lacing up my shoes as I read the text from Parker. I was just getting ready to head to Jill's to grab a few things for dinner, then walk over to her house.

I type out a response.

Me: Not mad. Just curious why.

Parker: Well, it's a funny story really . . . I forgot it was Monday.

Me: What's so special about Mondays? Except for the fact they were invented by the Devil, of course.

Parker: Dinner at Axel's.

Ugh. Fucking Axel again.

I roll my eyes, my thumbs flying over my phone screen as I ignore the incoming text from my agent asking if I got the script he sent over. It's the one I promised him I'd read, but the second I realized it was a superhero movie some comic book studio is trying to launch as a new franchise, I tossed it aside.

I know it would be a hell of an opportunity, but it would also mean a lot of filming, and I'm not sure I want to make those kinds of commitments now.

Besides, I have other things to worry about, like when I'm going to see Parker again.

Me: You mean to tell me you have dinner at Axel's on Monday, then Tater Tot Tuesdays at your mom's the next day? Do you ever cook for yourself?

Parker: Not if I can help it.

Parker: I also go to your gran's as often as I can, and you know she loves feeding people. I'm usually stocked for days by the time I leave.

Me: Spoiled.

Parker: Says the guy who requires all organic, freshly pressed orange juice in his dressing room with two ice cubes.

Me: I cannot believe they ran that story. It's so not true, and you know it.

Me: All I did was ask for one glass with NO ICE because I'm not Satan, and it got twisted into something else.

Parker: Hollywood is weird. I'd never want that life.

It's not the first time she's said something like that, and just like before, it leaves a bitter taste in my mouth because it feels like she's telling me no all over again.

Me: You don't even know the half of it. They make up the weirdest shit.

Like the time my friend Jude Rafferty took allergy medicine before a talk show and got a little goofy on them and tripped on live TV, showing the whole world his Snoopy underwear. It then spun into a whole story about him being on drugs, all thanks to one little mistake. It was wild to watch unfold, and I felt awful for the guy, especially since I know he hates the spotlight so much. Luckily for him, he's found an amazing fashion blogger girlfriend who helps him tolerate it just a little better.

Parker: What other weird stuff have they made up about you?

Me: If you haven't heard it, I'm not repeating it.

Me: Tell me again why you need to cancel?

Parker: First of all, boooo!

Parker: Second, I promised Axel I'd go to his house before I made plans with you, and I figured you didn't want to come.

Me: Who said I didn't?

Parker: Because you hate him?

Me: I don't hate Axel.

Me: I just don't particularly like the big fella.

Parker: See? I wasn't wrong.

Me: But I wouldn't mind being where you are.

Parker: You . . . want to go to Axel's with me?

Do I want to go and sit at Axel's dinner table so he can warn me away from Parker or frown at me the entire night? I'd rather eat a spoonful of Vegemite, and that shit is disgusting.

But do I want to spend time with Parker? Yes. A million times yes.

And I'll endure anything for an hour or two, just to make it happen, even if it's going to be pure torture.

Me: Are you inviting me?

Parker: Noel Carter, will you do me the honor of being my guest to tonight's dinner at Axel Cooke's?

Me: You're inviting me to be a guest someplace you don't even know if I'm welcome at?

Parker: NOEL!

I laugh, easily able to picture her stomping her foot with a hard stare.

Me: I'm kidding, I'm kidding.

Me: Yes, I'll come.

Parker: YAY!

Parker: Dinner starts at seven.

Parker: Oh, and bring some red wine. It's Axel's favorite. Maybe it'll be enough to push you into his good graces.

◆ ◆ ◆

I stand in front of a robin's-egg blue door, wine bottle in hand and ready to knock.

There's screeching coming from somewhere inside and the sounds of feet pattering against the floor.

Whatever I'm about to walk into, I have a feeling it's going to be chaos.

I suck in a deep breath, then knock.

Not ten seconds later, the door flies open, and my eyes go down, down, down to the three identical little girls staring up at me with wide brown eyes.

"Who are you?" one of them asks.

"Stranger," another answers.

"Bye," the third says, trying to push the door closed, but the other girls are in the way.

"Miranda, Matilda, Mavis!" Parker calls, and I look up to find her jogging toward the door, grabbing it before they can shut it. "What'd we say about opening the door?"

"Don't?" the one with pigtails asks, and I have to look away so the others don't see my smile.

"That's right. Don't do that. It could be dangerous."

"But it's Emerald Grove. Daddy doesn't even lock the doors."

"I do, too, you little snitch!" Axel calls from somewhere inside.

Parker rolls her eyes. "He doesn't," she whispers to me, before shooing the kids away. "Go on, now. Go play."

"Can we play with him?" A chubby finger is pointed my way, the girl's ponytail *whooshing* back and forth as she swings her head between Parker and me.

"Well, that's entirely up to him," Parker answers, peeking up at me.

I squat down to their level, waving with my free hand. "Hi. I'm Noel. It's nice to meet you."

They look to Parker for reassurance before stepping forward.

"I'm Miranda," the ponytailed one announces. "Are you here to play with us?"

I chuckle. "Depends. What are we playing?"

"I'm Matilda!" the one with pigtails screeches, launching herself at me and throwing her arms around my neck, squeezing me tighter than I expect from a kid. "We can play dolls!"

"I'm not sure Noel would enjoy that," Parker interjects.

"You kidding?" I say to Matilda. "I would *love* to play dolls with you."

I catch Parker's smile from the corner of my eye, then look to the one who hasn't spoken a single word.

"Hi." I offer another wave to the one with red ringlets hanging down past her shoulders, a sparkly purple tutu, and bright-orange rain boots. "If these two are Miranda—"

"And Matilda!" she yells again with an infectious giggle.

I laugh. "And Matilda, then that must make you Mavis."

She grins, a dimple appearing in each cheek. "I *am* Mavis, and I like turtles."

"You do? Do you know a lot about them?"

"I know *everything* about turtles."

"Well, then, you're definitely going to have to tell me about them at dinner."

"I promise." She sticks her pinkie finger out, and it doesn't take a genius to figure out what she wants.

I loop my own little finger around hers, and we shake on it.

I rise to my feet and look down at the brown-eyed kids. "Well, now that introductions are out of the way, may I come inside?"

Two of the three erupt into cheers. Matilda grabs my free hand, while Miranda tugs on my pants leg. Mavis leads the way, which I find funny, because I have no doubt this kid is likely the quiet leader of the bunch.

Parker steps out of their way, her eyes sparkling as they march me past her and farther into the two-story house.

Hi, I mouth to her, sending her a wink.

She smiles, and it's worth feeling like I'm being taken prisoner by children.

They drag me through the living room, which is littered with toys yet still looks completely cozy, then down the hallway lined with painted handprints and terrible drawings and straight into the kitchen, where we find Axel and his wife at the stove.

They're kissing.

"Ew!" the girls yell all at once.

The couple parts, grinning over at the kids, who are now in various states of *see no, hear no, and speak no evil* with their hands over their eyes, mouths, or ears.

"Go play," their dad instructs. "Or I'll bring out the tickle monster."

They all scream—even Mavis this time—then take off back toward the living room.

"Oh! Noel!" Axel's wife says excitedly when she finally notices I'm here. She wipes her hands off on the apron that's covering her swollen belly and comes around the island that's in the middle of the expansive kitchen. "Oh, gosh. I'm Mary. It's so wonderful to finally meet you."

I hold out my hand to shake hers, but she ignores it, going right in for a hug. She squeezes me just as tightly as her daughter did.

"I'm sorry we didn't get a chance to officially say hi before now," she says as we part. "I was hoping to chat at the auction, but this little one had different plans." She rubs her belly. "So I'm glad you could make it. Now we get you for the whole night, and I can hear all the stories about this one over here that she refuses to tell me."

Mary looks pointedly between the best friends as she makes her way back to the stove.

Parker holds her hands up. "Hey, I'm not ratting him out. He pays me."

"Technically, I don't. We're even partners."

"Does that mean I can say whatever bad things about you I want?"

Axel points a thick finger at her. "Watch it."

Parker laughs, then reaches for the bottle of wine I brought. She holds it up, eyes wide.

"I said *red*," she whispers.

I shrug. "Oops."

She narrows her eyes, knowing full well I brought white on purpose.

"Look!" She holds up the bottle. "Noel brought wine."

"Ooh. White. It's my favorite," his wife says excitedly. "Too bad I can't have any. Ax, have a glass for me."

Axel just grunts, then takes the bottle from Parker to open it. She moves to a cabinet, pulling down a few glasses, then to the freezer, plunking two ice cubes into one of them.

It's clear she's comfortable here, like this is a second home to her.

I can't deny the pang of jealousy that shoots through me.

I push it aside, then accept the glass of wine Parker hands to me.

She holds her own by the stem, tipping it toward me. She waves Axel over, and he steps between us with reluctance, eyes wary and lips turned down.

"To tonight," she toasts. "And to my two best friends. May they not kill each other over dinner."

Axel snorts. "We'll see about that," he mutters.

"Axel Joseph Cooke!" his wife admonishes, and he ducks his head.

It's the first time I've ever seen him even the least bit scared, and I can't help but laugh.

He cuts me a glance, but it doesn't even bother me.

Not tonight. Nothing can mess this night up.

CHAPTER FOURTEEN

Parker

"Well, that went to hell real fast."

I groan, dropping my head into my hands as we walk down Axel's driveway.

It's nearly 2:00 a.m., and we're just now leaving. About thirty minutes after Noel got there, all hell broke loose.

"You aren't kidding. I'm just glad Matilda's okay. And Axel too," I say. "There was so much blood."

"Nothing a few stitches can't fix for the both of them," Noel tells me, wrapping an arm around my shoulders and dragging me to his side. I snuggle against him, his warmth and cologne enveloping me like a safety net I so desperately need right now. "She's little but tough. She'll heal up okay. And Axel will be fine too."

"I know. Just scary, you know? And it could set us back a few weeks at the theater while his hand heals."

"Nah. I'm sure he's got his crew on it. Besides, you two have built a great business together. It's not all going to fall apart because of this."

"Yeah, maybe." I sigh. "I can't believe we didn't even get to eat dinner. But that lasagna was . . ."

"Charred? Completely burned to a crisp?"

"So, so burned. Does it make me a bad godmother if I was almost as upset over the lost dinner as I was about her getting hurt?"

I laugh. "I think it just makes you hungry."

"Ugh. *So* hungry. I wish we had a twenty-four-hour diner around here."

"I doubt we'd get as much foot traffic as you think."

"Probably not, but it would cure my sudden need for bacon and eggs. Oh, and potatoes. No, wait. Biscuits and gravy. And wa—"

"Come back to my place."

I halt, pulling him to a stop along with me. "What?"

"Come back to Gran's with me. She's got all those things and more in her fridge, and I can whip you up something to eat. I'm guessing since everyone else around town feeds you regularly, you don't have much at your house."

I don't even bother trying to deny it. "I have a couple of eggs, if we're lucky, and some ketchup. Maybe mayo. But that's it."

He shakes his head with a grin, swinging us in the opposite direction we were headed. "Then it's settled. We're going to Gran's, and I'm making breakfast."

"Are you sure Gran won't care?"

"Nah. Not one bit. Hell, she's so excited to have me home, she might just get up and make us food herself."

"Noel!" I poke at his stomach.

"Hey, hey." He tries to dodge me, but it's useless. "I'm kidding!"

He is, and he isn't. There's no denying how much Gran loves having him here—we all do.

In fact, I don't know what I would have done without him there tonight. When Matilda screamed, Axel jumped—as expected—and sliced his hand on the knife he was using to cut the garlic bread. Blood started gushing immediately, but he didn't care. His only focus was his daughter, which is why he went running through the house, trailing blood everywhere, and scooped her up in his arms.

They both landed at the local clinic for stitches—Axel with ten on his hand and Matilda with four on her chin, which she'd busted open on the coffee table.

Somewhere in the mix of all the mess, dinner was forgotten and burned, sending the fire alarm blaring, which freaked the girls out even more, which freaked *me* out.

But not Noel. He was calm. Completely collected. He didn't bat an eye or scream like I did when Axel started bleeding everywhere or when the triplets were screaming their heads off. He tossed me a towel, told me to keep pressure on Axel's hand, then scooped up the crying Miranda and Mavis like it was an everyday occurrence for him and helped keep them calm while Mary tended to Matilda and I took care of Axel.

Even while Mary and Axel headed to the doctor, Noel stayed behind with me to watch Miranda and Mavis, despite it being so late and our evening ruined. He cleaned up the messy kitchen and the vase Axel broke in his panic to get to the girls while I fed them mac and cheese and got them ready for bed.

He was our savior, and I shouldn't be surprised by it.

He saved me from falling into a pit of despair when my dad left, then saved me again every time Axel bullied me, or anytime anything bad ever happened.

And he's about to save me again, this time from starving.

On cue, my stomach growls, and he laughs.

"Hang on," he says, pulling us to a stop. Then he turns and crouches in front of me. "Up."

I grin, thinking back on the countless times we've done this before, and hop onto his back like it hasn't been forever since I've done it.

He stands, juggling me until I am in a comfortable position for him, and I hang on tightly to his back as he speed-walks us back to Gran's. I giggle the whole way, unable to contain my childlike excitement.

Or maybe it's just because I'm tired and the deliriousness is beginning to set in.

Noel's shoes crunch up the short gravel drive to Gran's house, and he drops me back on my feet before walking right inside.

See? Nobody locks their doors around here.

He pushes the door open and motions for me to follow him. We take our shoes off, then tiptoe into the kitchen I helped Gran remodel last year whenever I had some free time. It was a fun project and one that was long overdue. Plus, it meant spending more time with one of my favorite people. I couldn't pass that up.

"What do you want?" Noel asks quietly, pulling open the fridge as I settle into one of the kitchen chairs.

"Pancakes. No, wait. Omelets. No—"

"Focus, Peter," Noel interrupts with a laugh.

"I'm sorry, I'm sorry. Everything just sounds *so good*."

"Fine. How about I pick, then? You grab us some glasses for mimosas. I'm pretty sure Gran has some champagne tucked away in the back of the fridge. No telling how good it is, but booze is booze, right?"

"You want orange juice? I can't promise it's organic or freshly pressed," I tease him.

He rolls his eyes, turns back to the fridge, and begins pulling ingredients out, setting them on the counter. I go to the cabinet where I know Gran keeps her glasses and pull two down, then fill them up about halfway with the orange juice Noel left out for me. He's already at the stove, cracking open eggs and dropping them into a skillet while another warms up.

"Score!" I snatch the bottle of booze off the counter and peel at the wrapper around the top. "The champagne isn't open yet. Do you think she'll be mad if we drink it all?"

"I most certainly will."

My heart leaps into my throat for the second time tonight, and I whirl around to find Noel's grandmother standing in the doorway, a pink robe wrapped tightly around her and a flyswatter in one hand.

"Shit. Did we wake you?" Noel asks as if he's unsurprised to find her there.

"No. I'm just up for my nightly fly hunt." She rolls her eyes at his redundant question. *Of course* we woke her up, and she was coming at us with a flyswatter, just in case we were burglars.

Noel winces. "Sorry. We'll be quieter. Go back to bed."

She ignores him, tosses her weapon onto one of the chairs, and shoves her grandson away from the stove.

"You're doing it wrong." She turns knobs and shuffles pans around. "Let me do it."

"What? No," Noel argues. "Seriously, Gran. Go back to bed. We got this."

She points a spatula at the empty kitchen table. "Sit. Both of you. And pour me one of those mimosas, will you? If I'm going to be up at this ungodly hour, I'm at least having a damn drink."

And so Noel's grandmother makes us breakfast at 2:00 a.m., and when she's finished, we scarf it down like we haven't eaten in weeks.

It's the best breakfast I've ever eaten, and the second I'm finished I want to cry because now I have to trek all the way back across town to my house.

"You look like you're about to fall asleep," Noel says, grabbing my plate and putting it in the dishwasher. He's already sent Gran back to bed, which is exactly where I want to be.

"I think the long day and even longer night are getting to me."

"Stay."

"What?"

"Stay the night. Gran doesn't mind, you know that."

"I can't . . ." I shake my head, picking up our glasses and setting them on the top rack while he loads everything else. "I can't stay the night, Noel."

"Why not? It's not like you haven't before."

"Yeah, but we were kids then. *Little* kids. It was different."

He pauses, looking up at me with a mischievous grin I don't like one bit. "Why? Are you saying you don't trust me to keep my hands to myself?"

"Do I think you're going to fondle me? Absolutely."

"You'd love every second of it."

"Shut up," I mutter, turning away so he can't see how red my cheeks are. I continue cleaning the table and putting away the Tabasco sauce, butter, and syrup.

"I'll sleep on the couch," he offers.

"That's sweet, but I am not making you sleep on the couch in your own home."

"Then we'll sleep together."

I nearly drop the saltshaker I'm setting back by the stove, barely catching it before it clatters to the countertop and wakes Gran up again.

He says it so casually, like sharing a bed in his grandmother's house wouldn't be totally disrespectful to the woman who helped raise me. Sure, we're adults, and I truly don't think Gran would mind, but it still feels like we shouldn't.

Noel laughs from beside me, taking the shakers and setting them down in their place before I break them. "I'm teasing you. Sort of. I'll be on my best behavior, I promise."

I swallow. It's not that I don't trust him. I do. It's just . . . Can I trust myself?

A yawn slams into me out of nowhere, and I know then that yes, I can trust myself. I'm far too tired for anything other than sleep.

"Fine," I relent. "But I mean it." I point at him. "No funny business."

He holds his hands up. "Swear it."

"Then let's go, because I'm about to fall asleep arguing with you."

He chuckles. "Wouldn't be the first time."

It's true. We used to talk on the phone at night and debate anything and everything. Sometimes, the arguments would go on so long that we'd fall asleep and I'd kill the cordless phone battery.

My mother was always so upset with me for that.

"Come on," Noel says, taking my hand and leading me from the kitchen.

He turns the lights off as we go, stopping once we walk into his bedroom.

It's strange coming back in here. Of course I've been inside his room many times, but not as an adult. Gran has always kept the door closed, and it's another instance where we've pretended Noel didn't exist.

Noel closes the door, then crosses the room and flips on the light beside his bed, casting the room in a low, yellowish light.

Save for the luggage in the corner and the tux hanging off the back of his closet door, the room is the same as when he left. The walls are littered with movie posters, his action figures and awards are still sitting along the top of his old wooden dresser, comics and thrillers line his bookshelf, and—

I burst out laughing.

"What?" Noel asks, brows drawn tightly together. "What's so funny?"

I roll my lips together, trying to contain the laughter. "Nice sheets."

He glances down at the bed and shrugs. "You loved *Spider-Man* as much as I did. Maybe even more, *Peter*."

"Stop it," I hiss, pointing to the bathroom. "Safe in there?"

He rolls his eyes because he knows I'm referring to the time I walked in there when he was peeing and he made a mess all over the bathroom. We were both mortified, but it's not my fault he didn't lock it.

"Yes. Here." He turns to the dresser, pulls out a shirt, and then hands it to me. "You're short. This should work as a nightshirt."

"Rude." I take the shirt anyway, stepping into the bathroom.

I do my business, wash my hands, then grab a washcloth from the cabinet and clean my face the best I can. I strip out of my clothes and pull Noel's shirt over my head. He's right—I am short compared to him, and it hits midthigh on me. He's so big it hangs off me nearly everywhere. I like it, being in his clothes like this. He's lent me jackets or hoodies before, but those didn't feel the same as this does.

This feels . . . *intimate*. Before, it was innocent, but things are clearly different now. Being in his clothes feels like I'm announcing I'm his.

But then again, I guess I always have been in one way or another.

I squirt some toothpaste onto my finger, using it as a makeshift toothbrush. Then I pull my hair from my trusty bun and redo it, only to finally settle on keeping it down.

I'm stalling. I know I am.

I don't know why.

No. That's a lie.

I *do* know why.

I'm about to spend the night next to Noel. I've done it before, but that was before I had sex with him. Before I knew what it felt like to orgasm on his face. Before I practically confessed that I had feelings for him.

Everything feels so different now. So much . . . *more*.

And it scares the heck out of me.

I inhale slowly and exhale even slower. I do this several more times before placing my hand on the doorknob.

"Go out there, Parker. It's just Noel," I whisper to myself. "It's just the boy you used to love and could possibly love again, but big deal. You've faced harder things. You got this."

I take another deep breath, open the door, and come face-to-face with Noel.

He's naked.

Okay, so he's not *naked* naked, but he's in nothing but a pair of tight black boxer briefs, and they leave nothing to the imagination.

His legs are long and muscled, his abs—which I've memorized every ridge of—are perfectly sculpted, and his arms are completely jacked. His dark hair is untamed in a way that should look messy, yet it doesn't. His blue-green eyes are bright and command my attention.

I can see why Hollywood loves to cast him as the leading man, because he truly does look like a movie star.

He quirks a single brow. "Enjoying yourself?"

I give myself a mental shake, then walk past him as if I wasn't just checking him out and climb into his bed and under his *Spider-Man* sheets.

He laughs, then goes into the bathroom, only to reappear moments later as my eyes drift shut.

The bed dips as he crawls in next to me. He slides his arm under me, tugging me closer, and I go willingly, mostly because I don't have the energy to fight him on it.

He fits me against him like I was made to be there, then kisses my forehead.

"'Night, Peter."

"Mm-hmm," I mumble, and either he laughs so hard he shakes the bed, or I'm just that far gone.

Either way, it's the last thing I remember before I drift off to sleep.

"You're not supposed to be here."

I look up and find Noel standing at the edge of the Goodman Theater's stage in his favorite faded Ramones T-shirt he found when we went thrifting over Christmas break.

"You aren't either," I tell him.

He shrugs, climbing the stairs, his Chuck Taylors that he let me doodle all over squeaking loudly against the floor. "Yeah, well, looks like we both broke the rules."

He settles down next to me, his feet dangling off the edge like mine. The cologne I got him for Christmas wafts toward me, and I inhale the scent as best I can, committing it to memory, especially since I'm not sure when I will get to smell it again.

He sighs, then runs his hand through his hair, the same thing he's been doing for as long as I can remember. "I can't believe this place really got shut down."

I look around the theater. It's dark and quiet, save for the flood-lights that are still on for some reason. "I know. But I guess that's what happens when a tree falls through it and causes so much damage it's 'non-repairable.'"

"These big-ass trees around here . . ." He shakes his head. "I'm not going to miss them, that's for damn sure."

I'm sure he won't, given his history—losing his parents in an instant to a dark night, a slick road, and a tree.

"I still don't think it needed to be shut down," he says, changing the subject like he always does when we get too close to talking about his parents.

"Me neither. I bet anyone with the right skills could repair this place."

"They could tear it down and rebuild it. Make it better."

"No. There's no need to tear it down. It has good bones. It just needs some . . ."

"Magic?"

"Magic," I agree. I let my eyes wander over the high ceilings and down to the old, worn-out chairs that desperately need replacing.

"Well, who knows? Maybe the right person will come along someday with the magic this place needs."

"Yeah, maybe."

"So." He grins down at me. "Are you going to miss me, Peter?"

"Of course I will."

More than he knows.

If my best friend weren't leaving for LA tomorrow to try to become an actor, I'd tell him how I really felt, but I can't do that because he *is* leaving, and it sucks.

I'm happy for him. I really am. I want to see him get everything he wants out of life, but I'm also sad to lose my best friend and the boy I've loved for the last year.

I don't know exactly when it happened or how I knew, but one day I looked at Noel and thought, *I could love him.*

Then I realized I already *did* love him, and it wasn't just like a friend loves another friend. It was more.

The thought scared me so much I didn't talk to him for three days. When he asked why I was hiding from him, I blamed it on my period. He was either too embarrassed to ask more about it or bought it completely because we never spoke about it again. It was the longest we'd gone without talking since he went to camp when he was twelve, but even then, he left early because he hated being away from me—something he didn't tell me until long after.

It was like that with us. We were inseparable. Best friends. But that's all we were. All we were supposed to be. Then I messed it up by falling in love with him.

He snuck up on me, and suddenly I couldn't stop thinking about him in ways I never had before. Like how tall he was getting and how much I liked that he towered over me. Or how pretty his eyes were, framed by his dark lashes, and how it was my favorite thing in the world when they were trained on me. Or how his laugh was infectious, and I'd give anything to hear it. Everything about him made my body feel like it was on fire, and it's been so, so hard to ignore.

I think I've done a good job hiding my feelings. I don't think Noel suspects a thing—or, at least, I *hope* he doesn't. That would be embarrassing.

"I'll miss you too," he says quietly.

His pinkie brushes against mine, and I don't think much of it. We've always been that way with one another. But then he does it again. And again.

It's getting to be too much to ignore.

I glance over at him, but he's not looking at me. He's looking at where our hands meet, his eyebrows turned inward in concentration.

He's quiet. Something's up.

"What's wrong?" I ask him.

"It's . . . nothing."

"Come on." I bump my shoulder against his. "You can tell me."

"I . . . I really can't."

Now it's me drawing my brows together. "Why not? I thought we were best friends. We're supposed to tell each other everything."

I know how hypocritical I'm being right now, but my secret is different. That's the kind of secret that can ruin friendships, not strengthen them.

"I'm going to miss you."

"I know. You just said that."

"No." He shakes his head. "I'm *really* going to miss you, Peter."

"I'm *really* going to miss you, too, Noel."

He sighs. "You're not getting it."

I tip my head. "I guess I'm not."

"It's just . . ." Suddenly, he shoves to his feet and begins pacing the stage, back and forth and back again.

He does it countless times, running his hand through his hair every time he turns.

I'm about to ask him what's going on when he stops, looking right at me with his hands on his hips. "You know I care about you, right?"

I rise to my feet, dusting off the back of my jeans. "I know. I care about you too."

His lips pull up into a sad smile. "Not like I care about you."

"I doubt that."

And I really do. He has no idea how I feel about him. How every night I fall asleep thinking of him and wake up every morning with him still on my mind. He's the person I want to tell everything to. He's my confidant. My best friend. He's my whole world, and tomorrow, he's gone.

He crosses the stage to me, standing so close I have to tip my head back to look up at him. This summer, he went through a growth spurt, adding another two inches to his already tall frame.

He's staring down at me with a look I've never seen from him before, a mix of uncertainty and something else I can't quite place my finger on. It sends my heart racing and makes my spine tingle with anticipation.

He reaches out, brushing a hair from my face and tucking it behind my ear, then cradles my face, his thumb stroking against my cheek. Again, his touch isn't surprising, but this . . . It feels different. Like that look in his eyes.

"Can I . . ." He rolls his tongue over his bottom lip. "Can I try something?"

I nod, and he steps closer, the distance between us now nonexistent. His hard body is pressed against mine, and it's too much and not enough.

He grabs my chin, tipping my head back. His gaze bounces between my lips and my eyes, his chest rising and falling rapidly.

I know that look. I've seen it countless times in those Hallmark movies I watch with my mother.

Desire.

I swallow thickly because I know what's coming, and even though I shouldn't want it because tomorrow he'll be gone and I'll still be here, I can't help it. I do. I want it so, so bad.

Another brush of his thumb, another shallow breath.

"Can I kiss you, Peter?"

"Yes."

The word is barely out before his lips are on mine. They're softer than I expected them to be. *He's* softer than I expected him to be. Gentle. Tentative even.

His tenderness doesn't last but a moment before he's kissing me hungrily and expertly.

I've been kissed three times before. The first was during a game of Spin the Bottle with Axel Cooke, the second last year on my first date with Henry Redding, and the third at the Homecoming dance. None of them can compare to this.

Noel's lips move against mine like he's kissed me hundreds of times before and knows just what he's doing. His tongue sweeps against my lips, and I instinctively open them.

Then suddenly, his tongue is in my mouth, and I'm melting against him. I have no idea what I'm doing, but he doesn't seem to mind. He's too busy snaking a hand around my waist, holding me tighter to him.

He's kissing me like he may never kiss me again.

I love it, and I hate it, and I never want it to end.

But it does. Far too soon.

Noel pulls his lips from mine, his breath sharp as he presses his forehead against mine. "Come with me."

I jerk my head back. "What?"

He slides his tongue over his bottom lip. "Come with me. To LA, I mean."

"You're joking."

"I'm really not."

And I know by the look in his eyes that he's telling the truth. He wants me to come with him.

My mouth falls open. "You can't be serious. I can't . . ." I shake my head. "I can't come to LA with you."

"Why not?"

"Because I can't."

His nostrils flare, his jaw working back and forth. "That's not a reason. Give me one."

"Because . . . because . . . I'd have to ask my mom."

He snorts out a laugh. "You're an adult now, Peter. You can do whatever you want. Besides, Astrid's cool with me going. I bet she'd be fine if you tagged along and got out of this shithole town."

I bristle at his words. This town isn't as bad as he claims. I like it here. No. I *love* it here. And I don't want to *tag along* to LA to escape it like he does.

And don't even get me started on "tag along." What, like I'd be latching on to his dreams and following him there because I had nothing else better to do?

I *do* have something to do. I'm going to take college classes online and work at my mom's shop until I decide what I want to do with my life. I'm not some lost creature who needs Noel to step in and rescue me from my small-town life.

"No."

"What?"

"No. I don't want to come with you."

"You . . . don't want to come to LA with me?"

He stumbles away from me, his mouth falling open like he can't believe I'm denying him. "Why not?"

"Because I have college."

"You can take the courses there."

"But I want to take them here."

"Why? We can share my room, and there are so many restaurants where I'm going. I bet you can find something there. Maybe wait tables. That's what I'm going to do between the acting classes I've signed up for and auditioning. Then we can save up money and get our own place. We can leave this town, not be tied down here. We can explore the world together. It'll be amazing."

I shrug. "I know you don't like it here, but I do, Noel. I don't want to leave Emerald Grove right now. Besides, if you really wanted me to come with you, you'd have asked me sooner than the night before you left."

"That's . . . that's not true, Peter. I . . ." He shakes his head. "That's just not true."

"But isn't it? You weren't going to ask until we . . ." I can't say it, mostly because I still can't believe it happened.

"I was. I was going to ask, but I was afraid that *this* would happen. That'd you tell me no."

"So, what? You thought you'd butter me up by kissing me?" I huff. "You can't just play with me like that."

I turn away from him, stomping across the stage to the exit, needing to get away.

"Peter, wait."

I don't. I keep moving.

Why would he kiss me when he didn't mean it? Doesn't he realize what that means to me? Doesn't he realize what I feel for him?

"Come on, stop."

"Why should I?" I yell over my shoulder.

"Because I love you!"

I skid to a stop, my heart thumping so loudly in my chest that I can hear it in my ears.

I squeeze my eyes shut, sucking in breath after breath, trying to calm it.

He loves me? I know he just kissed me, but kissing is a heck of a lot different from loving. Could he really mean that like I want him to mean it?

"Parker?" he says quietly, nervously. His footsteps echo as he crosses the stage toward me. He's at my back. I can feel his heat. "Did you hear me? I love you."

I nod, not trusting myself to speak.

He grabs my elbow, and I let him turn me to face him, my eyes still closed.

"Parker, come on. Look at me." He cups my face with his hands. *"Please."*

The pleading in his voice is my undoing, and I peel my eyes open slowly.

He's staring down at me with nothing but sincerity, and I know at that moment it's true—Noel Carter loves me.

This can't be happening. This can't be real. He's leaving tomorrow and choosing to tell me he loves me now?

Why? Why is he doing this to me? And *now*?

"I'm not asking you to come with me out of pity or obligation or anything else. And I didn't kiss you because I was trying to butter you up. I kissed you because I've wanted to, because I've been dying to kiss you for years."

Years? He's wanted to kiss me for years*?*

"Around the same time that I realized I was in love with you, actually." He laughs to himself. "I . . . I don't know what happened. I don't. We've never . . . That's never been our thing. We've just been Noel and Parker, and that's it. But then suddenly, I realized you weren't *just* Parker. You were more, and I wanted more. I tried so fucking hard to not think of you like that. Tried to put it out of my mind. Tried to move on. But I couldn't. I couldn't stop loving you."

"But—"

"I know the timing is shit," he continues. "And I'm really fucking sorry about that. But I had to tell you before I left. Even if you don't feel the same—and it's okay if you don't—I want you to know. I love you, Parker Pruitt, and not just like a friend loves another friend. I'm in love with you, and *that's* why I want you to come to LA with me. Because I can't imagine my life without you, and I don't want to. So please . . . please come to LA with me, Peter."

Desperation clings to every word. I've never heard him like this before. Never heard him so frantic.

He wants me to come, and truthfully, a part of me *wants* to go with him.

But I can't. I can't leave my mom. I can't leave behind my town. Can't leave when I'm about to start college. My whole life is here, and I'm not ready to give that up yet.

I love Noel—so much more than he could ever know—but I can't go with him.

When I don't say anything back, he sighs. "You're not coming, are you?"

"No." The single word comes out as a whisper. I'm afraid if I say it any louder, it'll make this that much more real, and I *really* don't want this to be real.

"Not now or not ever?"

I swallow. "Not now. I'm just . . ." I shake my head. "I'm not ready."

He nods. "Okay. Okay. I can work with that. I can work with *not now.*"

"I'm sorry," I tell him, because I *am* sorry. But I'm also not ready to take the leap he's asking me to take.

"It's okay. It is. So you're not coming now. But maybe in a few months, yeah? I can go out there and get settled, and then you can move out with me."

"Yeah." I nod. "That . . . that sounds good."

And it *does* sound good. Truly, truly good. It sounds like everything I've ever wanted—a life with Noel.

But it doesn't feel *right.*

Why doesn't it feel right?

"Yeah? That's the plan, then?"

"That's the plan. I promise."

Promise. The word stings on my tongue, but I can't take it back. Not with him looking at me like he is—his eyes lit up and a smile stretched across his face.

It's easily the most excited I've ever seen him, so why does it hurt so much? Why does it feel like my world is about to implode?

"Good. You'll come out there and fall in love with it, and I'll become an actor, and you can work on sets, and we'll get to be together forever. It's going to be amazing."

"So amazing," I agree. "I can't wait."

And I *can't* wait. I want that too. I really do.

But something feels wrong. Off. My chest feels heavy, and not with elation. It's something else I can't quite put my finger on.

"Fuck, me neither, Peter."

Then he's kissing me again, and it's just as incredible as before.

No. It's *better.*

I lift my hand to touch him, to pull him closer, but it never connects. *Why doesn't it connect?*

I pull away, opening my eyes.

Noel's still there, but he's fading by the second.

What's happening? Where is he going?

"Noel?" I call out to him, but he doesn't answer. "Noel?"

Again, no answer.

"Noel? Noel? NOEL?" I yell, each call of his name becoming more frantic.

But it's pointless.

He's gone.

And I'm left standing on the stage alone, still calling out his name, tears rolling down my cheeks as sobs begin to rack my body.

He's gone. He's gone, and he's never coming back.

"Parker?"

I hear his voice. It's clear and loud. I whirl around, looking for him, but he's not there.

"Parker?" he says again, and the stage shakes.

What's happening? Is this an earthquake?

"Parker!"

More shaking.

"Peter!"

I wrench my eyes open, gulp in a big breath of air, and sit straight up.

I blink, looking around the room, expecting to see the Goodman Theater, but it's not there.

I'm in Noel's room, in his bed.

It . . . it was all just a dream. Or a memory, really.

It was the night Noel asked me to go with him to LA. The night I turned him down. The night we kissed for the first time. The last night I'd see him for a long, long time.

But he isn't gone. He's here, next to me, sitting up with the *Spider-Man* sheet bunched around his waist. His brows are pulled together with concern as sweat rolls down my back.

"Are you okay?" he asks softly, rubbing my back.

I nod. "I—I'm okay."

"Bad dream?" he guesses.

He doesn't know the half of it.

"Yeah. Bad dream."

He frowns. "You were whimpering. It woke me up."

"I'm sorry."

He shakes his head. "Don't be. Just come here."

He pulls me back down, tucking me against him like he did before. He continues to rub my back soothingly.

We lie like that until sleep begins to nip at me again. I'm almost pulled under its spell, but I fight it, too scared it'll happen again.

"Sleep," he says, like he knows what I'm up to. "Sleep, and I'll protect you, Peter."

He kisses my forehead, hugging me tighter, ready to fight my demons.

If only he knew what I really needed to be protected from was him.

CHAPTER FIFTEEN

Noel

"Put that over there."

"Here?" I move the vase of peonies to the wrong spot on purpose. Parker laughs, which is exactly what I was going for.

To say she's been stressed these last two weeks would be an understatement. I've tried to distract her the best I can with kisses and getting her naked as often as possible, but she's still running on high alert thanks to juggling the theater renovation on her own—with Axel being out of commission—and this damn fundraiser we're hosting tonight.

It's Saturday, and we're in the middle of decorating Bigfoot's Hideaway for tonight's second effort to raise funds for the theater reno. We knew going in that the bar-and-bowling-alley combo would require a miracle to make it look suitable for the event, but leave it to Parker to pull it off.

Sure, the dark log cabin–style walls are still lined with photos, mismatched bigfoot paraphernalia, and other random decor, but now it looks downright bright and cheery with all the balloons, flowers, white tablecloths, and signage we've hauled in here. Hell, she's even swapped out the light bulbs to get rid of the yellowish hue this place always seems to have going on.

"Ha ha." She pokes her tongue out. "You know I mean the table, not the stool. You're lucky I like you."

"It's the sex, isn't it?"

Her eyes widen, and she glances around the room, which is not as empty as she'd like if I'm going to be talking like that.

"Noel." She says my name like a curse, poking me with the pen she's wielding. "Stop it."

"Why? Afraid someone's going to get jealous?"

"Of me or you?" she challenges, and it feels like a trap.

"Both?"

She pats my chest. "Good answer."

Phew.

She grabs the flowers I've placed on the stool and moves them to the center of the table, arranging them just so.

"There," she says once she's satisfied. "Much better."

"You know, I think this deserves a test. Let's not put flowers on a few tables and see if the teams without them lose or win."

She rolls her eyes. "How about we don't?"

"Or we could just get rid of them entirely. Besides, it's one less thing I have to throw off the table when I ravage you on top of it later."

"Noel!" she hisses for the second time, and I can't help but grin.

God, I love messing with her.

Well, I'm not *entirely* messing with her. If we're left to cleanup duty again, that is *so* happening.

"You're impossible, you know that?" she whispers, her eyes still darting around to see if anyone is paying attention.

They aren't.

Fran is busy bringing in the extra chairs and tables, Astrid and Clifford are off flirting in the opposite corner, and Garth, the owner, is perfecting the audio system in the bowling alley so everyone can hear the door prizes we're offering throughout the night, an idea Gran had that we rolled with at the last minute. We reel them in with the promised trivia and bowling, then get them to stay and spend more money by offering up raffle tickets for cheap prizes and donated gift cards from local businesses. It's a win all around.

Nobody cares what we're doing, so I can do whatever I want.

So, I do.

I grab her waist, tugging her to me, and she comes effortlessly, falling against me like it's second nature.

"Hi." I smile down at her.

Her eyes sparkle with giddiness. "Hi."

"Whatcha doing after this?"

"Uh, going home to change into . . . well, not paint-stained overalls?"

"Can I watch?"

She laughs. "Again, impossible."

"Am not. I'm perfectly possible. I just know what I like."

"Yeah, and what's that?"

"You."

Her eyes widen, and I can't help myself—I kiss her.

She pauses for only a moment, then she's melting into me.

I guess she doesn't care about everyone else being here as much as she says.

She fists her hands in my shirt, tugging me closer, and I lose myself in her. The way she fits against me, the way she always smells like peppermint, the way she feels, the way she tastes.

I'm gone for Parker Pruitt, and I don't give a shit who knows it.

"All right, you two. Break it up," Astrid says, but the love in her voice is evident. "We're supposed to be working. We have four hours until the fundraiser starts."

That gets Parker to pull away.

She tries to wiggle out of my embrace, but I don't let her, even though all eyes are on us at this point.

She grins up at me. "See what you started? Now they all know."

"So? Does that bother you?"

"No."

"Parker . . ."

"Fine." She sighs. "Sort of. It's just . . . This town likes to talk, you know?"

There's worry in her eyes, and I'm not entirely surprised by it, given her comments on how she feels about my Hollywood lifestyle and fame and how it would bother her to have everyone in her business.

"And you don't want them talking about us," I guess, and she nods. "I could have my agent step in and shut down whatever trash the *Gazette* might try to print."

"I appreciate it, but I don't want it to come to that. I just . . ." Another sigh. "I don't know what I want."

"Other than me?"

"Other than you, Noel."

She pushes to her tiptoes and presses her lips to mine. This time, the kiss is brief and over far too soon for my liking, and when she pulls away, I let her go.

Two hours later, we're ready to call it a day so we can get ready before the event in T-minus two hours.

"Wow, Parker. It looks great in here," Garth says as he takes it all in. "I can't believe it's the same place."

"I do what I can." She grins at him. "You'll be ready to go at seven?"

"Yep. I got my team prepping everything in the kitchen. We got sliders, jojos, wings, and chili-cheese fries on the menu for the evening. They're our bestsellers, so we should bring in a lot of money for the theater, even with them on sale."

"Oh man. I haven't had jojos in far too long. I tried ordering them when I first got to LA, and they looked at me funny, then brought me a plate of potato wedges. Just regular potatoes, sliced up. No breading, no spices, and they weren't even orange. Definitely not fried like they should be either."

Parker gasps. "That's insulting! They're totally different!"

"I know."

She shakes her head, then looks to Garth. "And the booze?"

"Pints are three bucks, pitchers are sixteen, and bottle buckets are twenty."

"Mixed drinks?"

He smiles. "Don't worry, I have your whiskey sours on sale tonight."

He winks at her, she blushes, and I fucking hate it.

I step forward, wrap my arm around her, and tug her close.

There's no mistaking what I'm doing, and Garth tracks every move I make. His eyes widen slightly, then he meets my hard stare and it becomes clear.

Mine, the gesture says.

He nods subtly in understanding.

Parker leans into me, completely oblivious to what's happening.

"I got a little drunk *one time*," she tells him.

"One time a month, maybe. You and Axel have too much fun in here sometimes."

She wrinkles her nose. "We do, huh?"

"Oh, you definitely do. Anyway, I still have lots to do before we open, and I'd better help my staff prep. See you at six thirty?"

"On the dot," Parker promises him, then looks up at me. "I'm going to go tell my mom bye."

"I'll be here."

Once she's gone, Garth steps forward, holding his hand out to me. I accept it.

"I didn't know you two were together. I guess I should have, though." He laughs.

"Why is that?"

He tips his head to the side. "Come on, man, like you and Parker haven't always been inevitable. When I heard you were coming back, I had a feeling you'd end up together again."

"Again?"

He glances over at Parker, who is chatting with her mother.

"When she gets drunk, she talks a lot. She mentioned what happened before you left and how you were sort of together then. She rambles about it sometimes and how she wishes she would have said yes, whatever that means."

His words stun me.

Parker regrets not saying yes? Does that mean . . . Does she regret not going to LA with me?

I don't know how I feel about that. *Of course* I wanted Parker there with me. More than fucking anything else. And I've hated not talking to her for the last ten years.

But seeing how everything else has worked out, it's hard for me to wish we could change the past.

She has an incredible career. I'm not sure she'd have it if she hadn't turned me down, and I don't want to erase that for her.

"Sorry, it's none of my business. It's just us bartenders, you know. We hear stuff."

I nod. "Yeah, no. I get that."

"And really, you have nothing to worry about with me. I know love when I see it, and I'm not about to try to step in the middle of that."

My territorial moment aside, I wasn't worried, but I appreciate his words all the same.

"You ready?" Parker asks, bouncing on her heels back our way.

"Yep," I answer. "Let's go."

We say our goodbyes to Garth, then make our way out into the sunshine. Parker and I walk hand in hand down Borgen, and she only blushes a little when people stare or take notice of our touching, but she doesn't pull away. I *like* that she doesn't pull away. Probably a little too much.

"So," I say after passing The Chilly Cow, our frozen yogurt shop that I used to spend far too much time at. "Garth said you talk about me sometimes."

"Garth is a liar. Ignore him."

I laugh because I know he wasn't lying. "Bartenders never lie."

"Sure they do. They always lie when they say they're going to pour you a double. They add extra ice, the same amount of alcohol, and still charge you double."

"All right, I'll give you that one. But I don't think Garth was lying. Was he?"

She doesn't say anything for several moments, and it's all the confirmation I need.

"Axel and I used to hang out there often, especially before the triplets came along. It's where we became friends, actually. You were gone, and I was bored, so I went into the bowling alley one day, and there Axel was. He was sitting alone, looking as sullen and grumpy as I felt, with a basket of chili-cheese fries in front of him. We made eye contact but didn't speak as I rented a lane. I could feel his eyes on me the whole time I was bowling. So finally, after about my fourth gutter ball, I smiled and waved at him. He scowled and looked away, and I laughed. It was the first time I had laughed since you left, and it felt so good that I wanted it to happen again."

Fuck. The thought of her being so upset that she couldn't laugh is . . . well, it's fucking heartbreaking. It eats me up inside that she was feeling like that and I wasn't here. I hate myself for it.

"I went back in the next day, and there he was again," she continues. "The same table, a new basket of fries. So I rented another lane, took my Coke and old shoes, and sat across the way from him. Again, he stared, and again, I waved. That went on for a week, and as weird as it sounds, it felt nice to have something to look forward to, even if it did mean I was getting glared at while throwing an embarrassing number of gutter balls."

"How'd you two become friends then?"

She laughs lightly. "I got tired of it. One day, when he looked over at me, I flipped him off instead of waving."

I laugh because I can't imagine Parker doing anything like that. "You did not."

"I did too. And Axel had the same reaction you did. He laughed. It was so sudden it surprised him, and I knew immediately that he was broken like I was. His parents were going through a divorce, and all his friends had just moved away for college. He was alone. I was alone. So, we decided to be alone together. We've been best friends since."

I wait for the jealousy to hit over her calling Axel her best friend, but it doesn't come.

He's been there for her so much over the years, showing up for her, cheering her on, and, hell, he's even her business partner.

He *is* her best friend, and I'm finally okay with that.

No. The only thing that comes is heartache.

Broken.

Is that really how she felt? Like I broke her by leaving? It hurts, and that guilt I've felt all these years seeps back in.

"I'm sorry," I tell her, squeezing her hand as we turn into her driveway. "I'm sorry you had to go through that alone. I'm sorry that I left."

"Don't be. I mean, there have been plenty of times over the years when I've not liked you, but you're here now, you know? That's what matters, right?"

I swallow. "Right."

I am here now. Only for a few more weeks, but I'm here.

Yet I can't help but wonder . . . What happens when I leave? What happens to *us*? Will Parker stop talking to me again? Is it going to break her heart like it did before? Garth said she regrets not saying yes back then. If I were to ask now, what would she say? Would she turn me down, or would she go with me?

I'm too fucking scared to ask because I have a feeling I know exactly what her answer would be, and it's not the answer I want.

I want Parker to come with me. I want to show her my life in LA. I want to be with her—and not just for six weeks tucked away here in the Pacific Northwest. I want her all the time. In my bed, in my house, in my life.

I just want *her*.

But I know that's a tall ask. She has a life here. A career. The theater. Asking her to leave it all behind would be selfish, and I don't want to be selfish with her.

"Want to come inside?" she asks as we ascend the stairs to her front door.

More than she knows, but instead, I say, "How about I meet you at Bigfoot's later?"

She frowns, and I can tell she's sad I'm not coming inside to have my way with her.

I laugh. "I've got plans with Gran," I explain.

She sighs. "Fine. I'll allow it. But only because I think it's sweet that you're a total grandma's boy."

I press a kiss on her cheek. "Go inside before I change my mind."

"I'm going, I'm going."

She waves as she closes the door, and I jam my hands into my pockets as I make my way back down her driveway and turn onto Borgen to head to the other side of town.

Shops are starting to close early, and several are even posting signs on their doors pointing potential customers to the fundraiser.

My heart swells every time I read one. The town is rallying behind Parker with such force. They love her, and if there's one thing she's made clear over the years, it's that she loves them too.

It's just another reason I can't ask her to leave. She belongs here. These are her people. This is her home.

My phone buzzes against my leg, saving me from the spiral I'm on.

My relief is brief when I realize it's my agent for the third time in two days.

Aaron: Did you get a chance to read that script?

I groan. Is he really bothering me about this again?

Me: Not yet. Been busy.

Aaron: Read it. I think you're going to love it.

Me: I said I didn't want to do superhero stuff.

Aaron: I know, I know, but this is a huge opportunity. I think you'd regret passing it up.

Aaron: Besides, you owe me. I got you these six weeks off and have been keeping the press off your trail so you can enjoy your little vacation, right?

He's got me there. I know he worked some magic to reschedule things to keep me in Washington for these six weeks, but the second my time here is up, it's back to the grind. I'm flying to LA for just two nights, then I'm going to New York for a talk show run that will last another week.

He's saving my ass. I guess the least I can do is read the script.

Me: Fine. I'll let you know on Wednesday.

Aaron: Make it Monday. The studio is on my ass. They want you big-time.

I groan, grinding my teeth together.

Me: I have shit I'm doing this weekend.

Aaron: Well, then, make it work. They aren't going to sit around and wait on us forever. They need an answer soon.

I know he's right on all fronts.

Sure, I might not want to do the movie, but the least I can do is play nice with the studio, or else they might stop knocking at my door.

Me: All right, all right. Monday.

Aaron: Thank you.

Aaron: Oh, and I have a slight change of plans. You'll be in LA for just one night, and I need you in New York a night early. I got you an invite to the premiere of Jasper Rafferty's new film.

Aaron: I'll have Vince send you all the details.

Aaron: Talk Monday.

He's not giving me an option, and he's not asking if this is something I want to do. He's just informing me that I'll be there.

I love acting, but I could really do without all the extra shit that goes along with it sometimes.

I tuck my phone back into my pocket as I walk up Gran's porch. I sneak inside quietly, knowing she's taking a nap to "stay up and party with the young'uns," as she told me this morning. I've been instructed to wake her at six to walk over to Bigfoot's.

I check the clock hanging on the living room wall. I still have an hour to kill before I need to wake her.

I shuffle into my room with a sigh and then settle onto my bed. I grab my laptop from my nightstand and pull up the script I've ignored for the last week.

I guess now is as good a time as any to start it.

◆ ◆ ◆

"You know these old bones don't move as fast as they used to, right?"

"I know." I slow my gait. "I'm sorry. It's just that we're late, and I know Parker won't be happy."

"Bah." Gran waves her hand. "She'll be fine. She knows I'm poky. We walk around town at least once a week, which takes us forever. She's used to it."

I love that even though Parker and I had a falling-out, she never stopped including my gran in her life.

It's just another reason to admire her and why I hate that I'm letting her down by being late for something that means so much to her.

I'll admit it—I don't hate the script as much as I thought I would. In fact, I love it. It's more than just a superhero movie packed with action and CGI. There's true heart there, and it's something I'd be proud to be part of. I got so wrapped up in the story I forgot to wake Gran, and she had to be the one to come get me just as I was sending off an email to Aaron, letting him know I was open to a conversation with the studio.

The parking lot of Bigfoot's comes into view, and it's clear this event is already going well—and we're just fifteen minutes into it.

I curse myself for the umpteenth time for being late. I should have been here on time. This event is important to Parker, which makes it important to me. Though I'm sure Gran is right and Parker won't be upset that I'm late, I'm still eager to get inside, and the old woman next to me doesn't miss it.

"Go on ahead. I'll catch up, bub."

I shake my head. "Like I told you three times at home, I'm not leaving you."

Gran huffs. "So stubborn."

Music and laughter filter out as we shuffle up to the front door.

"After you, ma'am," I say, letting her pass.

"Call me ma'am one more time," she warns, and I laugh.

We walk inside, and my mouth drops open.

"This is . . ."

I don't have the words for it. There are people everywhere. Every trivia table is full, there's hardly any standing room at the bar, servers are buzzing back and forth, and Garth is popping top after top from beer bottles. One peek into the bowling side tells me it's just as busy.

"She's amazing, huh?" Gran grins as she takes in the scene before us. "I've never seen this place so busy before, and that's saying something because I've lived here forever."

"It's incredible."

"Where's Parker?" Gran asks, craning her neck to try to find my girl.

Just when I'm about to give up and park Gran near the bar so I can look for her, I spot her.

She's in the bowling alley, and her arms are raised as she does a little dance. Astrid high-fives her, then sticks her tongue out at Axel, who looks as grumpy as ever.

Parker looks so happy and at ease. She's in her element.

It's just another reminder of how much she belongs here, how perfectly she fits into every little space in this town.

As if she can feel my eyes on her, she glances my way, and her smile grows even wider.

She waves me over, but I point to the bar.

Whiskey sour? I mouth.

She nods enthusiastically, and I laugh. It's clear from the glassy look in her eyes that she's already had one, maybe even two.

"I'm grabbing a drink, Gran. Want anything?"

"A whiskey neat, please."

"You got it. Meet you over there."

"And some jojos!" she calls after me, and I nod to let her know I heard her.

When I approach the bar, Garth dips his head at me, and I relax against it, knowing it'll be a minute before he gets to me.

I look back at the crowd, still in awe of what Parker has accomplished.

I shouldn't be surprised. She used to run the set design team like a champion too.

"This is an impressive turnout."

I grit my teeth and look to my right. "Figs."

"It's Leonard," he tells me with a sneer.

I ignore him. "I'm surprised to see you here. Even more surprised you're praising Parker's efforts."

"I don't dislike Parker if that's what you're getting at."

"Could have fooled me."

"I don't. I just don't like that this town is wasting its time and money on something so . . . so . . . so asinine."

"You don't like theater?"

"I don't believe it's something this town needs. The Goodman Theater never sold out a show in its existence. Aren't there far better things we could build on the land that would bring revenue to this town?"

"Sure, but this town does well enough on its own. Can't we have something fun?"

"We can, but it shouldn't start with that silly little project your girlfriend is working on."

"It's not silly."

He snorts. "It is. And it's going to fail. Mark my words."

I push off the bar to my full height and step toward him. "It won't fail."

"You would say that. After all, it's named after you."

"It won't fail," I repeat slowly this time, so maybe he gets it.

"That's what Parker claims too. She's just too—"

"If I were you, I would choose my next words very carefully, *Figs*." Another step, so close I can smell his aftershave. "Because if you so much as utter one more bad word about Parker, I'm going to make sure you never write another article in this town again."

"You don't have that power."

"Oh, I don't? Try me, then."

He gulps loudly, blinking up at me. "I—I—I . . ." He puffs his chest out. "You can't stop me from reporting the truth, Noel. The *Gazette* helps this community."

"The *Gazette* is one step above a trash magazine you ignore at the grocery checkout. You know it, and so does everyone else."

He glares at me, and it's the least scary thing I've ever seen. "It's better than that theater."

"Yeah? Well, we'll see about that when the project gets fully funded, sells out crowds, and thrives no thanks to your shitty little paper." I take another step toward him. "Now get the fuck out of here before I throw you out myself."

He huffs but hurries through the crowd, and I watch him all the way to the exit.

"Thank god you said something," Garth says. He stares after where Figgins just pushed through the doors. "I never liked that guy. He's always causing trouble."

"Too much of it, if you ask me."

Garth shakes his head. "Anyway, you need a drink?" I nod. "Let me guess: A whiskey neat for Gran with some jojos and a whiskey sour for Parker?"

I laugh. "Are my women that predictable?"

"Considering they're in here at least once a week and never order anything else, I'd say yes. What can I get for you?"

"Gimme your best scotch."

"Neat like your gran?"

"Of course."

He taps the bar twice, then moves away to make our drinks.

I turn back to the crowd, watching the people of Emerald Grove look like they're having the best night of their lives.

Fuck Figgins and his articles. I don't care what he says. This event—and the whole theater project, for that matter—is great for the town. It's exactly what we need.

Garth reappears, setting the three drinks before me, and promises to send the jojos over once they're ready.

I try to hand him my card, but he waves me off.

"No. All your shit is on the house tonight."

I ignore him, pulling my wallet from my back pocket and tossing a hundred on the counter anyway. "It's for a good cause."

I balance the drinks, something I learned from the few months I worked at a restaurant when I first moved to LA, then head for the bowling alley.

The lanes are jam-packed, kids are running loose everywhere, and the noise level is at an all-time high.

I hand Gran her neat whiskey, then claim a stool. Axel nods at me from where he's sitting, and I nod back. We aren't going to be best friends anytime soon, but it's progress.

"You going to bowl, Gran?"

She snorts. "With these hips? Not again in this lifetime."

I frown. I hate that she can't do the things she once loved, but I guess that's part of getting older. You learn to adapt or find new things to keep you occupied.

Parker grabs a ball and walks to the end of the lane. She peeks over her shoulder, a playful spark in her eye, then shimmies forward. Another foot. And another.

Soon, she's halfway down the lane. She squats and then drops the ball, letting it roll slowly toward the pins.

"Cheater Peter!" I yell, but it's pointless.

They all fall, and she turns, throwing her arms into the air.

"I won! I won!" she chants as she races forward and launches herself at me.

I catch her easily, wrapping my arms around her waist desperately like I didn't just see her a few hours ago.

She grins up at me. "You made it."

I wince. "I'm sorry I'm late. I was reading."

"Reading?" She gasps. "Were you reading romance novels? Because I read those sometimes. The kissing ones are my favorite."

"Just kissing?"

"Oh no. I like it when they bang too. That's really my favorite part."

I laugh. Oh yeah, she's definitely tipsy already. "Good to know. Though I am sorry to burst your bubble, it wasn't a romance novel. It was a script."

"Apparently, it's a good one too. He forgot to wake me up," Gran complains, sipping her drink.

"Ah, right." Parker nods. "Sometimes I forget you're a movie star."

Sometimes I forget, too, especially lately. Being back in your hometown will do that, I guess. Nothing humbles you more than the people who knew you before.

I won't lie, a part of me has missed it. I've missed being *just Noel*, which is how everyone here treats me—like I'm the same kid they've known since I was a toddler. While I miss LA and my friends, it's a nice break to turn off the movie star side of me and be regular Noel again.

"You're still just the boy I fell in love with."

My heart thunders in my chest.

"Is that right?" I ask her, tugging her closer.

Her grin stretches wider. "That's right."

"How many drinks have you had?"

"Just the one. Plus one more. So that's two. But now that you've brought me one, it'll be three."

"That's some good math. Mrs. Kohlson would be proud."

"She's here. I should go tell her. Then maybe shake her down for a few bucks for the event." She pulls away to do just that, but I stop her, dragging her back to me.

"How about we get you a water, then we'll go shake down our sixth-grade math teacher?"

"Fine." She huffs. "But you have to bowl with me too."

"I think I can arrange that."

By the night's end, we've officially put a $35,000 dent in the renovation fund, and Parker is drunk.

She had a glass of water, beat me at bowling, *and* snuck two more whiskey sours.

After all the work she's been putting in, she deserves to let loose. Even if it does mean I have to piggyback her into her house.

"You know, you should really lock your door," I tell her as I step inside without a key.

"Why? Are you planning on breaking in?" she counters.

I laugh at her absurdity, then move to drop her onto the couch.

"No, no, no!" she protests, clinging to me so tight I can barely breathe.

"Choking. Me."

She loosens her grip, and I suck in a gulp of air.

"Oops. My bad." She giggles. "Just not the couch. I'll fall asleep."

"That's kind of the idea. You're drunk."

"I am not."

"You are, and it's adorable."

"Aw, you like me." She nuzzles her nose against my neck.

She has no idea.

"I like you too," she says, kicking at my sides like a horse. "To my bedroom!"

I laugh at her, carrying her back to her room as requested.

I deposit her onto the bed, snuggling back against her.

"I think this is where I'll sleep tonight."

"Yes. Don't go," she says, gripping me tighter so I can't move. "Stay here forever. Stay in Emerald Grove forever."

Her request hits me right in the chest. I know she's being playful, but what if she's serious too? What if she does want me to stay? Could I do it? Could I stay for her?

A part of me thinks I could, but I can't gamble on a maybe—not when it comes to Parker.

I push from the bed, my thoughts racing too much to stay still. I need to take a walk. Need to clear my head.

"Hey!" She pouts, sitting up. "Where are you going? Aren't you going to ravage me like you promised earlier?"

I laugh. "When you're drunk? Absolutely not."

"Boo."

I lean forward and kiss the top of her head. "Are you going to be all right?"

"Why are you asking me that like you're leaving?"

"Uh, because I am?"

"What? No. Stay," she begs. "I want that amazing breakfast you allegedly make in the morning."

"Even if it means I'm not going to ravage you?"

"Yes. I like sleeping next to you."

I like sleeping next to her too.

"Fine. But I get to be the big spoon."

"Well, duh. I'm not the big spoon. That's weird." She lifts her arms in the air. "Help."

I grab her shirt by the hem, pull it over her head, and toss it aside. "Pants too?"

"Yes. I'm not sleeping in jeans. You're so weird tonight."

I barely hold back my laughter at her annoyance at my questions as she lies back down. I pull off her shoes and socks, then unsnap her jeans and work them down her legs.

I crawl on top of her. "Better?"

"Much. But now I have to pee."

I laugh. "Do you need help with that too?"

"I think I can manage."

I roll off her, ensuring she gets to the bathroom okay before I take off my jeans and T-shirt and crawl under the covers.

She returns a few moments later wearing an oversize T-shirt, and I recognize it instantly—it's mine from when she stayed over at Gran's. She must have snuck it home, and I didn't notice.

Her hair is wild from her drunken adventure tonight, her makeup a little messy, and her eyes are glassy and tired. She looks as gorgeous in my T-shirt now as she did that night, and I wish she weren't drunk so I *could* ravage her as I promised.

She climbs into bed next to me, and I lift my arm. She snuggles against me like it's something we've rehearsed, and I pull her even closer until she's practically lying on top of me. It takes all of a minute until she's already snoring lightly.

I chuckle, then kiss her head. "Good night, my little drunk."

"Hmm." She rubs her cheek against me. "Night, Noel. I love you."

She's half-asleep, but there's no mistaking the words she just said.

I love you.

It's the second time she's used the L-word with me tonight, and the second time there's a pull at my chest.

Parker Pruitt loves me.

And fuck if I don't love her too.

Part of me always has, but not like this.

This love . . . It's different. Even different from when we were teens.

It's the kind of love that simmers for years. The kind that eats at you just a little every day, burrows its way into your heart and plants itself, a seedling that gets watered just enough to keep it alive. Then, one day, it blooms, and it's bigger than you ever expected.

I love Parker. I *have* loved Parker. And no matter the time, distance, or status of our relationship, I always will love Parker.

"I love you, too, Peter," I tell her, holding her closer as her snores fill the room.

I just hope we can make this thing work when push comes to shove.

I really don't want to lose my best friend again.

CHAPTER SIXTEEN

Parker

I love you.

That's what I said to Noel last night.

I remembered the moment I woke up.

It's why I've been lying in bed for the last twenty minutes, pretending to still be asleep while he moves around my kitchen making us breakfast.

I can't believe I told him I love him.

More than that, I can't believe it's true.

I thought I was over him. Thought I had moved on.

I was wrong.

I was wrong, and the thought terrifies me as much as it thrills me.

All it took was him being back in town, and I'm head over heels for him. I haven't felt this way since . . . well, since I was eighteen, only this time, sneaking around and hanging out with him is far more fun and naughtier.

I can't pinpoint exactly when it happened. Maybe it was when he stepped in to rescue me from Figgins and promised to stay and help with the theater, even though I knew he had much more important things to do. Or maybe when he took me out to the Falls and gave me the best orgasm of my life. Or how he looked after Axel's daughters and me during that disastrous dinner. Or that he takes care of me when I have too many whiskey sours.

Or maybe . . . maybe I just never stopped loving him at all.

I'm in love with Noel Carter, and I have no idea what to do about it, especially since he's leaving again and I can't go with him. I have far too much to do here, like finish the theater and run my business with Axel. I've worked hard on both, and I don't want to give any of that up.

Besides, I don't even know if I would *want* to go. I doubt I could handle the high-profile life he leads. That's his world, not mine. I have no idea where I'd fit in there.

But I guess that's not something I even need to worry about for a few more weeks.

I hear him grabbing plates from the cabinet, and I know it's my cue to finally crawl out of bed. That's good because I'm not sure I can handle thoughts of him leaving with this hangover.

I use the restroom, brush my teeth quickly, and pad out to the main quarters.

Noel is at the stove, flipping a pancake off the skillet and onto a plate. He's barefoot, wearing the same jeans and simple gray T-shirt he had on last night. His back muscles are jumping with every move he makes. Whatever workout routine they have him on in LA is clearly paying off.

When he finishes the pancakes, he turns off the burner and heads to the fridge, pulling out a carton of orange juice and two cups from the cabinet. He's moving around my kitchen like he's in his element, and all I can think is, *He fits here.*

He might have reservations about this town—and I get it, I do—but I think he belongs here more than he realizes he does, and that's the worst part of it all.

I could ask him to stay and prove to him that this place is his home as much as it is mine, but that wouldn't be fair. Just like I have my business to run here, he has his own career that's much better suited for LA than some tiny town in Washington.

My eyes drift to Pumpkin, who sits on the back of the couch, one of my Frosty the Snowman figures between his paws as he nips at it. He looks at me and meows, a sign he wants his breakfast.

Noel hears him and looks over, his face lighting with a smile when he sees me. "You're up."

"I'm up," I say, walking farther into the kitchen and straight to Pumpkin's bowl.

I stop when I see it's full.

He fed my cat.

My cat, the very same one who left scratch marks on his cheek just a couple of weeks ago. It's . . . well, it's sweet.

"You fed him."

"Huh?" Noel asks, turning to me.

I point to the bowl. "You fed Pumpkin."

"Oh yeah. He was meowing his little head off. I hope that's okay."

"That's . . . It's . . ." I race toward him, wrapping my arms around his middle, pressing my face against his chest. "It's more than okay. I can't believe you fed my cat."

He laughs. "I'm trying to feed you, too, but I kind of need to move to be able to do that. Sit. Breakfast is just about ready. You feeling okay enough to eat?"

My stomach rumbles as I pull away. "I'm *starving.*"

"Good," he says, turning back to the stove and grabbing the scrambled eggs to plate them, "because I made breakfast. We have eggs, home fries, sausage, pancakes, and fruit."

"It smells amazing." I slide into one of the chairs at the two-person table. He already has everything set out—hot sauce, shredded cheese for the potatoes, syrup, and butter—even salsa, since he knows I love it on my eggs. "But you didn't have to do all this for me. I was only kidding last night."

He pauses, and I don't miss it.

Crap.

Does he remember what *else* I said last night too?

If he does, he doesn't say anything and continues to plate our breakfast.

He brings them over, settling one in front of me and the other in front of his chair. Then he grabs the two glasses of orange juice and brings them over before sitting down.

He lifts one glass to his lips, then takes a healthy sip before smacking them together dramatically.

"Taxes?" I ask. He grins, then hands me the juice he just took a drink from. "I hate taxes."

"I don't know. I kind of love them." He winks as I take a sip, then points to my plate. "Now eat. We've got a big day ahead of us."

I set the glass down and raise a brow. "We do?"

"Yes."

"Care to tell me what we have going on?"

"Eat first."

"Fine." I slide my knife through the butter, then drop a big glob onto my pancakes before drowning them in syrup. I firmly believe that's why pancakes were invented—as an excuse to eat butter and syrup for breakfast.

I take a bite, and though I should be embarrassed by the moan that leaves me, I can't find it in me. Not when it tastes so good.

"Holy . . . This is the *best* pancake I've ever had. How do you get them so fluffy?"

"Do you go to a restaurant and ask the chef their secrets? My lips are sealed."

"Mean. Guess I'll just have to kidnap you and keep you here so you can make these for me forever."

He pauses for the second time this morning, and it takes me a moment to realize what I've said.

It's a reminder that his time here is limited. It's a reminder that I'm playing a dangerous game by getting so attached to him, but I don't care—not when it feels so good, so right.

I just want to relish this little bubble we've created for a bit longer.

When we've both cleared our plates, I move to start cleaning up.

"Whoa there. What do you think you're doing?" Noel asks as I lean over the table, reaching for his dishes.

"Um, cleaning?"

"Not happening. Sit. I'll clean."

"No. You cooked. I'll clean."

"Or hear me out, you sit, and *I* clean since I made the mess."

I sigh. "Noel."

"Don't *Noel* me. Sit."

"Fine." I toss my hands in the air, plopping back in my chair. "Be my guest."

So I begrudgingly sit there while he cleans up the kitchen, even grabbing the spray from under the sink and wiping the counters down. It's as sweet as it is annoying, but I know if I get up to help, he'll yell at me until I stop.

When he's finally done, he walks over to me and holds out his hand.

"Oh, am I allowed up now?"

He smirks. "Yes."

I let him pull me up, and he drags me right against him, pressing his lips to mine without any warning.

The kiss is hard and heated and has me tingling in all the right places.

I'm breathless when he finally pulls away.

"Good morning," he says, like he didn't just kiss me senseless.

"Good morning. What a way to wake up."

"Oh, if you think that woke you up, wait until you see what I have in mind next."

Without warning, he lifts me into his arms and sets me on the table.

"What are you doing?" I ask breathlessly.

"Having a second breakfast." Then he drops to his knees and parts my thighs. He arches a brow my way. "Any complaints?"

I shake my head furiously, and he chuckles darkly.

"I didn't think so. Now, lie back so I can eat your pretty pussy."

A shiver racks through me from his vulgar language, and I don't dare ignore his request, lying back as he hooks his fingers into my underwear and drags them down my legs. He grabs my hips, scooting me to the edge of the table where he wants me, then shoulders his way between my legs.

One swipe of his tongue and I'm arching off the table with a sigh.

I crash my fingers through his soft ink-black locks, pulling him closer.

"God, you taste good," he murmurs against me. "I could stay here all day."

"Do it," I challenge him brazenly, and he laughs, sending a shock wave through me.

He slides his tongue against me again and again, the stubble on his chin rubbing at my most sensitive place. The roughness shouldn't feel so good, but it does.

He continues to eat at me until I'm bucking against him, dying for a release.

But he doesn't give it to me. He just keeps teasing and teasing.

"Noel." I growl out his name.

Another laugh. "Yes, Peter?"

"You're killing me."

"Really?" He licks at me again, and I moan. "Because it doesn't *sound* like I'm killing you. In fact, it sounds like you're only moments away from coming on my face."

"And I would be already if you didn't stop tormenting me."

"That so?"

"Please," I beg. "I want to come."

He smirks. "I think I can arrange that."

Then he sucks my clit into his mouth, and I lose it. My back curves off the table, and I cry out as my orgasm crashes through me like waves slamming against a rocky shore.

It's magnificent, but it's over far too soon.

Noel kisses the inside of each leg, then up my body, taking my shirt—*his*, technically—along with him. He tosses it aside, then closes his mouth around a nipple, sucking at me gently while he slips his hand between us and works his jeans and underwear down his legs.

"You know, I've always wanted to kiss this spot right here," he says, then drags his tongue over the tiny freckle I have under my breast. "It's been taunting me for years."

"Years?"

"Yes, Parker. Do you have any idea how long I've wanted you?"

I shake my head, then remember he's not looking at me. "No."

"Too fucking long," he says, taking my other nipple between his teeth, flicking his tongue over it.

When he's done kissing both my breasts, he works his way to my lips and kisses me thoroughly. It's so good yet so not what I want.

I want him. And now.

I lift my hips, searching for his touch. He smiles against me.

"Eager?" he asks.

"For you? Always."

He pulls away, and his eyes rake down my body, hunger and desire swirling in his blue-green stare.

"You're so fucking gorgeous like this," he says, his voice thick with need. "Spread before me for the taking."

"Then take me." I lean up and wrap my arms around his neck, dragging him back down to me. "Make me yours."

He grunts, his erection pressing against my opening.

"As if you already aren't," he grunts out before sliding into me.

I sigh in relief as he fills me, not giving me even a chance to adjust to his size before pounding into me again and again. And truthfully, I don't want the chance. I want him just like this—raw and so ready for me that he can't control himself.

The feet of the table squeak against the floor with his thrusts, and I have no doubt that when this is over, I'll have to do some rearranging, but I don't care. I can't care. Not when it feels so, so good.

"Do you have any idea what you do to me?" he growls into my neck, one hand tangled in my hair, the other biting into my hip. "Any idea at all how good you feel? How badly I want to stay inside you like this for all eternity? How much I fucking want you? Because I do, Parker. I want you. All the time. Every minute of every damn day. That's never changed for me. *Never.*"

I don't say anything back because I can't.

My second orgasm barrels through me out of nowhere as Noel pushes into me harder and faster, chasing his own high.

Moments later, he gets it. He stiffens over top of me, his breaths growing sharper and sharper in my ear as he empties himself inside me.

He rocks into me slowly, working us both over until we're completely wrung out, then finally he stills, the only part of him moving is his mouth against mine.

When he pulls away, I know I look a mess. My eyes are heavy, my hair is tangled from his fist, and there's no way I'm not red all over from the stubble lining his jaw.

"Now *that* was a wake-up," he says with a grin.

All I can do is nod, and he laughs.

He scoops me into his arms and carries me back to the bedroom. He drops me into bed like he did last night before taking off his clothes and sliding in next to me, tucking us both under the blanket.

I'm nearly asleep when a thought hits me.

"Wait." I lift my head to look up at him. "You said we had big plans for the day."

"I did."

"Well, what are they?"

"You."

"What?"

"You. You're my big plan for the day. Just me, you, and this bed. Or the couch. Whichever. We can watch movies or nap, or I can let you take advantage of me. Whatever you want. You've been running yourself ragged. I just figured you needed a day to do nothing. That okay?"

My shoulders sink with relief. I'm not sure I could handle a day out and about. I'm tired. These last few weeks have been exhausting between juggling the renovation and the events. It's taking a toll in ways I hadn't even realized.

But Noel did.

Of course Noel did.

"That sounds like heaven," I tell him, tucking myself back to his side.

And it's exactly how we spend the day.

I do take advantage of him . . . twice.

◆ ◆ ◆

"Are you really just sitting and looking longingly out the window?"

I sigh, my chin resting on my hand as I look out at Borgen Avenue from my spot at Rossi's Café. "Yes."

Noel laughs. "You look like a little kid who's been told they can't go out and play in the rain."

"That's because I *can't* go out and play in the rain. It's halted all construction."

It's Wednesday, and we've been waiting out the rain for two days now.

It's frustrating because we take one step back for every step forward with the theater. There was a great turnout at the auction, then asbestos set us back two days and ten grand. Then Axel's hand got messed up, which cost us labor hours we can't get back. We had the bowling and trivia event where we raised a significant amount, only for it to rain nonstop for two days, and it doesn't seem like it will clear anytime soon.

While I know this project isn't going to happen overnight, I also feel like we're making very little progress, and I desperately want to make progress. I've been dreaming of this for so long, and I just want to be done so badly. Not to mention Leonard and his "reports" on the progress.

"Is this because of Figgins's latest article?" Noel asks, reading my mind as he sips the lavender lemonade that I got him hooked on, and just the mention of the guy has my blood boiling,

"No. Maybe. Yes."

His lips pull up on one side. "You know he's just trying to get a rise out of you, right? Hardly anyone reads the *Gazette* anyway."

"*Everyone* reads the *Gazette*, and you know it."

But I appreciate him trying to make me feel better about Leonard's latest dig in his *What's New* segment of the newspaper.

Under *Theater Construction*? He put *"nothing."*

And that was it.

Nothing!

It was like a slap in the face for everything I *have* accomplished even despite our setbacks. Like running two successful events with turnouts this town hasn't seen in years. Or lining up our first production—*Beauty and the Beast*—to open this winter. Or all the hours I've spent making sure every last detail is as perfect as possible.

Figgins will be lucky if I don't give him a piece of my mind the next time I see him—or kick him. I haven't decided which yet.

But I have decided that I'm now even more determined to prove to him and the naysayers who held the project back for so many years that this will be the best theater they've ever seen. Sure, we're still far from having this thing fully funded, and every day it's looking more and more like I'm going to have to take out a *very* hefty loan to complete it, but it'll be worth it to see the looks on their faces when I open the doors and the townspeople come flocking to see our shows.

They'll just have to wait and see.

"You're still getting plenty done. You were up half the night designing and redesigning the lobby, right?"

"I didn't hear you complaining when I"—I glance around the café to ensure nobody is paying us any attention—"took an extended break."

He grins wolfishly. "Oh, I'm not complaining. I quite enjoyed you on your knees for me, Peter."

My face heats at his words, and I rub my still sore knees, a reminder of our night of activities. I've never much been one for oral, but I'll admit I liked being on my knees for him too.

The one good thing about the rain delay is that it means more time with Noel. We've spent the better part of the last two days alternating between my bed and the couch—and, okay, the kitchen counter too. I'd have thought by now I'd have had my fill of him, but it's been the total opposite, and I can't get enough.

I have no idea what I'm going to do when he leaves.

How am I supposed to go back to life as I knew it before he breezed into town? How do I go on, not kissing him every day? Not hearing his laugh or seeing his smile light up a room? How am I supposed to move on from him after this?

I can't, and I don't.

I just need to accept the fact that I'm doomed to repeat my mother's history—I'm in love with a man who doesn't want to stay.

"Want to go do something reckless?" he asks out of nowhere.

I already am doing something reckless by loving you.

But I don't tell him that. Instead, I say, "Such as?"

"I don't know. Go egg Figgins's car or something?"

I laugh. "I will *not* commit felonies with you, Noel Carter."

"It wouldn't be a felony. I highly doubt we can cause five grand worth of damage."

I lift a brow. "Why does that number sound specific enough that it's exactly how much damage you'd need to cause for it to be considered a felony?"

He shrugs with a grin. "I don't know what you're talking about."

I shake my head, sipping my own lavender lemonade. "So what do you have in mind other than the destruction of property?"

"I got nothing. That was my only plan."

I bark out a laugh, so loud several heads turn our way. I glare over at Noel.

"What?" he asks innocently, though he knows it's *his* fault I'm getting stares. "But seriously, we could hike out to the Falls. I know how much you like it out there."

"I don't want to get muddy."

"We could go bowling?"

"We *just* went bowling on Saturday."

He leans across the table. "Then we can go back to your house, and I can fuck you again."

His words go right between my thighs, and I clench them together, wanting that more than I realized. "Let's do that."

He shoves to his feet, his chair scraping loudly across the floor, and now *everyone* is looking at us, including Gianna and Greta, who are behind the counter.

He holds his hand out to me, and I happily accept it, letting him pull me to my feet.

I can't help but giggle as he drags me to the door, and I wave to the café customers looking at us with wide eyes.

We look ridiculous, but I don't care. That seems to happen a lot with Noel, the whole not-caring thing. He makes me feel far too good to be bothered by much.

My giggles subside when we step outside and come face-to-face with Leonard Figgins.

I school my features, trying to hide my displeasure at seeing him. "Leonard, hi. How are you?"

"Me? Oh, I'm fantastic." He grins widely. "How are you, *Parker*?"

I hate the resentment he puts on my name, as if *I* have wronged *him*.

I paste on a fake smile. "Positively peachy. Couldn't be better."

His grin widens, and I hate it. I want to reach up and wipe it off so badly. "That's lovely. It's a beautiful day outside, isn't it? I hear we're getting even more rain tomorrow. It's good. We could use it."

No, we really couldn't. We've been drowned enough over the last few days.

"While we'd love to stay and chat about the weather, we've got plans. I'm sure you understand, *Figs*," Noel says snidely.

Leonard narrows his eyes at Noel. "Right. I don't want to keep you. I'm sure you're a busy man. I heard you're up for a new role. The next *Avengers*, I believe, is what they're calling it."

I look up at Noel. "You're up for a new role?"

Is this the same script he was reading the other night? The one he was so engrossed in that he was late to the fundraiser at Bigfoot's?

"Nothing's set in stone," he says, but he doesn't return my stare, and that giddiness I felt just moments ago is replaced by a heaviness that leaves my stomach feeling sour.

"Well, while this has been *lovely*," Leonard says, clearly knowing it's been anything but, "I'd better run. I have lots to do at the paper. There are so many *important* things to report on."

Leonard grins like he's just won a prize, pushes his rain-streaked glasses back up his nose, and continues on his way. He's only a few feet away when I hear his jaunty whistle, making me want to kick him all over again.

"Well, that was something, huh?" I mutter, looking back up at Noel.

He nods, still keeping his eyes anywhere but on me.

I loop my arm around his. "Are you still coming over?"

"Hmm?" he asks distractedly, then *finally* looks my way. "Oh. Yeah. Let's go."

We don't talk on the walk there or when we walk inside my cozy house, hanging our raincoats by the door. Not a word is uttered as Noel drags me into his arms, then down the hall and straight to my bedroom, where he makes good on his promise from the café.

And that dreadful feeling never does go away.

CHAPTER SEVENTEEN

Noel

A loud buzz wakes me, and it takes me a moment to realize where the noise is coming from—my phone.

It shakes across Parker's bedside table, and I reach for it as fast as possible, praying it doesn't wake her up.

Yesterday, she went back to work at the theater and stayed until 10:00 p.m. She was so exhausted that she ate the dinner I made in the bathtub, then promptly crawled into bed and started snoring before I was even out of the bathroom.

The phone quiets for only a moment before springing back to life.

Aaron.

Shit. My agent.

He's not going to stop calling until I answer.

I let the phone ring as I carefully extract myself from Parker's hold. She groans a little, a wrinkle forming between her brows, then she's back to snoring.

I smile down at her, wishing I could keep this moment forever.

Then my phone rings again.

I repress my sigh, then tug on my jeans and T-shirt before padding out of her bedroom.

Pumpkin meows at me from his perch on the back of the couch, a long string of last year's Christmas garland dangling between his paws. I shake my head at him, then pull open the front door, stepping into the cool morning air.

It's just six, and the town is quiet. I've been here a month, but I'm still getting used to peaceful mornings like this.

My phone goes off again, breaking through that peace, and I sigh, hitting the green button as I settle into the chair on Parker's porch.

"Hello?" I answer.

"They want you."

"Well, that's an interesting greeting. Good morning to you, too, Aaron. How's your Friday so far?"

He sighs, irritated. "I don't have time for pleasantries. Plume Pictures wants you—badly. They want a face-to-face meeting on Wednesday to offer you the role formally."

Fuck.

No, not *fuck*.

This is good news. Excellent news, really. This is the kind of news most actors hope for, can only dream of.

But it also means the one thing I was hoping it wouldn't—I have to leave Emerald Grove a week early.

I count on my hand how many days I would have until I have to hop on a flight back to LA.

Five.

That's all I have left here, and it's five days too few.

To be fair, I don't think any amount of time in this world would be enough with Parker.

I've gone ten years without her, and now I can't imagine going one day. The way she's nestled her way back into my heart in just a month . . . it's unreal. I wake up thinking about her, wanting her. I go to sleep doing the same. All my thoughts are centered around when I'll see her next and how I can make her laugh.

She's become everything to me all over again, and now I'm going to have to let her down.

I promised her six weeks, and I should have known the second I did that it would never be enough.

Not with Parker. Not with the woman I love.

"Noel?" Aaron barks. "Are you still there, or did you lose the connection in that little Podunk town you hail from?"

"It's not Podunk," I say defensively. It's funny because I would have said the same thing just a few weeks ago.

But something about being back in Emerald Grove is different. Maybe it's because I'm older and can appreciate the slower pace of life. Or perhaps it's because I've gained enough distance from all the bad memories I have here, and the good ones feel brighter and more important. Or maybe it's just because of Parker.

He snorts. "Whatever. Anyway, the meeting is on Wednesday at two o'clock, and I already have Vince booking your flight and car service to the studio so you can meet with the bigwigs and they can present us with a contract."

"How do you know they're offering me the role? We haven't even discussed salary."

Aaron laughs. "Please. That was taken care of before I even sent you the script. They've known they wanted you for months now. We just needed to get you on board."

I grit my teeth. If Aaron weren't so damn good at his job and didn't know exactly what he was doing, I'd be pissed as fuck right now. But at the end of the day, I trust him, and I know he'd never steer me wrong.

"I told you I didn't do these kinds of movies."

"Yes, so you've said, but you loved the script, didn't you? I knew you would. I just needed you to get past the superhero thing and give it a shot. So I guess you *do* want to make these kinds of movies after all."

Shit. He has me there.

"Let's make it, then," he says when I don't respond. "You have the time. This could be *it* for you. It's the start of a franchise. This could be your legacy. You could be the next Iron Man or Captain America. Don't let this opportunity pass you by, Noel. You've worked hard to get an offer like this. You deserve it."

I have worked hard. I've spent the last ten years working hard. I wanted a break. I wanted some room to breathe.

But he's right. This *is* a huge opportunity, and it's exactly what I've been working toward.

So why am I not jumping with joy? Why am I not feeling that flutter of excitement? Why am I not happy?

The answer is lying inside, snuggled up in a cozy bed that I wish I were in—*Parker*.

It always comes back to her.

I want to do this, but even if what we have survives my move back to LA, I know this movie would mean committing to spending some serious time away from her, and not just now. It will mean months of being on set, long days, and late nights. Then, country hopping, doing promos, talk shows, and everything else that comes with promoting something this big.

Do I want that? Do I want to be away from her for that long?

Yes and no.

It's complicated, and I don't want to make this decision right now, but I know I don't have a choice.

"Noel," Aaron prods. "What's it going to be? Are you in or out?"

I take a deep breath, then blow it out slowly, knowing my answer could threaten everything I have with Parker.

"Yes," I tell him. "Yes. I'm in."

"That's what I thought." I can hear the smile in his voice. "Vince will be in touch with your flight information before noon. I'll see you Wednesday."

Then he hangs up, leaving me with a whirlwind of emotions.

I drop my phone onto the table next to me, absorbing the silence while I still can. Soon, I'm going to be back in the mayhem of LA, going to meeting after meeting, then to interview after interview, and photo shoot after photo shoot, only to jet off to another project so I can start it all over again.

I'm unsure how long I sit out here, but it's long enough for cars and people to start moving about the town and for Parker to come looking for me.

The front door clicks open, and I hear her sigh with relief.

"There you are," she says, her voice still groggy from sleep. She pulls the door shut behind her and pads onto the small porch. "I was wondering where you ran off to."

She's wearing my T-shirt again, a pair of sleep shorts that barely peek out from under it, and nothing else. Her long auburn hair is a tangled mess, and her eyes are a bit puffy, yet she's still the most beautiful woman I've ever seen.

She slides onto my lap, and my arm goes around her, holding her close as she settles against me.

I could do this every day.

The thought slams into me out of nowhere, and I instantly know it's true.

I *could* do this every day. I could sit here in this tiny town with Parker on my lap and be just as happy as I would be back at my house in LA.

That's how I know that I love her. That she's completely it for me.

And how I know that what I have to tell her next is going to suck so fucking much.

"I'm leaving early," I announce after several moments of quiet.

She sighs, but it's not a sad sound. It's a resigned one, as if she knew this was coming.

And honestly, how could she not? Even I've had an inkling this would happen, especially if the news of my potential involvement is making headlines.

I was just hoping it wouldn't be so soon.

"When?" she asks.

"I have to be back by Wednesday afternoon."

She nods and rises from my lap, holding her hand out to me. "Then we'd better make the most of the time we have."

I let her pull me back into the house, where we spend the morning in bed doing exactly that.

◆ ◆ ◆

"Come on. I want to make sure we get a good spot."

Parker runs ahead of me, her steps light and excited, like a child getting free rein at a candy shop.

I thought she'd be more upset about me leaving, but she's keeping true to her promise of making the best of the few days we have left together.

Our Saturday began with breakfast in bed—her being the breakfast. Then we took Gran to lunch at Rossi Café, where I wolfed down an Italian sub *and* two cookies before heading to the theater, where I helped her and Axel settle many debates on paint and countertop colors. It's a good thing it's Saturday so the crew wasn't around to hear their bickering.

Now it's time for the monthly movie club to meet, and apparently, we *have* to attend.

I'm wary of her excitement as she dances across the park, weaving through the people already spread out on blankets until she finds the perfect spot.

"Here," she announces.

I unfold the blue plaid blanket that's usually bunched in the corner of her couch, which I've fallen asleep on too many times to count, and spread it wide for us. We grab our popcorn, candy, and drinks from the small basket Parker brought along, then settle down with just a few minutes to spare. Parker slides between my legs, her back pressed to my front as she snuggles into me.

"It's the perfect night for this," she says, tipping her head back to look at the stars. "No clouds."

I follow her gaze, admiring the night sky. Thanks to all the light pollution in the city, I don't often get to see it like this, and I almost forgot how beautiful it can be.

"It is. A little chilly, though."

"That's why we brought the second blanket." She reaches for the backup blanket she brought and drapes it over us before resuming her spot tucked against me.

"Smart woman." I kiss the side of her head just as her mother and Clifford come ambling our way.

"Well, look at you two, all cozy and whatnot." Astrid grins at us as Clifford shakes out their blanket, settling it next to ours. "Haven't seen much of you lately, little miss," she says to her daughter.

Parker looks up at me, a silent question in her eyes. *Can I tell her?* they ask.

I nod.

She looks back over at her mother. "Noel's leaving early."

"Oh." Astrid's grin fades, but it only lasts a moment. "Well, that's all right. You'll be back, won't you?"

Parker stiffens against me.

My return isn't something we've discussed.

Do I plan on coming back? Yes.

Do I know when I can actually make that happen? No.

I wish I had more for her than I do, but since I can't give her a definitive answer right now, I don't want to make a promise I can't keep.

"I'll be back," I tell her, deepening my voice like Arnold Schwarzenegger in *Terminator*, trying to keep the mood light.

It works, and even Clifford laughs at the impression.

I'm saved from talking about it anymore when the screen flickers to life, signaling the movie's start.

Parker relaxes against me once more. She reaches for the cheddar cheese popcorn she brought and pops a few pieces into her mouth before offering me some.

She giggles when I snake my tongue against her fingers and then wipes them dramatically on *my* pants.

I allow it because I'll do anything to keep her smiling.

"You never did tell me what movie we were watching," I whisper as the movie starts.

She shuffles in my arms. "I didn't?" she asks. "Well, I guess you'll see. Now, shhh. The movie's starting."

The music begins to swell, and vaguely familiar images flash across the screen. Then, briefly, the title flutters across the screen, and I suddenly know why Parker didn't mention the film's title. It's one of mine—a romantic comedy about an assistant who falls for his boss.

I groan, and she laughs.

"Well, would you look at that?" She grins at me. "It's one of yours."

"It's a good thing you never auditioned for any of the plays at the Goodman Theater. You're a terrible actress."

She gasps. "How dare you. And I'll have you know it's called the Noel Carter Theater now. Maybe you've heard of him. He's some hot-shot actor. We're about to watch one of his movies. I've heard he takes his shirt off in this one." She bounces her brows up and down a few times.

She's right. I *do* take my shirt off in this one.

"What if I told you it's a body double?"

"Please." She rolls her eyes. "I've seen you shirtless countless times. I can count your abs in my sleep. I'll be able to tell."

I shake my head with a smile. "Just watch the movie, Peter."

"Don't have to tell me twice. I love this one."

"You're lucky. I really, *really* hate watching my own stuff."

"I think most actors do. But tell you what. You get through this with me, and I'll make it worth your while later."

She grins suggestively, and miraculously, I am *thrilled* to watch my own movie.

"Deal."

She laughs, earning us a few glances from around the park, but I don't care. I want her happy. I want her laughing. I want these next three days to be full of moments like this.

When my character appears on-screen, the whole park erupts into cheers, and I wish like hell I could run far, far away.

Instead, I wave to them, accepting their love and support, then bury my face in Parker's neck, sending her into another fit of giggles as I pepper her with kisses.

By the time the movie is over, I'm more than ready to be done.

I shove to my feet, dragging Parker up with me, and practically throw our belongings into the basket. I don't even bother folding the blankets back up; I just stuff them right in there too.

"You ready?" I ask Parker, holding my hand out to her.

"Yep," she says, lacing her fingers in mine.

I start walking one way, and she starts walking the other.

We snap back together like rubber bands, and I catch her before she collides into me.

I smile down at her. "Did my incredible abs make you so loopy that you forgot where your house was?"

"Did you forget I promised to make it worth your while?"

"No? I thought that's why we're going back to your place."

She raises her brows. "Oh, you thought I meant *that*?" She grins impishly. "I was thinking something else . . ."

"You kids in for frozen yogurt or what?" Astrid asks, hitching her thumb in the direction of The Chilly Cow.

I glare at Parker, who is tucking her lips together tightly, practically bouncing on her heels.

"You tricked me," I accuse her.

"I did no such thing."

"Peter . . ."

"Noel . . . ," she mocks, deepening her voice.

I step toward her, and she takes off, sprinting toward her mother like she will save her, laughing the entire way.

I shake my head, following after them with a smile.

If frozen yogurt is what she wants, I'll give it to her.

Hell, I'd give her the whole damn world if I could. Anything she'd asked for, I'd give to her.

Even for me to stay.

The thought hits me out of nowhere, but it doesn't make it any less true.

If Parker asked, I'd stay here for her. I even think I'd give it all up for her.

But she'd never ask, and I'm not sure how I feel about that.

I shake away my thoughts and catch up with them.

We walk into Jules's shop with just fifteen minutes to spare until close.

From her pinched expression, it's clear she's annoyed we're coming in so late, but her attitude shifts instantly when her eyes land on me.

"Noel! Come in, come in. Can I get you some samples?"

I laugh, setting our stuff down on one of the tables. "No. I'm all set, Jules. I know my way around." I wink at her, just because I can, and I swear she pushes her shoulders back a little more, loving the attention.

Parker smacks my stomach. "Flirt," she whispers, a heat behind her words that I enjoy far too much.

"What? I thought that's what we were doing tonight—teasing."

That earns me a glower as she moves through the machines one at a time, trying to decide on the right flavor.

She finally settles on marshmallow and then moves on to the toppings, loading her bowl with four different kinds of candy and enough chocolate syrup to satisfy even the sweetest of tooths.

I fill my cup with vanilla, then add peppermint candies and nothing else. It's always been my favorite because it reminds me of Parker.

"You mind if we sit outside and enjoy this?" I ask her as I'm paying.

"Not one bit."

"Thanks, Jules. You're the best."

I toss her another wink, which earns me another smack.

We carry our stuff outside, Astrid and Clifford not far behind, then settle at one of the many tables on the sidewalk.

Even though I thought my reward for suffering through my own film would mean something entirely different, I'll give it to Parker that this is a nice alternative.

"So," Astrid says, taking a bite from her treat. "When do you leave?"

Those four words are all it takes to suck the goodness from the evening, a somber cloud settling over us in an instant.

Parker's shoulders tense, and I'm suddenly not hungry.

"Early Wednesday," I tell her. Vince originally had me flying out on Tuesday, but I made him push it back until the last possible second. I wanted as much time with Parker as I could get. "I have to be back in LA for a meeting that afternoon."

"Must be awfully important if you're cutting your trip short."

It's not a dig or a snide remark, just a genuine statement.

"I can't say much about the project, but it has the potential to be big."

"That's great. Really. I'm so proud of you, son."

My throat tightens with emotion, and I have to look away so I don't do something completely irrational like start crying.

I didn't realize how badly I needed those words right now.

Returning to LA was inevitable, but I didn't expect to feel so torn about it or get so attached to everyone again. It's going to make leaving even harder. I'll miss everyone here, especially this woman before me, who has always treated me like her own.

"Thanks," I mutter. "That means a lot, Astrid."

She pats my hand, squeezing it tightly before letting go.

"Well, that was a mood sucker, huh? Let's talk about something fun. Cliff, tell the kids about that thing you showed me in the bedroom last night."

"Mother!" Parker screams, and even *I* want to crawl into a hole and hide right now.

"What?" Astrid asks innocently. "I just meant a photo taken at the Falls." She grins. "Why, what did you think I meant, you little perv?"

Parker sighs loudly in relief, but while the lightness of the evening mostly returns, a solemn cloud still lingers in the distance, ready to bathe us in darkness at any moment.

We say good night to Astrid and Clifford and make our way back to Parker's.

We're quiet as we walk inside and barely exchange words as we get ready for bed.

I slide into my side of the bed, and she slips into hers, crawling toward me and wrapping herself around me.

I kiss the top of her head, and she sighs.

"Thank you for tonight," she says into the darkness of the room.

"Thank *you* for tonight," I counter. "I had fun."

"Even though you had to see yourself shirtless?"

"Do I always stand like that? My hands on my hips?"

She laughs. "No. And you looked great, so hush."

"Yes, ma'am."

She burrows into me more, tucking her face against me and pressing soft kisses against my chest. "I'm going to miss you, you know."

It's the first time she's brought up my leaving. The first time either of us has.

Even though it's not forever, it's still just too damn real to talk about.

"I'll miss you more," I tell her honestly because I have no doubt it's true. I *will* miss her more.

I'll miss everything about her—her laugh, her smile, the way her eyes light up when she sees Tater Tots. Or how even after all these years, she still looks at this town with wonder and love. I'll miss how kind she is, like when people stop to chat with her when she's in a hurry or is so tired she can barely stand but she still makes time for them and genuinely listens.

Then, of course, I'll miss other parts of her—the ones I get all to myself, like how the sun dances off her skin in the early-morning glow. The way her hazel eyes brighten to almost a full green after an orgasm. That damn freckle that sits under her tits. And how she breathes my name like a sigh of relief whenever she comes.

So, yeah, I'll definitely miss her more.

"Go to sleep," I tell her. "You'll need the rest for the plans I have for you tomorrow."

"Hmm. Fine. But only because I'm exhausted." She kisses me again. "Good night, Noel."

"Night, Peter."

Her soft snores fill the room only a few moments later.

As for me? I don't get an ounce of sleep, and I know it's because I'm too afraid to miss a moment of this.

CHAPTER EIGHTEEN

Parker

When Noel told me he was leaving early, I wasn't as surprised as he probably expected me to be.

That day we ran into Figgins, I felt something brewing. I prepared myself for the possibility that Noel would leave before our six weeks were up, and I swore that no matter how soul-crushing it felt, I would put on a brave face and make the most of our days left together.

I think I've done a good job of keeping that promise.

We've spent the last several days wrapped in nothing but one another. It feels just like before, with us being so attached at the hip. Wherever he goes, I go, and vice versa. I even went to the gym with him yesterday, and I've lived here twenty years and never once stepped foot inside it until then. I learned I hated burpees but would suffer through a hundred if it meant one more minute with Noel.

"You're walking like you fell down a flight of stairs."

"That's because I *feel* like I did."

He laughs. "It was one day in the gym."

"And for someone who never goes, it was rough."

I shuffle through the aisles of Jill's Bait & Tackle. We're grabbing supplies for Tater Tot Tuesday. When I asked Noel if he was sure this was how he wanted to spend his last night here, he looked at me like I'd just asked him to fly to the moon.

"What's on the list again?" I ask him.

"We don't have a list, remember? You insisted you'd remember everything and then stole my pen while I was trying to make a list because I knew you were lying."

"I would never do that." *I totally* did *do that.* "Now, tell me what you forgot."

"*You* forgot jalapeños, Fritos, shredded cheese, onions, and sour cream."

"See? We never needed a list." I stick my tongue out at him.

He rolls his eyes. "Let's just grab the supplies, smart-ass."

We wander through the aisles, adding a six-pack of Watermelon Lime wine coolers and a bottle of wine to our basket before heading to the checkout.

Peggy is her usual not-so-chatty self, and we grab our bags and head out toward my mother's house.

I limp up the sidewalk. We're just a block from our destination, and then I can sit at the counter, make my Tater Tots, and get a break. I heft the grocery bag in my arms up higher.

Noel sighs. "Would you just let me hold that?"

"No. You're already holding all the other groceries."

"Yeah, and that's the heaviest bag. Just give it to me."

I cut him a glare, and he snaps his mouth shut. "Fine. Then struggle."

"You're so annoying," I mutter to him as we turn into my mother's driveway.

"That's not what you were calling me this morning. I believe the words *sex god* were used once or twice."

I roll my eyes. "You wish."

Though, to be fair, that assessment wouldn't be far off.

He just laughs, then helps me up the porch steps.

I whirl around to face him once we reach the door.

"Now, I'm going to open this door, and we are *not* going to discuss our sex life. At all. Understood?"

He nods, barely holding in a grin. "Understood."

"Good."

I push open the door, not bothering to knock.

"Mom!" I call out, taking off my shoes. "We're here!"

"And we are definitely not talking about our sex life, so don't even ask!" Noel yells.

"Noel!" I hiss, glaring at him, and I hear my mother laugh.

"Good to know," she hollers back. "We're in the kitchen!"

This time, I'm not surprised by the use of *we*. Clifford's been joining us for Tater Tot Tuesdays since he and my mother went public.

At first, I wasn't sure how I felt about my mother dating. Not because I didn't believe she shouldn't, but because she never had before. But she and Clifford are perfect together. They complement each other so well that I've often wondered why they didn't get together much earlier.

We make our way back to them, and I'm unsurprised to find her at the stove, stirring away.

"Chili is just about ready," she says over her shoulder.

"Perfect, because I'm starving," I tell her, setting the bag of groceries on the counter and practically falling onto a stool. My shoulders sink in relief. "Oh, gosh. That feels good."

Mom lifts her brows. "I'd ask what's wrong, but I'm a little scared, given Noel's announcement about what topics are and aren't up for discussion tonight."

I throw the man in question another glare, and he laughs it off.

"I took her to the gym yesterday," Noel explains.

"We have a gym?" Mom asks.

"See?" I say to Noel. "I told you I'd never heard of it before."

"How . . ." He shakes his head, stopping himself from asking a silly question. "Never mind. I forgot who I was talking to. Yes, we have a gym. It's behind Jill's."

"Shut up." Mom looks at her boyfriend. "Did you know this, Cliff?"

He nods. "I knew."

"Wow. And to think you know a place." Mom goes back to stirring the chili, muttering about what other secrets this town could be hiding.

Noel begins pulling the supplies we brought from the grocery bags and setting them on the counter. "Is there anything I can do to help?" he asks my mother.

She smiles over at him. "Just sit your butt next to Parker. It's your last night here. You're not helping me cook."

"I tried to offer too," Clifford says, "and it's not my last night here. Why can't I help?"

"Because, love, you eat baked beans for dinner at least four nights a week. You're hopeless in the kitchen."

He shrugs. "She's got me there."

Noel settles on the stool next to me, his leg pressing against mine like it's where it belongs.

I'm going to miss this. These little moments. The small ways he finds to touch me. Or having him here for Tater Tot Tuesday. The familiar scent of his cologne. Just *him*.

I've always felt content in life. I have a house I love, a cat who is a monster but I still adore, a mother who is one of my best friends, and a business that is doing well.

Then Noel came back and showed me that while things were good, they could be great.

And I want great. I want him back in my life. I want everything I didn't know I was missing.

But I'm not going to get it. He leaves in less than ten hours, and I have no idea when he's coming back.

Mom announces the chili is done, and we get to work making our pans of tots. Noel and I split one, topping ours with fresh jalapeños, shredded cheese, and bacon bits before sliding it into the oven.

"Noel, Cliff, why don't you two head outside and start the fire?" my mother suggests. "Parker and I can bring these out when they're done."

The guys take off outside, and the second the door snaps shut behind them, my mother turns to me.

"How are you holding up?" she asks, leaning her elbows against the counter, her stare boring into me like she's looking into my soul.

"I'm okay."

She gives me that look only a mother can give. The one that says, *Come on, it's me.*

I sigh. "Really, Mom. I'm okay." She doesn't look like she believes me, and so I force a smile. "I swear."

But even *I* can hear the shake in my voice.

"Have you talked about what this means for you two?"

"No."

"Why not? Don't you want to be with him? You've loved him since you were a kid."

Of course I want to be with Noel. More than anything. But it's not that simple.

How could we even make this work? Would Noel live here? Would I live in LA? Would I have to give up my business with Axel? And what about all the chaos that comes with being a star? Would I even *want* to deal with that? *Could* I?

I don't know.

"What's the point? We both want different things. Noel wants to live in LA, and I want to stay here. Nothing's changed over the last ten years."

"I don't think that's true."

But it *is* true. He still wants a life I'm not sure I want to live. Or even *could* live. It's the same thing he wanted when he was eighteen and the same way I felt when *I* was eighteen.

We might be older, but we're at the same spot we were when he was leaving last time.

"Can we talk about something else?" I ask.

She opens her mouth like she wants to argue but thinks better of it, instead nodding.

"Okay," she says.

Relief floods me. *Thank gosh, she's dropping it.*

"But can I just say one more thing?"

I groan. "Like you weren't going to anyway."

"For what it's worth," she continues like I never spoke, "Noel is worth the work. I think this thing you two have is worth it too. Seeing you this last month with him here . . ." She shakes her head with a soft smile. "I haven't seen you like that in a long, long time. You're happy with him. *He* makes you happy. He always has, even when he's annoying you. That kind of love . . . It doesn't come around often, trust me. So whatever is holding you back, I'm here to tell you that you're strong enough to work through it. Especially if it means having a shot at the kind of love you and Noel have."

She pushes off the counter, then moves to the oven and pulls it open.

"Grab some plates, will you?" she asks like she didn't just drop that bomb on me.

Noel *does* make me happy. He always has. Some of the best memories of my life include him, and I don't think that's a coincidence. I know it's because of him and the impact he's always had on me. From the day I met him, something about him drew me in. I don't know if it was his smile or how he complimented my backpack or what, but I liked him instantly. He made me feel welcome. He made me feel safe. He made me feel *loved*.

Twenty years later, he still makes me feel all those things.

I push from the stool and do as she asks. We plate our dinners and then take them outside, where Noel and Clifford have a fire roaring.

We make light conversation as we eat our dinner, and I participate, but my mind is halfway on the ticking clock hanging over our heads.

And when Noel pushes up from his chair, I know it's time.

"Astrid," he says, crossing the lawn to my mother as she rises to meet him. He wraps her into his arms, hugging her tightly, and I love how they cling to one another. They've always had a bond, and I'm forever grateful for the way my mother took him in as her own over the years.

I turn away from them, giving them a moment alone.

I jump when a hand lands on the small of my back.

"Sorry," Noel says. "You ready?"

I give him a small smile. "I'm ready."

I hug my mother goodbye and promise to check in with her tomorrow, then I wave to Clifford before Noel navigates us back through the house and out the front door.

We're quiet as we hit Borgen Avenue. It takes me a minute to realize we're not headed toward my house, but I know instantly where Noel is leading us without him saying a word.

Five minutes later, we walk down the lane to the Noel Carter Theater, then push inside.

We sidestep the mess Axel and his crew have made, careful not to touch anything, then make our way to the stage.

Noel helps me up, and we walk to center stage, sitting at the ledge and letting our feet dangle over.

It takes me back ten years to the last time he was leaving and we did this exact thing.

"So," Noel says.

"So," I echo.

We laugh, and the tension is broken.

"I still can't believe you're renovating this theater."

"Me neither," I say, looking around the empty room. "It's going to look so different when you see it next."

His feet stop midswing, and I realize what I've just said.

"You are, right? Coming back, I mean."

"I am," he says quietly.

"When?"

He considers the question for a moment. "I don't know. I know we haven't really talked about it, and that's my fault. I didn't want to fill you with empty promises, so that's all I have for now. I don't know *when* I'm coming back, but I know I *am*. I wish I had a better answer, but I don't."

I wish he had a better answer too.

I wish *I* had a better answer for the situation we're in. But I don't. We're stuck until one of us decides to budge.

We sit on the stage for another half hour, then finally make our way back to my house. The walk that usually takes five minutes takes us twenty, both of us trying to stretch this out as much as possible.

I don't bother asking Noel if he wants to come inside. He walks in behind me like we do this every night.

We go straight to my bedroom.

There are no words exchanged. We know exactly what's happening here.

This is it. This is our goodbye.

Noel steps up to me, takes me in his arms, and kisses me like he never has before—like he never will again.

He pulls my shirt over my head, then undoes my bra with deft fingers before unsnapping my jeans. I shimmy them down my legs, kicking them aside.

Noel steps back, drinking me in with hungry eyes.

"You're perfect," he says. "So fucking perfect."

Then he's kissing me again, and we fall onto the bed. He crawls on top of me, fitting himself between my legs, then tugs his shirt over his head, tossing it aside before his lips are back on mine.

I unbutton his jeans, pushing them down as far as possible, and then he finishes the job. I sigh in relief when his naked body presses against mine.

He keeps kissing me as he slides inside me with a gentleness we've thrown right out the window the last few days. He thrusts into me slowly and softly, our lips never once breaking apart.

My orgasm barrels through me, and Noel's follows soon after.

When he's finished, he rolls off me, tucking me into his side.

I fall asleep, and when I wake up, Noel is dressing near the foot of the bed.

Moonlight streaks into the room, and I use it to memorize every inch of him, from his raven hair to the scruff lining his jaw to his strong shoulders and corded arms. Every part of him I can see, I commit to memory . . . just in case.

When he goes to turn my way, I slam my eyes closed, not wanting to see him go.

Noel tiptoes back to the bed and then kisses my head.

"Goodbye, Peter," he whispers.

Goodbye, Noel. I love you.

But I don't say that. I don't say anything. I lie there, pretending to sleep.

Pretending like my heart isn't breaking in two.

It's not until I hear the front door click shut that I finally let the tears fall.

CHAPTER NINETEEN

Noel

"Noel? That you, bub?"

I smile. It's exactly how she greeted me when I arrived five weeks ago.

"It's me, Lou Lou," I call out to her, taking my shoes off. I pad through the house, unsurprised to find her sitting at the kitchen table. "What are you doing up?"

"Couldn't sleep." She shrugs, then lifts her coffee mug—the one I made for her that says WORD'S BEST GRAN—to her lips. I forgot the *L* and was so upset over it, but she just laughed and said it made the gift even more unique than it already was. It's the only cup I've ever seen her use. "The better question is, What the hell are *you* doing here? I thought you were staying with Parker until you had to leave."

"I *do* have to leave."

She glances up at the clock that hangs on the wall. "Oh. Well, shit. I guess it is about that time, huh?"

"I have a few minutes still." I head to the coffeepot, grab a mug from the cabinet, and pour myself a cup. I don't care that it's the worst coffee ever. Right now, it's exactly what I want—one last moment with Gran and her terrible coffee.

I settle in the seat across from her, barely hiding my grimace as I take a drink of the piping-hot java.

"So, what's on your mind, bub?" Gran asks, pulling her pink robe tighter around her shoulders.

"Nothing."

She flattens her lips into a straight line. "Noel Benjamin, you can't bullshit me."

I cough out a laugh. "All right. Fine. I'm going to miss Parker."

She nods. "I kind of figured that."

"And you too."

"Well, no shit."

I laugh again. "And I guess . . . I guess I'll miss this town too."

"It does tend to sneak up on people. What else?"

"What else what?"

"What else is on your mind? Because I know it's not just that."

I pick at the floral tablecloth that Gran is always switching out for holidays and seasons. "I want to ask Parker to come with me but I'm scared she'll say no again."

"Would that surprise you?"

"No. Yes. I don't know."

"She has a life here."

"I know." I sigh. "And I have a life back home."

"You do." She sips at her coffee. "Did you know your parents did the long-distance thing before they had you?"

My brows pull together. "They did?"

"Sure did. Your dad got a job offer in New York, and your mother didn't want to leave Washington. She was going to college in Seattle."

"Dad lived in New York?"

She nods. "For two years."

"I've never . . . I didn't know that. That's . . ."

"A hell of a lot farther away than California?"

I swallow, understanding what she's getting at. They made it work with much more distance between them, so why can't Parker and I make it work too?

Because it's still a lot to ask her to give up, and a lot to put her through. I'm not just working some job in a different state, I'm traveling all over the world, practically unreachable for days at a time, thanks to shooting schedules. It's not just *some job*. Asking her to come to LA with me . . . It would be throwing her into the lion's den, and I can't do that to her.

"I know your situation is different," Gran says. "But I also believe your love is strong enough to withstand whatever comes your way. You two kids . . ." She shakes her head with a smile. "You two have always been something together. I was heartbroken when you couldn't make it work after you left, but I understand why. You were young. You didn't know any better. But now . . . now I think you know exactly what you want, and you're just too scared to go after it."

She's not wrong. I *am* scared, and I know Parker is too.

"Can I confess something to you?" she asks.

"You can tell me anything, Gran."

"I'm the reason you're here."

I tip my head, not following along. "What do you mean?"

"That anonymous donor? The one who wanted the theater named after you? It was me. I donated the money for the renovation."

My jaw slackens. "No fucking way."

"Yes fucking way." She grins, looking smug.

And I guess she has a right to it. She fooled us all. I would have never thought in a million years that it was Gran who donated that money. I know Parker knows nothing about it, either, or she'd be having words with Gran right now.

"Why? How? *Why?*" I repeat that last question because it's that damn important.

"Why? Well, part of it was for purely selfish reasons. I missed having you here and knew you would have to return for the ceremony. How? I'm old, Noel. I have money squirreled away that you have no clue about."

"I . . ." I shake my head. "I can't believe it."

"I'm immensely proud of everything you've accomplished in your short life, bub. It astounds me every day. But your fame . . . your career . . . None of that matters to me. None of that changes how I feel about you or how I still see you—that little boy who looked at me with tears in his eyes at his parents' funeral. The little boy I love. I want you to be happy. And I fully believe that Parker is a key to achieving that."

"But she and I hadn't talked for ten years. How did you know that we . . . ?"

"Because you're you."

She says it with such conviction, like she believes it with her entire being.

It's almost enough to make me believe it too.

"Look, bub, I know you're scared. I know Parker's scared. But how will either of you know you can make it work unless you try?"

Deep down, I know she's right. But that doesn't change the fact that I still have to leave.

That Parker still wants to stay here.

I glance at the clock. I have just a few more minutes to spare before I need to hit the road to make it to the airport on time.

"Can you do me a favor?" I ask her.

"Anything."

"Can you get me the information for the restoration committee?"

◆ ◆ ◆

"Sir?"

I look up to find the flight attendant staring down at me with pinched lips.

"Did you need a refill on your drink?" she asks impatiently, making it clear this isn't the first time she's had to repeat this. "This is the last call."

I had no idea she was even standing there, I was so lost in my thoughts.

I hand her my empty glass. "Yes, please. Another scotch."

"Sure thing." She gives me a tight smile that tells me she'd rather be anywhere else than catering to me right now.

I don't blame her. I'd rather be anywhere else than on this plane right now too.

It's early as fuck, and I didn't sleep a wink last night.

How could I? It was my last night with Parker, and I wasn't about to miss a single second of it.

Luckily, Gran's terrible coffee kept me awake during my drive to the airport. I raced through security and made it just in time to board.

I hoped to catch a few hours of sleep, but it eludes me now.

All I can think of is Parker.

Parker and her auburn hair.

Parker and her hazel eyes.

Parker and her laugh.

Her smile. Her sense of humor. Her general badassery.

Parker, Parker, Parker.

"Sir?"

I shake myself from my stupor to find the flight attendant back, that same frustrated expression on her face.

"Sorry." I take the scotch from her outstretched hand. "Thank you."

She gives me another tight-lipped smile, and I don't miss her rolling her eyes as she walks away.

Normally, I'd do something to try to fix this because it inevitably leads to a blowup on social media, but I don't care, not today.

Not with my mind back in Washington.

I can't believe Gran was the one who donated the money for the theater renovation to reunite Parker and me. Either she's a genius or completely delusional.

Since I'm currently sitting on a plane, flying away from the woman I love for who knows how long, I'm going with the latter.

If Parker wanted me to stay, why didn't she ask me to?

The thought stays there throughout the rest of the flight and even when we land.

I slide into the car Vince has waiting for me and close my eyes as the driver navigates us toward the studio.

We sit in traffic—because there's always fucking traffic—and I do my best to try to block out the noise from all the honking horns and loud cars.

Fuck, has this city always been so noisy? Has it always been this overstimulating? Or did I just get far, far too used to the slow pace of Emerald Grove while I was there?

Almost an hour later, we pull into the studio lot, and I'm escorted inside the big gray building where Aaron is waiting for me in the equally gray lobby.

"Noel!" he chirps, rising to his feet to greet me. "You made it!"

"Did you think I wouldn't?"

My words come out much harsher than I intend, but I guess that's expected when I haven't had any sleep or food and am running on shitty coffee and scotch.

Aaron's brows lift, but he doesn't comment on my demeanor. "Right. Well, we should probably go over a few things. Ensure we're on the same page before heading in there."

We sit, and he pops open the briefcase he was holding. He pulls out several papers, shuffling them around.

He begins going over timelines, salary, and script changes.

I nod along with all of it, not really paying attention.

I should be fucking ecstatic to be sitting here. I know at least ten other actors who would kill to be in my shoes right now.

But I can't muster a single ounce of enthusiasm for some reason.

Maybe it's the lack of sleep or overdoing it on the caffeine. Or maybe all the travel I had to do this morning, the traffic I had to sit in on the way over here, or these gray walls making me more and more miserable by the second.

Or maybe it's just that I miss Parker, and I think I left half of my heart back in Washington.

"Noel?" Aaron asks. "Are you still with me?"

"Hmm?" I scratch at my scruff, which is steadily turning into a full beard. "I'm good. It's just been a long day already."

He frowns. "This is why Vince had you flying in yesterday so that you could be rested for today. But no. You wanted to stay in your crummy little town until the very last second."

I grind my teeth, barely holding back all the words I want to sling at him.

It's probably not a good idea, especially since he's worked so hard to get me here and I'd basically be spitting right in his face.

He snaps his fingers at the employee sitting at the front desk. "You. Can we get some coffee, please?"

They roll their eyes but rise, then walk to the coffee bar near the elevators. They make a big deal out of putting the pod in the machine and pressing the start button. When it's finished, they bring it over to us, stomping and sending the coffee sloshing out of the paper cup the whole way.

Aaron takes the coffee with a groan and then hands it to me.

"Thank you," I tell them. "You didn't have to do that, but I appreciate it." I smile, trying to ease the apparent tension my agent has created.

They give me a curt nod, then walk back to their desk.

I take a sip from the cup, not caring that its contents are hot enough to burn my mouth, and it's good.

I *hate* that it's good.

I want lousy coffee, peppermint kisses, and a town that's too nosy for its own good.

But all I have is good coffee, a gray waiting room, and my agent, who won't stop talking.

I'm fucking miserable.

I yank at the collar of my dress shirt, then tug my tie loose. Why the hell is it so hot in here? I rake my hand through my hair.

"Mr. Franks? Mr. Carter?" the receptionist says, saving me from Aaron droning on and on. "Mr. Plume will see you now."

We rise from the chairs and follow them down a long corridor to a hidden second set of elevators.

We pass by a restroom, and Aaron points at it.

"You want a moment to collect yourself?"

I shake my head. "I just want to get this over with so I can sleep."

He presses his lips together, clearly displeased with my answer, but nods anyway.

We step into the car and take it up to the thirtieth floor, where we are led down another long hallway that feeds directly into a conference room.

Aaron sticks his arm out, halting me.

"Are you sure you're up for this?" he whispers. "This is a big deal. You know that, right? They only invite people here when they're planning to woo them. Is that something you can handle today?"

"I'm fine," I bite out.

"Really? Because your clothes are a wrinkled mess, you smell like scotch, and you look like you've run your hand through your hair twenty fucking times." He steps closer, his brows pinched together. "So I'll ask again: Are you good?"

I fully understand what he's asking: *Can I trust you in there?*

I nod. He can trust me. I don't plan on messing this up. I flew all the way here and left Parker behind. I'm in this.

"I'm good," I tell him.

He nods. "All right. Let's go in there and get this deal done."

We walk inside the conference room, and all the men at the table rise.

"Mr. Carter!" the man at the other end of the room booms, rounding the table to meet me, his hand sticking out. "It's a pleasure to meet you."

"Likewise, Mr. Plume." I shake the CEO of Plume Pictures' hand firmly, giving him my best smile. "Thank you for meeting with me today."

"Oh, of course. Aaron and I go way back—we were old drinking buddies from our college days. When Linus"—he gestures to the man sitting next to him with thin wire glasses perched on his nose—"pitched this idea and said he wrote the script with you in mind, I knew we had to do everything we could to get you in here. It's a good thing I had a connection with Aaron." He releases my hand, then pats the back of my agent. "Good to see you, old pal. How have you been?"

"Good. Great. Even better now that we're here."

Mr. Plume laughs heartily. "Always were the straight-to-business kind, weren't you?" He waves his hand toward the chairs. "Please, gentlemen. Have a seat."

Aaron and I sit in two empty chairs as Mr. Plume rounds the table, giving introductions to the other men seated around us.

I nod to them all, and we get down to business.

"So, Mr. Carter. Aaron here tells me you once refused to do any superhero roles. Why the sudden change of heart?" Linus, the writer and director, asks.

"Please, Noel is fine," I tell him. I clear my throat. "I won't lie, I've never really enjoyed the superhero stuff because I find it stale. Ninety-nine percent of the time, it's the same thing recycled over and over. But with your script, it felt different. The hero was complex, the villain felt authentic, and the romance aspect of it was subtle. I liked that I wasn't waiting for the kiss at the movie's end."

"We were quite proud of that," Linus says. "And I'm glad you liked my fresh take on the role. Are you worried about your character's growth at all? Because we're planning for a three-film saga, where he turns bad in the second film and his redemption arc will conclude in the third."

"I'm fine with that. It shows his human side. We're all flawed, aren't we?"

The director smiles widely. "You get it. God, I'm so glad you get it. Please, please, *please* tell me you liked the script so much that you'd consider changing your stance on superhero films?" he asks hopefully.

I nod, feeling a spark of excitement despite myself. "This is a project I'd be proud to work on."

"Excellent. We're happy to hear that. In that case, we're pleased to offer you a contract. Marty, you got that ready?"

"Of course. Here you are," Marty says, sliding a paper Aaron's way.

"Hmm. I see," my agent says, looking it over. "But right here, line . . ."

I tune them out as they all begin talking among themselves.

This part doesn't pertain to me.

It's all legal mumbo jumbo and details that I'll be reminded of a million times later.

My phone buzzes in my pocket, and I pull it out.

Gran: It's drunk

Gran: Damn tit

Gran: No tit

Gran: D

Gran: O

Gran: N

Gran: E

Gran: Hate this damn phone

I smile. She's still not yet mastered the art of texting.

Gran: U know she is gonna B mad

Me: Let her be mad then.

Gran: Brave man

She can be mad all she wants. I'd rather she be mad and still think about me than forget me.

Gran: How is your meat

Gran: Meat

Gran: U know what I mean

Me: Good so far.

Gran: Proud of you

Gran: Love you

Me: Love you, too, Gran.

I look up, and Aaron is standing over Marty's shoulder, still reviewing the contract.

I turn my attention back to my phone, my fingers hovering over the name of the person I'd kill to have next to me.

I read over the last texts we sent yesterday while I was grabbing breakfast.

Parker: If you're walking past Fran's, can you grab me a slice of apple coconut? Pretty please?

Me: You know I HAVE to walk past Fran's to get to the café. This feels like a setup.

Parker: Oh, do you? I never really thought about it.

Me: Uh-huh. Sure.

Parker: Please? I'll be your best friend.

Me: You already are my best friend, Peter. You're stuck with me.

Parker: I hope so.

I hope so.

At the time, I took it as playful banter and nothing else. But looking at it now . . .

Now I wonder if she really does want to be stuck with me.

Because I want to be stuck with her.

I want to be stuck with her right now. Back in her bed that's almost too small for two people. Back in her house that's small in a cozy sort of way. Back in Emerald Grove, where everyone talks too much about other people and smiles back when you smile.

I want to be there. Full stop.

"Noel?"

I whip my head up at Aaron. He's standing over me, holding a piece of paper in his hand.

"Care to take a look before we sign this thing?" he asks.

I take the paper as he sits, then read over their offer.

There are a lot of zeros behind that number, and while that is very appealing, the shoot time isn't.

Six months.

And it doesn't include reshoots.

They want to shoot all three films back-to-back.

It would mean six months away from Parker—six months of grueling work, and six months that I absolutely do not want to spend on set.

I look at Aaron because I know I'm about to do the one thing I was sure I wasn't.

I'm going to mess this all up.

"I can't."

Every head swings my way, their expressions ranging from shocked to confused to furious.

"Pardon?" Mr. Plume asks.

"I can't do this project."

Aaron shoves to his feet. "Give me a moment with my client."

He grabs my arm, hauling me from my chair and dragging me out to the hallway and away from the conference room.

"Are you out of your fucking mind?" he hisses at me. "This contract is unbelievable. You can't turn this down. I'm not letting you."

"I have to, Aaron. I can't do this. It's too much work. Too much time away . . ."

"Away? Away from what? You've never had an issue with a schedule like this before."

"Because I didn't have her!" I explode.

He blinks up at me. "What are you . . ." Realization dawns on him. "You met someone."

"No. Yes. Sort of. It's . . . it's complicated."

He shakes his head. "I can't believe you're turning this down for a piece of ass."

I take a step toward him, then another. I back him to the wall, my nose just inches from his. His eyes are wide with fear, and his breath hitches in his throat.

"Parker is not just some piece of ass. She's everything to me. And I am *not* walking away from her again."

Aaron swallows. "Are you good?"

I back away. "I'm good."

He pushes off the wall, straightening his jacket. "I'm not asking you to walk away from anyone. I'm asking you to give this a shot."

"It's six months, Aaron. At *minimum.* Do *you* want to take six months away from your family?"

"I . . . Well, no. Not particularly."

"Then how can you ask me to do it?"

"It's a huge opportunity, Noel."

"I know that!" I yell. "I fucking know. But I can't. I can't commit when I . . ."

I can't commit when I left my whole heart back in Washington.

Before signing anything, I have to figure out what's happening with me and Parker. If there's a chance for us to work, I want to take it before I sign away six months of my life.

"I'm sorry, Aaron. I am. But I have to go."

I turn on my heel.

"Go?" he calls to my retreating back. "Go where?"

I ignore him.

"Noel?"

I press the button for the elevators.

"Don't walk out," he warns. "I mean it."

I step into the elevator.

"Noel!" he yells just as the doors close.

I know I just screwed up. I know I probably just cost myself the biggest deal of my career. I know it's likely the most foolish thing I've ever done, but I don't care.

I'm going back to Emerald Grove.

And I'm going back for Parker.

CHAPTER TWENTY

Parker

It's been three days since Noel left, and somehow, it feels like three years.

So much has happened.

After he left, I stayed up crying for hours. I called Axel, and one "hi" from me told him everything he needed to know. He instructed me to stay home, and given how tired and heartbroken I was, I wasn't about to argue. I finally fell back asleep from exhaustion when the sun came up.

It dredged up too many old feelings I thought I had moved past, like when my father did the same thing, leaving in the wee hours of the morning. Or when Noel walked out of my life the first time.

It wasn't until my mother showed up around 6:00 p.m. that I finally crawled out of bed and did something with myself. She made me shower and eat, then put me back to bed.

The next day, the town was buzzing with the news that the *Gazette*'s doors had been padlocked overnight and the entire staff had been relieved of their duties. It was so sudden and shocking that it was all anyone could talk about . . . until the next big news broke, the one I'm still trying to understand.

The Noel Carter Theater project was fully funded, saving me a mountain of debt. I got the call this morning from the restoration committee that a donation was made the morning Noel had left.

I've been reeling since . . . and I think I know exactly who is responsible for it.

If it was Noel who donated the money—and it makes the most sense that it was—how could he do that? How could he drop a load of cash, then disappear again? How could he walk away with a vague promise of returning and nothing else? How could he do something so rash without talking to me first?

And how could I let him go without telling him how much I love him?

I'm a fool. The biggest joke there is.

I let him walk away, and I said nothing.

I didn't ask him to stay. I didn't go with him. I just let him go.

I'm as angry with myself as I am with Noel for leaving again.

So I'm at the theater doing what I've been doing for the last ten years—burying myself in work.

Axel and the crew called it a day two hours ago, but I stayed behind to work on the main foyer because I couldn't stand the thought of going home.

I've always loved my house, but right now, it's the last place I want to be. Everywhere I look, I see Noel, and I can't stand those reminders right now.

I grab a stack of lumber—far smaller than anything Axel would carry—and move it out of my way to get a better look at the area I'm working with.

I've been debating what to do with the foyer for days, and last night, it finally came to me in a dream.

While cleaning the theater, I found several old photographs tucked away in Ms. Goodman's office. They were from the years I spent here and even before that. I kept them in case I found something to do with them, and now I have.

A memory wall.

I want to blow the photos up and put them on canvases to display inside the foyer so that the memories and history of this place are the first thing our guests see.

It's the perfect combination of new and old, and I think the town will love it.

"I should have known."

A loud squeal leaves me, and I do a full jump-spin to find Axel leaning against a doorframe, taking up the entire thing.

"Axel!" I glare at him, and he shrugs, unaffected by my outburst. "What are you doing here?"

"Looking for you." He pushes off the door, grabs a much larger stack of lumber, and moves it aside for me. It's absurd to me that even with his banged-up and bandaged hand, he can still lift far more than I can. He drops the wood down with a loud thud. "What are *you* doing here?"

"Working."

"I can see that. But why? We called it a day hours ago."

"Because I can," I tell Axel, picking up another small stack of materials.

"So you're avoiding going home and thinking about how miserable you are?"

I don't say anything. What's the point when we both know what the answer is?

Yes.

He sighs. "Want to grab a drink?"

I let the wood in my hands clatter to the floor, wiping my dirty palms off on my trusty overalls. "Yes, please. I could go for a whiskey sour or two right now."

Axel laughs. "Let's start with one."

I grab my purse, sling it over my head, and follow Axel out of the theater.

The town is bustling, all the shop doors propped open, laughter flowing out as we walk by. Everyone's so happy, but I don't understand how they could be. Noel is gone. What's there to be happy about?

We walk into Bigfoot's Hideaway, which is just as busy as the streets, and grab our favorite stools at the bar.

"I was wondering when I'd see you two in here again," Garth says, tossing two coasters before us. "I figured that theater has you busy, but I didn't expect you to be out this late. Is everything all right?"

"Long day is all," Axel tells him, covering for me.

"I hear that. It's looking great, by the way. Can't believe the progress you've made despite all the rain."

Take that, Leonard Figgins.

Garth is right. We *have* made a lot of progress. Well, Axel and his crew have. I've been . . . distracted.

But still, the theater is coming along nicely, even with the rain delays. We still have months of construction, but I couldn't be happier with how things are going.

"Thanks, Garth."

"Thank *you.* My niece squealed so loud when she heard you were doing *Beauty and the Beast* as your first show. She's been nonstop singing that song Belle does as she walks through town, so rest assured you already have at least one ticket sale." He taps the bar top. "Anyway, you want your usuals?"

Axel and I nod, and Garth runs off to grab our drinks.

"Did you hear that?" I turn to Axel. "We already have a sale!"

"I was sitting right here, so I definitely heard it." He might *sound* like he doesn't care, but I can see the smile tugging at the corners of his lips. He's as thrilled as I am about this.

This is exactly why I wanted to resurrect the Goodman Theater: to bring the community together, to get kids interested in the arts, and to have fun.

It lifts my otherwise sullen mood just a little.

Then Garth slides a whiskey sour before me, and the gloomy day gets a bit brighter.

"So," Axel says, and just like that, I'm back to feeling somber because it's a loaded *so.*

It's the kind that leads to questions I don't want to answer and conversations I don't want to have.

At least, not now.

"Are we really doing this again?" I ask.

"Doing what?"

"You getting me to spill all my deepest, darkest secrets to you?"

"I don't know what you could possibly mean." He smiles innocently, then takes a sip of his whiskey sour.

But his intentions right now are anything but innocent. I know that's *exactly* what he's after.

"To be fair, I didn't ask you to tell me about your Noel woes back then. You did that all on your own."

"Yeah, because I was trying to make *you* feel better about *your* shitty situation with your parents' divorce."

He grunts. "Well, it worked. All I wanted to do was kick Noel's ass for hurting you."

"And now? Do you still want to kick his ass?"

He runs his hand over his beard. "No. I kind of like the guy now."

I raise my brows in disbelief. "Really? What changed?"

"I saw how happy he makes you."

He says it so matter-of-factly, like it's the most reasonable answer in the world.

And I guess it is. Noel *does* make me happy.

"I didn't want him to leave," I whisper. It's the first time I've said it out loud.

I didn't want Noel to go back to LA. I wanted him to stay. I wanted to build a life with him. I *still* want a life with him.

But I can't ask that of him, especially when I know how he feels about this place and that he has a career he needs to get back to. I can't ask him to forget all about those things just because I'm scared of being forgotten again.

"Have you told him that?" Axel asks.

I shake my head. "It's . . . complicated."

"It doesn't seem that complicated to me."

It's easy for him to say. His wife loves this town. She doesn't have a big, fancy job waiting for her. And even if she did, he wouldn't be afraid to leave it all behind and be with her. He'd know how to make our business work or let me buy him out or whatever he had to do to make it work because he's fearless like that.

But me? I *would* be afraid to go with Noel. Heck, I *am* afraid to go with Noel.

But none of that matters because Noel's gone, and he never asked me to go with him.

What's done is done, and I'm stuck here, waiting to see when he'll return this time.

Axel takes another drink and then settles his glass against the bar. "Can I tell you something I've kept a secret for a long time?"

I gasp. "You've been keeping secrets from me? Is that why you've never called me your best friend? Because you know best friends don't keep secrets, and you couldn't call me your best friend with such a huge, life-changing secret up your sleeve?"

"Yes, that's exactly why, Park." He shakes his head with an eye roll, like he's already exhausted with me. "This is something that nobody else knows except for two people."

Okay, I so did not expect that.

"Wow. We really aren't best friends, are we?"

He ignores me. "I saw you first."

I squeeze my brows together, not following. "What do you mean?"

"I mean, when we were kids, I saw you first. Noel and I . . . Well, you know we used to be friends."

"I remember. When I first moved here, you two were together a lot, then suddenly you weren't."

"We were. I'd even wager we were best friends, which is totally acceptable since we were kids," he tacks on when I start glaring at him.

I nod. "Fine. I'll allow it."

"Anyway, we were out on the playground—that one in the town square—and jumping off the swing set, daring each other to do flips and whatnot. Then we saw you. You were riding your bike down Borgen just a few days after the moving trucks left your driveway. You were heading into your mom's new shop, and I instantly thought, *That's my soulmate.*"

I pause, my drink halfway to my lips. I slide my eyes over to him. "I'm sorry. You thought *I* was your soulmate?"

"You had a Huffy and a *Spider-Man* lunch box. Of course I thought you were my soulmate."

I laugh. "That lunch box was sweet. I'm pretty sure I still have it in storage somewhere. Do you want me to get it out so you can fall in love with me again?" I bump my shoulder against him, though I'm sure he barely feels it.

"*Anyway* . . . I was so excited for school to start so I could officially meet you, but it wasn't *me* you wanted to sit next to. It was Noel."

I laugh. "I remember that. I thought you were terrifyingly large—kind of like now—and Noel was, well, not."

A smile pokes through his thick beard. "I was so awkward then. So much taller and bigger than everyone else. It was a nightmare, and I even scared myself sometimes, so I get it."

Coming to a new school was hard, and I was so young back then that I never even considered how it was for the other kids. As tough as Axel was on Noel and me, I'm sure he was even tougher on himself.

"What happened?" I ask. "With Noel, I mean."

"You mean, why did we stop being friends?" I nod, and he sighs. "It was because of you."

"Me?" I point to myself. "What'd I do?" I ask with a frown.

"You chose him."

"I did not!" I argue.

He laughs. "You did. I don't think you even knew you were doing it, but you gravitated toward him from Day One, and he did the same with you. And me? I was *pissed.* As angry as an eight-year-old could be. I was so damn jealous because *I* wanted you to be *my* friend. I wanted you to show me your *Spider-Man* lunch box. I wanted to ride my Huffy with you. But he was all you saw. So I decided I didn't want to be either of your friends."

"And then started tormenting us?"

"I didn't *torment* you."

"You did too. Calling me Potty Parker and a theater geek, telling everyone I was a terrible kisser, yelling *nerd alert* any time I walked by," I say, ticking off each mortifying experience on my fingers. "Should I keep going?"

His cheeks turn a deep shade of red. "I'd rather you didn't." He screws his lips up. "Man, I sucked, huh?"

"You did." I pat his shoulder. "But you were also a kid, Axel. You didn't know better. None of us did back then."

"That's no excuse. Not really, and I'm sorry about that, Park."

I wave a hand dismissively. "I know you are. We've rehashed all this already. But you're not that person anymore. You're much better than that little twerp ever was."

"I am, huh?"

"Well, yeah. There's no way my *soulmate* could be such a jerk."

The redness to his cheeks that was fading comes back in full force. "So now we're back to being soulmates?"

"Oh, Axel. We've *always* been soulmates. Platonic ones. Even when you were being a buttmunch to me. You pushed me back then—to be better, to be smarter, to be *me*. In a way, you were helping me much more than you ever hurt me. And now, as an adult, you do the same."

"I do?"

I nod. "I wouldn't even be in the renovation business if you hadn't convinced me I could do it. Without you, I wouldn't have adopted Pumpkin or started my obsession with whiskey sours, though I secretly hate you for that last one sometimes." I wink at him, then take a sip of my drink.

"I guess I am a good influence, huh?"

"The best," I agree.

"Good. Then that brings me back to why I'm here—Noel."

"You're here for Noel?"

"No. I'm here *about* Noel. You're being a dumbass."

I rear my head back. "Excuse me?"

"You heard me," he says, stroking his thick red beard. "You're both being pigheaded about this. You want to stay, he wants to go, but neither of you is willing to compromise."

I shake my head. "You don't get it. It's complicated. It's—"

"It's really not," he interrupts. "I know why you didn't go when you were younger. That made perfect sense. You were just starting your life, and you were scared to leave. But now you're an adult. You have your life figured out. You know who you are. You can do whatever you want, Park. You just need to be brave enough to go do it."

I tip my chin up. "I'm plenty brave."

"Just because you watch scary movies through your fingers now instead of hiding under the blankets doesn't mean you're brave. You're strong, that's for damn sure, but you're still running scared. Why?"

"It's—"

He cuts me a glare. "Don't you dare say it's complicated, Parker Bernice. That's a shit excuse, and you know it."

"Wow." I whistle. "You're going to middle-name me right now?"

"Yes. Because this is that serious."

I sigh, pushing my whiskey glass back and forth between my hands. "I don't know," I tell him. "I mean, I *do* know a little bit. There are parts of it that make a lot of sense. But . . . he lives in a whole different world than I do. We're two completely different people. What if I can't handle it?"

"Are you kidding me? I see you yell at grown men all the time. Hell, you made our lumber guy, Ike, cry. You've almost made *me* cry. You can handle Hollywood, Parker. Especially for Noel."

I don't say anything because I don't know what to say. Axel's right. I have done those things, but they're different than uprooting my life for a guy who has left me twice.

And that's the real root of my issue. Everyone is always leaving. My father, Noel . . . Noel, again. What's to stop him from taking off a third time?

"What if . . . what if he leaves?" I ask quietly. "Like my dad did?"

"Then I'll personally hand his ass to him. Twice. No. *Thrice.* But honestly, I don't think it's something you have to worry about. That man loves you. Everyone can see it. Hell, everyone could see it back then too. Even me."

Noel loves me?

Sure, he's said so before, but that was years ago, when we were teens who knew nothing about the real world.

Is it true he could love me now? Is that what I want?

Yes. More than anything, because I love him too. So much more than I ever thought I could.

"Look, if you want to go, go. I can take care of our business. You can work remotely and fly back here when needed. We could even expand into LA—there's plenty to renovate there too. So don't let that stop you from making a decision. But don't let your fear stop you either. There's no point in spending your life just coasting by when you can spend it happy—like truly happy—and with someone who loves you as much as you love them. Just be happy, Park, okay? Let your fear go and be happy."

Fear—the ugliest F-word of all. It's held me back for far too long, and I'm tired of it.

I've shut down the idea of living in LA so many times, but has my judgment really been fair? I don't truly know I can't handle it. I've just assumed so much about a potential life there because I've been terrified of getting hurt again. Sure, I know there are plenty of aspects of it I won't like—such as the paparazzi and everyone being in my business—but is that really such a bad trade-off when it means a life with Noel?

Axel is right. Maybe I need to shove my fear aside and find my happy.

And right now, my happy is in LA.

I shove from my stool, digging into my purse and tossing cash on the bar top for Garth.

"Wait, wait, wait," Axel says. "What are you doing?"

"Leaving."

"Leaving? What? Why?"

"Because I have a flight to book."

Slowly, a smile spreads across his lips, and he nods. "There she is."

"Who?"

"My best friend."

I launch myself into his arms, letting his warmth envelop me.

"You called me your best friend," I whisper, hugging him tightly.

"Shut up," he says, squeezing me back just as hard.

I laugh, pulling away. "I don't know how long I'm going to be gone. Are you sure . . . are you sure you can handle everything? Ordering the right supplies and putting everything where it needs to go?"

He rolls his eyes. "Mess up a paint color one time . . ."

"Three times, Axel. Three times."

"Just go before I revoke the status of our friendship."

I let out a squeak, and he laughs. "I'll call you."

"Please don't."

I throw my arms around him again, kissing his rosy cheek. "I love you, *soulmate*."

"Love you too . . . *best friend*."

"Shit. Fuck."

I sit straight up in bed, my heart pounding like I just ran a mile.

I glance at the clock. It's 3:00 a.m.

I have an alarm set to go off in two hours so I can drive to the airport for my flight to California.

I'm surprised I even fell asleep, my nerves are so high over my first time flying and seeing Noel again.

Will he freak out when I call him from the airport? Will he think I've completely lost my mind for flying out there when I have no idea where I'm going?

Will he want me there?

A loud crash breaks through my thoughts, and I pause.

"Son of a . . . Ow! Ow! Fuck!"

I hold my breath the best I can, straining to hear because I swear I just heard Noel's voice, and it sounded like it was coming from my living room.

But that's not possible, right?

"Mother of . . . Fucking hell!"

No. That is 100 percent Noel's voice.

I throw my covers off—the ones that still smell like him—and race from my bedroom to the living room.

There, standing by the door, is Noel.

And there, attached to his leg, is Pumpkin.

"Dammit! Stop it, Pumpkin! It's me!"

The cat hisses, his teeth clamped on Noel's leg, his claws digging in alongside his teeth.

I'm touched that my demon cat loves me so much, but Noel's safety is my top priority.

"Pumpkin!" I yell, snapping my fingers at the orange tabby. "Down!"

Noel's head whips my way. His bright blue-green eyes are wide.

"Parker," he says softly, never mind that the cat is still tearing into him.

"Hi," I say, racing toward him and grabbing Pumpkin.

It takes a moment to coax the cat from Noel's leg without causing more harm, but when I finally get him off, he races toward my bedroom, his tail thwacking against the door as he passes.

"Holy crap, is that little guy strong," Noel says, sucking in heavy breaths. "I thought he would never let go. I tripped over . . ."

He stops talking, his eyes drifting down.

He looks back at me. "Parker, why is there luggage by your door?"

"*That's* the greeting I get? Not a *Hi*, *Hello*, or a *Thank you for rescuing me from your cat*?"

He grins. "You're right. Where are my manners?"

Then he hoists me into his arms, and my legs go around his waist of their own accord. I throw my arms around his neck, and he plants his lips against mine.

The kiss is heated and heavy, and if we're not careful, it could lead to something more.

I want something more. Badly.

But there's a lot we need to discuss first.

Like what the heck he's doing here.

I pull my mouth away, my breaths coming in sharp, and smile down at him.

"Better?" he asks with a cocky smile.

I laugh. "Much."

He sets me back on my feet but doesn't let me go, holding me to him still. "*Now* can I ask why your luggage is by the door?"

"For you."

He lifts his brows. "Me? What do you mean?"

"I was going to LA to find you."

He tucks his lips together. "You realize that LA is huge and not like Emerald Grove, and you can't just *find* people there, right?"

"I know that. I . . . I was going to call. It was going to be a surprise. Kind of like this is." I squint at him. "What *are* you doing here?"

"You."

"Noel . . ."

He laughs. "I'm serious. I came back for you. I would have been here three days ago but I had some things I needed to take care of first so I didn't completely lose everything for walking out."

"Walking out?" Realization hits me. "Your meeting . . . The deal . . . You didn't take it?"

"No, because it doesn't matter. None of it does. I . . . I want you, Peter. You're what matters."

"Noel, you can't . . . We can't . . . That's not how this was supposed to work."

"Then how was it supposed to work?"

"You were supposed to ask me again."

He cocks his head to the side. "Ask you what?"

"To go with you. Ask me to go with you again."

He sighs. "I can't. I can't do that, Parker."

"Why not?"

"Because it's not fair. You love it here. This is your home."

"It's yours too."

"I know." He nods. "I know that now. I've tried to leave it behind and move on, but I can't. I can't because . . ." He licks his lips, running a hand through his hair. "Fuck, because you're here, all right? You're here, and you're my home, Parker. You always have been."

"So then ask me."

"I can't," he says again. "I can't do that. What if *you* wake up one day and realize it's not what *you* want? What if you realize you made a mistake? What if you start to resent me? Then what? Will it be me without a home? Will it be me left alone in LA again?" He shakes his head. "I can't do that. I can't take you away from this place."

"And what if I wake up one day and realize I'm the happiest I've ever been? That it's *exactly* what I've always wanted? What if I realize it's the greatest decision I've ever made? What if I look at you and fall even more in love? What if *not* going with you is the biggest mistake of my life?"

He opens his mouth to speak, but nothing comes out because he knows I'm right.

"That's a big risk," he eventually says.

"Yeah, and it's worth it. *You're* worth it."

His ocean eyes bore into me like he's searching for a hint of a lie. He's not going to see one. I've weighed my options on this. Heck, I've been weighing them for the last ten years.

I'm sure.

A life with Noel Carter is what I want.

"Are you sure?"

"Surer than I've ever been about anything."

"It's going to be a lot, Parker. There will be late nights, star-studded events, paparazzi, and people in our business."

I nod. "I know. I know it is. It's going to be an adjustment. A big one. But so have the last ten years without you. They were hard. It was painful slugging through them. If I can survive that, then I can manage a few fancy parties and photographers being annoying. I don't want to spend these next ten years sitting here and wondering what my life would be like if you were in it. I want you in it now. I want you now. I . . . I love you, Noel. So much it hurts sometimes. And I want a life with you. I want you to be my best friend. Forever."

"Fuck." He drops his forehead to mine. "Fuck, Peter. I love you too. I want all those same things. I really do. I . . . I have one caveat."

Worry races through me. "Okay . . ."

"We live here too."

I pull back. "What? But you hate it here. You . . ."

"*You* love it here. This is your home, and I don't want to ask you to leave. Besides, it's growing on me. So let's live here too. We can split our time between here and California. It'll take some work, but I think we can manage it. Besides, you have a theater to run here. I can't let you build your dream and leave it behind while I get mine."

I bury my face against his chest, trying to hide the tears falling from my eyes.

"Hey, hey. Come on." He pulls my face up to him, using his thumbs to wipe away my tears. "Why are you crying? I thought you'd want that. I thought that would make you happy."

"That is what I want. It does make me happy."

"Then why the tears?"

"The theater. You paid for the theater."

"Oh. That."

I laugh. "Yeah. That."

He winces. "Are you mad?"

I shake my head. "No. I wanted to be, but . . . no. I'm just happy—so dang happy."

"Good. I know you can do it on your own. I have full faith in you that you can. But you shouldn't have to. I want to be there to help. I want to be your partner in everything, including this."

He presses his lips to mine in a soft and slow kiss.

"I love you, Parker," he says, his mouth brushing against mine with every word. "I've loved you since I was eight years old and you came riding through town on your bike. I loved you when I was nine and you told me why your father left. I loved you when I was ten and you didn't talk to me for a day because I said Batman was better than Spider-Man. I loved you from twelve to eighteen, even when you turned me down. And I've kept loving you these last ten years, even when I never thought I'd have another chance with you. I love you more than anyone I've ever loved, and I will always love you. You're my best friend. My everything, Peter, and I want to spend the rest of my life proving it to you."

I sigh. "It's not fair. You're an actor. You have all these pretty speeches memorized."

He chuckles. "Nothing about that was rehearsed. I said every word straight from my heart."

I know he did. I can feel it in mine.

"I love you, too, Noel Carter, in those same ways. I think I have since I was eight, before I knew what love was. From the day we met, I knew you were mine and I was yours. That's never changed—not once when we were kids and not even when you were gone. And it never will change. You're my best friend, and I want nothing more than to give forever a shot with you too."

He captures my lips again, kissing me like he'll never get enough of me.

I get it. I do. I'll never get enough of him either.

As good as it sounds, forever might not be enough, not with Noel.

"I do have one question, though," he says.

"Anything."

"What the hell are we going to do about Pumpkin?"

EPILOGUE

Noel

Eight Months Later

Despite Parker's talk about the theater and being part of the renovation, I still never expected it to turn out like it has.

This place . . . It's incredible.

I look up at the foyer's high ceilings, remembering the asbestos-filled hole that was once there. It's covered now, and a shimmering chandelier hangs in its place.

My gaze drifts to the walls, which are adorned with a rich tapestry of old black-and-white photographs. Each image tells a story, a chapter in the theater's history, from the first iteration to this masterpiece Parker has created.

"Parker, this is . . ." I can't find the words.

"I know." She bounces excitedly on the toes of the same black high heels she wore to the bachelor auction. "But wait until you see the rest."

It's been killing me not to be part of the final stages of the restoration, but it's been for a good reason. I'm not sure how Aaron did it, but he salvaged the meeting with Plume Pictures, and they still offered me the role. They wanted me so badly that they pushed the production by three months and guaranteed a month between films. It means we'll be shooting for longer, but I get to have a life too.

Which is how I'm here right now. We're just thirty minutes from officially opening the doors of the Noel Carter Theater, and to celebrate, we're hosting the premiere of *One Night*, the movie I filmed last year when this theater was still just a dream.

Now it's more than a dream—it's a reality, and damn, is it stunning.

When I got back into town last night, I wanted to come straight here to see the theater, but Parker made me wait until today to get my first glimpse of it all finished.

Honestly, I wasn't *that* upset, considering I had her naked and under me in less than a minute.

"Come on." She grabs my hand, tugging me through the foyer, farther into the theater.

Parker waves toward the impressive concession stand that smells like freshly popped popcorn and butter. "Popcorn guests don't have to bring from home!"

I laugh, remembering how everyone used to sneak snacks into the Goodman Theater. "It smells incredible."

"Tastes even better," she promises. "I might have had a bucket for dinner last night."

She looks guilty, which tells me that's *exactly* what she did.

"I promise to cook you a fantastic dinner tomorrow, deal?"

She sighs dramatically. "Thank goodness. I'm not saying you've spoiled me with your amazing cooking skills, but I've been eating at Rossi's *a lot* lately."

"And that's a bad thing because . . . ?"

Parker peers around, smiling at the few people we've let in before the show starts, then leans in conspiratorially. "Because you're a better cook."

She kisses my cheek, and I grab her by the waist, hauling her closer.

I've missed this. I've missed *her*.

We've only been apart for two weeks, but it feels like a lifetime, especially since it's the longest we've been separated since the night I came back to Emerald Grove and tripped over her bags.

Parker came to LA as promised, and to both of our surprises, she didn't hate it. In fact, I think she kind of loves it. Not more than Washington, of course, but still enough that she's made herself right at home in my penthouse and has even mostly gotten used to the paparazzi that follow us around. Pumpkin loves it, too, and he does much better with the flights than any of us anticipated.

Being with her these last eight months has been incredible, and I can't believe I went ten years without her.

I know one thing is for damn sure—it will never happen again.

"What are you thinking about?" she asks, grinning at me.

"You."

"Me?"

I nod. "Yes."

"Are they naughty thoughts?" she whispers.

I laugh. "Surprisingly, no. I was just thinking about how much I love you."

Her grin widens. "I don't think I'll ever get tired of hearing that."

"I'll never get tired of saying it. I love you, I love you, I love you."

She laughs. "All right. That's enough of that."

"Why? Am I getting you all riled up?"

"Yes," she states matter-of-factly. She wiggles out of my hold, grabbing my hand once more. "Come on. Let's see the rest."

We walk through the theater, and I spy Astrid and Clifford, who she recently moved in with, sitting near the bar. She sends me a wave, and I give her a wink.

I nod at Axel, who is holding Molly, his adorable baby girl, as we walk down the hallway. The triplets are at his feet, giggling over something, while Mary chats with other guests. Parker's best friend nods back. We've found a good rhythm, he and I. There's less grunting and more talking. We won't be giving hugs anytime soon, but we have advanced to handshakes.

Progress is progress.

Parker points out all the posters of upcoming films we're showing and the subtle details she's added, like filmstrips embedded into the trim pieces, and then pulls me through the double doors that lead into the theater.

My jaw drops.

The old, worn-out seats and the horrid popcorn ceiling are long gone. In their place are shiny black seats that look cushiony, and the ceiling has been replaced with beautiful ornate tiles.

But that's not the best part. The best part is the stage.

"It's the same one," I say, unable to take my eyes off it.

"It is," Parker says. "I didn't have the heart to tear it down. With a few reinforcements under the stage and some hard buffing, we were able to restore it and keep it going."

"I can't . . ." I shake my head, looking over at her. "I can't believe you did all this. This place . . . It's . . . I really don't know what to say. It's perfect. I couldn't have imagined anything better."

"Really? So you don't think that the wall color is too—"

I capture her lips with mine, cutting off whatever silly-ass thing she's about to say.

Everything about this place is perfect, down to the most minute detail, and I couldn't possibly be prouder of her.

The kiss is soft at first, but it progresses into something more almost instantly, and now it makes me wish we were anywhere else right now so I could rip off the gorgeous skintight navy-blue dress she's wearing and have my way with her.

"Okay, okay. Stop sucking each other's faces off before the show even starts."

We spring apart like two teenagers caught in the act.

"Gran!" I say, looking over at her as she walks through the theater doors.

She grins up at me. "Bub. Why didn't you come see me last night, hmm?" She lifts her stark-white brows at me, and I feel like a kid getting reprimanded all over again.

I point at Parker. "It was her fault."

"Hey!" My girlfriend smacks my hand away. "It was not!"

But it so was. We both know it.

"Well, I'm glad you're here now." Gran opens her arms, and I fall into them effortlessly, hugging her tightly and inhaling the aloe vera she always smells like.

"I missed you," I tell her.

"You just saw me a month ago," she says, pulling away, but I know she missed me too. She steps up to Parker, taking her face between her wrinkled hands. "You, my sweet girl, have done an outstanding job, and I am so, so proud of you."

Parker's eyes well with tears instantly, and she wraps Gran in a tight hug.

I never told her about Gran being the anonymous donor. Not that I think Gran would mind if she knew, but I like that it's a little secret she and I have for now.

"Parker!" Fran yells, skidding into the room. "There you are!"

"Fran? What's wrong?" Parker asks.

"Have you been outside lately?"

"No." Parker shakes her head. "I've been here for hours, making sure everything is perfect before we open at five. Why?" She pulls her brows together. "What's wrong?"

"You just . . . You have to see this. Come on."

Fran grabs Parker's hand, tugging her from the room.

She looks back at me over her shoulder, her eyes full of worry, but I just shrug.

I look to Gran, but she waves at me, silently telling me to follow Parker.

The girls make their way to the front of the theater, and I trail behind.

Parker pushes open the door, and her mouth drops.

"Peter?" I ask. "Everything okay?"

She nods but doesn't look away from whatever has her in shock.

I sneak up behind her, looking over her head, and my jaw slackens along with hers.

When I pitched the idea of premiering *One Night* here, Parker was a little wary that we'd never get anyone to come out who's not local, especially with it being so far from the airport. But two minutes after tickets went live, they were sold out. So we added another show, and that sold out too.

It's one thing to sell out a theater, but seeing the crowd in person is another.

There's a line wrapped around the building, so long it bleeds onto Borgen, and all I can think is, *Take that, Figgins.*

I couldn't stand all the shit he pulled with Parker, so to stick it to him and all the other gossipmongers at the *Gazette*, I bought it just because I could. I fired Leonard Figgins first, then the rest of the staff who were stirring up trouble, and I rebuilt it with honest and unbiased journalists. It took a few months to get it off the ground, especially with my travel and filming schedule, but now it's doing better than it ever has and even has an online version that I get sent to my inbox daily to keep up with the happenings of Emerald Grove while I'm away. It's been a real blessing for all of us.

"Holy . . . crackers! This is . . . Wow! I don't know what to say." Parker shakes her head in disbelief. "I . . . I never expected this."

"Really? I sure as hell did."

Parker turns to me, letting the door close behind her. "You did not."

I nod. "Oh, but I did, Peter. From the second you told me about this, I knew this theater would be the most incredible thing ever."

"You . . ." She grins. "You're amazing, you know that?"

"Me?" I wrap my arm around her waist, bringing her closer because I can't *not* touch her right now. "I'm nothing compared to you, Parker.

I never have been. People think I'm the one with all the star power because I'm an actor, but it's not me. It's you. It's always been you."

"Say that last part again."

I smile. "It's always been you, Peter. And it always will be."

I kiss her softly, slowly, lingering just because I can. When I finally pull away, she's still smiling, and I love it.

I love *her*.

"I love you, Noel Carter," she says.

"And I love you, Parker Pruitt. Now, let's go open a theater, huh?"

ACKNOWLEDGMENTS

I can't believe this is my second traditionally published book. Hell, I *still* can't believe I published the first one!

I wouldn't be able to continue on this journey without so many people, and I feel they all deserve a moment of recognition.

First—*always* first—my wonderful husband, who I love *and* like. Thank you for driving to the camper van every single day of this deadline and letting me sit out there for hours while I wrote because it was what was working at the time. You've always been my biggest supporter, and there's no way I could do this without you. I love you.

Thank you to my amazing agent, Aimee, and the rest of the team at Brower Literary for making my dreams come true.

The team at Montlake for believing in me.

My editors for whipping this into shape.

Valentine PR for being the *best* PR team ever. You ladies rock!

Laurie, my friend and PA, who is always there when I need her.

My mother and my sisters for always cheering me on.

Ashley and Becca for being the biggest cheerleaders ever, gasping at my plot twists, and for the six-hour (or longer) dinners.

Davenport Coffee for all the incredible lavender lemonades that kept this shit show running so I could meet my word counts.

The Book World for sharing my work and telling their friends about it. Word of mouth is truly the best advertisement, so every review, post, comment, and like means more than you could ever know.

Finally, thank *you* for taking a chance on this book. Parker and Noel popped into my head one day and refused to leave until I wrote their story. I hope you loved it as much as I loved writing it and fell for them as hard as I did.

ABOUT THE AUTHOR

Photo © 2019 Perrywinkle Photography

Teagan Hunter is the author of *The DM Diaries* and other steamy romantic comedies written with lots of sarcasm and a side of heart. She loves pizza, hockey, and romance novels, though not in that order. When she's not writing, you can find her watching entirely too many hours of *Supernatural*, *One Tree Hill*, or *New Girl*. Teagan is also mildly obsessed with Halloween and prefers cooler weather. She married her high school sweetheart, and they currently live in the Pacific Northwest. For more information, visit www.teaganhunterwrites.com.